Death extends
A lip to the earth,
A lip to the heavens,
A tongue to the stars.
—*The Ugaritic Baal Epic*

Sheol and Abaddon are never satisfied, and never
satisfied are the eyes of man.
—*The book of Proverbs*

She kept on; went on out of sight, journeying always
further into death.
—C. S. Lewis, *Till We Have Faces*

About the Author

Eric Ortlund teaches Hebrew and biblical studies at Briercrest College and Seminary in Saskatchewan, Canada. He's fascinated by modern fantasy and horror and by ancient myth, and loves finding ways to interweave the two. His short fiction has appeared in *The Midnight Diner* and online at *Mindflights* and *Fear and Trembling*. When he's not writing, he's reading Gene Wolfe and Neil Gaiman, playing with his two kids, and shooting his bow.

DEAD PETALS

An Apocalypse

Eric Ortlund

FINGERPRESS LTD
LONDON

Dead Petals—An Apocalypse

ISBN (pbk): 978-1-908824-29-5

Published by Fingerpress Ltd

Production Editor: Matt Stephens
Production Manager: Michelle Stephens

www.fingerpress.co.uk

Dedicated, with profound respect, to Dust,
a true and noble knight, who understands this story.

Thank you to:

Ray and Jani (who reads everything I send her), John and Krista, Dane and Stacey, Gavin and Esther, David, Dustin, Rob, Michelle (without whom...), Amanda (my best editor), Lyn, Jeff, Logan, Andre, Dale, and finally Erin, Kate, and Will, who mean more than I can say.

DEAD PETALS

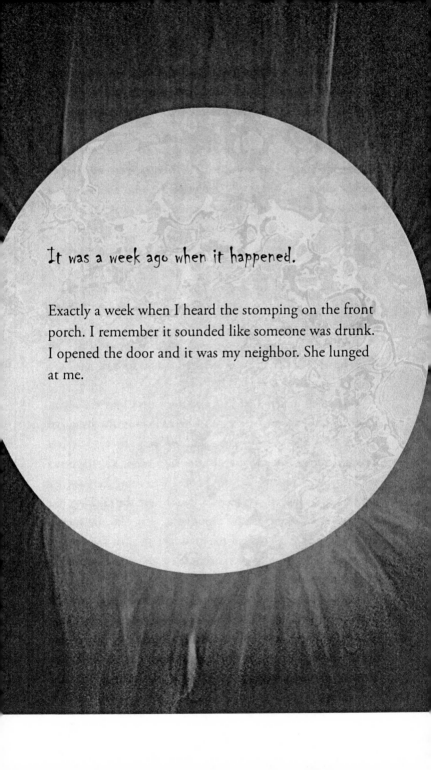

It was a week ago when it happened.

Exactly a week when I heard the stomping on the front porch. I remember it sounded like someone was drunk. I opened the door and it was my neighbor. She lunged at me.

It lunged at me. Not she. I had the door slammed shut and locked before I could think, but as soon as I saw her, I knew she was a corpse. She looked like walking gangrene.

Eight days? A week.

I leaned against the door as the arms pounded on it and my heart thudded in my ears. The hinges were starting to buckle when it shuffled off. I crept to the window and saw a car slowing down. Then it accelerated, but it was already too late. The body had shuffled onto the road. I'd rather not remember the heavy, wet sound it made when they collided, or the screams of the man when he got out to look under the front of his car and my neighbor grabbed him. What was left of her, spread out on the road and under the car in a mass of white and red.

Perhaps I should have shouted, tried to warn him. Can they hear? Would it have crawled back toward me and knocked the door down?

The smell lingered all that afternoon and into the night. It wasn't until the moon was up when the motorist struggled to his feet, the ghostly light bathing him in black paint which dripped from where his arm had been. He staggered off into the fields beyond my home. The thing beneath his car was still snapping its teeth. I could hear the clicking like tiny bones breaking in the moonlight, just like the moonlight whispering all around me now, as I sit with my back to a tree, glancing around every minute to make sure nothing is staggering toward me.

Been driving for three days. I'm exhausted and soon I'll have to go lock myself in that wretched car so I can sleep. But I can't close my eyes to the stark beauty of this moonlight, turning the night sky a pale blue flecked with diamonds. The soft iridescence plays on the rolling hills and makes them look as if they were in motion. The moon is so quiet and confident, a dead face grinning at the world as if amused.

I've been telling myself I'd just pack up and leave for years, and now I finally have, but it doesn't feel like I'm going anywhere. I keep turning around, expecting to see my old house behind me. How can you go anywhere when there aren't any boundaries anymore?

Night again and my eyes are drooping. I woke this morning to the car being rocked like a boat in a storm by eight or ten ragged bodies. It felt like they were going to turn it over. One was pounding against the glass on the driver's side, and even though its hands were bloody and it looked like one wrist was broken, the glass was cracking. I kept the windows cracked during the night, and I could hear the wind whistling through the opening, and their moaning voices.

I got the key in the ignition and started driving forward slowly, stupidly hoping they'd take the hint and let me pass. The two at the front of the car just kept backing up. This went on for an idiotic minute. I saw a tall man standing off to the side, watching, but the Dead seemed more interested in me. Eventually a corpse climbed over the front bumper and started pounding on the front windshield. I squealed and sped up, and the sound of the things that used to be people getting crushed under the car was too much, and it was all I could do to keep the car on the road while I threw up onto the seat next to me. When I looked up, the thing on the front of the car had fallen off because of my swerving.

I kept driving in the stink of my own puke until I saw something moving on the seat to my right. It was a severed hand, trailing white strings of cartilage which floated in the air. Crawling toward me. I slammed on the brakes and grabbed my backpack and ran. I was lucky the car didn't flip. Eventually the empty wheat fields broke in a small town with a car dealership. I let myself in and found a key and was driving again ten minutes later.

I wrote about their voices earlier, but that's a lie. A voice is something you can laugh with. You have to have a heart and mind for a voice to come out of your mouth. The wandering wind is more human than the sound they make. And they don't have mouths, just holes where their faces used to be. I opened the door and she came for me—not she, it, it. I keep wanting to call it a her, but the corpse in front of me was the furthest thing away from a "she," the furthest thing away from the music between man and woman. A rock has more personality than the thing that pounded against my front door.

What was her name? She had borrowed sugar from me before. Was she flirting with me? Why can't I remember her name?

I'm almost sure he was one of them. He was dirty enough, anyway, waving his arms around and shouting by the side of the road. I didn't even slow down.

Corpses of animals, everywhere I go. Deer, rabbits, dogs. None of them moving. All rotting. Even saw a bear. What does it mean?

Drove past a graveyard today and saw the exploded earth in front of the tombstones. Something inside my head was yelling at me to just keep going, but I got out and looked around. I guess if they're strong enough to knock down a door or turn a car over, they can dig themselves out of a casket. Some graves had undisturbed earth; some of the dead still slept. But I saw at least one from three years ago which had overturned earth in front of it.

I wonder if she's found my ex. She always did go to her first.

She'll never catch me. Ever.

Whenever I felt like this before, I would take another trucking job and leave, and when I returned I'd be able to stand my apartment for a few more weeks. But now I can move all I want and I'll still find those things, staring at me without really looking and shuffling toward the car they'll never catch. They've made every town the same: no matter the different layout or stores, as long as those bodies are shuffling around, it might as well be the last town I drove through. It's almost like I'm the prodigal son they're welcoming back.

So what's the point of moving on to one more place when everywhere has become the same place?

Maybe without any home to come back to, all one can do is run.

But why doesn't that make me feel better?

Lost track of the days since I last wrote. I've found a forest. I traveled south until I hit what must have been Arizona or Texas or something. I didn't want to be in the desert—too visible. So I drove east. A couple days later, I had driven my latest car dry. I was somewhere green with mountains. I got out and walked into the scattered trees, feeling like I was the one standing still and the trees were all walking toward me in an ever thickening crowd. I was a child, walking away from

5

his parents and getting himself lost and quite enjoying it.

I've found a nice little river and a slope with bushes at the top where I can sleep without being too noticeable. Cleared it of the bodies of birds and squirrels.

I'm out of food. Have to search tomorrow.

Finally back under the cover of trees. Never thought I'd feel so strange out in the open after so many hours in my truck. There's a town just a little further down the road that will take a long time to bleed dry. I even found some barbed wire, which I dragged back to my camp and strung around the trees in an egg shape. My hands are bleeding from a dozen mistakes, but I doubt anything could get through it. I had to leave a little room between two trees for me to get in and out, but with some camouflage it will not be too noticeable.

I do not know what the town was named. The welcome sign had been defaced. I'm stealing from it, and I don't even know what it was called. In fact, I haven't found a single city that had an intact sign for its name. They've all been torn down. I don't know how that's possible.

This morning, when I set out, I walked past the car I had driven without even realizing it until later. It was already the car of a stranger.

I always told my students to write it out, if they were in pain, but it's not helping. It makes it more real. But I can't stay away from this cheap spiral notebook.

That hand, on the passenger seat, crawling toward me.

I'm sitting here with the notebook, trying to enjoy myself. In my old life, this would have been a perfect evening: camping, alone, with time to write and think and express the world around me through the words on the page. Hell, it doesn't even hurt when I think about the teaching job I lost or all the useless degrees I'll never use again. Instead I just stare into space. The forest is too quiet. Can't hear any birds or that relaxed sound crickets used to make. The moon is only the curve of a fingernail now, but as I read these short lines, I can imagine a ghostly skull in the night sky keeps grinning at me. (That hand, reaching for me.)

But I'm under the cover of forest now. I made it this far.

Have to go lie down soon. Hopefully I won't have that dream again. It's so hot and muggy I probably won't sleep anyway. I'm so tired I'll just lie there, and the earth will spin beneath me, and I can think about the trackless globe I'm on, smooth and without markings like a skull, grinning at me. Maybe I can grin back at it, through these pages.

Dreamt it again last night: I'm lying on the ground in the forest, and suddenly I realize I'm asleep, but I don't wake up. A face forms in the air above me and talks to me. I don't want to hear what it is saying, but the air is rushing all over my skin, and I try to get up and run but I can't. A whirlwind is above me, pushing me down and shouting.

I saw another one of them two days ago. (Three? Four? I don't trust my memory. Time has gone fluid.) It was crunching its way through the forest. Green-brown skin and dead eyes and blood all over it. Walked by my camp a dozen feet away and never turned to look. It was like death had reached backwards through time and was working the body like a puppet.

Time stopped. I couldn't look away.

7

An Asian man showed up yesterday. I think he's in shock. His voice is too calm. He follows me around like a sleep-walker and does whatever I tell him. His name is Masaaki Shinogaido. He said the English name his parents gave him was Eric, but I don't understand why anyone would cover up a perfectly good Japanese name, so I call him Masaaki. When he asked my name, I hesitated too long before decid-ing on Oz, but I don't think he noticed.

The day after, a set of identical twins showed up, Jack and Selene. Selene has a beautiful pale face and jet dark hair but will not meet my eyes. She and her brother engage in numerous whispered conferences, but she talks to me only when she has to, and not much above a whisper. Now that I think about it, Jack is usually standing between me and her. Jack is pretty quiet too, with his short black hair and narrow shoulders and wide eyes, but he does anything I ask without complaining. Selene spends every moment she can reading, turning those pages as if her life depends on it. I told her it wouldn't help and it might hurt. She didn't even look at me. I shrugged and walked away.

I couldn't take my eyes off of them the first day the four of us were inside the barbed wire, but then I laughed at myself. What was I worrying about, that they were secret FBI agents? That they were going to report me to... who?

I wonder if others will show up, and what it will take to convince them to go somewhere else.

In the evenings, we sit and sweat in the sultry summer heat and the dying sunlight. Nobody talks.

At least the camp is turning out well. We've each got our own sleeping areas and a system for boiling water. But we need more supplies. If our camp is going to be consuming three times as much food, then they should get their own. I can draw them a map.

Evening again. I am exhausted from the day's work and want nothing more than to close my eyes, but I have been avoiding this notebook for more days than I can count. Now that I have had some time to collect myself, I must face facts: I very much want to leave, but it would be futile to do so. No matter how I fantasize about simply walking away, I'd only wind up hiding somewhere else, and more survivors would cluster around me, looking to me to lead only because I appear less homeless than they. And they would not understand that it's only because I've been homeless longer. What to do?

The world, the same, everywhere.

And those things, roaming through their new home.

ONE

The Flower

Oz's eyes opened in the dull sunlight of early morning. He had slept without a blanket, but was still slick with sweat. He lay for a moment in the unbroken silence of the forest. Then he sat up and saw the pages covered with his tiny handwriting from last night. Looking around to make sure everyone else was still asleep, he put them in his backpack and stuffed the trusty North Face under his sleeping bag.

He was eating a can of cold corn in front of a dead campfire when Masaaki sat up, blinked, walked over to him and sat down. He looked as if we were still asleep.

"A few cans of food remain, if you're hungry," Oz said.

"No," Masaaki said.

Oz held his fingers close to the ashes from last night, threw a few leaves and twigs on them and blew. By the time Jack and Selene had joined them, a small fire was crackling in the shallow pit Oz had dug a few days earlier. It was nearly invisible in the morning sunlight. Jack and Selene each had a tin can in their hand as they sat down with bleary eyes.

"You may boil water, if you wish," Oz said, indicating the fire. Jack nodded but didn't move.

10

Oz scooped out the last spoonful of cold corn, chewed, and said, "Now that you three have joined me, the food is being depleted more rapidly. There's barely enough left for today. But, you know, a town lies just down the road." Masaaki, Jack and Selene stared at him.

"So, the three of you may, ah..."

"Very well," Masaaki said. "I will go with you."

Oz shook his head and started to speak, but then turned to Jack when a broken sound came out of the boy's mouth. Jack swallowed and managed to ask: "Oz, what has happened?"

Oz sighed. "The world died."

Jack's eyes fell and he stared at the fire. He glanced at his sister, who gave him an urgent look, and asked Oz, "So what do we do?"

"I don't know."

"So it's just one big camping trip." The words wandered out of Jack like lost moles, blinking in the sunlight. "We'll get supplies every once in a while and tell campfire stories and live here. For the rest of our lives. The end."

"Whatever you choose to do," Oz said, standing up. "The town is simple enough to find, but if you wish I'll draw you a map." He walked back to his sleeping bag and patted it down, making sure he could feel the notebook hidden under his sleeping bag. Not wanting to stop moving, he picked up his backpack and sorted through it. He picked up the blanket he'd been using for a pillow and folded it.

He glanced back at the campfire: three sets of eyes stared at him. Oz put his hands on his hips and sighed. He walked back to the campfire.

"Which way is the road?" Jack asked.

"Over yonder," Oz said, pointing. "Only a short distance.

Take a left and you'll see the town in less than a quarter of a mile, if I'm not mistaken."

"You won't accompany us?" Selene asked, her wide eyes like two moons between the night of her long hair.

"I believe I will take a walk," Oz said.

"Is it safe?" Jack asked.

"As safe as any place is now."

"We should stay here," Jack said to his sister. Oz saw the disapproval on her face, and the fear in Jack's eyes as he minutely shook his head. Oz grimaced, an old wound throbbing inside him.

"I'll go with you to town, Oz," Masaaki repeated, standing. He sounded as if he were talking in someone else's dream.

Oz threw up his hands. "Very well, children. We can all get backpacks once we get there and carry more back." He walked toward the opening in the barbed wire and muttered, "Blind leading the blind."

*

Ten minutes of sweaty tramping brought the four of them to a quiet road. A few empty cars sat on it. Oz followed the road to the right, and within a few minutes the trees were gone and empty houses started to move past them. The yellow sun throbbed above them like an eye.

They passed a field where weeds and sunflowers reached almost to their heads in vibrant green and yellow. The sunflowers seemed to stare at them as they walked. Oz realized he had started to run, and that the others had fallen into a jog behind him. He forced himself to walk.

They passed a short strip mall with silent, peaceful mannequins in the windows. Oz saw something pass over Jack's face and asked, "What is it, Jack?" Jack jumped, glanced at Oz, and then glanced at his sister on his other side, who stuck close to her brother. "Nothing."

"Tell me what you see."

"The worst Disneyland ride I've ever been on."

"Care to elaborate?" Oz asked.

"It's just... none of this seems real," Jack said. His voice was gravel. "I keep trying to see everything, and my eyes slip over it. All these houses and stores are still standing, but they may as well have had a nuclear bomb dropped on them. It's like everything is a movie set, and soon the workers will come out and kick us out. And they'll all be dead."

"Just so," Oz said. "What do these ruined buildings mean now? Before, one would see a broken down building in relation to the other buildings that weren't broken down. Now it's been reversed. All these buildings will be in ruins soon enough."

They passed a four-story brick building, *O'Brian's Insurance* painted on the front window. Jack pointed to it. "It will take that one a long time to fall down. Centuries."

"A memorial to all our great achievements? 'Look on all my shopping malls, ye mighty.' No, Jack, with mold and birds flying into the windows and no upkeep, it'll be rubble soon enough."

Selene whispered to Oz, "You certainly seem cheerful." Jack shot a warning glance at his sister and turned back to Oz.

Oz gave Selene a long look and said nothing.

Her eyes drilling into Oz, Selene muttered, "Your true name isn't Oz, is it?" Oz again said nothing, but a smile played over his lips as he looked ahead and walked.

Jack's eyes widened. "Is that true?"

Oz glanced at the twins and shrugged. "If people are going to die, it's just as well that the whole world die too. It makes one death less... jagged. Less jarring. And we were all going to die anyway. Perhaps we're seeing the truth which was there all along—all this desolation, I mean. Maybe all our ant-scurrying before the world died was only self-distraction, so we didn't have to think about the void above our heads and beneath us, and how soon we slip into it. Maybe all this is more honest." Oz smiled again. He stopped walking and turned around. "Friends, you'll notice the convenience store on the corner, two gas stations, the hardware store, and some more stores down that street. Remember you'll have to carry everything you take back to camp. So..."

"So this is where you leave us," Masaaki said.

Oz's eyes opened wide as the amusement fell away from his face.

Masaaki said, "Your directions to town were incorrect. You meant for us to become lost, and not return to your camp. When that failed, you led us here. But you never intended to return with us." Selene was nodding as Masaaki spoke.

Masaaki looked past Oz and said, "But it seems you will be frustrated."

"And what do you mean by that?" Oz asked.

Masaaki pointed. Oz turned and gave a little scream. A body in ragged clothes with a bent spine was shuffling away from them further down the street.

They stood, frozen, as the world held its breath for the corpse to keep walking. Jack's mouth started to work. Selene grabbed his arm and put a hand over his mouth. Jack shook it off and hissed, "There's someone over there, down the road! Should we try to help him?"

A tall, stocky man with ragged red hair stood further down the street with his back pressed against a wall. The corpse was wandering at such an angle that it didn't seem to have noticed him. The man had a gun in one raised hand. His wide eyes flicked back and forth between the four survivors and the thing shuffling past him. When the corpse had moved past, the man scampered toward them.

"Why didn't you shoot it?" Jack hissed.

"They might hear the sound," the man grunted. "You folks came from that way?" The man waved his gun vaguely.

"Yes," Jack said. "It's clear." Oz glared at him.

The man glanced behind him: the arc of the corpse's path had turned a little toward them. A little more, and it would see them.

"Let's go," the man said, breaking into a trot back down the street.

"Now, hold on," Oz hissed, but stopped when the man fell backwards onto the pavement.

A tall corpse blocked their route home. It was wrapped in a black cloth which rippled in the breeze. Its bald head stared, but it did not seem to see them. Its diseased fingers quivered. Its lower jaw hung open, locked by straining muscles. Its back arched beneath the clear blue sky and the watching sun. The eyes clouded over with a gray fluid. The dead flesh on the front of its face rippled and then peeled back like a blossoming flower. It turned its head upward to the sun.

The red haired man, still prone on the pavement, gasped and scrambled backwards without getting to his feet. He shouted and wriggled sideways when he brushed against the corpse they had seen moving down the street. It shuffled past him toward the tall, rigid corpse, ignoring the other humans. Oz, Selene, and Jack all backed away into an alley. Only Masaaki stood still and watched.

The ragged thing stopped in front of the shrouded body. The head of the taller corpse waved like tentacles underwater. Within the circle of those tentacles, the five survivors could see a flat, craterous face with two gray, dead eyes and a perfect circle of sharp teeth. It did not look at them. The crater was turned to the shorter corpse, whose face rippled and then peeled back like the first. It looked up at the sun.

The red-haired stranger gained his feet and started running, grunting in anger as if having to force his feet to move. Oz ran down the street as well. Neither looked at the other.

Jack stared at the corpse, tears dripping from his cheeks. His sister grabbed him by the hand and pulled and they ran together. Masaaki turned and walked after them.

And behind Masaaki, other bloody and ragged bodies shambled toward the tentacled thing, closing in from all directions. One by one, their faces opened like flowers.

*

The red-haired man stopped at the field of sunflowers and waited for Oz and Jack and Selene to catch up. When they did, they leaned over, huffing. The red-haired man scowled and barked, "We need to keep moving."

Jack gasped, "Wait for Masaaki."

The red-haired man snapped, "Who?"

Jack pointed back as Masaaki walked toward them.

16

The red-haired man stared at Masaaki until he was standing next to them. "You took your sweet time," he muttered.

Masaaki said nothing, turning instead to look at the sunflowers. He stared for a moment before saying, "Each one staring, blind, into the sun." Then: "It is beautiful, is it not? And terrifying."

The newcomer gave Masaaki a hard look, turned, and began to run again. They followed.

TWO

Man-Made

The forest had closed around them when Oz turned back to the others.

"What... what was that thing?" he asked.

The trees leaned close above them, tall judges or guests at a funeral. Oz put a hand on the nearest tree, feeling its bark. Dappled shadows played over his bald head as he whispered, "I can still see it. Curling starfish arms. Slow flames around the center of a sun."

No one spoke.

"Where's our camp?" the stranger asked.

Oz asked, "'Our'?"

The stranger said, "The name's Mason. You got a camp you're heading to?"

"You think my camp means anything now?" Oz yelled.

Mason's face became a locked door.

Oz whispered, "Sure, come on back to our camp. We can wait for dark and tell spooky stories and wait for those things to join us."

Mason moved until his face was an inch away from Oz's and growled, "I dunno if we'd survive if those things found us. They can get hurt, but they just grow back. But it's still

18

better if we stick together. At least we can try to put some clues together."

The whisper of a smile played over Oz's face again. "Man-made?" he asked.

Mason's eyes narrowed and he nodded. "How else?"

Jack sputtered, "What's man made? And what do you mean grow back?"

Mason and Oz continued to stare at each other. Oz snorted and stepped back from Mason. "Did you know they could do that with their faces?"

"No," Mason said. "I never saw that before."

"And they grow back, you say?"

Mason snorted. "Guess you never tried killing one before."

A gleam played in Oz's light blue eyes. "My name is Oz, Mason. This is Jack, Selene, and Masaaki. Our camp is this way." Oz walked away, his boots crunching leaves, turning left after he walked past a thin red strip of cloth tied around a high branch which Jack had never seen before.

They walked through the straight lines of the trees, through the fresh smell of pine and the quiet, speckled shadows. Oz hummed to himself as he walked; Mason bunched and unbunched his fists, his head down. Jack blinked watering eyes as he held his sister's shaking hand. Masaaki walked last, unhurried.

Oz was about to enter the circle of barbed wire when he froze: a tall blonde man was standing with his back to them within the circle, at the opposite end from the entrance. He was gesturing with his arm. A green cap was on his head; sweat darkened his plaid shirt.

Oz stood for a moment and then looked back at Mason. When Mason gave an almost unnoticeable nod, Oz lifted his arms and threaded his way through the narrow opening in the barbed wire between two trees. He walked into the center of the camp.

The man whirled and stared at them. His face didn't change, but his unblinking eyes narrowed within golden curls of hair. His hands clenched into fists and his forearms flexed.

"Get out," Oz said, pointing with a finger to the entrance of the camp.

The man didn't move.

Oz watched the blonde man for a moment. Then he shrugged, unshouldered his backpack, and put it at the head of his sleeping bag. He sat and began unlacing his shoes. As if on cue, Masaaki and Selene sat down under separate trees. Mason stood and watched.

Jack walked over and sat next to his sister, putting his arm around her. She scooted away from him, got a book of Emily Dickinson's poetry from her backpack, and sat against a tree opposite him. She flipped the book open and stared at it, her eyes unmoving. Jack hung his head.

The blonde man's eyes moved among them. He turned to the forest, took his cap off of his head and waved it. A fat man with curly brown hair bumbled out through a clump of bushes and waddled through the opening of the camp as if he was late to a party. A thin strip of skin showed between his shirt and his belt. Beer stains blotched the shirt like small continents.

"The name's Bob, sir," he said to Oz, extending a hand without meeting Oz's eyes. Oz, still seated, raised a limp hand which became engulfed in a vigorous handshake. "A pleasure, a genuine pleasure. This here is my friend and longtime associate, Luke. Real nice place y'all got here! Some real good work put into this. How can I help?" His slow voice was like syrup.

Oz introduced himself hesitantly, as if not listening to himself. Bob began to talk about defenses and pits and traps. Oz turned to look at the trees outside the barbed wire, as if something in the dappled shadows of the forest were calling to him.

*

Mason stood up to his considerable height as the members of his new camp wandered to different trees and sat with bleary expressions. Eventually he found his own tree and let his head rest against the hard bark. Sweat trickled down his back, but he didn't move. The image of the corpse's face unpeeling flashed over his mind. He sighed and forced his thoughts away from the sunflower—which opened again, even as he pushed it away, to show a scarred, barren planet orbiting a different kind of sun. He turned his attention to the witnesses sitting around him. He tried to recall the pleasant, mindless fatigue of working so many late nights at the station, hour upon hour to dull memories he didn't want.

Mason watched Oz. Oz was staring at the forest outside his camp as Bob drawled on about defenses. Mason watched the empty, airy look in Oz's eyes, and wondered when the balding professor's mood would shift again. He wondered why Oz didn't show more signs of trauma, and if Oz would cut and run when they needed him most.

Mason turned to the Japanese man. He was staring into space as if watching TV. A steel wire in Mason's gut twisted as he wondered when the man would break.

He looked back at Bob. Bob was still droning on about fences and traps, oblivious to Oz's boredom. As Bob turned this way and that, pointing to different parts of the camp, his gut almost brushed the side of Oz's head. Mason watched how Bob's eyes never met Oz's.

Mason turned to Luke, who stood at the far end of the camp, his John Deere cap shading his face. Luke stood as if he were ready to start sprinting or fighting if anyone talked to him. The steel wire in Mason's gut tightened a little more.

Luke's eyes locked with Mason's, and Mason quickly shut his eyes, forcing himself to take deep breaths as if he were sleeping. In the silence of the forest, without any wind blowing through the trees, the whispered conversation of the twins sitting near him was easy to hear.

"Remember how he never came up to the loft?" Jack asked. "There will always be a safe place for us."

"Yes," his sister said. Her voice was dead.

"We got away from the farm eventually. And we survived while we were there."

"Yes."

Eventually, the brother asked, "How could you tell those things about Oz?"

"What things?" a distant voice asked.

"That his name wasn't Oz."

"I thought upon the moon," Selene murmured. "It lingers still, above the trees."

"What does the moon have to do with it, Selene?" The question was a gentle stroke on her back.

"Before all this disaster, I would think about the moon whenever Father came to me within my dreams. I would think about it shining, how it made the velvet darkness beautiful. And when I think about it now, things become clear. Do you remember how it used to shine within the window of the loft?" As her question hung between them, Mason realized the color had come back into her voice.

"Okay, weirdo, don't tell me," Jack murmured, and Selene laughed quietly.

From the opposite direction, Mason heard Bob say, "You sure I can't help make this place more secure?" Mason opened his eyes. Bob was still standing in front of Oz, who still stared into the forest.

Mason stood and walked toward them. "Mind if I ask you a few questions?"

Oz didn't move.

Mason snapped his fingers in front of the professor's face. Without blinking, Oz turned and looked up at Mason.

"I keep thinking about it," Oz said in a voice as soft as a breeze. "Opening."

Mason kept his voice low and motioned to the far edge of the camp. "Let's talk."

They walked around the small mound where they slept and stepped over the bubbling stream. Mason walked until he could touch the barbed wire and sat down, his back against a tree. Glancing back, he saw they were nearly hidden from view. Luke's eyes followed them, but there was nothing Mason could do about that. He motioned for Oz to sit, but the older man stood, looking down at him.

Mason shrugged and gently rubbed his finger against one of the tiny spindles of wire. He said, "You know it's better if we stick together."

Oz said nothing, standing still as the air around him.

"I've been in two other groups before this one that didn't last longer than a couple days. People just lost it. Some actually went looking for corpses so they could get bit. But it's better if we stay together."

"Given how your other groups ended, do you think your chances are better with us?" Oz asked.

"You people aren't like the other groups. You seem kinda calm after what we just saw. All of you. Real calm." Mason looked at Oz for a moment before asking, "Should we tell the others?"

"Tell them what?"

Mason glared.

"Sure, let's tell them," Oz said.

"It might cause a panic."

Oz shrugged.

"Look, the first thing you do is try to contain the scene. Then you try to interpret the evidence. If bystanders panic, it can ruin everything."

"You were a policeman." Oz seemed minutely more relaxed.

Mason shifted and looked away. "Yeah. So?"

"You think this is some kind of crime scene. And you're investigating."

Mason glared at Oz. "Everyone's guilty. And there's always evidence. You can run if you want, but I'm gonna..."

"You'll solve the case and execute justice on the evildoers."

Mason ground out the words like he was chewing broken glass: "You can say whatever you like. I'm asking you if we should tell the others."

"It doesn't matter."

Mason's jaw dropped. "It doesn't matter if we tell these people a man-made agent has turned half of the population into zombies? And that most of the other half have been eaten?"

"It doesn't matter if we tell them or if we don't. Nor does it matter if our suspicion is true or false. Death was everywhere before this happened. It's only taken on a new form."

Mason looked at Oz for a moment. He said, "I'm telling them tonight."

"Sometimes it's best to leave the truth alone."

"Sometimes figuring out who's guilty hurts. But unless you do, the evil just lies there."

"The old world has died, Mason. Why not let its sins rest in peace?"

"Like your sins, Oz?"

The color drained from the professor's face. "You're chasing something that doesn't exist, policeman. Justice barely existed before, and there is no justice now. I think, for your own sake, you'd better accept that."

Mason stood. He looked back and forth between the camp and Oz. "What a way to lead!" he snorted.

"I'm no leader."

"You better at least figure out how to lead yourself. You'll go over the edge if you don't."

"I've been there a long time," Oz said.

Mason stood and started to walk back to camp. He stopped and said, "Bob doesn't have much more time, but watch out for Luke."

Oz's face made a question mark. "He's white trash."

"Maybe not. See you tonight." He walked away.

THREE

Conference

As the setting sun reached long, yellow arms through the trees, Mason walked over and sat down at the camp's shallow pit near the stream. He stared at Oz until Oz, who had moved back to his sleeping bag, happened to look at him. Oz rolled his eyes and joined him at the shallow pit.

"This a fire pit?" Mason asked.

"Correct. But it's too humid for a fire."

"And too dangerous," Mason said.

"Why?"

The sunset made Mason's short red hair and red stubble look fiery. "They're attracted to fire. Did you know that? Have you thought about it? If you haven't, would you like to start?"

Keeping his eyes on Mason, Oz shouted, "Circle round, friends. Citizen Mason wants to have a town meeting."

Masaaki, Jack, Selene, and Bob came and sat. Luke hung back, arms crossed, smiling.

"Coming, Luke?" Mason asked. Luke hesitated, then sat on the ground a few paces away.

In a wobbly voice, Jack asked, "Are you two going to tell us what you were talking about on the way back here?"

Mason said, "It's possible that something just accidentally happened that turned most of us into zombies. Some kind of disease, or some experiment gone wrong. Lots of guys in white lab coats running around in a lab a mile beneath Nevada." Luke snorted, and Mason shrugged. "Just laying out possibilities."

"They're not zombies," Jack said softly. "The actors in zombie movies are way more human than what we saw today."

Mason eyed Jack. "You like scary movies? You?"

"He used to hide them in his room," Selene whispered. Jack rolled his eyes.

Mason kept his eyes on Jack for a heartbeat. "The way that thing's face changed..."

"How is that different from any of the others?" asked Jack.

"Disease breaks a body down," Oz said. "It doesn't give it new parts."

"So something happened that's changing us, but the cause is natural," Masaaki said.

"I can't rule it out," Mason said. "But it's more likely this is intentional."

"Couldn't it have been released accidentally?" Jack asked.

"I suppose," Oz said. "But whoever made the chemical meant it to be used eventually, so their intentions have been served regardless."

"So, terrorists?" Jack asked.

"No," Mason said. "Terrorists are trying to make a point to everyone else to change something. Whoever did this didn't leave much of anyone else, and they changed everything. And what point are they trying to make by destroying everything?"

No one spoke. The silence filled the circle the way smoke would have if there had been a fire, rising into the evening sky which stood above them like a blank face, staring and silent.

*

Jack asked, "What did you mean about the... the flower-head things growing back?"

Mason said, "When you shoot them, they stop for a while, but this white stuff grows outta them. Like cartilage. Heals them. Best you can do is slow them down so you can get away."

No one said anything for a moment. Then Jack asked, "Why is this place so quiet? I expected to hear crickets or something, but it's like we're in an empty room."

Mason blinked. "That's another thing. When's the last time you saw an animal?"

"We saw a lot of dead animals on the way down here," Jack said.

"Long dead and rotting," Selene added.

"I ain't seen a live one since this happened," Mason said. "Anyone else?"

Nobody spoke.

"So, here's what we know," he said, leaning in. "We know …"

Masaaki interrupted, "Someone has unleashed death on us. That is what we know."

"I remember the day it happened," Selene whispered. "Some people just changed. But not everyone."

"Hey, what was that?" Jack turned to look into the deepening gloom.

"I didn't hear anything," Oz said.

Mason stood, eyes wide, and pointed. "Did you see that?"

Jack stood as well, nodding. "Right over there."

The group turned, but only the shadowy lines of the trees were visible.

"Would you care to fill the rest of us in on your little mystery?" Oz asked.

"I saw someone, standing over there. Jack, you did too?"

Mason and Jack stared into the forest. "He was tall," Jack whispered.

Mason sat slowly, blinking. "Uh, what was I saying?"

"You were laying out the evidence for your case," Oz said.

Mason said, "Yeah. Right. What I wanted to ask was, why would someone do this? And can we find them?"

"I doubt this individual had a rational reason for what he did," Oz said.

In a soft voice, Selene asked, "What do we do now?"

"We need to find a way to kill them, for starters," Mason said; but Selene was shaking her head. Mason stopped, waiting for Selene to speak. When she would not, her brother said, "I think she means, what do we... do?"

"Figure out as much of this as I can," Mason said.

"Why?" whispered Selene.

"I've seen a lot of crime scenes where I was too late to do anything about it. But figuring out as much as you can about what happened and why and who did it... it helps. You can fix a lot of the wrong that's been done."

"I do not believe there is any way to fight this," Masaaki said.

"And why do you say that?" Oz asked, smiling wryly.

"It is death we are dealing with. One does not fight it."

"How do you figure that?" Mason asked.

"I saw many sick when I was a physician. I saw many elderly, who were close to death. I knew most of them would get better. Now, it is like we are seeing a corpse and asking what can be done. The world is a corpse. There is nothing to be done." Masaaki turned and saw the burning in Mason's eyes. He looked down and quickly said, "But let us try to see it, all the same, as Mason says."

Oz nodded. "Very well, detective. Help us decipher this mystery."

"All right," Mason said, still looking at Masaaki. "The first thing is always to..."

The words froze in Mason's mouth. His eyes widened and he scrambled to his feet. A few feet away in the thickening darkness, Luke stood and turned; a girlish yelp escaped him. A dark outline shuffled through leaves and pine needles toward the line of barbed wire. As if a cloud had covered the sun, the shadowy forest around them grew dim before the presence of this nullity. It stopped. In the deepening gloom they saw dark tentacles blossom around its shadowed head. It hissed and walked toward them. The barbed wire flexed and bounced as the corpse tangled itself up in it. It tried to keep walking, hands out, as the wire tugged at its dead flesh.

"Get rid of it," Selene hissed, shaking her twin's shoulder. "Jack, get rid of that thing!" But Jack sat with his head down, hands over his face. He rocked back and forth and moaned.

Mason ran a dozen steps toward the center of camp. He crouched, then moved toward the corpse, his arms full of logs which he dropped a foot away from the line of creaking barbed wire. A crumpled map from Mason's pocket fell onto the logs, and a single match popped into life. The sap and pine needles brought easy, licking flames.

"What... what..." Oz gasped.

The thing had been reaching torn hands to embrace Mason, but it grew still before the fire which danced in its gray eyes. Its tentacles drooped. Taking one of the longer sticks, Mason inched the logs closer to the thing in the barbed wire. Twice the flame died, and Mason had to blow on it to revive it. Luke got down on one knee with a stick and pushed and blew as well. Soon they were in reach of its hands, which now hung limp before the mesmerizing flame. Something caught Oz by the throat when he saw the thing was wearing Converse All-Stars.

Behind Oz, Masaaki said, "Wait." His voice resonated in the quiet of the forest, broken only by the creaking barbed wire.

Mason, crouching over, gave him a look that said, *This better be good.*

"Why not leave it?" Masaaki asked, his face glowing against the light of the fire. "This thing is lost and lonely. It is trying to die, and to be with others in death. Is burning it any way to treat it?"

Mason's jaw flopped open. He turned back to nudge the logs closer.

"Maybe he's right," Oz whispered. "Look at his shoes. You can see his big toe sticking out. He was alive, not so long ago." He gave a shuddering, weepy groan. "We're the monsters now. It's already tangled up, so it won't follow. I'll make a camp somewhere else."

Mason stood and looked around as if he was the last sane person on earth. He turned to Luke in exasperation, but Luke was absorbed in the thing and not listening.

Mason crouched again. One more nudge from his stick, and the thing in the wire gave a soft, piercing whistle as the flames licked up and around its legs. Dirty jeans melted into dead flesh. Jack pressed his hands against his ears and collapsed to his knees next to Bob, who had remained sitting, stunned. Selene joined her wail to the corpse and staggered away.

The flames ate their way up its legs. The tentacles writhed and its gray eyes looked upward, as if searching for the sun. The pit which had once been a mouth opened and several black tongues flicked and slithered past jagged teeth. Its hands jumped as if electrocuted, and one pawed at Luke. With animal quickness, a knife flashed from Luke's belt and the hand fell to the forest floor. Luke fell backwards and backed away on all fours as the severed hand started to pull its way with questing figures in a slow curve back to its owner, trailing short white tendons from the wrist. The tendons hung in the air as if underwater. The hand crawled into the fire and burst into flames with an audible *thud* and began to melt into a white mass. The flames momentarily leapt above their heads. Long, white lines like streaks of smoke rose from the fire.

As the flames gradually receded, Oz saw a feminine face reflected in the firelight among the trees. He shouted incoherently and it disappeared.

The corpse, now engulfed in flame, shook and shuddered. Its high, rising wail finally faded into the crackling flames. It held its arm out, away from the fire. Where its hand had been, white cartilage grew into something which looked like a flower.

*

An hour later, it finally collapsed on itself, pulling the barbed wire down with it. Oz's tears had dried on his cheeks, and Jack's sobs had quieted in exhaustion. Selene had wandered to her brother and sat next to him at the fire pit. The rest sat in a semi-circle, facing the thing they had burned, their faces lit by the orange glow. The slow flower growing out of the thing's wrist had been pulled into the flames. Soon it was only a bubbling puddle of white.

Oz's voice was a wandering whimper. "Do you still want to figure this out, Mason?"

The low, sputtering fire played across the flint of the stocky man's features. Although Mason said nothing and didn't turn to Oz, he could tell that, even now, Mason's mind was scurrying for clues.

Oz wanted to turn away from the bubbling white puddle, but instead he sat, and sat, and wondered what the point was of building another camp if he would have to watch this all over again. Then dawn was prying his eyes open. He was lying on his side where he had fallen asleep.

Walking over to the charred remnants of the fire, he saw the barbed wire had returned to its normal height, blackened but unbroken. Where the corpse had collapsed, glistening white petals overlapped slowly, like tectonic plates forming a new world.

FOUR

Two Gunshots

The next day was spent in useless wandering inside the camp. That evening, Mason came over and sat down beside Oz.

"There's someone out there," Mason muttered.

"I know, I saw her last night."

Mason paused. "I didn't see a woman."

"Oh."

"It's hard to find someone in a forest if they don't want to be seen. And none of us are up for it anyway. But we got two people watching us. At least two. What does that tell us?"

"It tells us there are people out there who are even more scared than we are."

"It tells us," Mason barked, "that there are other survivors out there. Are they a threat? Do we need them?"

"The more people we have here, the more complicated matters will become."

"I ain't leavin', if that's what you mean. Oh, and Luke is acting pretty weird, too. He keeps talking to Bob, but I can't tell if Luke's pissed off or scared. I guess Bob wet himself last night. Doesn't have a change of pants."

Oz snorted and tried to keep from smiling. "What do

you want me to say, Mason? Do you want to take a trip to town and get laundry detergent?"

"I want you to start thinking about other people and what might be best for them."

Oz looked at the ground. "We're all alone. We were before, and we are now. You can't help someone who doesn't want to live. Ignoring that and trying to carry someone just makes it worse in the long run." He hesitated. "You said yesterday we were surprisingly calm."

"Well, you weren't calm when that thing came last night, but you people bounce back better than anyone else I've seen."

"I would venture that the reason for our resilience is that the people here have already learned you cannot depend on others."

Mason frowned; Oz turned away.

Masaaki walked over to them. "The Flower we burned last night is growing again," he said.

Oz and Mason looked at each other.

"Yeah," Mason said.

Oz looked away, into the forest, and said nothing.

*

Selene sat with her back to a tree and a book open in her lap. Her brother sat next to her. Selene stared at the pages. Her eyes didn't move. Every minute or so, she flipped a page.

"Maybe the ocean," Jack said. "We could find an island."

Selene turned another page, then sighed and shut the book. "I'd give anything to taste a cappuccino," she whispered. "Just to sit and sip and read."

"I read a zombie comic once where a group of survivors found a prison. It was a perfect fortress."

Selene grabbed Jack's hand and squeezed, hard, her nails biting into his skin.

"I'm not giving up," he said.

She let go. "Can't you feel it, brother? The world has changed. We are no longer on the farm. How we survived that place... it won't help us now." She looked down. "The dirty man keeps staring at me."

Jack looked across the camp to where Luke sat, adjusting his hat around his golden locks. Bob sat nearby, taking large breaths, his eyes wandering over the trees as drool slipped from his sagging mouth.

The tall blonde stood, brushed down his filthy plaid shirt, and walked over to them. He stood for a moment before saying, "Emily Dickinson."

Selene glanced at the book in her lap and nodded.

"There's somethin' quieter than sleep," Luke said. Selene's eyes flared in surprise.

Jack got to his feet and stood in front of Luke. He had to tilt his head back to meet his eyes. The corners of Luke's mouth curled. He cocked his arm. Jack flinched, took a step back, tripped on a root, and landed in a graceless pile on the forest floor. Luke chuckled and turned back to Selene.

"I'm nothing like you think," Selene hissed. "Stay away."

Luke's face darkened. He walked away. Jack scooted back to sit with his sister. His eyes were watering and he was biting his lip.

"I'll kill him if he comes near you again," he whispered.

"No you won't." She stared at Luke as he walked away. The muscles in his back showed against his sweat-stained shirt, and she felt something stir within her.

*

After the sun set, Oz lay down on his sleeping bag and looked up at gentle stars. Gradually the others settled down and the noises around him subsided. He felt the sweat drying on his skin. He watched the stars. His eyes closed.

Oz flew in shining moonlight, and knew he was asleep, and dreamed still. Above the forest he soared, beneath the velvet beauty of the night and the unworried, childlike stars, high above the undead which swarmed like bloody ants on the surface of the earth, free of the sad man lying on his sleeping bag and the other survivors hanging onto him. He passed over a lake and saw his tiny body reflected in the surface of the water.

In the distance, something roared. He craned his neck and saw the whirlwind on the horizon. He remembered the dreams he managed to forget by day, and fear gripped him. He dropped to the ground to hide in the forest and waited, frozen, as the rainless storm passed by. When the air was quiet again, he saw a woman walking through the forest. Her footprints glowed green, and little flowers grew wherever she stepped, and Oz knew, as one knows in dreams, that she was walking toward their camp. Her sharp lips and green eyes and red hair flashed in the moonlight. Oz followed.

She came into camp and sat by the body of the man who called himself Oz. She looked at his body, and asked, Can you come back? It's easier to talk to you that way.

He shook his head and he felt the ground beneath his skull. He blinked and realized he was lying on the ground.

You're another man, she said. I can see the disease in you. Why aren't you dead?

I have been dead a long time, Oz answered, looking up at

the woman from the ground.

Were you good to your women? she asked.

No, he said, and the quiet hum of the night seemed to pause.

The woman said, The colors stopped here. Will I be safe if I stay?

I swear on my daughter's life I will do everything in my power to keep you safe, he said, but something inside him wondered if he lied.

Why are you looking at me that way? she asked, tilting her head.

Because it is so wonderful to see something green and verdant after so much death, Oz said.

The woman frowned and looked away. The first timid lines of sunrise began to streak her face. Something boomed in Oz's dream like distant thunder from a graveyard.

The woman said, Another man is getting what he deserves.

A second boom sounded.

*

Oz sat up, blinking. A woman with pale skin, sharp green eyes and red hair stood next to him.

He blinked at her for an instant. "Don't tell them what I said about not being good," he said, and then he was up and running to the other side of the camp. Luke ran past him toward the stream, covered with something which looked like black paint in the dim light of early dawn.

Oz stopped at the place where Luke and Bob had slept. He took one step, then another, toward Luke's sleeping bag and the body lying next to it. He heard splashing behind him, but Oz couldn't look away from the hand lying on the ground and the gun dangling from it, the beer-stained shirt, the pot belly.

Oz turned around and saw Luke standing in the stream, blinking and dripping water. His shirt was stained with blood. The others had assembled around him. Luke's wide eyes jumped among the people staring at him.

Mason walked toward Oz, looked at the body, and walked back to Luke. "Why were there two shots, Luke?" he asked.

Jack whispered, "He was trying to stop him. I saw."

Mason's eyes remained trained on Luke. "If you were trying to stop him, why were there two shots?"

Luke said nothing, his body tense. But suddenly everyone turned away from Luke and toward Oz. Standing over Bob's corpse, Oz had thrown back his head and begun to wail.

Decorum would have had them turn away, but there was nowhere in camp where they could not have seen Oz, and they would have had to walk far to go beyond the range of his shuddering sobs. When the storm finally blew itself out and Oz turned around, no one had moved. They stared at him.

Oz stood for a moment, a bald bent man with a sagging stomach in a sweat-stained shirt in the growing sunlight. Then he croaked, "Time to have a group meeting. Now." He walked toward the fire pit and sat down.

No one argued.

FIVE

Write the Pain Out

"The first thing we're talking about is Luke." Oz was glaring at the shallow pit in the ground. "What happened and whether he is staying."

Luke sat across from them, rigid. He muttered, "You know what? I'm gone," and stood up.

"Afraid I can't let you do that, friend," Mason said without looking at him.

Luke sneered, "How you figure that?"

"Would I find your fingerprints on that gun, Luke? In my experience, suicides don't shoot twice. And I saw you talking to Bob all yesterday. Care to relate your conversation?"

Luke turned and started walking away.

"Jack here said he saw you trying to stop him. If that's true, why are you running away?"

Luke turned and glared at Mason.

Oz said, "If he wants to go, let him."

"You gonna let someone guilty go?"

"Are you saying he murdered Bob? Even if he did, what can we do about it?" Oz looked around for confirmation, but Selene was fighting back tears and said nothing. Jack was staring at his shoes, hands gripped together. Masaaki was looking at the edge of camp, where Bob's corpse still lay. Oz sighed. The new woman stared back at Oz, her face unreadable.

"We can't just let criminals go," Mason growled. "Now more than ever."

"Why?" Oz asked.

"Because there are so many of them now."

The balding professor frowned. "You mean the dead? Is that how you perceive them? As criminals?"

Luke turned and started walking away. Mason stood and took out pair of handcuffs. He said, "You're not going anywhere, Luke."

Luke stopped and pulled a knife from his belt. He didn't turn around.

Mason was pulling the handgun out of one of his pockets when the new woman said, "You men. Even after you killed the world, you're still ready to kill each other."

The stocky policeman turned to the new woman. "And who might you be?" The flame-haired woman gave Mason an even look and said nothing. "I don't believe I caught your name, sweetie."

"My old name is lost," she said. "But I'm going to find my new mother. She'll give me my new name, and I'll know it's real as soon as I hear it."

Mason looked like he wanted to start laughing but was too surprised. Luke stared at her as well.

Looking back and forth between Mason and the redhead, Oz said, "The second thing we need to talk about... well, it isn't the second. We need to introduce the newest member of our happy little camp. Then we need to decide what to do with..." Oz swallowed. "With the body. And we need to decide if it's worth staying together. What are we doing here? If it's only survival, I can survive on my own."

"Not as well as we could together," Mason said.

Oz snorted. "Said the ex-cop, ready to kill a suspect."

Mason glared at Luke and said nothing.

Oz opened his mouth to speak and then shut it.

"Speak," Selene whispered.

"There doesn't seem to be much point if we are going to part ways," Oz said. He realized everyone was looking at him intently.

"Speak your mind," Selene said.

He took another breath. "I don't care if individuals stay or leave. But if we stay, let's be clear about why." He looked back at the place where Luke and Bob had slept, and shivered. He whispered, "And please, please, if you're going to end it, have the decency to leave first and do it far away." His voice cracked like a twig under a boot.

Silence, then, in the quiet forest and the warm morning light.

When no one spoke, the professor's eyes fell to the ground. After a minute, he said, as if to himself, "When you're in pain, you write it out. Write the pain out of you. That's the advice I was given early on, and that's what I told my students. So this is what we are going to do. We are going to write out our stories. How we got here, what things were like for us before all this, and what we noticed. Try to find clues." He glanced at Mason. "Try to make as much sense out of this as we can. And we'll decide what to do once we've all had a chance to speak. I have paper in my backpack that I'll give to everyone."

No one spoke.

"I'll go first," Oz said. "We'll meet this evening and read

what we have written. Agreed?"

"I'll do it," the red-haired woman said. Selene nodded, as did Masaaki.

No one else seemed to be disagreeing, so Oz said, "Now if someone will help me, I'll bury the body. I have a small shovel."

"I will," Masaaki said, and started walking toward the body before Oz could agree. Oz followed him without looking at any of the others.

As they walked away, Jack whispered, "What's wrong with Masaaki? Is he in shock?"

Mason said under his breath, "He's not acting like it."

"You've seen a lot of people in shock," Selene said, her voice quiet as moonlight.

"That's right."

"Then why is he so calm?" Jack asked.

Selene whispered, "You know why Oz began to cry, do you not?"

Mason said, "Obviously this has happened to him before."

*

Masaaki and Oz dropped the wrapped sleeping bag after two dozen paces of tramping through the woods. Oz said in a low voice, "I know this is close to camp, but I just want to get this done." The Japanese man nodded.

After an hour of taking turns with Oz's single short shovel, there was enough of a long trench for them to toss the sleeping bag in. As it came to rest in the earth for the last time, the half of Bob's head which was still intact rolled from under the fold of the sleeping bag. He seemed to be looking at something in the distance which interested him. Oz reached out to cover Bob's face, but his hand trembled and stopped. Masaaki put a hand on his shoulder and did it for him.

They stood for a minute. Then Oz said, "Thank you for helping."

"I have to help." He stared at the ground.

"Well, thank you for helping me."

"Not you alone," Masaaki said. "Them. Him."

"The people back at the camp?"

"No," Masaaki said. "Them."

"How," Oz asked, "are you going to help the dead?"

Masaaki stared at the sleeping bag. "I do not know yet. Perhaps your exercise tonight will help."

It took less time to cover the grave than to dig it. Oz crouched and spread leaves across the overturned earth; then he stood and looked at their work. When he saw Masaaki staring at him, he said, "I don't want to remember where this grave is."

"It is important to have markers for the dead."

"I sincerely doubt he cares."

"It is still important. If you try to erase the memory of the dead, it will only..." He stopped as he saw the professor's hands begin to shake.

"I apologize," Masaaki said. "In Japan, my fathers would bury their dead near the village. It was hard. But I think it was wise."

He smoothed a few more leaves over the grave with his boot. "I'd never stay in a village like that."

Masaaki looked thoughtful. "Anyone who stays in one place long enough will find pain. But it is better than sleeping alone in the hills and the rain."

"No it is not," Oz said and walked away without looking back. Masaaki waited for a moment, then followed. Neither saw the newly turned earth start to shift, as if someone beneath were turning over in their sleep.

*

After Oz and Masaaki had rolled up Bob's corpse in his sleeping bag and left camp, Jack walked over to the nameless girl and stood next to her. She was sitting against a tree with an empty look in her eyes.

His hands looked as if they wanted something to clutch, but had nothing, so they grabbed each other.

He opened his mouth to speak, but Nameless cut him off without looking at him. "Are you going to be, like, my Knight in shining armor? Really? I won't go to prom with you. Walk away, asshole." When Jack froze, shaking his head and trying to speak, Nameless turned her face toward him with razors in her eyes. "Stay. Away. From. Me," she whispered.

He heard the hint of hysteria in her voice. He went to the other side of camp and sat where his sister couldn't see him.

Six

Stories

That evening, Oz arranged a crumpled map, twigs, and four smaller logs inside the fire pit. When Mason walked over, Oz said, "I know a fire is dangerous. But if we're going to tell our stories, we ought to have a fire. Besides, yesterday's was the first I've seen in the forest."

Mason nodded and sat down. Soon flickering flames threw yellow and orange rivulets on Oz's wrinkled, bald face. Mason's close-cut red hair and stubble burned in the sunset. The other members of the camp sat around the fire, most holding sheets of paper. Jack seemed of even slighter frame in the gathering darkness; Selene's skin seemed paler, her hair darker. The red hair and green eyes of the nameless woman glowed as she stared into the fire. Masaaki sat next to her, but Luke sat outside the circle in the shadows.

Oz picked up his paper and cleared his throat.

"Hold on," Mason said. He turned to the redhead. "Who are you and why are you here?"

"You five are different."

"There are six of us here," Oz said, nodding toward Luke.

"He just lives nearby," the nameless girl said. "He came here by accident. The rest of you are special."

Mason rolled his eyes. "Just read," he muttered to Oz.

Oz looked at the paper in his hands, opened his mouth, and shut it. He sighed.

Selene asked softly, "What stops you?"

He stared at the pages and said nothing.

"C'mon." Mason's tone was a coiled serpent. "You're the one who said we gotta talk about our feelings."

"It's just that I was writing before you all came here. Writing always helped in the past. This time, it helped a little, but it made it worse, too."

"How?" Jack asked.

"It made everything more real."

"And now you don't want that to happen again," Masaaki said. Oz would not meet his eyes.

The fire glimmered in Mason's hooded eyes as he said, "What else?"

Oz slumped over. "It's not very good writing."

The guffaw in Mason's throat was gravel tossed down a well. "That's it? You won't read it 'cause it's not poetry?"

"I used to write often. I did it well. This," he indicated the paper in front of him, "is terrible. But it still reminds me of someone I left behind long ago."

"Just read," Selene said. "We will hear the truth you want to say." Oz looked at her, and saw a half moon high above her. The celestial body shone with the same ghostly radiance of Selene's beautiful face. Oz realized he was staring and looked away.

Masaaki said, "Speech is given to the living. There are no words in the grave. Speak to us, Oz." His ivory face was like a statue of an angel looking over a graveyard.

Oz spoke.

*

"I was living in Alberta when it happened, north of Edmonton. I took trucking jobs whenever I could and stayed out of the city as much as possible."

"You don't talk like a trucker," Mason said.

"That was the job I had when it happened." He glared, and the policeman shut his mouth. "I hated my life then, but there were a lot of sunsets on my front porch, even though I couldn't so much as open a book. I would sit out there and drink, the whiskey making me dizzy and... hold on..." He scanned the page in front of him. "'The whiskey making me dizzy and pulling currents through my head like the wind drawing the wisps of clouds across the sky.'"

Selene smiled. "That's not bad."

"So tell us about the day it happened," Mason said, as if he had another meeting to get to.

"My neighbor was shuffling around on my front porch, and when I opened the door, I could see it wasn't my neighbor anymore. I slammed the door and leaned against it as it pounded..."

"I thought you told me your neighbor was a woman," Jack said. "That's what you said when we first came."

"The thing pounding on my door still had long brown hair and earrings," Oz said, "but it wasn't a woman. It would have broken down the door except it got interested in a motorist who had slowed down. I stayed inside the rest of that day and watched, but didn't see too much of anything else. I drove into town the next day. All during the drive, I was telling myself the trail of smoke on the horizon was from a fire. By the time I was inside the city, I could see three more. And those things, shuffling, grabbing, eating, slow and strong and slack-jawed, bored and ravenous. Their blind feet and their dead eyes. I'd had to drive into the city so many times before, but it wasn't the same city.

"I wanted to drive further into town, but I couldn't get very far with those things swarming everywhere, so I went home."

"Why are you smiling?" Mason asked.

"I am not."

"Yeah you were," Luke said.

"Everyone's guilty," Mason said. "You can't hide it."

The words rushed out of Oz like wind: "I was thinking about those things swarming through the head office of the trucking company where I used to beg for jobs, and how I'd never have to go back there and sit across from the boss who smirked at the guy with a PhD on his resume who didn't know a thing about trucking and who was plainly desperate." A smile broke over Oz's face again. "For a couple days after that, I just enjoyed it. The world had given me a gift. I stayed inside, of course, but I lived in a remote area, so it was relatively safe. I could hole up inside without my house ever turning into a prison, and in the evenings, after the TV was only static, I would put a chair by the front window and watch. It was as if I was travelling, or that any other place I went was as real, or as unreal, as the place I was right then. Perhaps I shouldn't have left."

"Why did you?" Mason asked.

"Because... I actually wondered that myself on my way down here. Part of it was the winter which would eventually come. Part of it was a dream I had. I was back in my old office and wind was blowing everywhere, knocking books off the shelves. I looked out my one office window to see it was broken, letting in all the wind, and the undead were stumbling around outside in circles which almost made a pattern. The secretary for the department came in, and I started to apologize for the mess, but I saw she was dead. Then the Dean walked up behind her to tell me I was fired again, and he was dead as well. I woke up gasping. It was hard to be inside my house after that.

"Another reason was the knock on my door five or six days after it happened. I froze as soon as I heard it, not wanting anyone to hear me inside, even though I knew they would never knock. Eventually I cracked the door open. I told him he couldn't come inside.

"He talked a while in circles and hints, but it was clear that he was a part of another group of survivors, and he wanted me to come with him. He made a number of veiled threats. Eventually I pointed behind him with a scared look on my face, even though there was no one there. He jumped and whirled around, and I slammed the door in his face and pressed my shoulder against it as he banged on the door, thinking about how my neighbor had pounded against it to be let in for a meal. I left that night." Oz paused to clear his throat and take a sip from the cup of water. The fire danced in his eyes.

"I slept inside cars with doors locked and the windows cracked. Only once did I wake up to blind pawing on the windows around me." He shuddered. "The moaning fingers and yawning hunger. One started to hit the glass. It shattered as I drove away.

"I kept moving south, sometimes walking and sometimes driving. Always the wind was at my back. The dominant memory I have is of emptiness: moving from emptiness into emptiness. After a while I didn't see the devastation, the empty buildings with broken windows. Always moving under bright blue skies down nameless roads, each border and county line now only a curiosity, the satisfaction of crossing it gone, thinking about why I'd left, whether I'd made the right decision, and what basis you could have for making any decision anymore. And I wondered if there was a reason why it had happened. If there ever could be a reason adequate to what has happened."

"There must be a reason," Mason said. "That's part of why we're here, to look for clues."

Oz said, "Well, they're attracted to fire. We know that already, of course."

"Tell me about how you learned that."

"Should I have a lawyer present before I answer that question, Mason?"

Firelight caressed the policeman's granite face. "Those things are out there, doing things the worst criminals could never get away with. If you're not helping me do something about it, you're part of the problem."

"Very well. Here's how I discovered it: I went by an oil refinery. I was looking at it when I jumped like I'd been stung, because I heard that shuffling moaning behind me. One of them was making its way toward me. I fell over and started to crawl away in the dust, only to see more of them. But they all went right past me and just walked into the flames. They would start to melt when they got close and open up in those white tendrils, but they'd keep going anyway and melt entirely. They were more interested in the fire than me." He sighed. "It was actually one of the safer places I'd been, but I left regardless."

"If it was safe, then why?" Selene asked.

Oz hung his head as if ashamed. "When I was running from the dead, I at least felt like a human being. As if I were

51

still alive. When they ignored me, it was as if I disappeared."

"Where was this?" Jack asked.

"I don't know. They tear down every road sign. Didn't you know that? If that's a clue, I don't know what it means."

"So what else?" Mason asked.

Oz sighed again. "I've told you more than I wanted to already, but... I had a hallucination I won't soon forget. It must have been a hallucination, it must have been, since I couldn't really trust my mind then. I wasn't sleeping very well in any case. During part of my journey, I got sick of being inside a car all day, so I walked for a while, regardless of the risk. I found it impossible not to keep whipping around to look behind me, ready to run, but it was just my mind playing tricks.

"In any case, I was weaving through dead cars like animal carcasses on a highway into some city. Then I walked out into the hills. The wind rushed in endless twisting paths through the tall grass. It was the first beautiful thing I'd seen in weeks. And it started to whisper to me. The wind, I mean. I stopped, and the whispering surrounded me. Then the wind... it pooled around me. Like a helicopter was just above my head. There was a face impressed on the grass. I got back to the road in a hurry and made sure I stayed on the roads after that."

"It's an appropriate metaphor for you, Oz," Selene said.

He stiffened. "And what does that mean?"

Selene looked around and saw that everyone was staring at her. Her eyes fell and she folded into herself and said no more.

Luke chuckled. "Bunch of geniuses."

Oz continued, "When I got to what I think was Arizona, I found myself heading east. I couldn't rest in the desert. I told myself it was because it would be harder to grow things there, but I don't know the first thing about gardening, and I had enough to eat from canned goods in any case. The real answer was I wanted traveling to be exciting again. I collected maps with a greed I couldn't control, even though they were useless. I was trying to make it exciting to cross boundaries again, but I failed. The whole world was one vast blur. I could walk through it forever and feel like I've never gotten anywhere. Eventually I hit what must have been Tennessee or Mississippi. I found my way to this forest and the rest of you showed up. And those things started to change, or at least some of them did."

He stared at the paper in front of him. "This is quite different from what I wrote down," he said. He flipped a page and read, "'I know I said we should engage in this exercise to look for clues and try to understand as much as we can. But why? Even if you could find the source of all this destruction, would that change anything? Would it mean anything at all? If an ant was caught in a fire in the middle of a skyscraper, could it understand, even if it crawled to the source of the blaze? Perhaps we should stop talking about this now and just make a decision, any decision. Perhaps talking is the worst thing we can do. Maybe the closer we get to the blaze, the less we'll be able to cope.

"'And how much has really changed? Even before all this disaster, destruction came to ants easily enough. The mortality rate for our species is still 100%. Now it just comes looking for us sooner. How much of a difference is that?'"

"Is that truly how you feel?" Masaaki asked.

"Very well," Oz sighed. "I want to try to understand what's happened. Not that I really care about the truth. But I want to know how to get some space from them. And it's not as if there's much else to think about."

He paused, then flipped to the last of the yellow sheets and read, "'I can't even give a name to what's happened. Only clichés come to mind: The Thing. The End. The Disaster. The day the TV stopped blaring and even AM radio went dead, the crackpots who finally had a genuine apocalypse to rant about. The passing of an age.

"'We'll never be able to give a name to what's happened, because death is nameless. Death is not one more thing in the world we can put in a certain category. Death is the denial and annihilation of every category. And that's what happened: death. They are the Nameless. The contradiction, the denial, the annihilation of what we were. I'm still breathing, and trees are still growing, but the world has died.

"'Look on all my works, ye mighty, and all that. Call me Oz.'

"That's what I wrote, anyway."

He held the pages close to the fire for a moment, then stuffed them into his pocket.

Mason said, "So nothing has really changed, and you're more at home in this world than the old one. That's what you're saying."

They all looked at Oz. He sat, head down, then looked up and said, "Yes." In the firelight, his eyes were like glowing pennies.

*

Masaaki said, "I will speak," and began to read.

"'My name is Masaaki Shinogaido. My parents called me Eric when we moved to America to help me make friends, but others rarely used it. I lived in Nashville and worked as a doctor. But I feel far away from that man. I can remember him, but he is a stranger. He did not marry and his parents had given up trying to find a suitable bride for him. The man had listened to his parents when they moved from Nagoya to the new country. They told him that he must be industrious and polite, or they would not be accepted. He had ignored the insults at school and worked hard. He became a doctor and he helped others. He did not take sick days.

"'When the dead came, the man continued to drive to work because it was the place where he worked. One day, he was sitting in the office of his small practice when the power went out. He sat in the dimness, wishing for an e-mail or phone call he knew would never come. The battery in his laptop died a few hours later. The man started to hear the deep silence of the building. He began to think about what had happened.

"'There was a scraping on the window. He turned and saw them outside, staring at him. In his fear, the man wondered if they were trying to get inside so they could speak to him about their disease. The man thought of all the bodies he had treated over the years, and wondered that a corpse should walk. The man left by another entrance and drove home with the absurd feeling that he had been terminated. He had always wondered what his last day would feel like. He drove through blank stoplights and sat at home, feeling that he was in the home of a stranger.

"'The man left soon after. He walked through empty streets, looking through the windows into the tombs, wondering where he might find a place in this new society.

"'Eventually he found a forest. His first night in the forest, as he slept in the leaves, the man dreamed of a huge insect with large, trembling wings. The man woke the next morning with a fever and something squirming on the back of his neck. When he slapped at it, an insect buzzed away, larger than his hand and black as night. In his fever, the man saw swirling patterns like smoke, shifting on the insect's dark wings. He saw the same patterns in the shapes of the branches against the sky, and then again in the night sky, when darkness came. In his fever, he dreamed that someone waited for him beneath the forest floor. Silent. Unmoving.

"'I woke the next morning with the fever gone, but I was weak from hunger. I'd had to run from the dead before. But when I saw one in the forest, it grew calm and only stared at me as I walked by."

"And you just walked past it," Mason snapped.

"Yes."

"And it just let you go."

"Yes."

Mason stared at him and said nothing.

"'If I had not discovered Oz's camp later that day, I probably would have died.

"'At times I think of my life practicing medicine. The man who did that is dead, but his desire remains. I already learned how to live in a new country. Now I must find my path in the midst of this death."

Masaaki took the page of Japanese characters and held it in the fire until it caught, holding onto the last corner until the flames claimed it.

*

"'Our names are Archer and Selene and we are twins. I go by Jack. We both lived north of Milwaukee in Wisconsin. Selene worked in a bookstore and I was a bank teller.

"'I was making breakfast one morning when I saw Selene drive up. I knew from how she was driving that something was wrong. I lived by a lake without neighbors and had not seen anyone that day.

"'I went to the window and saw Selene run out of her car without turning it off. She was in her bare feet but didn't seem to notice the gravel driveway as she ran. She slammed my front door and locked it. I asked her what was wrong and she just stared at me. Then I asked her why the front of her car had so much red on it." Looking up from the pages he clutched, Jack said, "Selene didn't want me to say this, but she still will not tell me what happened before she drove out to find me." His sister, sitting with her eyes fixed on the fire, seemed to shrink into herself.

"'Selene only said that we had to go to a hospital, to the police, go underground. I tried to get something coherent out of her until I heard a banging on the front door. I went to open the door, but Selene went white and grabbed my wrist and wouldn't let go. When I finally ripped my hand out of hers, she looked at me for a second and then ran out the back door. I could see her pushing my boat into the water, even though she can't swim. She sailed slowly outward on the lake and turned and stared at me.

"'I went out the back door and waded into the water and clambered inside, getting a lot of water in the boat and frightening my sister even more. Then Selene pointed behind me. I turned around and saw the owner of the gas station down the road walking down to the shore. Except..." Jack stopped reading and bit his trembling lower lip. Looking around with broken eyes, he said, "It was a perfect summer day. Huge, gentle trees looking down on the lake like grandfathers, the lapping of the water, the warm sun breathing in the air. And it stumbled down in the middle of that. I can't even remember his name."

The fire crackled in the silence.

Jack wiped his eyes and read: "'I started to say to Selene that he looked like he needed help because of the twigs sticking out of his arms and the cuts on his face, but the words stuck in my throat when I saw the cut that had opened up his cheek. Even from the lake, I could see his molars. I kept looking at it, searching for what I'd seen in every other human being that wasn't there anymore.

"It wasn't a zombie. It was like death had reached up into a human body and was jerking it around like a puppet. Its eyes were toward us, but it wasn't looking at us. When a human being looks at you, you see that spark as they recognize you. That thing had eyes in its head, but it couldn't see like that. It stumbled after us into the water.

"'We'd pushed off without any oars, so we floated for a while until something bumped against the side of the boat. Gray fingers broke the surface of the water, but the thing pushed us out of range.

"'We both started paddling with our hands and slowly curved back toward the shore, further down from my cabin. By the time the boat nudged the sand, its head had broken the water behind us. I helped Selene out and we started running back to her car. I looked back once and saw that it had gotten tangled up in a jungle gym. The way it banged into the metal bars made me sad, even though it was trying to get us. An ugly fluid from its wounds was eating away at the metal. Its grunting wasn't that loud, but I guess others heard it, because they started to shamble after us in a slowly shrinking circle through the trees. The trees and bushes slowed them down. The ones that still had eyes never blinked, but they didn't see the trees in front of them—all they saw was us, because they'd walk right into a tree if there was one between us and them.

"'I don't remember being scared as we got into Selene's jeep and drove back into town and holed up in a gas station. Selene wasn't talking by that point. It was tough checking out all the aisles to make sure we were alone in there, but I did it. We stayed there for hours. It made me sad to see the sun shining through the grimy windows on the bright containers of junk food. It was like the store had died.

"'Selene sat in the dim light as if she was never going to get up again. I sat next to her, not touching her, trying to think. We both froze and Selene stopped sniffling when we heard something shuffling around back, and a heavy grunting. I was so frazzled, I half thought it was our father searching for us. That made me think of the first time I'd ever felt free of him.

"'I pulled Selene to her feet and drove us to the airport. They would turn and shuffle after us as we drove past, and then start to wander again once we were gone. When we got to the airport, I drove into one of the hangars toward the smallest prop plane I could see. The keys were in it already; I guess they never thought anyone would steal it.

"'Sitting in the plane, I turned around to yell at Selene to climb up when I saw more of the dead walking through one side of the huge door of the hangar. Selene was standing outside the car, staring at them. Then she started walking toward them.

"'I sat wondering what it would feel like to turn it on and

59

just go, and then I was running and grabbing Selene and dragging her up into the cockpit and the propeller was roaring into life. I moved us toward the runway without hitting any of them and didn't even look at Selene until we had been in the air for a couple of minutes. Then I told her we were heading south-southeast and asked if that was OK. Her voice was a little too flat as she said it was, and I realized we'd have to come down sooner or later and wondered what I would do if she didn't snap out of it. I started to feel like I was choking.

"'You've got to come back, Selene, I said. I can only take care of you so far.

"'But she just stared straight ahead.

"'Looking outward, past the droning engines, I felt like I could see the curve of the earth even though we weren't high enough. The trails of smoke rose like offerings in every city we flew over. The radio gave either static or screaming.

"'I kept staring at the line of cloud in the horizon, but flying didn't feel the same. It had been great to fly before because I could think of my father as just a speck on the ground. Now I was just getting a better view of everything that had happened. It started to feel like I wasn't flying at all, only driving a tiny car through mist, and at any moment one of those things was going to walk forward and grab us. The instruments went blurry and I felt like I was going to throw up. Selene had to hold the steering. I banged my fist against the window and told her I couldn't take care of her anymore, that there was no more taking care of anything. When my eyes cleared I looked at her, and saw her look back at me. Really look at me. That made me feel a little better. I took the controls again.

"'I kept flying as long as I dared, but eventually the fuel

60

gauge got too close to "Empty" and I landed us in a big field. I had wanted so badly to fly, but I'll be happy if I never do it again. I never want to see so much again.

"'Neither of us said anything as we ran for the line of trees on the horizon. We found a highway and followed it, staying as far within the trees as we could. We scavenged at gas stations when it was safe. A couple days later we reached the ocean. We slept that night in an empty beach house. I woke halfway through our first night there and walked down to the shore." Jack paused, scanned what he had written, and then said, "One direction was as good as another."

"Hold on," Mason muttered. "What are you leaving out?"

Jack's jaw tensed and he glanced at Selene; but Selene was ignoring him. Oz said softly, "You and your sister have nothing to be embarrassed about. You can hardly be more pathetic than the rest of us."

He lowered his head. "'I woke halfway through our first night there and walked down to the shore.'" His hands shook as he held the paper. "'At least, I think I did; I may have dreamed the whole thing, because I don't remember being frightened or wondering if I would get eaten by the huge snake in the water I had been dreaming about. I sat down on the shore, trying to clear my head of the dream and instead seeing the huge thing in the water even more clearly. When I went into the water, I touched its side. It could have swallowed me." Jack stopped and gave Luke a nervous look, but Luke seemed absorbed in Jack's story.

"'I wanted to get away from the ocean after that. One direction was as good as another, but forests seemed to be safest. After I had lost count of how many days we'd walked, we went two days without eating. Eventually we both sat with our backs to a tree. Neither of us saying anything.

"'I was sitting there, trying not to think about how thirsty I was or how big the forest was, telling myself to put my arm around Selene. She put her arm around me instead and I leaned my head on her shoulder. We heard sounds, rustling, but neither of us moved. If it had been one of them, I don't think we would have tried to get away. The noise continued for a while before I finally looked up and saw, through intersecting branches, a man standing inside a ring of barbed wire, working on a shelter. As I watched, his face would crack—he would focus on the trench he was digging for a few heartbeats, and then he would look up and, without making any noise, start laughing or crying without making a noise. I couldn't tell which. Then he would shiver and get back to work. When Selene walked over to him, he didn't tell us to leave.

"I'm glad to be here"—Jack glanced at Oz—"because it's easier to stay protected than on our own." Jack's mouth worked, but he couldn't speak.

His voice as gentle as Jack had ever heard it, Masaaki said, "Please finish what you have written."

"I can't," Jack said. "I wrote for a long time about responsibility and protection. Trying to convince myself. But it's like I said. There's no taking care of anything now." Selene finally turned and gave her brother a bottomless look. Then she turned to Oz. Oz quickly looked away from her.

"But I want us to stay together," Jack said, looking again at Oz. The professor didn't meet Jack's eyes.

*

Oz asked, "Who's next? Luke?"

Luke smiled at the group and held up his beer in a toast.

"Where did you get that?" Mason asked.

"You can't have none," Luke said, and belched.

"Very well," Oz sighed. "What about you, Mason?"

"What?"

"Care to share what you've written?"

"I didn't write anything. When you come across the scene of a crime, you don't write about your feelings. You do what you must do to make it right. The whole world's a crime scene now. But that doesn't mean I'm off the hook." He turned toward the trees and added in a loud voice, "And anyone who wants to join me is more than welcome."

Oz stiffened, eyebrows raised at Mason. The burly policeman nodded.

"What's going on?" Jack asked.

Oz said, "Mason here has seen someone watching our camp."

Mason, his eyes scanning the dark shapes of the trees, whispered, "Everybody go lie down. I think I can get him to come out if I'm alone."

Selene's eyes were wide. "I don't want to sleep if someone lies in wait for us."

"There are a lot of monsters out there, sister," the nameless woman said. "Be braver."

Masaaki said, "This meeting was to resolve Oz's anguish over Bob's suicide. And to try to find clues about the new world." He turned to the professor. "Have we accomplished what you asked?"

Oz held up his hands. "I'm not running this meeting. I won't tell anyone how to live their lives. But let us do as Mason says."

"I did not think you wanted more members of the group," Masaaki said.

"I don't. But it's something to do. Maybe we can talk with him. Now go."

Nobody moved.

Looking at them, he added softly, "You were expecting some kind of resolution. I was as well, and I suppose I led us to believe that meeting like this would give us that satisfaction. But the world has died. There are no more satisfying conclusions. Please get used to it."

They sat, silent and staring, as if each one were waiting for someone else to speak. The moon appeared from behind the clouds and shone silvery light on them. Selene stood and said in a small voice, "Bob tried to make friends and help us the best he could, but he couldn't bear the fear he carried. Let us be to his faults a little blind." The heaviness in the air lifted, as if they had each let out a soundless sigh. She turned to Oz and said, "Thank you. I'm glad we did this."

His eyes opened wide. "Did you hear what I just said?" he asked.

"Nevertheless, I thank you." She smiled, her pale face lit with ghostly fire. Then she walked away and laid down on her sleeping bag. Her brother followed, as did the rest. Soon only Oz and Mason sat at the fire.

*

Mason sat, keeping his head toward the fire while his eyes ranged over the shadowy trees. Without moving his head, he hissed to Oz, "What do you want?"

"Two questions."

64

"Keep your voice down!"

"You didn't challenge Masaaki's claim that he simply walked away from the corpse in the forest."

Mason said nothing.

"Was he telling the truth?" Oz asked.

"He wasn't lying," the policeman said. "He didn't think he was lying, anyway."

"Are you certain?"

"I got a pretty good radar for that stuff."

"And you're not curious about that?"

Mason stopped looking at the trees and glared at Oz.

Oz said, "You mentioned earlier that we were different from other groups you had encountered. What about the hallucinations we related? Why moths and snakes? Wouldn't you expect hallucinations about the dead?"

"I dunno. I had one like that, actually."

"A similar hallucination?"

Mason nodded.

"Tell me, please."

"You shouldn't be enjoying this," Mason said.

"Aren't you curious? Even a little?" He struggled to keep the smile from his face and failed.

Mason's jaw flexed. "No, I'm not curious. It's like I said. It's the same game. I've seen death and corruption before."

"This is not at all the same game. Something strange and new is happening. Everything has died, but something else is waking up."

"What's your second question?"

"Tell me your hallucination." When the policeman scowled, Oz said, "Come now. If it's just a hallucination, there's no harm in telling."

"I thought I saw this big red thing."

65

"Thing?" Oz asked.

"It looked like a man, but it wasn't human. The dead were bowing in front of it. It... bit me. My hand. It burned, but it felt good."

"And you're not in any way curious about what that might mean?"

"In any crime scene, there'll be details that don't matter. Part of getting to the bottom of things is finding the real clues."

"And you imagine you're going to solve the case. You are going to solve the mystery of the world."

"Death and crime haven't gone away. They just got bigger. And they still obey the same rules."

The professor smiled.

Mason growled, "What else do you want?"

"One more question. Can we trust Luke?" He paused, and added: "Or what about Masaaki? Or the woman who won't give her name?"

"I don't trust any of you."

Oz pulled back and crossed his arms.

The policeman muttered, "You ain't acting the way you should. You having any nightmares?"

"I was while I made my way here. But not anymore."

"Me neither. You still jumping, like you feel one of them just behind you? Like you talked about in your story?"

"I suppose not. I hadn't thought of that."

"You should have. Go away, Oz. Try to think about how you can make this right."

"Do you honestly think right and wrong mean anything anymore?"

Mason ignored him. Oz stared at him for a moment, then stood and walked away. He lay down, glancing once at

Mason's face lit in gentle red by the embers of the fire. The professor stared at the moon. He interlaced his fingers behind his head and sighed. He didn't know why he felt so calm. As he drifted toward sleep, something tickled the back of his mind. He turned on his side and let his eyes play over the vague, dark shapes of the trees.

Suddenly, he was on his feet. "Mason!" he hissed.

Mason ran toward him.

"I saw him! Out there, among the trees! Then he disappeared!"

Mason turned and ran through the opening in the barbed wire and off into the darkness. Fifteen minutes later, he returned from the forest with scratch marks on his face. "Couldn't find him," he panted.

"You look as if you got lost," Oz said. "Actually, you look as if you still are."

"Weirdest thing," the policeman murmured.

"What?"

"Earlier, I saw a dirty face with a beard looking in on us. But when I was out looking for him, I saw someone else."

Oz leaned closer. "Tall? Strange in a way that's difficult to describe?"

Eyes wide, he nodded.

"I believe I have seen people like them before. Have you, Mason?"

He said nothing, but Oz saw the answer in his face.

"Strange new world," the professor said.

"Some things never change," Mason said through clenched teeth. He walked away and lay down on his sleeping bag.

$\mathcal{S}$EVEN

Dreams

The nameless girl waited inside the circle of strangers as the men finished their arguing and everyone realized they had nothing to say. Then Selene stood and blessed the group, a sentiment that the men could never give, as the moon shone on her face. Nameless watched where she lay down next to her twin, and walked under the gently shifting trees and lay down next to her. The moonlight seemed to pool on Selene's face.

"That was, like, really beautiful, the way you did that," Nameless said, and touched her hand.

"I always feel more calm under the moon."

"You're her sister," Nameless said.

"That's a metaphor."

"No, it's true. The earth is our mother. We're lying on her warm skin right now. Can't you feel all the trees growing out of her?"

"No, I can't. But..."

"Tell me," the nameless girl whispered.

Selene stared at her for a moment. Then she whispered, "I can feel the moon. All the time. Even when I don't see it."

"See? You can feel our connection to Gaia. You're not

totally a slave."

"A slave?"

"Men enslave women and make us forget that we're closer to Gaia than they are. We create life. Men don't."

"Jack has not enslaved me," Selene said.

"What did your brother ever do for you?"

"Protected me from father, first of all. He sang me to sleep when I was young. We would hide in the barn when he was drunk."

Nameless didn't speak for a moment. Then she said, "Can you see the colors?"

"Colors?"

Still lying next to her, Nameless took one of Selene's hands in her own. "Just focus," she said. "Think about the moon. Remember that you're a woman."

Selene was silent and then she gasped. "Beautiful!" she whispered.

"Yes, sister."

"Have they always been there?"

"I only started to see them myself a little while ago."

"I don't even know what words to use. They're just gorgeous. How... how..."

Nameless said, "Gaia came to me and touched me. She let me see these colors. She said she would come back for me."

Selene's eyes were still moving back and forth, as if trying to follow each bird in a flock. "But how..."

"Men never see Gaia's colors. All they do is, like, mess stuff up. The women they enslave stop seeing the colors. You stopped seeing them, too."

Selene turned toward her brother, who lay a few feet away. He didn't seem to have heard their whispered conference above the occasional *pops* of the fire and the wind shushing through the trees. "He's blue!" Selene gasped. "How can a blue be that deep?"

Nameless took her hand from Selene's. Selene gasped, "They disappeared! Bring them back!" She reached to take Nameless' hand again, but Nameless moved her hand away.

"You have to free yourself from your brother," she said. "The world men built has died. Don't die with it."

Selene, still lying on her sleeping bag, looked at Nameless for a moment. She turned on her side to face her brother. When Nameless slipped a hand into hers, Selene squeezed it once before letting go.

*

When Selene finally fell asleep, she dreamed her father was in their camp, shuffling toward her. In her dream, she knew her father wanted help taking his life. Jack was standing behind him, trying to be angry, trying to threaten their father and keep him away from her; but his voice was only a whisper. Selene dreamed that Nameless sat next to her, watching and ready to disapprove. Selene tried to say to her father that it was impossible, that he was already dead. Then she saw the moon above the farmhouse where she had grown up. She remembered the moonlight, whispering all around her, and the stars pulsing in faint pressure, humming in infinite silence. Selene remembered her father had been killed years ago in a car accident. When she looked around their camp, he was nowhere to be seen. She looked at the moon, aware that Jack was asleep next to her, and that Nameless was on her other side, tears streaming from her closed eyes.

In her dream, Selene stared at the moon. She felt that there was something she needed to give to Jack, but couldn't think what it was. Eventually her moon fell below the horizon. Dawn glowed through the trees and the sun rose. She watched it, unable to remember when she had woken.

*

Jack walked away from the campfire and lay down, knowing he would be able to sleep after what his sister had said. The stranger came and lay down next to Selene. Jack forced his eyes closed and tried not to think about her red hair, her sharp lips, her fingers, and what it would be like to touch them. For once, he was glad of the darkness and tall trees standing around him like frowning sentries.

He heard the gurgling of the stream nearby, and wondered where it led. Jack imagined it joining a river, and that river joining another, until it emptied into the ocean. He thought about how the earth really had only one ocean, and how the names people had used to divide it were arbitrary. The thought filled his mind.

He dreamed that he stood on the shore of the sea, the sea which surrounded the dry land and was itself surrounded by nothing. Lightning ripped again and again across the darker-than-black sky, showing the dead walking toward him like a strobe light, arms out, mouths open. He dreamed there was a serpent in the water, gliding, coiling, looking at him through cold emerald eyes. Each lightning flash showed the dead moving closer, closer. He walked backwards toward the ocean, but didn't walk into it.

When sunlight opened Jack's eyes, he realized he had not been afraid. He wondered how far away they were from the ocean.

*

As Masaaki slept, he dreamed that he again lay on the forest floor, and a kaleidoscope of fluttering beetle wings bit the back of his neck and returned underground. As he dreamed, the forest grew small, and he saw a yawning chasm beneath it where the giant beetle lived. Masaaki saw the shifting patterns of the thing's wings, and the shifting patterns of the forest paths above them. He saw where the paths joined the patterns on the beetle's wings, and understood how simple the new world was.

He awoke, sweating in the morning summer heat. The dream faded, but he chased it in his mind, trying to remember the paths, and how he could guide the others on them.

*

After their conversation, Mason walked away from Oz to the far edge of the camp. He lay on his sleeping bag without unlacing his boots and tried to shut out Luke's drunken snore. Mason thought about the dirt and the weeds and plants beneath him, growing however they wanted, and how they would keep on growing even if no one was here to tend them or benefit from them.

He blinked, and the image of the thing burning in the barbed wire flashed across his eyes as he looked up into the trees. He thought about a fire starting in the woods, and how it could wipe clean all the useless weeds and plants. The embers from the campfire were still hot.

He sat up, but his fatigue made his head spin. He lay back down. This would not be the last night they had a fire.

Soon his eyes closed. He dreamed of the corpse struggling in the barbed wire as flames licked up its body. He saw the tentacles open around its face, and felt something open inside him. In his dream, he saw again the Flower reach a hand toward Luke, and saw Luke cut it off. He dreamed that the hand crawled toward where he slept. It embraced his own hand like a lover, and he suddenly saw the tall red man again. Or rather, he saw that the tall red thing was watching him dream, watching the colors and mysteries which came and went across the stage of his sleeping mind. Joy burned in Mason, and he dreamed of a cleanness and simplicity which would have been impossible in the old world.

*

Oz slept deeply and peacefully. When sunlight coaxed his eyes open, his dreams rushed away from him. He lay on his sleeping bag, resting, wishing again for coffee but not minding that there was none. He heard a twig snap and saw Luke outside the barbed wire, walking away from the camp. Luke had on a thick plaid jacket and walked with one arm unbent. He disappeared among the trees.

Mason sat up. His face was a volcano about to explode. The grizzled policeman stood and walked out of camp, moving through the trees in Luke's direction.

Oz looked around: everyone else was still asleep.

He got to his feet and followed Mason.

EIGHT

A Silent Conversation

The dullness of sleep fell away from Oz as he walked. He remembered how he used to enjoy taking walks and realized how cooped up he felt in his camp. Branches interlaced in a cathedral-like effect above him. The air brushing his face was not exactly cool, but it dried the sweat on his forehead. It occurred to him that he wasn't walking in a straight line. He wondered if he would be able to find his way back and smiled. He pushed a branch out of his way and looked upward. The sun was blunted as it shone through the branches, softened by the leaves. No starfish arms circled it. He smiled again.

He looked back to the path and realized he had lost sight of his mark. He hurried forward, but stopped when he saw, some distance ahead, a familiar blonde figure in a green cap. Oz held his breath. Luke had stopped in a little clearing and was pulling a shotgun out of the arm of his jacket. He leaned it against a tree and took off his jacket, hat, and sweat-soaked T-shirt. He ran his fingers through dirty blonde curls and the muscles on his arm and back leapt against his skin. The professor frowned at Luke's shaggy, leonine brawn as he silently moved closer. Did white trash normally spend hours at the gym?

When Luke turned around, his eyes passed over Oz. Oz flinched, but Luke didn't notice him. The muscular back-woodsman sat on a tree stump with his gun across his knees. He took a small notebook from one pocket, flipped through several pages, and tapped the notebook with his pen. He sat and waited.

Oz had never been a hunter, but he had heard other truckers say that the chirpings and rustlings of a forest will return if a hunter remains still for a quarter of an hour. Luke waited at least that long in eerie silence before an uneven crunch snapped Luke's attention to his right. A bloody, damaged head appeared between the leaves. Empty eyes and gray skin moved through speckled shadow and sunlight. Something cold curled around Oz's spine. He watched himself watch Luke sit with back arched, still as the forest itself, until the thing started to walk past. Oz let his breath out.

Luke knocked the barrel of his gun against a tree. Oz's mouth dropped open.

The ragged shuffling stopped, the neck turned, and death walked toward Luke.

He rose with the gun in one hand and positioned himself between the shambling corpse and a tree that had a trunk jutting in two long branches at chest level. The dead thing got one arm and its head inside these branches and the other arm outside. It continued to shuffle its legs, arms outstretched and eyes vivid and hollow.

He lay his gun on the ground and slowly walked toward it. Dodging the clumsy grasping arms, he stared into the skin which had once been a face.

Oz took a few steps to his left. He looked at Luke's chiseled features and saw the light which played in the guy's eyes as he stared. Something in Oz's gut tightened. He took one step closer, then another, his eyes moving back and forth between the two, trying to catch what was passing between them.

A rough voice barked behind Oz, "What are you doing?"

Oz whirled to see Mason, his face a fiery exclamation point. Luke turned and shouted at the sight of Mason and then Oz, and shouted again when a gray hand grabbed the back of his head. Bruise-green fingers pulled tufts of tawny hair closer to a chasm of rocky teeth. Luke squealed and tried to pull his head away from the thing behind him. Oz lurched toward him and picked up the shotgun at Luke's feet.

"Shoot it!" Luke yelled. The muscles on his arms and chest danced, but Luke couldn't stop his head being pulled toward the thing's mouth.

Oz pointed the barrel at the corpse's head. The eyes moved to it and turned dark gray. Gray-green skin curled back as tentacles flared in slow flame around a newborn sun. Several snake-tongues flicked out of its mouth and it hissed. The hissing rose in waves and started to break in staccato stutters. Oz's finger grew limp on the trigger. The forest fell away as he stared, searching for the thing that was gone from the being opposite him, and the thing that was trying to be born.

"Is it... is it trying to talk?" Mason gasped. He had moved next to Oz and was pointing a finger at the thing.

Luke reached his arms and grabbed the gun from Oz. Eyes straining, Luke pushed the shotgun through the crook in the tree behind him and pulled the trigger.

The head opened in a white blur. Tentacles flew in the air

and plopped onto the ground. Luke's head stopped its slow movement toward the corpse, but the hand didn't let go.

He shouted, "My knife! Back in the camp!"

White feelers were growing out of the thing's neck. The shape of a skull started to form.

"No time," Mason said, his voice a steel wire. He pulled a knife from a sheath in his boot and swung it down on the arm. Luke staggered away, grimacing in pain as the fingers tightened on his hair. He dropped the shotgun and shouted for the knife. When Mason gave it to him, he started to cut the hair on the back of his head.

Oz ignored this, staring as the white feelers began to re-form into the shape of a flower. The feelers made a tiny sound, like tin foil being crinkled. He noticed the tentacles inching like worms across the forest floor back to their master.

When the last of Luke's hair fell away and the hand dropped to the ground, Luke wrapped his arm around Oz's neck and pressed the knife into his back. Oz blinked, as if coming out of a daydream.

"Put the knife away, Luke," Mason said. His eyes glanced only once at the hand as it crawled back to its owner.

Luke gasped, "You had a chance to kill that thing and you waited. Were you gonna get your jollies watching it eat me?" Oz jumped as Luke pressed the knife harder into his back.

Oz wondered how his voice could be so steady as he said, "Fine. Let me go on my way and I won't come back."

The hand crawled up the corpse's leg. The severed wrist moved, and the white feelers coming out of the arm joined those of the hand. Soon the wound was noticeable only as a thin white circle around the wrist.

Luke snarled, "I'm gonna gut this s.o.b. and you're gonna say one of 'em got him. Got it, Mason?"

"Fine," Mason said. "He deserves it. And then I'll kill you." He picked up the shotgun

The arm around Oz's neck loosened. "What?" Luke asked.

"You both were making nice with the enemy. You both deserve to die. So make up your mind, Luke. Let him go, or face me."

Luke spat on the ground and stepped back from Oz. He threw the knife into the chest of the corpse. It stuck in the white feelers and was quickly covered by them, like waves washing over a beach.

Oz said, "Goodbye," and turned to go.

Mason grabbed his arm. "You're coming back with me, friend."

"How is this a concern of yours?"

"You've betrayed us," Mason said. "You're not getting away. Let's get back to the group. Now. Before that thing starts walking again."

"It won't even be able to see us."

"I wouldn't be too sure about that. Move."

"You seemed just as interested as me."

Mason blinked. "That doesn't matter."

"Doesn't it?" Oz asked. "I'm not sure that... Where's Luke?"

Mason whirled. Luke was gone.

"Whatever," the policeman said. "We need to warn the others. March."

They jogged away from the thing. Oz turned back once and saw white tentacles starting to wave around the thing's new head.

When they saw the barbed wire through the trees, Mason slowed them to a walk. He snorted and said, "You don't make any sense, Oz. If you're gonna fall in love with them, why not just go join them?"

"You have to admit that they're the most interesting thing out there, now. You seem to find them interesting as well."

Mason grabbed Oz's arm again and turned him around so that his back was to the camp. The policeman shoved his face close and opened his mouth to snarl at him. But his eyes widened as he looked behind Oz. The professor turned and saw Jack, Selene, Masaaki, and the nameless girl standing around a stranger in the middle of the camp.

NINE

The Pale Men

When Oz and Mason walked into camp, the newcomer turned a bald head and thick beard and hooked nose toward them. His movement revealed the scab where his right ear had been. He asked in a Slavic accent, "One of you is leader here? I can get nothing from these."

Oz looked to Mason, but Mason stared at the ground. His jaw flexed and his face seemed to burn.

"We must resolve this. You will come with me," the man said.

"Very well," Oz said.

The man blinked. "What?"

Jack whispered, "Are you sure, Oz?"

Mason said, "He's right. We came across one of... them. It's near. It might find its way here."

"That was the gunshot we heard?" Masaaki asked.

"Who had a gun?" Jack asked.

"Oh, don't worry," Mason growled. "Oz here can answer all your questions. Next chance we get, we'll give him plenty of time to talk. Now let's go."

Jack asked, "Where's Lu..." but Mason cut in with, "So you're the man I saw spying on us?"

"Yes."

"Why were you waiting?"

Something passed over the man's face like a cloud blocking the sun. "One must be cautious these days."

"What's your name?" Oz asked.

"Miroslav."

The nameless girl asked, "Are there women in your tribe?"

"What if there are?"

Mason rolled his eyes. "How could it possibly compromise you to tell us that?"

"Yes. There are women there."

"Then I'll come," the nameless girl said, a smile in her voice. She walked toward the opening in the barbed wire. Mason and Oz followed, and Masaaki behind them. Jack came last, leading his sister by the hand, looking around at the camp with a sad face.

Miroslav, still standing in the middle of the camp, called after them, "The thing you burned is growing back."

No one stopped walking.

Miroslav asked, "Why is it you grow them?" They turned. He tilted his head, looking for a moment like a vulture.

Mason said, "We are not growing them. If you were watching, you saw what happened: it got tangled up in the barbed wire. Nothing to do but burn it."

"You will not betray us?" Miroslav asked.

Mason gave a frustrated laugh. "Betray you to who?"

Miroslav asked, "You have not met other groups?"

"That doesn't matter. We're not safe here," Mason barked. "Show us your camp."

Jack whispered, "Are you sure about this?"

"I got all kinds of bad feelings about this, but we need to not be here for a while. A larger group is probably safer."

Miroslav hesitated a moment longer and then followed them out of their camp. He gave Mason a dark look as he walked past and led the group into the forest.

After a half-minute's walking, they passed a large mound of churned earth. Oz gasped and turned to Masaaki. "Is this where..."

Masaaki nodded.

"What?" Mason asked.

"This is where we buried Bob," Oz whispered.

Jack opened his mouth to ask a question, but Oz turned away, his eyes on the ground. Soon they crossed the road they had taken to town and entered the trees on the other side.

"So it's only a matter of time," Mason said in a low voice, eyes on the needles and leaves in front of them.

"Only a matter of time," Oz said. "No rest for us in the grave."

Mason muttered, "And whatever it is that changed everyone is still in the air, or wherever it is."

Jack said, "So it's hopeless? Then what's the point of going with Miroslav?" The Slav turned again at the sound of his name, but no one looked at him.

Oz continued in the same low tone: "I don't care if it's hopeless. I'll stay away from death as long as I can."

Mason said, "We will find a way to fight these things. We have to," and ignored Jack's persistent, whispered questions.

Eventually Jack fell quiet and they simply walked, eyes wide and feet heavy. Miroslav turned to give them brief looks as he led them, but none of them looked back at him.

After a while, the nameless girl said, "They are coming."

They stopped. "How do you know?" Masaaki asked.

The sound of cracking twigs and crunching leaves reached them, and the sight of three shapes, moving through the trees. The quiet growth and clean smell of the forest fell away before the bodies shuffling toward them. It seemed almost as if the three corpses were standing still and the earth was moving beneath them, drawing the few remaining living toward them. One wore a woman's body, but had lost every echo of the woman it had once been, even though it was still wearing the blue Wal-Mart apron with a nametag which said "My name is Carol, How can I help you?" Behind it, a thing in black leather boots, black jeans, and a black T-shirt walked, its black crew cut a spiky bush on a dead skull. Its missing lower jaw gave it an eternally hungry, frustrated look. A gray janitor's uniform followed.

Miroslav screamed: "Your gun! Your gun, angry man!"

"They just grow back," Mason growled. "Run!" But Miroslav's feet were rooted to the earth, his eyes bright as he stared at the dead.

Jack saw the agonized elation twisting Miroslav's face, and something twisted inside him. He felt his sister's hand gripping his shoulder and heard her panicked breathing. It felt as if every nerve inside him were gathering breath to scream as he took one step, and then another, until the Wal-Mart apron was in front of him. He didn't want to touch the ruin which had once been a face, so he planted his fist into her chest. It was like punching wet concrete; the corpse didn't even stagger, and Jack's wrist and shoulder flashed with pain. A cold hand gripped his other shoulder. He fell to his knees and gasped, feeling as if the weight of the dead new world were bearing down on him. The mouth moved closer to his face, its tongue quivering. And then he was being pulled away, and Masaaki was helping him to his feet. The three corpses were standing still, staring at the Japanese doctor. They stood like sleepwalkers mesmerized by some new dream.

"Go," Masaaki said. "I will follow soon."

"How..." Miroslav asked, staring at Masaaki; but Mason grabbed the Slav by the shoulder and pulled him down the path. The rest hurried along. Masaaki rejoined them a few minutes later, after the trees had blocked their view of the dead.

"Who are you people?" Miroslav asked.

"The camp," Mason said. "Get us to your camp before those things find us again."

"Who are you people?" Miroslav asked again.

Mason pulled out his gun. "We're out of time," he growled.

"This way."

They walked. Leafy branches passed over them. Their footsteps were the only sound in the forest.

*

Hours later, the trees thinned before a small, huddled collection of trailer homes. Each window held dirty, staring faces.

Oz froze. "Mason," he hissed. "How did Miroslav lose his ear? If one of the dead attacked him, he would have been infected."

Mason's eyes widened. "An accident?" he asked.

"Perhaps." He opened his mouth to say more, but fell silent and stared as the houses expelled their homeless residents. Disheveled, empty faces circled them and stared.

Mason had a moment's queasy deja-vu at the sight of so many slow bodies surrounding them. One woman looked from face to face among the newcomers and muttered, "How could this happen? I was good, I was tolerant, I worked hard and didn't hurt anyone, I don't deserve this, I don't deserve it." Other mumbled pleas for help surrounded the newcomers.

Miroslav shoved his way through the group and opened the door to one of the trailers, indicating that they should enter. The six found themselves in a dusty room empty of furniture. In one corner, a pile of laptops and Blackberries sat beneath a thick layer of dust. The rest of Miroslav's camp filed in and sat on the ground in the dim afternoon light. They looked up at Mason, Oz, Masaaki, Jack, Selene, and Nameless. Each one bore some wound, some missing an ear, some with teeth missing, some with arms which ended at the wrist.

Miroslav stood before them and raised his hands. "Friends," he said, "you know I had many doubts. Even when I brought them to us, I was unsure. But I have good news. The end of our struggle is here. These new friends do not fear the dead as we do, and the dead obey them." A sigh breathed from the group.

"That's not true," Jack whispered, and Mason said, "We need a way to fight these things. What do you know?"

The nameless girl said in a loud voice to Miroslav, "You said there were women here."

Miroslav blinked. "Our women are right here."

The nameless woman said, "These are cattle. You totally lied to me. They were better off in the old world."

Mason gripped Miroslav's arm. His face burned as he grunted, "How do we kill them? We must find a way."

Something cleared in Miroslav's eyes, as if he was seeing the newcomers for the first time. "We do not," he said slowly. "You must know that we cannot kill them. They just grow back. So we use them, and you will help us. Come." Miroslav turned away from the group and led them down a corridor of closed doors. He stopped at the end and put his hand on the doorknob.

Oz glanced back. Everyone from the camp had followed, but the rest of Miroslav's group sat with blank faces as they gazed down the corridor.

"Why does everyone in your group self-injure?" Oz asked.

"What's behind that door?" asked Mason.

"The thing you cannot fight, angry man," Miroslav said, and opened the door. Two sets of manacles hung from the walls, holding two dead bodies, one tall, one short. The taller one opened, and they saw the same flat, bruise-brown skin encircled by waving arms, two gray ovals which had once been eyes, and a hole with teeth which might have been a mouth, if there had been a soul within to speak. And everywhere present but nowhere visible, a light, as if a flower was opening to a sun only it could see.

*

Oz stared. He again felt something open inside himself. He closed his eyes, wishing he was outside and under the sun; but the sun he imagined stared at him from within starfish tentacles which would follow him wherever he ran.

*

Masaaki looked on the sunflower and something inside him broke. This mute, lost thing should be resting in the earth, but instead it was chained here, forever homeless. A tear slipped down his cheek.

*

The nameless woman looked into the room and her mouth curled in disgust. The men running this camp were no better than the things they had chained up. She wondered if there was a way to free Miroslav's women. If she led, would they follow?

*

As Jack watched, a knife edge cut through him. He flexed his fists and took a step forward. Selene slipped her hand into his, and he read her expression easily: what more damage could be done to this thing, or the smaller one which had been a child?

*

Mason stared and felt the rage inside him grow hotter. Better for the world to be empty than for it to come to this. Trying to use them! For what?

But his rage died when he looked at the smaller corpse. Tears he couldn't control slipped down his cheeks as he imagined what it had been like, when it had been a girl, and he remembered another girl he had held once, and her warm blood soaking his uniform, and the sting in his knees from the concrete of the driveway, and the limp body in his arms which he would not let go even when the sergeant shook his shoulder.

*

The arms of the taller one snapped straight against its sides and the tentacles around its face stretched taut. The smaller corpse turned toward it, starfish arms rigid, two lifeless planets circling each other. Slinking sibilants like razorblades sliding together passed from the taller to the smaller. Black tongues flicked out of their holes. The smaller one turned toward them, thin arms straining in their direction. Tiny bits of brick fell from the wall where the shackles had been attached as it struggled.

"Is it... is it trying to talk?" Selene asked. Mason gave Oz a stricken look.

Without turning to them, Miroslav said, "You see! You see what powers you have! Never have I seen the dead respond this way." He closed the door and pulled a knife from his belt and offered it on upraised palms to them.

"What are you doing?" Jack asked.

"Join us," Miroslav said. "You will lead us against our enemies."

Mason said, "That thing is your enemy."

"No," Miroslav said, still holding out the knife. "They are our weapons. When other groups of the living raid us for supplies and take us as slaves, we hide underground and release one of the dead upon them. Eventually it wanders off, and we come out from hiding. But with our group so obedient, there are few of them left. With you, we can herd the dead like cattle."

"You have more?" Mason asked, incredulous.

"When my father came to America, he was wise enough not to trust the government here. He built a large room under the ground with tunnels and hidden doors that connect our houses. We strengthened the door to the basement to keep them in, and can open another door to the outside without the dead seeing us."

Oz asked, "What do you mean about the group being obedient?" He sounded seasick.

Miroslav said, "If we are to survive, we must be strict. Those who give in to fear and steal or hurt others, or those who run to another group, are sent to the basement." Jack gasped; the nameless woman shook her head.

Mason's thick neck flexed as he said, "There's no way you chained that thing up in there. They're too strong."

Miroslav almost smiled. "You are correct. She was the first rebel, an example to the others. We chained her and hid and let one up from the basement."

"And the little girl?"

"She wandered in after her mother. She is small enough that six of us managed to chain her."

Mason's fist seemed to come out of nowhere. Miroslav was sprawling on the floor before Jack realized the brawny policeman had hit him. The knife clattered down the corridor out of reach. Mason leaned over Miroslav's prone form and said, "You're sick," and raised his fist again.

The corridor filled with men. Each had a weapon—knives, sticks, a few guns—and each had a wound. Mason straightened up and Miroslav slowly got to his feet. Mason looked to the men and said, "Get out of my way." They didn't move.

Confusion clouded Miroslav's face. "Why... Why are you not..."

Oz said, "Mason's right. You people are sick." The nameless girl nodded.

Miroslav's eyes grew distant. "You think to betray your own kind?"

One of the men standing near Miroslav said something in an Eastern European language none of the others recognized. He had a thick black beard and one eye.

"No," Miroslav said, his eyes on the newcomers. "We will give them time. They will join us. And if not..." Miroslav turned to the black-haired man and shrugged.

Jack whispered, "Mason. Your gun."

Mason grimaced. "I only got two bullets left."

"You will come with us," Miroslav said.

Mason tensed, but Selene put her hand on his back. "They are too many. You would only injure yourself." He slumped.

They were led back to the main room, through the staring eyes of the still-seated group, and outside. Miroslav walked to another house and pointed for them to enter. They found themselves in an empty room with one other door. Standing in the doorway, Miroslav put the knife on the carpet in front of him. "You may come out when you have sacrificed a part of yourself to the group. Drop it through the crack in the front window. If you do not join us by tomorrow, you will serve us by joining those in the basement."

He left. The lock clicked behind him.

TEN

Nameless' Story

The six prisoners stood for a moment. Jack walked to the room's only other door and tried the handle; it was locked. He sighed and hung his head. "Wish we were back at the farm," he said. Selene looked at him.

"What do you mean?" the nameless girl asked.

Selene said, "He speaks about the farm where we grew up. Our father was an angry man. Jack protected me." Her voice was like a mouse peeking out from a tiny hole in the wall.

"You wish you were back there?"

"Only one monster to worry about," Jack mumbled and crumpled into a sitting position against the wall.

Mason shook his head and strode to the back door and kicked it several times, and then kicked the front door; they shuddered on their frames but didn't give. "They've reinforced them," Mason said. "We'll have to break a window and escape tonight."

"Easier said than done," Oz said, standing at the window. Outside, three men stood a dozen paces away, their backs turned. One had a rifle slung over his back.

"We outnumber them," Mason said.

"They'll only shout for the others," Oz said.

Mason growled, "I'm not going to rot inside here, and I don't think anyone else wants to." He looked around at the others, but saw only exhausted looks as they found different places to sit. They looked like piles of dirty laundry, collapsed in random heaps. Mason's shoulders sagged. He leaned against the wall and slid into a sitting position.

They rested in silence for some minutes before Oz said, "Feeding humans to them. The whole world has gone crazy."

"They are afraid," Masaaki said. "They call the dead their weapons, but they are slaves to them."

Mason grunted. "Smartest thing you've said yet."

The lock clicked on the front door and it opened. The man with one eye entered, looked behind him, and shut the door. He stood and stared at the nameless woman. His breath was coming out in short spurts as he pulled a knife from a sheath in his belt. "We don't have many women like you," the man said, and walked toward her. She cringed; the whine of a whipped dog escaped her throat.

The man stood over Nameless and suddenly stiffened, his eyes bulging. Mason was behind him, pulling one of his wrists behind his back and up toward his shoulder blades.

The man gasped. "You can't... You're our prisoners!"

"You think I'm going to stand by while you rape that woman? I'm insulted." Mason pushed the man's wrist further up his back. "Drop the knife or I'll dislocate your shoulder." The knife clattered to the floor. Mason put his foot on it and said, "Good man. Now let's have some fun." Still holding the man's wrist, he reached down for the knife and pointed it toward the man's eye.

Selene stood and walked to them. "Mason," she said. "Please."

He stopped moving, but didn't look at her. Selene put a hand on his shoulder.

"For my sake," she said.

Mason met her eyes, grimaced, and released him.

The black-haired man scampered toward the door. "You will not tell the others," he said. "They'll send me to the basement."

"First chance I get," Mason said.

The man locked the door behind him. Through one of the opened windows, Oz saw him talk to their guards, wave one arm, and run away.

Silence filled the room. Afternoon faded; the sun set and night entered through the windows. Stars appeared, tiny pinpricks in a black curtain. The moon rose high in the front window and light fell in a trapezoid on the floor. Selene moved to sit in the middle of it. She looked at them and said, "Of all the groups to fall in with, Jack and I could have done worse."

Oz smiled and Jack gave a quiet laugh. In the gloom, a smile creased Masaaki's pale face as well.

Masaaki asked, "Jack, may I ask you something?"

Jack nodded.

"Why did you strike the corpse on our journey here?"

"Because I'm a coward," Jack whispered.

"No you're not," Selene said.

"Do you know what happened the first time I got in an airplane, Selene?" Jack asked. "My hands were shaking so bad I could barely hold the control yoke. I was too scared to even move the plane onto the runway. Eventually the flight instructor told me to go home. It took a half-hour phone call to convince him to give me another chance. I managed to get the plane off the ground that time. Then I landed and went to the bathroom and threw up."

"So?" Selene asked. "You're a good pilot now."

Jack's head fell so that his face was covered in darkness. "The only reason I learned to fly was because I'm terrified of heights," he whispered. "The only reason I fought Dad was because he terrified me. It's the only reason I do anything."

Selene asked, "Why are you smiling, Oz?"

Oz's smile disappeared. "Because..." He sighed. "Because I remember what it was like to think I could change the world. And change myself, just through what I did."

"And now you see how stupid that is," said Mason.

"It isn't easy to learn how powerless we are," Oz said. He gave Jack a long look. "But it's probably best to learn it sooner rather than later."

Masaaki said to Jack, "Fear has been the source of your courage so far, and you have faced fearsome things. But there are deeper sources of courage. You must find them, or fear will be the only thing you have left."

Mason shook his head. "I've seen it before, kid. Don't try to be something you're not."

Jack looked at the policeman. The darkness seemed to pool in his eyes. He said nothing, but his fists trembled as he stared.

With hooded eyes, Selene asked, "Why did you cry when you saw that girl, Mason?"

Mason's face tightened as if he were holding his breath. Then he let out a long sigh and his shoulders relaxed. He was quiet for a minute and then, in the fluid no-time of that moon-drenched night, words started to wander from his mouth.

"My first week on the force, the station got a call from a hysterical woman, talking about what her husband had been doing to their daughter, and what she was gonna do to him. My partner and I got there first. He was on the front lawn, holding the daughter hostage with a handgun. He yelled at us for a while as other cars pulled up and they set up a perimeter. The little girl's eyes... Never forgot those. They were beggin' me the whole time to get her away from the man that was her Daddy. He yelled at me to stay back, but I couldn't. I got too close and he pulled the trigger. The sniper they had set up four roofs away took him down in one shot, but it was too late. I held her as she died. There was so much blood on my uniform. Couldn't wash it out. They gave me a new one, but I kept the old one in my locker and brought it home when it started to stink. It's probably still back there in my old house.

"Everything was different after that. Even after the captain finally stuck me behind a desk, I saw it on the face of every miscreant and whore they brought into the station. Decay and disorder. People giving up and breaking all the rules. I think that's what kept me from cracking after it happened. I saw more than one crazy person before I ran into you weirdoes. They just weren't used to the chaos."

"But you were," Masaaki said.

"I didn't feel too different after it happened. Except that whenever I saw one of them up close, one of the dead, I'd remember her."

"So what are you going to do now, officer?" Oz asked.

"We can't fight them. I was telling myself the whole way over here that if we just got enough people together, we could think of something. But they're too strong, and they grow back if you wound them. And how do you kill something when it's already dead?" Mason frowned and stared at the floor, his forehead casting shadows over his face. "There's nothing to be done against those things. But I'll kill myself before I stop trying." He shook his head. "I shouldn't have listened to you, Selene. I should have dislocated that guy's shoulder and then used the knife on him."

Oz said, "You're engaging an enemy too vast to be defeated. Adjust the way you view the world."

"Oh, like admiring those things, Oz?" Mason asked. "Is that what you mean?"

Jack asked, "What are you talking about?"

Mason said, "Luke set out this morning on his own before anyone else woke up. I followed him from a distance. He was sitting there, waiting for one of those things. And then Oz here shows up, walking up close enough to touch Luke's back, without making a single sound. I dunno how I missed him, because I was checking my perimeter the whole time. One of the dead walked past and Luke managed to get it stuck in a tree so he could stare at it. He was takin' notes or something. And Oz here joined in. Looked like they were going to snap a photo of it for a scrapbook."

"What did you see?" Masaaki asked.

"The thing got ahold of Luke and Luke shot it. He'd brought a gun with him, I forgot to say that. We got away as its head was growing back, but Luke slipped away from us."

Oz looked at the others: the room had suddenly developed a single set of eyes which were staring at him.

"It's not... It's..." Oz said, his hands up. He looked to Selene, and the words died in his mouth. He looked at the moon outside, luminous and calm. "I saw everything and nothing, Masaaki. I saw the world, and the only interesting thing left in it. And it was nothing. I always told my students that even a moderately good poem can have some kick to it, can surprise you and nourish you. But there wasn't anything there. And I couldn't turn away."

"Pathetic," Mason said.

Jack said, "People used to stare at car wrecks and horror movies in the old world. It's hard not to."

Mason was shaking his head in disgust, but the professor mused, "Why did we make horror movies back then? Did we, at some level, wonder if this might happen to us?"

Jack sighed. "I'd do anything to watch a zombie movie now. It'd be like comfort food. To watch how badly we imagined it."

"What do you mean?" Masaaki asked.

Jack said, "In the Romero movies, he used zombies as a way to talk about something else—politics and things like that. But now there's nothing else except them."

"Didn't everyone always die at the end of those movies?" Selene asked.

"In the good ones," Jack said. "If it had a happy ending, you'd feel kind of cheated."

"And why would we show ourselves that?" Oz asked. "Were we trying to make death less horrifying by making it more entertaining? Were we trying to recognize something about ourselves up on the screen? Confess something to ourselves? Or were we trying to comfort ourselves that we were better than the monster? Or were we doing all those things at the same time?"

Mason said, "So quit avoiding the question and tell us what you and Luke were doing, staring at that real thing up close."

Oz shrugged. "I'm no hero," he said. "As long as we're pointing fingers, why is it the dead act as if they are hypnotized around Masaaki?"

"I do not know," said the doctor.

Mason said, "Here's another one: why doesn't Oz tell us how he can move so quietly in the forest while the rest of us crunch along? Or why he's so hard to see when it's shadowy? I couldn't see him this morning until he was practically in front of me."

"Is that true, Oz?" Jack asked. The professor said nothing, but the moonlight in his stricken face was answer enough.

Mason said, "Whatever it means, Oz should be the first one to try to escape. He's got the best chance. He can clear the way for us."

Oz's eyes grew wide. "I already told you I'm not a hero," he whispered.

"Obviously," Mason said. "But you couldn't do any of that before the dead came, could you? And Masaaki, did you have a calming effect on people before?"

"No. People were rude to me many times."

Oz said, "So it started when..."

A sob sounded in the darkness. In one corner, the nameless girl held her head in her hands. Tears dripped down her forearms. Selene went and sat next to her, wrapping one arm around her shoulders. The nameless woman leaned into her.

Her voice shuddering, Nameless said, "You men, analyzing and arguing and blaming and thinking how to win and fight. Gaia has already punished you, but you're still the same." She gave a shuddering sigh and looked at them, tears glistening on her cheeks.

"Uh, didn't I just save you from an assault?" Mason asked.

"You expect me to thank you for saving me? The men inside this room are as bad as the ones out there."

"I ain't feeding people to the dead, sweetheart."

The nameless girl shook her head. Her long hair waved in the darkness like a red waterfall. "You were going to castrate that man right in front of me. You're sick! I wish you all would kill each other and be done with it." Her jaw tightened. "I will never let you hurt me again. Never. You hear me?" She swallowed in an audible click, as if willing away her tears.

No one spoke.

"Jason was the only one of you I ever met who was different," Nameless said. Her eyes grew distant. "I saw the football players shoving him around in the cafeteria one day and cheerleaders laughing at him. I stared at him when he slunk passed me. Our eyes met, and he didn't look away, even though he was about to cry. I stared at him every time I saw him after that until he finally sat with me at lunch. After a while, I started to tell him about my parents and the store I wanted to go to where they sold crystals and tarot cards. I was too scared to go on my own. I was still a slave back then. But he understood." Another sob coughed through her. "I still remember the look on his face as he listened, and I could tell he knew what I was talking about. I told him how I couldn't stand my father's eyes any longer. My father hardly ever talked, but there was something hungry about him that was creepy. And my Mom was so perky. I just couldn't stand it. And Jason listened, and held my hand, and told me he'd go to the store with me.

"It wasn't, like, really different from any of the other stores in town. They just painted the walls black and sold different kinds of trinkets. But I didn't know that then. I talked with one of the slaves working there and I bought some things. When we walked home, Jason told me about the books he kept under his bed. Stuff about druids. It was men who wrote them, but I would read them again if I could.

"A Wiccan priestess did a talk at the store a few weeks later. I brought Jason. He was the only man there and he got some looks, but he didn't mind. I didn't either." A smile lightened her face. "She told me the earth was alive and that men had hidden how beautiful she was with marriage and war and work. She said in the seventies, when women started to want something more than the kitchen and the bedroom, men had given them a place at work. But that just made women more like them. She said that when I reconnected with Gaia, I'd be free. And she was right, even though she didn't know what she was talking about. But I know, and I'm freer now than she ever was.

"Jason and I walked home afterward and sat on our front porch. I kissed him, and he ran his fingers through my hair. The moon smiled on us like an older sister. I tried to tell him with my lips how beautiful I was with him. I fell asleep that night wondering how my father would look at me the next morning, and whether he'd be jealous. For the first time, I didn't care.

"I woke up the next day and went into the kitchen. A thing wearing my father's body was on its knees underneath the kitchen table, snorting and chewing. My mother's legs were sticking out from under the other side. She moaned, and reached a hand toward my leg. The thing under the table stopped eating my mother and started to crawl toward me. It still had my father's glasses on its face. It still had that same hungry look.

"I ran out the front door. Felt like the sidewalk moving beneath me from miles away. I saw men eating each other and eating other women. After a while I looked up and saw I was at the New Age bookstore. I went in and sat down and watched. Eventually I prayed to Gaia, sometimes with words and sometimes without. I asked her where she was and what I should do. I think Gaia answered me, because after a while, what I was seeing outside the store window made more sense. The men were finally acting like real men. They were doing what they'd always done. Gaia had just made it more obvious. It, like, really scared me. Was this how the Great Mother punished her children? It made me wish that Gaia had done nothing. Made me wish she didn't exist. But I was still a slave back then.

"I kept the door locked all that day and didn't eat. I waited in the back of the store, in the shadows, and watched the men do their thing. One of the cheerleaders from my old school ran past. I suppose she saw me because she ran back and started banging on the window." The nameless girl paused, and something cold entered the room. "I watched as they ate her. She lay on the ground for a while and then got up and walked after them. She was just like the rest of them before, and she's just like them now. If the earth had really been her mother, she could have saved herself.

"I sat and rested my head against the wall. I was thinking that I needed to go look for Jason, but I must have fallen asleep, because the next thing I remember I was lying on the ground. A man was lying on top of me, jerking against me and gasping the way men do. His hand was over my mouth. I couldn't breathe. I struggled, but everything went red and then went dark. The next thing I saw was my own body, lying on the store of the floor. I floated up toward the ceiling and saw my body lying on the floor, not moving. My eyes were fluttering. At first I thought it was one of the dead on top of me from the way he was moving against me, but then

I saw the side of his face, and his skin was still pale pink and his eyes were not dead.

"Then I heard a voice. It wasn't my voice, and it wasn't his grunting. As the voice sang to me, I sank down into the earth. It was dark and warm down there. I saw a woman, a giant woman, green and more beautiful than anything I'd ever seen. She spoke to me, and I didn't feel so afraid anymore. I had never heard her voice before, but as soon as I did, I knew I'd been searching for it all my life. Her warm hand touched my back. I felt myself starting to come back to my body, and I fought it, because I just wanted to stay safe and warm with my real mother forever, but I opened my eyes and I was back in the store.

"It was like I was waking up for the first time. I screamed like a newborn child. I grabbed the man by the scruff of his neck and told him to look me in the eye. To at least pay me enough respect to look me in the eye if he was going to do this to me. His eyes got wide and he tried to pull away, but I held on to him and grinned. He was yelling at me to let go but then then his eyes closed and he gasped and shuddered and I knew I had beaten him.

"He got off of me and pulled up his pants and scampered out of the store. He made it across the street before the cheerleader who wasn't a cheerleader anymore met him. I smiled.

"I went to the bathroom to clean myself up. I looked in the mirror at the woman looking back at me, and I tried to remember what Gaia had just said to me in my vision. I could still feel the love of her hand on my back, but the words were fading. I started to freak out, like when I had seen my father that morning. I totally didn't want to forget. I just wanted to find her again. Then I saw the colors for the first time."

"What's the point of..." Mason asked.

"Let her finish," Selene said.

"Green, floating around my dirty face like smoke," Nameless said, as if she hadn't heard. "I moved my face around the mirror and it followed me. I couldn't leave the mirror. I could barely breathe, it was so beautiful. I felt like I was seeing something real for the first time, that everything I had ever seen before was just a shadow."

Selene was staring at Nameless, her eyes fixed on Nameless' face. As she spoke, a tear slipped down Selene's cheek. But Nameless was staring at the floor in front of her and didn't see it. She continued, "Then I understood the beauty the priestess had been talking about. I understood better than she did. I saw how much she had been a part of the old world, even though she had tried to get out of it. I saw how much I had been too. I realized I had been punished along with it by a man, just like every woman who trusts them. But not like the others. Gaia was kind. I realized I wasn't afraid of her anymore.

"I cleaned the punishment off of me and, when the street was clear, followed the color outside the store and down an alley. When I got out of town, I saw more colors. I don't have any names for them. I followed them. Whenever they turned gray, I knew the dead were near, and I would hide until they left. I thought about Gaia and wondered when I would see her again. I kept going until I got here.

"Why did you stop?" Selene asked, sniffing and wiping her eyes.

"The colors stop in the sad man's camp," Nameless said, indicating Oz. "They go into the ground."

"So these colors of yours are all around us?" Mason

asked.

"You breathe red," the nameless girl said. The policeman's eyes widened.

"What is it?" Selene asked. Her voice was a gentle invitation. Mason looked at Oz, who shrugged.

"I was hallucinating," Mason said. "Right after it happened. I wasn't myself."

"Tell us anyway," Selene said, the moon full in her face.

As if he couldn't resist her, Mason said, "I was sleeping in the back of a store, and I dreamed I saw this big red thing in the street. All the dead were bowing down to it. Then it was in the store. I don't know how. It leaned down and touched my forehead. It burned, but it felt good."

"I thought you said it was a hallucination, not a dream," Masaaki said.

"Whatever."

Oz said, "I though you said it bit your hand." Mason glared at him.

Jack asked, "What's my color?"

"The blue of the sea," the nameless girl said. Jack's mouth dropped open.

"Do other people have colors?" Masaaki asked.

"No," Nameless said. "I saw a few survivors, but I've never seen them coming out of anyone except you five."

"Five?" Mason asked.

"The white trash guy. The blonde one. He didn't have anything coming out of him. Only you five do. Red, deep blue, the white of the moon, black, and the pale blue of a summer sky."

"How can you see this?" Selene asked.

"Gaia touched me. I am different." Nameless paused and something broke in her face. A tear traced its way down the curve of her cheek. "I thought Gaia would be at the end of the colors. Instead I found you. People who have been touched and don't even care. Gaia came to me once. Where is she now?" She took a deep breath. "Jason is dead. I'll never meet anyone like him again. But my true mother is deep beneath us. She must be. She must be. I'll wait until she tells me what to do. At least I'm not a slave anymore."

"You ever gonna tell us your name, sweetheart?" Mason asked.

"My old name doesn't matter. When Gaia finds me, she'll tell me my real name. I'll ask her to show you mercy."

Jack gasped. Masaaki asked, "Why? I am a man."

"You five get it that the old world is dead. You're not still trying to live in it."

Mason guffawed quietly. "She'd be scary if she weren't crazy," he muttered to Oz; but Oz was staring at Nameless.

"I have many questions as well," Oz said, "but she could tell the dead were coming in the forest before we saw them. Did the colors stop, Nameless? Is that how you knew they were coming?"

The nameless girl nodded. Oz gave Mason a significant look.

With her arm still around her, Selene said, "You were not being punished when that man hurt you. Don't say such things."

Nameless shook her head. "Gaia was punishing the men of the old world and the women for going along with it. It touched me, but only a little." The nameless girl turned toward Mason, red hair falling over her ears, hiding her face from the moonlight, so that her eyes shone like two diamonds in a setting of black velvet.

Mason suddenly sat up straight. "What is that?" he

gasped.

They all turned in the direction he pointed. On a hilltop outside the circle of houses, a tall man walked. His skin shone gold, brilliant in the darkness. Even at that distance, they could see the man's naked body, his bald head, the smooth space between his legs where his genitals should have been, and the third eye of perfect gold in the man's forehead above two eyes of dead gray. That eye looked back at them in sleepy incomprehension. A scream sounded from a nearby house, followed by a gunshot. The man walked down the opposite side of the hill and out of view. The six prisoners looked at each other.

"What..." Mason whispered.

Outside the window, a low voice said, "I didn't kill him."

Like frightened children, their faces crowded into the window. Sitting in the crystal moonlight, a muscular man sat next to a rifle, arms around his knees. Lanky curls which would have been blonde by day showed silver. His John Deere cap was black.

"I didn't kill Bob," the man said. "I was telling him not to. When he shot himself, I was beggin' 'im. He only injured himself. I helped him pull the trigger the second time."

"You lost your friend," Selene said; but Mason cut her off: "Luke, help us get out of here." Another scream drifted through the moonlight, shouting, banging doors.

"The thing they chained up broke free. It went downstairs and let the others out of the basement." Luke stood and moved off into the darkness.

"That's it," Mason said. "Everybody back." The tinkling of glass from his boot was quiet compared with the now constant screaming. Mason walked toward the window, but the jagged outline of glass kept him from touching the windowsill. Firelight began to glow near the center of the compound.

Mason turned toward Selene. "I won't fit," he said. "Somebody smaller needs to go." Selene's eyes flared and she shook her head. The fiery glow colored her face blood red.

Oz sighed, walked toward the window, vaulted off of one of the chairs, and tucked and rolled when he hit the ground outside.

"How did he do that?" Jack asked, his mouth hanging open.

The professor stood and dusted himself off. He turned back to the window. "I'm no hero," he said. Then he walked out of sight.

After a moment's silence, Mason said, "Looks like we need to find some other way out." An explosion boomed. More screams. "Quickly."

A loud gunshot punctured the waves of shouting, and the lock on the front door clumped onto the floor. The door opened, and Oz stepped in, holding a gun. "One of the guards dropped it," he said, as if apologizing.

Mason exhaled loudly. "Time to go," he said.

They ran outside. The house where they had been introduced to the group was on fire. Through the front window, they could see people inside struggling and succumbing to Flowers with blooming heads. The shadows they cast writhed on the walls in a wild dance.

Oz turned to Nameless. "Does Luke have an aura or whatever that you can follow?"

Mason was nodding. "He probably has a hiding spot. Smart."

Nameless shook her head. "You five have different colors, but he's ordinary."

Mason shook his head. "Whatever. Let's move, people." He ran toward the row of trees. They followed, and soon they were stumbling over roots and plants as if the forest itself were trying to slow them. Jack looked back once; a bonfire was visible through the crisscrossed trees. A tree branch exploded above their heads with a whining sound of a ricochet. Mason whirled. "They're chasing us. Let's move it, people."

Another shot sounded, followed by a scream. "The dead are near," Nameless said, looking around. In the crisscrossing branches, against the background of the fire, the small shape of a starfish appeared, arms waving, with another behind it. A hiss seemed to surround them. Nameless' face flared in fear and she stepped backwards and yelled as her leg disappeared into the ground. "There's a hole," she said.

"Sounds fine," Mason said, pulling her out and clearing away the brush. Pulling a flashlight from his pocket, he looked inside.

"There's stairs," he said. He lowered himself in and disappeared from view. The thin beam of his flashlight appeared, and he called for the rest to follow.

Jack was the last one in. He walked down a few of the wide stairs, and Mason moved past him to pull some of the brush over the hole. Then Mason descended to the front of the group, holding his flashlight up. The light jiggled in shaky circles as he took one step after another. The others followed.

A minute later, a door with a picture of an oddly shaped eye appeared. Mason pulled it open and motioned them through. The hissing sounded again. They looked up at the hole far above in the ground to see a dark globe with waving arms. It reached through to crawl after them. Mason slammed the door shut. The door hissed and settled into its frame. Small dents popped in the door as the thing on the other side lashed against it, but the door didn't move.

"Whoever built this knew what they were doing," Mason said. Lights turned on at the sound of his voice. They were standing in a corridor of unearthly white. It ended in a blank wall to their left. He turned to the right and started walking.

"Are you sure you know where you're leading us?" Jack whispered.

"You sayin' you want to go back to them?"

The corridor ended. Another door on their left stood ajar. Mason opened it and led them down another long flight of stairs. Another closed door met them at the bottom. He opened it, gasped, and walked through. The rest followed.

They were in one corner of a vast warehouse, lit in spotless white by fluorescent tubes above. Stairs descended to a floor beneath them which held rows of machinery, spreading all the way to the distant opposite wall. Offices stood along both walls with desks and dead laptops. On the opposite side, a matching set of stairs ascended to a small platform. A man sat there in front of a tent and a small fire. A thin tendril of smoke rose toward the high ceiling. Even at the great distance, they could see the man's tangled black beard and the look of joy on his face. He waved to them.

ELEVEN

Beneath the Bottom of the World

The six survivors stood on the platform, frozen. The man waved again, and then descended the stairs and walked in their direction.

Oz started walking toward him. Mason took a step to follow, but Jack touched his arm and hissed, "After the group we just left, shouldn't we be careful?"

"We may as well see what he knows," he said, "but good point. Let's stay frosty." Then he followed Oz. The rest followed him.

It took a minute of walking before they met the man. He stood in front of them in shabby green pants and a plaid shirt. His beard covered his chest. He stared at them, plainly awed. Jack looked down one of the rows of massive gadgetry as he waited for whatever would happen next. He saw different kinds of jetpacks, whips which ended in splayed tendrils, huge machines with two arms and two legs and a hollow space for a human body. Although Jack had never seen anything like them before, they somehow looked like pieces in a museum.

He turned back to look at the newcomer. The harsh lights shone on his bald skull. Jack realized he couldn't smell anything; after the unending scents of the forest, it was unsettling.

Masaaki, staring at the man, said, "You... Why are you nervous?"

The man shifted on his feet, eyes darting between Masaaki's face and his feet. "Zeke's the name," he said, in a slow southern drawl. "It's an honor to finally meet you."

Zeke walked toward Masaaki, pressed his hands together in a posture of prayer, and bowed. A stream of Japanese syllables came from his mouth.

Masaaki's eyes widened in surprise. He bowed and said, "You honor me, but it is you who must guide me."

"The best I can," Zeke said, and turned toward Jack. He gripped one of Jack's thin arms, saying, "It's an honor, sir." Selene, standing behind Jack, had her hand taken and kissed with perfect sincerity.

Oz was favored with a huge grin. "Oz, I'm honored," Zeke said. The professor's mouth hung open, as if he wanted to laugh but had forgotten how.

Zeke turned to the nameless girl. Taking both her hands in his, he said in a soft voice, "Holy Mother, greetings."

The nameless girl's eyes opened wide. "No, I am looking for my mother," she said. Zeke gave her a knowing look, and turned to the policeman. Zeke kept his head down and turned his palms up.

"Mason," he whispered. "It's an honor, a genuine honor."

"Uh, yeah. And who might you be?"

"I'm, uh..." Zeke looked at them from within the forest of his beard. "Well..." He sighed and held up his hands. "I'm a prophet."

"Then speak your prophecy, Ezekiel!" Oz said, his own eyes dancing.

Mason said, "Oz, hold on…"

"Are you kidding me?" Oz asked. "This guy is a picnic compared to Miroslav. Speak, prophet!"

Zeke kept his eyes on the ground as he said, "I've got some things to show y'all, and some things to tell y'all." He looked up at them. A joy shone in his features which made Selene give a tiny gasp. Zeke's voice trembled. "But the main thing is that there ain't nothing you can do. The new world is comin', and it's only a matter of time before it catches up with y'all."

*

"Hate to break it to you," Mason said, "but the new world is already here."

"No, no," Zeke said. "Somethin' completely different. I've seen it. Except, well, this'll make more sense if I show you first." He sighed unexpectedly. "What I mean is, it's more likely you'll believe me if you see it first." Zeke turned and started walking back the way he had come.

Jack said, "Uh, Zeke or Ezekiel or whatever, no offense, but we just narrowly escaped a group of survivors who locked us up. How do we know it's safe?"

"Really? Were any of them manifesting?"

"Manifesting what?" Mason asked.

"They had locked up a bunch of the dead."

"Then they'll be dead themselves soon enough," Zeke whispered. "Two rows down on your right is a row of weapons. Take as many as you like."

Mason shoved his face into Zeke's. "If you stab me in the back, you'll get my first bullet."

"Sounds fine," Zeke said. "You do whatever you need to do."

Mason, Oz, Jack, and Masaaki walked down the aisle; Selene and the nameless girl hung back. Mason picked up a yellow and green handgun and discharged it in the air. A quiet *chink* sounded, and a splatter of holes appeared in the roof far above, fire flickering out of them briefly. Mason looked at the thing in his hand and then shoved it into his belt. Oz slung something resembling a rifle around his shoulder. Masaaki stood, considering.

"Nothing for you, Shinogaido Masaaki?" Zeke asked.

Masaaki stepped away from the row of technology and said, "This is not for me."

Zeke bowed again. "Of course not," he said, his eyes twinkling.

Jack picked up a long scabbard colored in two lines of deep blue and pearl white. It was heavy in his hands and cold like marble. Drawing out the sword with one hand, he held it upright. The sword showed a thin line of cloudy blue which flowed in one half of the blade and a milky white in the other. As Jack eyed it, the sword tipped slightly toward the floor, and suddenly it rested against the concrete in a tiny divot, pebbles of concrete pattering along the floor to either side. Jack grimaced in pain and grabbed his wrist as he dropped the sword in a clatter.

Zeke said, "That was a prototype. It was originally meant to release a charge of energy when swung. The idea never got further than filling the blade with chemicals which would make it heavy and light by turns. With the right kind of training, you could be a deceptive opponent."

"Who uses swords these days?" Mason asked.

Zeke shrugged. "It was an experiment."

Jack put the sword back and picked up two smaller guns. Walking to Selene, he handed one to her, but she shook her head.

"You're not thinking clearly," Selene said. "You can't make decisions out of fear." Jack gave her a sharp look and put both guns in his belt.

When they had all turned back to Zeke, he said, "This was originally the staging area for a company..." He put a hand to his forehead, as if suddenly struck with a headache. "A company called Horus Industries, which produced experimental weapons for the government."

"Anything that... " Mason asked, but Zeke cut him off: "There's nothing here that's any use against the Flowers, Mason."

"How did you know we called them that?"

Zeke sighed again, and drawled, "I do apologize. I'm gettin' ahead of myself. I have a tendency to do that. The point I'm trying to make is, this is only a front. Horus Industries kept it up as a subterfuge even after the company had... had moved in a different direction."

"What direction?" Mason asked.

"It's better if I show you." Zeke turned and walked toward the opposite platform again. The six survivors gave each other silent, tense looks and followed.

After a minute, Mason growled, "Why are you so happy?"

"What?"

"You're practically bouncing," Oz said with a grin.

"Oh. Well, I guess you might say I've waited a long time for this."

"It's only been a few weeks since it happened." Mason spat the words like the first flicking raindrops before the thunderstorm.

"It's typical," the nameless girl said, looking at the rows of machinery passing by them like marching soldiers. "Men build weapons, but they can't stop the monsters they create." She shook her head. "The colors are dim here."

"You're surely right," Zeke said, without looking back as he walked.

"Are you making fun of me?" she asked.

Zeke stopped and turned, his face an exclamation point. "No, ma'am, no, not at all. We did make a monster we can't fight. I'm trying to show you how." Zeke stared at them for a moment, as if he was worried they might turn and join another tour group. Then he trotted off toward the stairs; soon he was taking them two at a time. One by one, they followed.

At the top, Zeke walked past his tent and smoldering fire and toward a single door which stood within the long white wall opposite them. He punched numbers into the pad beside the door, and it opened to show an elevator.

"We must descend, must we not?" Masaaki asked.

"True," Zeke said, stepping inside.

Mason gave a laugh which sounded like a gun being cocked. "I don't believe any of this."

"I'm aware of that," their host said from inside the elevator. "You'll get your answers soon enough. I promise. I can see the rest of you are reluctant to follow me. Richard, I know that you don't like being here, and that you'd rather be outside with the wind on your face. Selene, this may be difficult for you as well. But it will be worth it."

"Who's Richard?" Mason asked.

115

"Oz," Zeke said. "I meant to say Oz." He shook his head and rubbed his eyes. Mason turned to Oz, but Oz kept wide eyes on the ground and quickly walked into the elevator with Zeke. Jack followed Oz, and Selene followed her brother. Masaaki and Nameless crowded into the small elevator, Nameless giving Zeke a long, curious look. Still outside, Mason shrugged his shoulders and entered.

The elevator dinged, a loud sound in the long silence of the warehouse, and the door slid shut. A humming sounded as they fell.

*

A full minute later, it slowed to a stop and opened on a long, dimly lit corridor of closed doors.

"Why are the lights still on in this building?" Mason asked.

Zeke glanced back at his followers before starting down the hall. "They had alternate sources of power. The board is at the end of the wall. The board room, I mean, at the end of the hall." Zeke walked forward, and so did not see Selene staring at a door which was standing ajar. Nor did he see her push it open and look inside.

She saw a single dim light in the ceiling which shone on a bare room with black walls. On the opposite wall, the features of a mask glistened under the silent light. Selene walked toward it and the face opposite her shaped itself into a sneer. Harsh syllables streamed from it in a seasick, drunken slur. Selene moaned and collapsed backwards at the sound of the voice. She fell into Oz's arms, who had followed her in; as he caught her, the face in the wall shifted in his direction. A girl's plaintive voice filled the room in a wordless wail. Oz's eyes opened in shock.

Zeke ran into the room and grabbed Oz by the shoulders and pulled him backwards. The two of them rolled into the hallway. Before Oz could stand, their black-bearded host leapt to his feet and carried Selene from the room. He kicked the door shut before he put her down.

Still prone on the floor, Oz mumbled, "Did she say..."

Curled in a ball, Selene gave a muffled sob. "I told myself he was dead forever."

Zeke stood with his hand on his hips, panting, and looked at his charges as if he were about to bark an order. Then his shoulders slumped and his head fell into shadow beneath the light bulbs set in the ceiling above.

"I was goin' to take y'all below and show you," he said. "But you jus' got yourselves a taste of it. The company started with weapons, but they soon got on to other experiments. After a while, they stopped trying to make new products and started finding ways to manipulate the patterns most scientists thought were laws. The head of the company kept searchin', kept digging and digging until he got beneath the laws of nature."

"And what did he find?" Oz asked from the floor. His question was like the wind wandering over an empty plain. Selene stood up, wiping her eyes and sniffing.

"Nothing. The emptiness outside all order. The darkness outside every light. The void that gives birth to the cosmos. And he found a way to use it. That's what I'm trying to show you."

"What was that voice saying to you, Oz?" Jack asked.

"You didn't understand it?" the professor returned. When Jack shook his head, Oz's eyes widened. "Nothing. I just

117

heard nonsense."

Zeke said, "Now y'all come with me, and don't open any more doors." He turned down the corridor.

The door at the end of the hallway opened to a narrow room with a long, polished table and high-backed chairs. The same dim light from the ceiling shone in this room as well. A laptop stood open at the furthest seat, where a blonde-headed figure typed. Beyond him the walls and ceiling continued into darkness.

"Luke?" Mason said. The figure at the desk jumped to his feet, startled.

"He's been coming here for the past few weeks," Zeke said.

"How did he get into the elevator without knowing the code?" Mason asked.

Zeke said, "A keypad like that can't stop someone like him," and made his way past the chairs toward Luke. Luke looked at them like a child caught with the cookie jar.

"Luke," Zeke said. "It's an honor." The redneck stared at Zeke without saying anything.

"This here's the company's board room," Zeke said. "The Head sat right there, where Luke was. Luke's probably hacked into their system, so he doesn't need me to repeat what I've already said. It was here that the decision was made."

"What decision?" Mason asked.

"You know what decision."

"None of this makes any sense. I'm leaving." He turned away.

"Any less sense than the dead rising?" Zeke asked. "You've a keen mind, Mason. But a case is solved against a larger order which exists outside the case. This is the place they decided to reverse that relationship."

Mason turned and looked at Zeke.

"Six chairs for six board members, and one more for the Head," Zeke said. "The Head promised these six places of honor and power in the new world. They agreed. He wouldn't have given them a choice, but they were hungry for what the Head had. There's one more thing to show you, and then we'll talk, and you can ask whatever you'd like."

Zeke walked past the table and into the dark corridor beyond the table, but stopped and turned after a dozen paces when he realized he was alone.

"Are you coming?"

"Yes," Oz said, looking at his feet; but he didn't move.

"Ah," Zeke said, walking back to them. "It has that effect sometimes. I'm going to show you what the Head discovered, and what he used to get the Dead up and walking. But it's hard to go toward it. It took the members of the board some time before they could walk to the end of their own board room. Wanting to get there helps. Do you want to, Oz?"

"Do I want to?" Oz asked. He looked like he was about to laugh, or scream.

The nameless girl said, "So I need to rely on a man one last time to find my true mother. Fine." Furrowing her brow, she put one foot out, then another. The others flinched and grimaced, as if each suddenly had a headache. When she finally stood near Zeke, the group exhaled a sigh of relief.

"And I," Masaaki said.

"Why?" Zeke asked, his eyes sharpening. He seemed to be holding his breath.

"I can guide no one until I learn how we became lost," Masaaki said. Although he walked without effort, the same uncomfortable blur fell over the rest; even though he didn't slow, the dozen steps Masaaki took seemed to last for minutes.

Oz started to swing his arms, but his feet remained on the carpet. He gaze Zeke a frantic look.

Zeke said to Luke, "You have seen designs and plans and notes from meetings. Do you want to see the reason the company existed?"

Luke's eyes widened, and he made the same eye-watering, prolonged journey which took only seconds.

"Don't bother, Jack," Zeke said. "Just give up."

Jack's mouth curved down. He grabbed his sister's hand and would have walked past Zeke into the vague distance if Zeke had not put a hand on his shoulder. Oz now stood by himself.

"My mind is playing tricks on me," he called to the others. "Just give me a minute."

Zeke said, "It's not only your mind. You've been close to chaos for so long. I'd a thought you'd dive right in. Don't you want to know what is beneath the world, Oz?"

"Do you?" Oz asked.

"Seen too much of it already," Zeke said. "But I'll do what I need to, to get you movin'."

"There is no beneath," Oz said. "No above the world or beneath it. There is no world, except what our minds want to see."

"Then there's no reason for you not to walk forward," Zeke said. Oz grimaced but didn't move.

Zeke took a step toward him and said, "Don't you want to see the rottenness eatin' the foundations of everything you know? Isn't there anythin' inside you that wants to look?" Zeke's voice was flat, as if his words had a bitter aftertaste.

Oz laughed then, an unhinged sound which echoed through the corridor as he finally took a step. They waited, and waited, and suddenly Oz was standing beside them.

"Let's cross that last boundary," Oz said. A wildness was in his eyes.

"Good," Zeke said. "It'll be easier now." He walked down the dark corridor. They followed.

*

"I can't recall what the walls look like. They are right next to me, and when I look at them, I can see them. Then I turn away and I forget."

"It tends to have that effect on people. Even people as smart as you, Oz."

"The colors are so rich here. Are you leading us to their source?"

"I suppose you could say that, Mother."

"I heard my father's voice inside that mask. I told myself I never again would see him, but his face was inside that mask. How? How?"

"Old voices echo in that mask, Selene. That was one of the ways the Head intimidated people. It responds to the chaos inside. It's connected to the place I'm taking y'all to. Who knows, seeing that mask may have been good preparation for what I'm about to show y'all. Ah, here we are."

Wide stairs ahead and below. Their footsteps made no sound as they descended into darkness. If the walls continued beside them, they couldn't see them.

"I wish there was a handrail."

"Do ya' feel dizzy?"

"No. I guess not."

"There ain't no danger of falling. Even if you did, you wouldn't hurt yourself when you landed."

"Why do I feel so relaxed?"

"'Cause we're further from the surface of the world and the dead than if we'd traveled beyond the solar system."

"I couldn't get it out of my head. The sunflower blindly opening to the sun. It printed everything. I'd even see starfish arms encircling people's heads who weren't dead. But it's gone now."

"Your mind is bein' washed clean, Mason. For now."

"How long till we get to the bottom?"

"You can't never really tell. Sometimes it's a few steps. Sometimes its an hour. But you always get there eventually. Yup, here we are."

Before them, the dim outline of the stairs ended before a rocky floor. A few more paces brought them to a rock face with a doorknob.

"There's no light. How can we see this?"

"What is beyond this door reflects light from above. It only becomes real by stealing from other things that are real. It has to reflect something, or it wouldn't exist."

The man they had called Zeke pulled on the handle. The door opened. They walked through. The door shut behind them.

*

The door opened, and they walked out again. Zeke shut it, and led them away into the glistening, shimmering darkness. Their path may have sloped upward.

"That was water, correct? Behind the door?"

"Tha's close enough, Oz."

"What do you mean, 'close enough'?"

"I'm pretty certain it ain't actually water. But that's the only way our minds can see it."

"Was it storming in there? I thought I heard thunder."

"I heard rocks crashing together."

"Wasn't that screaming?"

"No human voice can scream that way."

"How big was that room?"

"It ain't no room. I ain't never found any other wall except the one with the door."

"Why did you tell us not to touch the water?"

"It'll react to you in some strange ways. That's one of the things I'll try to explain. Here it is." Dim light shone through a hole in the rock above them. A man walked toward it and looked up, and as he did, Ezekiel's face appeared. An interweaving tangle of white roots hung down through the hole and penetrated the earth beneath their feet. Using the roots, Ezekiel pulled and huffed his way up through the hole and disappeared.

They stood in the darkness, ghosts who had forgotten their names. Ezekiel's face appeared in the hole, moonlight shining on his bald head. Speaking to them as if from out of the sky, he said, "Now, every single one of you will get out of that hole." There was flint in his voice.

They did, helping and pulling each other up, to stand in a panting semi-circle around their guide.

"Good," he said. "It can be as hard to get people out of there as it is to get them in. Now tell me where we are."

Each of them turned first to the tall white tree which glistened in the moonlight.

"It has barbed wire around it," Mason said in a hushed voice. "This is..."

Ezekiel asked, "Who remembers the shape of the moon when you last saw it?"

Luke muttered, "It was full. Now it's waxin' gibbous." They stared at him.

"You mean we've been beneath our camp for almost a month?" Oz asked.

"Or more than one," Ezekiel said. "No way to tell. Why do you think y'all were attracted here in the first place? Y'all sensed something about this place. And that's why the thing you burned has grown so large. Its roots reach all the way down to where we were. It'll be a long time before that thing stops growing. Now come with me."

They followed their prophet through the narrow entrance, through the disarray of their plundered campsite (clothes and old food scattered everywhere), and sat around the campfire. Ezekiel began to speak.

Twelve

Ezekiel's Prophecy

"A man whose name is well lost started Horus Industries. His official business was government contracts for special weapons development. He wasn't a scientist himself. He didn't even pretend to understand the technology he sold. He jus' knew how to find scientists who did. But something deeper drove him. He started to develop drugs which would create super soldiers. Give you night vision, let you jump twice your height, react faster than any human being naturally can. The military bought all of it without asking the right questions..."

"Wait, this stuff already exists?" Mason asked.

"It's been around for years. Y'all think the government would allow a free market on that kind of technology? But still the Head was restless. He started to think about how most of the human body is empty space. He wondered if there might be some potential in that emptiness.

"Then one of his chief scientists had a heart attack. Nobody else could interpret the notes he left behind. It looked like he had been working on some pretty important stuff. The Head was furious. People started disappearing."

"He murdered them?" Mason asked.

"Yessir. People wanted out, but there's no way the Head would let them go back to civilian life. In any case, it was death that the Head started to think about. The final darkness, when the body returns to emptiness. Could it be used somehow? Manipulated to his advantage? He kept searching, seducing the best minds he could find and chaining them to their desks with threats and pleasures. His workers kept reaching deeper and deeper, until it wasn't so much mathematical formulas they were comin' up with as much as metaphors. One day the Head was told one of his brilliant drones wasn't workin' any more, jus' sittin' at his desk, mutterin'." Ezekiel paused, staring at the dead firepit. He said, "The Head confiscated the drone's notebooks and found, among the rambling and numbers and equations and guesses, a map to a place that don't exist. It was the place the Head had searched for for so long. The chaos surrounding all scientific laws, the formlessness beneath all order, out of which everything we know is born. Another level to the company, beneath the board room, was constructed. And tha's where he stored it. Or, tha's where it is. You can't really store it, because it's not real. But tha's where it is.

"People drowned there. He lost workers who'd jus' walk in and not come back. Their bodies never washed up on the shore. If you ask me, it's endless. You never touch bottom.

"The Head met with the board. Told 'em he was gonna release a chemical compound into the air which had traces of the chaos. It was supposed to kill everyone and resurrect them."

"But some people survived," Mason said.

Ezekiel nodded. "Jus' one of the ways things didn't go according to plan for the Head."

"I saw some exploded graves," Oz said.

Ezekiel nodded again. "Makes sense it would work its way into the earth. Anyway, the Head promised that he and the board of his company would be given a different version of the same drug. It'd give them new bodies that could do things no human body could. The Head wanted to make 'em gods over a new humanity. The Head was gonna make himself the strongest, but the six board members would live forever, like him.

"They would have been fools to refuse. The Head had killed over much less. But they were so hungry for what he was sellin' that they agreed right away.

"They were gonna rule over a new earth, a new pantheon like the Greek gods. He promised one as a god over the sea, one to rule the air..."

"And one as goddess of the earth?" Nameless asked.

"Tha's right, sweetheart. The sea, the air, the earth, the sun, the moon, a god over death, who'd shepherd the dead, and a god of war, who would keep the stuff in his own body like a container. The Head was gonna name him after some old god of plague."

"Well, this Head you refer to failed," Oz said. "He made them less than animals. They're walking corpses."

"Well..." Ezekiel paused, the moon glistening on his skull. His beard seemed to be one with the night, as if his eyes floated above his chest. "Re-animating the dead was only the first stage. The chemical was going to stay active in them and keep changing them."

"That explains why some of them open up," Jack said.

"They open up?" Ezekiel asked.

"Where have you been for the last month? Or however long it's been?" Mason asked.

"Inside the company. Too dangerous to leave."

127

"Some of the faces of the dead open, like flowers," Masaaki said.

Ezekiel was sitting very still.

"You can't kill them, either," Mason said. "They grow back. That a surprise to you, Ezekiel?"

"I've seen some things yet to come," Ezekiel said, "but I haven't seen everything. I guess it makes sense the Head would want his children to be indestructible."

Mason groaned. "Wait a second. New bodies, you said? For the Head and his board?"

"That's right," Ezekiel said. "Why?"

"Was the Head supposed to be golden?"

Ezekiel's eyes widened. "You seen him?" he asked in a tight voice.

"Yeah," Mason said. "He was walking on a hill far away, but I could see him clearly. He was..." With moonlight filling his face, Mason whispered, "He was a monster, but he was beautiful."

Ezekiel whispered, "The version of the virus he injected into himself and his board was gonna take a while to work. The best calculations the Head had told him they'd regain consciousness after a couple of months. But he's already up and around. Well." Ezekiel let out a sigh. "The main thing I have to tell you is that the Head's plan didn't work—at least, not entirely. Now I'm learnin' new ways he failed."

"He failed?" Jack asked.

Ezekiel favored Jack with a fatherly smile. "Jack, you keep on doin' what you're doin'. You'll find your stride, and there won't be no one able to stop you once you do. Not even the dead." Jack's eyes widened and his mouth opened in a hungry question mark.

Ezekiel continued, "The Head failed because... well, the

new world he's tryin' to create, where he's god, won't happen. Something so much better is goin' to happen instead. And you seven are going to be at the heart of it."

"How do you know that?" Mason asked through gritted teeth.

"I saw it."

"How? Are you psychic?" Mason asked in a conversational tone.

"No. I was..." His voice trailed off and he looked away.

"Something worrying you, Ezekiel? You knew the code for the elevator. You worked there, didn't you?"

"You can kill me for being Judas if you want. It won't stop the miracle that you're gonna do."

"Just tell me the truth."

Ezekiel sat, rigid. As if on its own, his mouth opened, and words wandered out in low tones: "The Head drowned me. That was my reward for discoverin' something that would have put everyone who won a Nobel Prize to shame. Discoverin' something that can't be discovered because it don't really exist. You think 'cause I talk like this I'm white trash? I was top of my class at MIT. Top of the pack among the Head's drones, too. I was sitting at my desk the morning it happened. For weeks I had felt it in my mind, like a knot about to come loose. I hadn't seen the sun for months and I didn't care 'cause I knew I was close. I had taken to writin' in notebooks 'cause I couldn't get what was inside my head onto my computer. And one morning, it all broke open. I was writin' and drawin', and something shifted inside my head while my hand scrawled, and I knew I'd found it.

"And I stared down at what I'd written like it was someone else's work. As soon as the lock opened and I reached inside, another clicked shut behind me, and I couldn't remember how I got there. Two of the Head's goons held me in my chair while I raved at the Head that I'd forgotten it all, all the science I'd ever learned, like baby talk I'd outgrown. When the Head realized he couldn't get anything out of me, he took my work to some other scientists to look at. Then he came back to my cubicle with that awful smile of his, and I knew he didn't need me anymore. I got solitary confinement for a week, listen' to bangin' and drillin' and other sounds as he built something beneath my cell. Then a troop of guards opened the door and led me to that cavern I showed you. The Head was at the front of them. I was yelling at him the whole time that his secret was safe, that I couldn't understand it anymore, but the Head kept smiling all the way down. They forced me into the water and pushed my head under. The Head was smilin' so big it looked like his face was gonna split open.

"I struggled for a while. I think I probably coulda' swum if I tried, but I wasn't thinkin' of much of anything by then. They pushed me further under, and I sank. I could see the legs of the guards who drowned me, and the sand they were standing on, but I sank beneath them.

"I said I saw things beneath the water, but that's not really it. I think the years ran together. Time and space don't exist there, 'cause it's the opposite of time and space. I touched the future the way we're in the present right now. I saw the Head being worshipped by the dead. I saw the board trying to take their place with him in the new world. And I saw how they couldn't because they're startin' to die. It will take a long, long time before they do, but they're fading already. They're not true gods."

"The Mother is fading? The earth goddess?" Nameless asked. "How is that even possible?"

"The stuff the Head used to transform the six board members is unstable. It's chaos." When Nameless shook her head, Ezekiel said, "I know this hurts you, and I'm sorry. But I saw it."

"You're wrong," Nameless said, her voice like a knife-edge.

Ezekiel gave her a look that suggested he wanted to put his arm around her but was afraid to. He said, "I saw what you seven will become." His lower lip trembled. He seemed very far from the figure who had commanded them out of the hole back to their camp. "And it's beautiful."

"What do you mean?" Selene asked.

Ezekiel paused, as if glad simply to look at her. He said, "You know how it feels when you make up with your sweetheart and kiss? When the snow finally melts and you see the green and hear the birds? When the doctor tells you they got it all wrong and there's no cancer? It was like that. I thought I knew what joy was. Y'all showed me how wrong I was."

They stared at him, a row of tired, anonymous faces in the moonlight.

"I know how strange this must sound. It's hard to put it into words. Your whole lives have been lived in the middle of the argument, in the dead of winter, under a terminal disease. And when the dead came, you slipped deeper in. But it's coming." A ghostly smile broke over his face in the moonlight. "The end is coming."

"And what makes us different?" Mason asked.

"Y'all been touched. The six board members got together after they changed. They knew they were dyin'. They knew they couldn't face the Head, but they wanted revenge. They decided they'd pick six new ones and give them their power."

"But you were talking about us seven," Mason said.

"I didn't see it happen, but Luke here will have a golden body."

"The Head is... is gonna give him magical powers?" Mason asked, his mouth pulled back as if the question disgusted him.

"I didn't see how it happens. But I saw the end result." Ezekiel opened his mouth to say more, but then shut it and looked around at them as if expecting applause. They stared at him, looking like they might never talk again. Ezekiel's smile slowly fell away. "You don't believe me."

Nobody spoke.

Ezekiel's face fell. He said, "I sank and sank. Eventually I sank into a darkness... It wasn't so much darkness as the absence of light and dark. I didn't care. I couldn't even remember my own name. Then I started seeing things. And the further I sank, the higher I could see." Ezekiel's voice dropped to a whisper, and it seemed the night held its breath as he spoke: "I saw a light which makes the light we know look like fog. It was smiling down on the darkness beneath it. I saw you in that light, each one of you. I saw what you become, and the good you do. Then I wasn't sinking anymore. I was rising, and as I rose, time began to move backwards. I saw the Head bein' worshipped by the Dead, and then this conversation, right here with you, and then I saw me meeting you in the old warehouse. And I saw how, even during this conversation, that light was beginning to shine. That's why I was so excited to see you. I had to talk to you or none of it would happen. Then I was on my hands and knees in the sand, coughin' the water out of my lungs and laughin' while I did, 'cause of what was gonna happen and 'cause I was gonna be a part of it. I had been the instrument of so much destruction, and I'd have the privilege of guiding the people who would set it right. So I kept watch and waited in the place I'd seen us meet, and a couple weeks later, you were clattering down the stairs."

"You're crazy," Mason said.

"Can't see the things I have and stay sane. They're too wonderful."

Mason asked, "Why do the Dead eat us? Why didn't the Head just kill everyone right away?"

"Men like him are terrified of death. Having the Dead serve him was a way to try to control it. He wants Death to worship him."

"But why do they eat us?" Oz asked.

"Death is always hungry. Not even the Head can change that."

"Why do they only eat a part of someone else?" Mason asked. "Why not eat the whole body?"

"It's not the physical body they're interested in," Ezekiel said. "They're tryin' to eat the life outta you. Once you recomb a sight like them... I mean, once you become like them, they lose interest."

"Well, I believe you," Selene whispered.

"You the only one?" Ezekiel asked, looking around.

"You have made several errors in speech without seeming to realize it," Masaaki said.

Oz said, "He was in the stuff he says turned everyone into a walking corpse. If it's affecting him, how can we trust him? And if he sunk in it, how did he come back?"

Nameless said, "I can believe that a man killed everyone. But Gaia can't be dead. The trees are growing all around us. She is growing them."

"When's the last time you heard a bird sing?" Ezekiel asked. No one answered. "Any of you been swattin' mosquitoes lately? Or finding any ticks? Y'all been livin' in a forest. Anyone? The virus the Head released killed all animal life. And there's no comin' back for them. Any of you find yourself getting hungry less often?"

"I still get hungry," Luke said.

"That's just a psychological reflex," Ezekiel said. "When the head released the virus, it changed everything. Y'all will find you can go a long time without eating or sleeping and not even notice. Once it gets lighter, you'll see the white that looks like frost startin' to appear on trees and plants. That's part of the Head's plan. He killed the food chain, and plant life, too. Everything is goin' to turn white. Turn to ash." Ezekiel looked outward at the forest. The first hints of dawn glimmered through the trees. No one spoke.

"So..." Ezekiel said.

"So what?" Mason asked.

"So what y'all gonna do?"

"You're asking us?" Oz asked. "You're the one who supposedly knows everything."

"You have to do somethin'. You have to." His voice was rising. "Otherwise..."

"Otherwise what?" Masaaki asked.

"Otherwise I ain't nothin' but the tool the Head used to kill the world."

"We can't fight them," Mason said. "I don't know what you were expecting us to do."

Jack said softly, "It's a little much to believe." He didn't notice Selene glare at him.

Mason nodded. "A great light, shining on everything, making everything better? Do you really expect me to believe that, after everything I've seen?"

"It wasn't supposed to be like this," Ezekiel said. His face was ashen in the faint dawn.

A soft hiss sounded. Turning, Oz saw a tall body in a black sheet, seven starfish arms waving around a shadow-darkened head. Behind it, more bodies walked, dead sunflowers opening in the dim dawn light. The shout in Oz's throat died into a groan as the peace he had felt ever since his descent (almost unnoticed) soured.

Soon the perimeter of the camp was surrounded, each tall guardian hissing, the short tentacles around their faces swaying like slow waves of heat, arms rigid by their sides with tensed gray fingers. Each stared blindly from cloudy gray eyes at something far away. In the growing light, the survivors could see the thing they had burned at the edge of their camp was now a great white tree. Even though no wind touched its branches, they stroked the dead nearest it like a mother touching her children. Mouths opened at different points on its trunk; tongues hissed.

The Flowers stood, rigid hands curling and uncurling, arms and backs locked, tentacles waving. Tongues flicked in and out in a soft, hissing drone. Then something happened they had never seen before: the starfish arms on one of the dead started to fold back over its faces. For a moment, the Flower looked again like one of the early dead with stitches on its face branching outward from its mouth. It flared open and closed again, and others began to follow suit in an undecipherable Morse code.

The guns had been in Jack's back pockets so long he had forgotten they were there. Pulling one out, he aimed and pulled the trigger. A quiet *chink* sounded, and staccato holes appeared in three of the dead across the camp. A tiny flame appeared in each of the holes and quickly flickered out. The quiet susurration of voices quickened for a moment, then relaxed. In the strengthening dawn, Jack could see tiny white tendrils reaching out to close over the wounds. Jack looked at the gun and then threw it with a puff of ash into the firepit.

"I think..." Masaaki squeaked, and stopped as each Flower instantly closed, starfish arms folding to create the thin lines radiating up from each mouth. The sound of their whispering fell into utter silence in the clean light of dawn.

"I think they want us to follow them," Masaaki whispered, sweat beading on his pale face.

Mason hissed, "How do you..." but stopped as each Flower opened again.

Masaaki said, "That is what I think," and again, each face folded into silence.

The doctor stood. Beyond those directly outside the barbed wire, many more rows of corpses appeared in the growing dawn, silent and attentive. He walked toward the two trees which had formed the entrance to their camp, when it had been one.

The nameless girl, fear contorting her sharp features, rose and followed.

Jack discovered Luke was staring at him with desperate eyes. He glanced at Selene. She was looking at him with eyes that begged him to act.

"I don't think there's anything we can do," Jack said to her.

Oz said, "They're not coming in. If we can last a long time without food..." He stopped as the corpse standing nearest to him put two hands on a line of barbed wire and pulled it apart.

Jack stood and pulled his sister to her feet. She was shaking her head, but then she looked at the Flowers and something seemed to break inside her. Her head fell and her eyes closed and she let Jack lead her. Luke stood and followed. Mason, grinding his teeth to hold back tears, stood and walked out of the camp as well. Eventually Oz stood. His eyes darted each way, looking for an opening, but his heavy footsteps told another story.

Ezekiel came last. "It can't be this way," he whispered to himself. "They'll think uh somethin'."

The dead moved to surround them in a wide circle. They each turned their backs to the camp. None of the dead looked at the eight survivors as they started to walk, keeping the circle intact. Huddled together in the middle, the survivors began to walk with them.

THIRTEEN

The Head

The Dead walked, and the survivors stumbled and shivered with them. The circle in which the six men and two women moved became a stationary thing, the dead surrounding them like ancient trees. Flimsy brown things with dying leaves passed by them as they walked. Once one of the survivors saw a tall figure on the horizon; but when she looked again, it was gone.

It was not until they cleared the forest that they saw how many myriads accompanied them, some with faces closed and some not yet changed. Each one walked forward without looking at the survivors in the middle. The thousands of dead turned the gently undulating fields to gray-black waves. The only grass visible was beneath their feet. The survivors turned to it often when they couldn't bear the sight of their guides; but instead of the comfort of green, only yellow stalks showed, with splotches of white like frost.

The front of the ring around the survivors dissolved and re-formed around a corpse on its knees with its back to the survivors. The dead stopped walking and turned to the corpse at their center. A telegraph pole stood in the space cleared by the dead, the remains of a road, and a small hill.

The corpse in the center stood and lifted its head toward the rising sun.

A current began to move in the long circle of dead flesh. The first line of the dead edged sideways. Their faces flared open then shut. The line behind them moved in the opposite direction. They suddenly changed course and moved with the first line; then the opposite way. The movement rippled backwards across line after line of the dead. The movement of the lines began to weave among each other, like interlocking gears. Sometimes lines of sunflowers would open, sometimes they would shut. The waves became a whirlpool around a new center of the earth, random and no true place at all. An inkling of a larger pattern in the movement would steal over the eight survivors, only to slip away.

The corpse in the center turned and walked toward them.

It had two long and seemingly fresh scars along its jaw which ended in its mouth. No lines were visible running up its cheeks where tentacles had been pressed together. Its skin was a blotchy gray-green and open wounds festered on its bald skull; but it was also somehow more than the monsters encircling it. Something unearthly lit up its jaw and forehead and played along its fingers like electricity. Darkish gray tears slid down its face. The vast dance around the thing in the center (if it was a dance) somehow became more complex as it walked toward the survivors.

As it stood before them, the sun seemed to shine more brightly. Something black, deeper than the world, yawned open as the thing's gray eyes popped softly and more gray tears spilled down its face. A sigh escaped its lips and the scars on its throat peeled open in a perfect circle in the breeze. They waved in serpentine perfection around the crater with a mouth inside. It unmistakably looked at the survivors from its empty eye sockets.

The starfish arms closed again, forming a parody of a human face with long scars along the jawline. The same slithering whispers the other Flowers made were growing louder in her mouth, and more complex: "Yess... yesss... it returns. It returns to myself. I remember." The things circling her quickened, opening their tentacles, hissing. The Flower in the center turned empty eye sockets upward to the sun, its face flaring open again. "I finally see."

One of the dead in the circle surrounding the survivors stopped moving, dropped to its knees, and fell forward into the grass. Stillness rippled outward like rushing wind as the movement of the lines of Flowers stopped. The thing lay on the ground for a moment. Then the hands connected to the torso pushed down into the grass. It got to its knees and stood. Two smudges of gray fluid were left on the ground where it had fallen, and only cavities where dead gray eyes had been. Turning its face upward, sounds came out of its mouth: "Thllasssee... ethlassee... I return... thlass... I see... the sun..." Its starfish arms closed into a parody of a human face, the same scars on its jawline and caverns where its eyes had been. "I remember," it said.

Another Flower fell, and another. Domino-like, the line collapsed to the ground. The eight survivors huddled together on the grass. Some moaned as they watched.

In the rising, hissing babel of return and remembering, as the waves of dead fell and rose to their feet again, one of the dead broke ranks, shuffling toward the Flower at the center. No starfish arms were visible, nor any marks where they had been retracted. Half of its head showed white tendrils, the other, a head of curly brown hair. One of the survivors gave a long groan and shouted, "Bob!" The corpse didn't turn. The man shouted again and began to weep.

The thing that had been Bob walked to the Flower at the center, who pointed at the sun. The corpse with red hair looked upward. Red lacerations traced themselves from its neck up to its skull, and four waving arms peeled back from one side of the thing's swollen neck, floating in unseen currents: another sun born into death. Then the starfish arms closed to re-form half of its face. It walked back to rejoin its place in the lines of the dead.

"It begins," the thing in the center said, its face closed. "It ends and begins. It becomes one of us, and will return to itself." It flared open, mouth opening and jagged teeth clicking. It walked toward the survivors so that its head blocked the sun. Its starfish arms opened and wriggled like black solar flares. "Now the Father can come to us."

The stubby, festering tentacles waving around its face stretched taut and the body became still. The myriads of worshippers froze along with it. The survivors were suddenly surrounded by thousands of diseased statues.

The sun continued its long climb into the sky. None of the statues moved. A breeze wandered through the survivors. Hours or minutes later, the sun reached its highest point and began to fall. Slowly it sank and fell past the horizon, and the survivors sighed in relief, for they had not been able to stop seeing slow, waving arms around it as it gazed on the world. They sat, huddled and sweating, in stuffy twilight.

The thing in front of them still stood without moving. It seemed to be concentrating on something far away. The moon rose, covering its face in dim, liquid light. Faint moonlight played over the endless circles of Flowers around them. Night deepened.

"I remember," the thing said in a leathery voice. "It

141

remembers the woman I used to be." It stood, utterly still, as distant stars spiraled in ungraspable patterns. "I worked in a building in the center of the city. I worked where the rulers of that place kept the poor alive through food and medicine. They streamed in every day, empty in eye and empty of hand. I never saw any of them, never spoke with them when we exchanged words. I signed papers and typed messages.

"It remembers that I died. They came into the building, eating and eating. One came for me. It ate. I fell to the ground. The muscle beneath my chest stopped but my eyes stayed open. I remember now that the body I used to be ate anything that was alive, along with the rest of them. No thought was within me. Then I changed. I returned to itself."

Silence for a moment in the moonlight.

"I remember each one of the living I have eaten," it said. "Each one of their warm pink bodies, glowing in the moving gray. Each one lives within me. I feed on them still." Its voice changed. Without losing its reptilian, metallic tone, it became the voice of a little girl, speaking from a long way away: "Quiet, it will hear us and come back." Then an old man's: "How deep until I drown?"

Its face closed and the tension drained from its body. In the darkness, its outline looked almost human, and became even more frightening. It said, "I do not know where my true father is, he who brought me life without end and power. But he will find it. He will come."

It stopped speaking and stood, a dark statue against the deep blue of the twinkling night sky. It looked as if it would have sighed if it could remember how.

A bright, dead face continued its slow journey across the sky.

Later, it asked: "When will my father come to me? He spoke to me, before I returned to thought, but I understood him. We were to forget the other survivors and bring you. Then he would meet us. Where is he? I saw the light of his glory, and finally it was not hungry." Silence. Then: "Will you help it? Can you bring the Father back? You are important to him. Can you summon him?"

Another quiet hiss slithered through the darkness. "Take them. We will offer them as a gift to the Father." It sounded as if the speaker was standing next to them, even though their guard stood alone.

"No," the Flower in the middle said. "The Father commanded us not to touch them."

"But they are so beautiful. Life grows in them like no other."

Other hisses swirled across the empty space. Suddenly other Flowers were close, faces and waving starfish arms black against the streaks of pink glowing on the horizon. Their hunger was palpable, like a breath of frost playing over the survivors. Moaning and sobbing, they huddled closer to each other.

"No," their guardian said. "We cannot disobey our Father." Hissing was the only response, a hissing which rose to a sizzle. Dead hands began to paw at the survivors, but they then suddenly fell back. A vivid yellow light shone in the faint dawn sky. Without turning, the dead seemed to sense it. They snaked backwards to their line.

The light on the horizon grew ever more beautiful, but didn't rise into the sky, for it was not the sun. The light floated toward them, through the rows of dead, each of which turned and gazed on it, their starfish arms trembling in agony or ecstasy. As the orb of light grew closer, the survivors saw a massive naked man inside. His eye sockets were white cavities; they looked as if they were covered with mildew or ash. When he entered the clearing, a third yellow eye opened on his forehead. Both hands held dozens of wriggling, worm-like fingers. The growing dawn behind him paled before his glory.

"My children," he said. "I was unexpectedly delayed. But now I come, for your salvation." His voice was soft thunder.

FOURTEEN

You Will Be Gods

The man inside the aura of light turned to Ezekiel. "You," he said.

Ezekiel's eyes were wide as he sat on the ground and stared upward. He slowly shook his head from side to side, dumbfounded. Then recognition flared in his face. "The Head!"

The man inside the light said, "You are the slave who worked best for me. I had you baptized in your discovery as an honor. What are you doing here?" His single eye was fixed on Ezekiel like lightning about to strike.

Ezekiel stood. His legs and his voice trembled as he said in a quiet voice, "You drowned me. You tried to kill me."

"I dispose of my slaves as I see fit. I did not choose you for the new world. So why are you here?"

"I have seen your demise," Ezekiel whispered. "You're no god."

A rumbling sound came from the god's mouth like a mountain trying to laugh. "Open your eyes. I have defeated death. My new body is proof." As the Head floated above them, a thin cloud of white mold puffed from the two eye sockets beneath his single livid eye.

"You thought I was gone, but here I am," Ezekiel whispered. "It's only the first of your failures."

Streaks of gold like slash marks appeared in the globe of light surrounding the Head and faded as he floated above them. "Very well, slave. Answer my question, and I may accept you back into my service. And tell me why these six humans are different. I see the life of my chosen favorites in them."

Ezekiel looked to the seven other survivors, but none of them would look at him. "They're going to kill you," he whispered.

The deep rumble came from the Head again, like an earthquake trying to talk. He floated close to Ezekiel. "If you had not made such a great discovery, I would have destroyed you for that." The Head's single yellow eye stared at Ezekiel. Ezekiel trembled but didn't look away. "You claim you have seen this?" the Head asked. Ezekiel's eyes fell to the ground and he said nothing. "Well, slave? Do not test my patience."

Ezekiel glanced at the terrified faces of the other survivors and said, "It has to pattern." He blinked and pressed his fingers to his eyes. "Happen," he said. "It has to happen."

"Already the chaos is at work in you," the Head said.

Ezekiel stared at the ground as if he might be sick. Then his eyes flared and he looked back at the Head. "Where are the six board members? The ones supposed to rule with you?"

The Head's aura darkened for an instant. "Nothing can stop my rule. Nothing." He rose into the air and lifted his hand. Lightning shot up into the sky.

"I saw a world without you where they reigned." Ezekiel pointed to the seven other survivors.

"You saw me die by their hand?" the Head shouted.

Lightning crackled around him.

Ezekiel's head dropped. "I saw... I saw..."

The Head floated closer to the ground and the lightning storm stopped. He raised one arm in the direction of the circles of the dead. They stepped aside to create a narrow path, stretching away across the rolling plains. "If what you say is true," he thundered, "killing you will avail nothing. Go and stir up discontent and survive for as long as you can."

Ezekiel looked between the Head and the freedom stretching ahead of him.

"They will not harm you," the Head said. "My children dare not disobey me."

Ezekiel looked at the seven other survivors. "Can't you do something? Anything?" he whispered. They stared at the ground, mute and terrified.

"If you truly believe I am not a god," the Head said, "then go."

Ezekiel hung his head. "I don't want to leave them."

"Are they your saviors?"

"I don't know," he mumbled. "I don't know."

"Then resolve your doubt and worship me."

Ezekiel stared at the ground and said nothing.

The Head said, "You are not fit for my new world, even as a rebel and a vagabond." He waved his hand again and the path through the Flowers closed. The Head nodded to the Flower who had spoken to them, which still stood a few paces away. It stalked toward Ezekiel, hissing, its starfish arms stretched forward.

"Wait," Ezekiel moaned. "Throw me back in. Kill me that way."

"Why?" the Head asked.

"I might see something."

The Head rumbled. "Pointless. But I am generous in victory." He turned to the Flower closest to them. "You. Take him to the void. Hold him under until he sinks." The Flower's face collapsed again and he took Ezekiel by the hand. Another path appeared as Flowers stepped away, stretching back the way they had come. Ezekiel hung his head and let himself be led away. He glanced back at the Head once, and the seven survivors saw a flash of jealousy twist Ezekiel's face. Then the dead reformed their circles around them.

The Head looked at the seven for a moment as he hung in the air, a new sun which made the yellow disk behind him dim in comparison. He sunk to a foot above the dead grass and folded his arms. The wide mouth and sunken nose and trinity of eyes, two dead and one livid, wrinkled like a piece of paper crumbling in a fire. Only later would it occur to the survivors that the Head was trying to smile.

"My precious children," the Head said. "I have destroyed the old order of things. Death and decay are past. My children blossom in my light. I am their savior. And yours." The Head's orb grew brighter, and the tentacles of the Flowers surrounding him reached forward, drinking in his light.

The Head stared at the seven survivors. None of them could meet his gaze, but every once in a while they glanced at one of the Flowers. The Head rumbled, "You are dismayed by the glory of my children. I suppose it is natural enough. But it shows the smallness of your minds."

"Death is not a thing of the past," Oz whispered, keeping his eyes on the ground. "You made death even more ugly."

"I would not call this death," the Head said. He had the air of a patient adult speaking to a slow child. "And if it is, does it not have its own beauty? Do you really prefer your body? You are a sack of stinking chemicals."

Oz stared at the ground.

The Head floated toward him. "Well? Do not trifle with me, mortal. How do you answer?"

"There is beauty in the Dead," Oz gasped, like a man inside a headlock. His eyes turned to the rows of dead surrounding them. "My eyes linger."

"And I am their Creator," the Head said. "When ancient peoples imagined their gods, they prophesied of me. I am Ra and Osiris, but murdered by no one. I am Baal and Marduk, Zeus and Odin, Brahman and Vishnu and Shiva in one. I am the new Christ. I am your god and perfect man. I am the resurrection and the life. I have made all things new."

"You killed everything," Mason croaked.

"New life always rises from death," the Head said. "But no longer will species after species rise from the slime to crawl a few feet and mate before they die. Only one species covers the earth now, no longer weakened by hunger and need. And I will rule in the worship of my children."

"I know you've won," Mason said. His voice sounded like someone trying to balance on a broken ankle. "I know there's nothing we can do. But why bring us here? Why not just kill us?" Something played over Mason's face which made it difficult to tell which he preferred.

The Head floated closer to the seven seated survivors, his single eye fixed on them. "It breeds differently in you," he said. "From all the other scattered survivors, you are special." The survivors stared, uncomprehending.

The yellow god floated higher above them. "I forget that you cannot see the medicine by which I healed the old order."

"Medicine?" Jack asked.

"Virus. Pathogen. Plague. Whatever word you please.

Those words have lost their meaning. The death and the life I released. It is still in the air. And because it pleased me ever to gaze upon my tiniest servants, I ordered that my new body have the ability to see it." The Head's eye roved across the air above their heads. "Myriads of tiny red bodies, flowing on the air. The air carries them, and it is from the air that I rule. I can see them living in my children, their hosts. And I see them in you. But you are different."

The seven survivors gave each other furtive glances, but none spoke.

"We will baptize you, and it will energize the chemical latent within you. It will transform your bodies, so that you will be able to rule with me. You will be greater even than these my children." As the Head had been speaking, the countless rows of Flowers had been opening and closing their faces in waves; but they suddenly all opened and stretched taut. For a moment, the Head was surrounded by a thousand exclamation points.

The Head looked at the stricken faces, sweating and tinged with pink in contrast to the green-gray sea around them. No one spoke.

"I see I rush ahead of you in my counsels," the Head rumbled. "I suppose it is not the first time." Another puff of mold exhaled from his dead eye sockets. "When I planned the new world with my board, I gave those six authority under my rule. I thought to bring them with me here, as I presented myself to you. I gave them a different version of the serum and submerged them in the void. But none of them survived their baptism. The few I have found are not the powers I was told they would be. But Gaia told me about a group of survivors who were different..."

"Gaia!" the nameless girl said. "You spoke with her?"

"I created her," the Head said.

Confusion clouded her face. "But... but she spoke to me, comforted me when that man was... was... Where can I find her?"

"She is beneath your feet even now. She is present in the earth. She has taken on characteristics of the place she rules. Thus, she is Earth, even as she was to rule over it. But she is fading."

"No," Nameless said, seeming to speak to herself. "Whatever power you have you took from her. She created you."

The light surrounding the Head sharpened into pearly opacity, and the survivors closed their eyes and rolled away before a blinding flash. When they could open them again, the nameless girl lay on the ground, twitching. Spittle fell from her mouth. Selene crawled to her and held her in her arms.

The Head thundered: "She created me! She created me! Do you know how she fawned before me when we last spoke? When I summoned her to appear before me, and she obeyed by shaping the soil of her earth to form a face to speak with me, do you know how she begged? How she tried to trade information about six survivors different from all the rest, six who would be valuable to me, if only I would save her from her decay?" The Head's voice had sunk to the growl of a distant storm. "Only your ignorance lets you blaspheme so."

In Selene's arms, Nameless' shaking had quieted. She blinked several times and her eyes came into focus. "Sister," she moaned, "is the man telling the truth?"

Selene's pale, round face moved from Nameless to the Head and back again. "I think he is," she whispered.

Nameless turned away from Selene, curling up in a ball

on the ground.

As if he did not see, the Head continued, "I am a god and greater than any god. Every other god ruled over part of a larger order. I have rewritten the rules of all order. If I choose to join the personality of a human to some part of nature, letting her retain consciousness and will under my authority, then it will be done. I extend this privilege to you, and you do not thank me. It is true that I did not completely foresee the exact nature of my new rule. My virus did not transform all of humanity at once, as I was told it would. My first vice-regents could not withstand their transformation. Even my hasty judgment upon this child's blasphemy would have killed one of the old race of men.

"But that is why you are so valuable to me. I did not realize the full extent of my genius, the further stages by which my reign would be realized. And I offer you a share in it. I will transform your lowly bodies into the image of my beauty. You will be freed from your old lives." The Head touched down on the grass and stepped close, peering at them. "Is it fear which holds you back? Does the glorious freedom of my children overawe you? You will never be free of your fear as long as you cling to the old world. Give yourself to me, and I will re-create you. You can live as your own gods." None of the survivors could look away from him, but none could speak.

A voice, dry with ancient decay, floated across the sun-swept field: "It was as I said. It should have taken them. It could have offered them as a sacrifice to the Father." The tentacles of a row of Flowers were quivering. "It will take them now, and convert them to your cause." It seemed the entire line of the dead was speaking as they moved forward.

The Head shot into the air. Streaks of pearl and gold

spun in his aura like swords. The same blinding flash forced the eyes of the survivors closed; when they could open them, one section of the green-gray sea surrounding them was burning. The bodies of the Flowers inside the fire were quivering, faces stretched taut, their dead flesh boiling into white. A high keening sounded across the plain.

"You would destroy my pantheon?" the Head thundered above them. "You would reduce them to such as you?" More lightning strikes leapt from the Head's aura to strike the charred ground. The Flowers standing around the blaze didn't move. They kept their open faces upward to their god.

The Head sank to float just above the cowering survivors. "You will worship me yet. You will." He rose again and floated away, lightning crackling around the edges of his aura. The wide circle of Flowers followed their Head, again tightening around the seven survivors, who scrambled to their feet and huddled closer together and stumbled along inside the moving circle. The burning dead were collapsing in bubbling puddles of white.

Once again, the feeling that the earth was moving beneath them swept over the seven survivors as they crept along within the small island of dead grass. Above them, the Head floated onward. Occasional strikes of light flashed to the ground and ignited his children. The rest of the dead walked around these pyres like water flowing around a rock. Each face was open and hissing.

They entered a forest. One of the women whispered, "Is this..."

A man said, "He's taking us back the way we came."

"Why?" another asked. No one answered.

Tree branches exploded and fell when the Head's aura touched them, setting on fire more of the dead. They could see their camp ahead of them through the trees when the Head stopped in the air. The circle of Flowers around the survivors stopped as well. The Head's aura grew blindingly bright, and an earth-shattering explosion threw the survivors to the ground. Jack fell against the unmoving circle of dead and rolled away with a little scream, wiping his shoulder. Then the circle moved them forward again, down the tunnel the Head had created like water flowing down a channel. The survivors descended ever deeper into the earth. The Head's radiance lit up the tunnel he had created, showing roots and rocks cut clean through.

After several minutes of stumbling and tramping, the ground leveled off. To their left, the survivors could see the stairs they had descended with Ezekiel. In front of them, the remains of the wall stood. Beyond it writhed the churning abyss, like Cerberus straining against its chain. Endless black waves glistened with flecks of light. A muted, keening whine made the eyes of the survivors water—a sound trying to become a voice and failing.

The Head floated above them, his face twisted in ecstasy as he gazed on the abyss. The Dead massed around him, ready to wait for millennia with their Father. Then the Head rotated in the air to fix the seven survivors with his one eye. He opened his mouth to speak.

*

Oz bent over, pressing his fingers against his eyes and remembering the keening whine the void made, and how they had all heard it when Ezekiel had led them here for the first time, and forgotten it as soon as Ezekiel had shut the door behind them. Even as he winced, Oz could not help stealing glances at the void. Soon he simply stared, feeling it worm its way into him. Behind the back of his mind, Oz could feel a void opening, and thought he understood what it must feel like to be a Flower.

His legs buckled and he sat on something which was not sand. He let it sift through his fingers, and thought about worlds ground fine and left as detritus on the last shore of the last infinite ocean.

From far away, the Head was shouting. Fingers of cold parchment picked the professor up, fingers which could have crushed the arms they grasped. Somewhere, a part of his mind shrieked and focused on his still-pink skin, still pink with life. But for how long?

Oz was led to the edge of the void and pushed onto his hands and knees. The no-smell of Novocain pressed against his face. A few feet away, dark water lapped toward him and receded, panted toward him and receded. The void at the back of his mind opened further. He couldn't take his eyes from the faint glimmer of light which touched each wave. He looked around him and saw the other six survivors on their hands and knees before the void, all surrounded by the Dead, each one of them staring into the abyss. He could see by the fascinated looks on their faces that he was not the only one who was changing, already starting to die.

Time for repentance, the new god was booming behind them, time to repent of their ingratitude and acknowledge their master. Still on his hands and knees, Oz craned his neck to looked behind him, feeling absurdly like a dog looking back at its master. What he saw made his mouth drop open: a man who could not be Luke was walking through the Flowers toward the brilliant light at their center.

He prostrated himself before the Head, his shaggy blonde hair covering his face. In their journey, Luke's shirt had ripped, revealing muscles which bunched and rippled like waves stirred by a storm at sea. With his physique and yellow hair, he formed a mundane counterpart to the muscled body in golden light above him.

The Head looked at the man for a moment. He boomed, "Why do you bow, traitor?"

"You're my new master," Luke said. "You." The man craned his neck to look into the Head's single eye. With his face lit up by the Head's light, the shy backwoods man he had been seemed far away.

"And what do you offer me which makes you worthy of acceptance?"

Luke paused, opening his mouth and shutting it again. The Head shouted, "Don't stammer, worm!" Luke pointed a single finger to the side of his head, almost miming pulling the trigger. The glowing god sank to the ground, walked toward him, and put his hand on his forehead.

"What a mind you have," the Head said.

"I've always been smart," Luke whispered and winced, as if it was the hardest thing he had ever had to say. "I can understand that stuff in your old labs. And I think I can do it better."

A few feet to Oz's right, Mason shouted, "Luke! What're you doing?" His voice was a bird falling after the crack of the hunter's gun.

Luke turned to Mason, a look of purest misery passing over his chiseled face. "Been pissin' my life away this whole time. He's gonna give me something to do." Something washed over Mason's face which Oz couldn't decipher; but Luke's face bunched in a snarl as he growled, "Don't you pity

156

me. Y'all are gonna throw away your chance at greatness? I don't want your pity!"

The Head was smiling as if this exchange hadn't happened. "What a mind you have, child," he repeated in a thunderous whisper. "You do not have the same colors these other six do, but I think you will accomplish great things. I give you the honor of being my slave." The Head reached his arms out and touched both sides of the redneck's bowed head. Luke's face rippled with painful ecstasy as tiny stalks of electricity walked over Luke's body.

One by one Luke's six remaining friends dropped their eyes to the sand beneath the head's wriggling, worm-like toes (not sand, less real than yellow sand, and more complex). As the Head's aura grew brighter and Luke began to scream, the sand shone in faded, lusterless colors which almost formed the rough shapes of plans, ideas, and loves which had been consumed long ago, or soon would be.

The Head stepped back from Luke. "I have given you a little of my power. Rise, my slave." Trembling and weeping, Luke stood and looked into the face of his new Father. The Head rose off of the ground. "Hold them, my children," he thundered. The Flowers moved to form a semi-circle around Oz, blocking his sight of his friends. The Head rose high in the cavern, his aura crackling. His face was a contorted mask. He turned and floated toward the tunnel he had made. Without looking back, he said, "The void may behave strangely when I am not present. I do not think you will enjoy it. When you are ready to listen to my reason, tell my slaves."

The Head began to move back up the tunnel. Even though he was rising out of sight, it looked like the sun was setting, leaving behind darkness which was unbroken except for sporadic flashes of dim light from the curling, yearning chaos. The shattered glimpses of light played over the dead suns surrounding Oz, the open mouths and empty eye sockets and serpentine starfish arms, now seeming to smile, now to weep.

FIFTEEN

Baptism

Oz collapsed onto the sand. His mind reached for the image of the sun like a hungry man imagining a meal. He pictured it free and hidden far above, and the wind rushing over the earth. Then it sprouted stubby tentacles. He pressed his fingers against his eyes and stood up. He shouted the names of his companions, but no one answered.

It was hard to look at the creatures that formed the curving wall of his cell, but somehow harder to turn his back to them. He did it anyway and turned to the void. In the faint and intermittent strobe-light flashes, the water seemed to reach forever. He walked toward it. It seemed as though the void concentrated itself as he drew nearer, and he felt something behind the back of his mind tense.

Oz took a step into the cold water. He froze and gasped, told himself it was not caressing his ankles, and forced himself to take another step. When he was deep enough that the water was curling against his shins like a cat, he turned and walked toward the line of Flowers to his right. It was difficult to be sure, but he didn't see any more of the Dead outside the line making his prison.

A hissing sounded in the glimmering darkness. In the

dim, fractured light, the Flowers nearest the edge turned toward him and took a step into the water. Something cold snaked around the base of Oz's spine and he took a step back. The Flower stepped backwards into place and its head turned away from him. Its tentacles continued their slow, waving curls. It felt like the Flower was no longer aware of him, contemplating something Oz could never see. He took a step forward again, and again he fell under the sightless gaze of the Flower. He couldn't stop himself from backing away.

He turned his back to the Flowers and waded further out. He would swim in the loathsome stuff if he had to. The water reached his thighs and then his waist, coiling and knotting like a muscle flexing, but never quite able to grasp him.

In the darkness before him, a black figure was rising, visible only because of the faint radiance playing over the surface of a head and two arms and torso. The figure resolved itself into the delicate form of a young woman.

The professor froze for an instant. He staggered backwards, splashing clumsily. He fell into a sitting position on the sand, his shoulders heaving. The apparition opposite dissolved into the water.

Whether the moan that sounded came from the void or his own mouth, he couldn't tell. His breath huffed and he stood and found a place to sit which was equidistant from the void and the line of Flowers. He lay back on the dusty sand, his arms straight against his side. He closed his eyes and tried to be completely still.

Starvation, something inside him said. *Zeke said you wouldn't need much food now, but you'll starve eventually and it will be over.*

He thought, And get up as one of them and go call the Head my father.

Is that so bad? At least you'll be dead.

And eventually remember everything, he thought. Everything.

He lay still and tried not to think about the Head and his terrible, brilliant light.

*

As he lay there, the professor's thoughts turned to the formless, ever-flowing abyss just beyond his feet. Strange images floated across his mind. He fell asleep, and knew he dreamed, but did not wake.

He was teaching again, back in Room 111 of Archer Hall, back in one of his countless Intro to Western Literature classes. He was lecturing on Norse myth, and Oz (watching himself dream) felt the first pull of discomfort, because that area had always been his weakest. The students each had the Prose Edda open on their desks. He was describing the Norse gods when a man opened the classroom door and stood in front of the class. He had one eye.

"Is that Odin?" asked a young woman from the front row.

"No," said Oz, again feeling a pang of embarrassment, and wishing that the Dean and President were not sitting in the back row next to his ex-wife. Oz saw a letter in the Dean's hand and knew, in the way one knows in dreams, that it was the one telling him he was fired from the university for reasons of mental instability.

"But," the young woman said, "he's got a broad hat and

long staff and a raven on his shoulder, just like Odin."

"And I am missing an eye," the man thundered, "lost so that I might drink from the spring of wisdom."

"This is not Odin," Oz said. "Odin didn't have an eye in the center of his forehead. And he wasn't yellow."

The false Odin walked to the front of the class. The faces of each of his students peeled back in waving tentacles, their eyes gone, but their skin still pink and warm.

"All-Father," they hissed.

Oz struggled to wake up like a swimmer pulling for the surface. The classroom disappeared and he sat up on the dirty sand in a gasp. He blinked away the image of the yellow gleam of Odin's eye until all he could see were the occasional flashes of faint light, seeming to come from everywhere and nowhere at once. The void gave a moan which almost became syllables. He heard a shuffling and turned to see the row of Flowers to his left opening, moving not with feverish attention, as they usually did, but sluggishly and stooped, as if they were asleep. The hallucinogenic flashes showed the line lazily re-forming itself as a small man walked into his circle.

"Who's there?" Oz called. Something like the word *there* echoed from the abyss.

Another flash showed the man walking past him. Oz stood and grabbed his arm. "Masaaki?"

The Japanese doctor stopped, staring straight ahead. Oz realized that as soon as he let go of his arm, the man would continue walking, as if he had never seen him.

"Masaaki, what's wrong?"

Silence.

"How did you get the dead to move?" Oz stared, waiting. "They always calm down around you. You just told them to

162

move and they did, didn't you? How can you do that?"

"Silence.

"You don't know, do you? Why aren't you talking to me?"

"Speech is given to the living." The words sounded as if they had been recorded on a cassette tape.

Oz waited for more. When none came, he asked, "So?"

"I am neither living nor dead, so I have no speech."

"Masaaki, speak to me."

Masaaki turned and looked at him for a long time in the quiet jangling of the flashes of light. His face was a statue. A tingling cold spread in the professor's gut. His mouth dropped open. "You... you're not even afraid," Oz gasped.

"Don't go near the abyss," Masaaki said. "Your past will speak to you. It will tell you truth you do not want to hear." His face turned away, so that he stood stock still, facing forward.

Oz tightened his grip on the doctor's arm and blurted, "I went near the black water and something came up that looked human. I backed away and it melted into nothing. Is that what you're talking about?"

"You were wise to back away."

"Masaaki," Oz said, "Eric, whoever you are, what are we going to do?"

Without turning, a feverish smile swept over Masaaki's face. "You come to me for guidance? You saved my life in that forest, Oz, but I have done nothing but follow and watch since. I have been useless. I thought I might care for those around me somehow. Even the dead. How foolish." Masaaki's legs started to walk again.

"Where are you going?" Oz whispered, walking with him in the grimy sand, keeping one hand wrapped around Masaaki's thin arm.

"Nowhere." He kept walking.

"Don't," Oz whispered. "Please."

"I am nowhere. There is no more guidance." They were getting close to the opposite curve of the line of the dead. He stopped a couple of paces in front of it and asked, "Who could guide such as these? They have no destination. Or they have already arrived, forever."

The broken doctor moved to within arm's length of the nearest Flower and muttered a few syllables of Japanese. It shuffled aside. Oz, still standing several paces behind, whispered, "Please don't leave me."

"If you remain here, you are the one abandoning yourself," Masaaki said, and walked away. Oz sprang forward with a shout, but the Flower had moved back into place. It stared at Oz, its tentacles never in the same position in the weakly flashing light. He cried out and fell backwards. The Flower returned to its meditation, and Oz was again naked and invisible.

*

Far above, Masaaki looked full upon the face of the Head and said, "Tell me how to find the way in your world."

The Head boomed: "Will you set aside your old body? Will you blind yourself to the old world, that you may truly see?"

"I will drink corruption down," Masaaki said. "You may have my old eyes. I give myself to you."

The Head's smile was a rip in his face.

*

Oz sat.

He lay back on the sand.

He sat up.

He stood and walked toward the edge. This time, he didn't need to wade into the water. With each step closer to the shoreline, the spectral form rose higher out of the formless murk.

"Who are you?" Oz shouted. *Who am I?* echoed across the roiling, hungry waves.

"It is your reflection," the thing said. It shrunk until it was a head shorter than Oz. The hands it extended were delicate, the fingers thin.

Oz stiffened. "You're not real," he said. *I'm not real* echoed in the darkness.

"No," the form opposite him said. "It is only what you think of most often, your mind turning and returning and revolving around your daughter. As soon as you back away, it will dissolve forever."

"Then I'll stay here forever, sweetie." *You'll stay here forever*, the void said. Oz tasted the salt of his own tears as he opened his mouth and said, "I'd forgotten what your voice sounds like, love." *You'll forget your voice.*

"It is not your daughter," the shape said. "It is the reflection of your own mind."

"I left your mother to forget about you. I lived like a hermit and drove back and forth across the continent, always trying to leave you behind." *Left me a hermit, drove me to forget.*

If the shape's face opposite Oz had been visible, it would have been smiling as it again opened its arms. "You never left me, Daddy. You can't." The shimmering light grew brighter around the shape's face, and the image of wet skin became faintly visible, as well as the edge of a bathtub around its head like a halo. The specter's brown hair waved slowly around its head like the arms of a starfish.

"You never left the bathroom where you found her, Daddy," the thing said, a girlish lilt entering its voice.

He collapsed to the ground and threw back his head and howled.

The abyss howled with him.

*

When Oz had wept himself into exhaustion, the shadowy shape of his daughter was still there, staring at him facelessly. He stared back in silence.

"I'm tired of you hurting me," he said in a cracked voice. "I'll find you again, and we'll fix this." He stood and began to back away from the shore. "I'll see you soon, sweetie." *You'll see me soon.* The shape opposite sunk into the murk. Oz turned and walked toward the line of Flowers. When he stood in front of the nearest Flower and felt its attention on him, the blackness that had been growing in his mind blossomed.

"Let me see him," he said. His voice didn't crack.

The line parted. He saw a faint glimmer from the mouth of the cave. He walked toward it and started climbing up the perfectly smooth tunnel. His legs began to burn and he didn't stop. As the light grew stronger, he saw Flowers lining both sides of the tunnel like decorations on an ancient temple. He looked up once at the small shining circle of the cave's entrance and thought he saw a tall figure standing there; but when he looked again, he saw nothing.

Eventually the path leveled off in the forest where he had lived in a past life. Sweat dripped from his nose and his legs trembled, but he didn't think about this. He looked at the circles of Flowers standing in the forest and the glowing deity sitting on a rock in their center. The Flowers faces were open and hissing, tentacles waving gently, as if they could drink in the light radiating from the Head forever. The Head sat with his back to Oz, head down. Masaaki and Luke sat next to him, looking at Oz.

Oz stomped toward the golden god. When he stood within a few feet of the god's aura, he stopped. The Head did not turn around.

"Hey," Oz said. The Head did not move.

The professor picked up a rock and threw it. It disintegrated as soon as it touched the churning yellow light.

"Can you raise the dead?" Oz asked.

"I already have," the god said without turning around. "And no one thanks me."

"Are you... are you pouting?"

The Head leapt into the air and whirled toward him, lightning crackling in his hands. Pain shot across Oz's body. He fell backwards onto the bed of needles and leaves and convulsed. When the blinding light stopped, he blinked and forced his eyes to focus on the Head. Before the Head could speak, Oz gasped, "None of your children are angry. None of them remember the wrongs done to them."

"How could they?" the Head boomed, brighter than the sun. His face was bulging and livid. "I have liberated them."

"No." He climbed to his feet. "I mean the wrongs done to them by others."

"I have saved them from their old lives," the Head said.

Oz forced himself to sit up. He said, "The man who

worked for you, Zeke. The one who discovered how to use the chaos. He talked to us at length about how we were some kind of saviors, about some great light that was coming. He said it was hopeless. I think he spoke better than he knew." He paused, then whispered, "You're the only light left." As the words fell from his mouth, he felt something far beneath him sharpen in attention. He stood up.

"You own me as god?" the sun opposite him boomed.

"I've been running from my daughter for three years. But you brought her back to me. Every time I see one of your children, I see her."

"And?"

Oz said, "I was happy at first, when the Dead came. Thought it would make it easier for me to keep running and hiding. But I can't outrun her. And I don't even want to anymore. You rule over yourself, don't you? Nothing hurts you."

The Head gave a booming laugh which hurt Oz's ears. "Do you own me as god, worm?" he asked.

A smile twisted the professor's face. The wind whipped around him as he got down on one knee, bowed his head, and stretched his arms out so that his fingers played over the stinging edge of the Head's aura. "O great Odin and Christ!" Oz laughed. "O true light and salvation! I serve you and accept my place in your rule." He suppressed a snicker. "Give me free reign over this new world, to seek and punish who- ever I will."

"You will not punish, slave. My children need no pun- ishment."

"Of course, of course. Just let me rule with you. Under you, I mean. There's someone I want to find and... have a talk with."

"Very well. I accept you in my service. And here come two of your companions, who have also come to their senses."

Craning his neck, Oz saw the nameless girl walking toward him, with Mason walking behind her. The nameless girl's face had the look of a woman who had cried herself dry. Mason's face was full of thunder.

*

The girl who had left her old name behind sat at the edge of the infinite ocean and tried not to think about the man who had finally gained what all men wanted and become a god. She tried not to think about the long line of dead women who had let the new god take their beauty and life from them in exchange for power. She tried not to think about how much she missed the colors.

If the voice had not been so clear, Nameless would have thought it was only the quiet, toneless buzzing which came from the water. But then she heard the word *Daughter*, deep and warm and desperate.

Nameless started, one hand gripping the other. "Mother?" she whispered. "Is that you?"

I must speak with you once more before I die.

Nameless froze. "What?"

The gentle words rolled across the dark waters. *I was created to move in all the earth, but I cannot move as I used to. I have watched you when I could, but the Head hunts for me, and would kill me if he found me. I used what little strength I have left to escape him the last time he found me.*

Question after question choked Nameless, each trying to get out of her throat. Eventually, she whispered, "You're dying?" The syllables wandered from her like lost children.

I am coming undone. I am dissolving. The Head injected me with a special form of the chaos you see before you, and it transformed me. But now I am turning into the chaos.

"How can the earth goddess be dying?"

The Head was a fool. He did not understand what he was doing.

Nameless shook her head. "That doesn't make any sense. Gaia could not have been created by a man. You're the one who gave birth to everyone."

If there were an earth goddess, I would have found her. We are alone.

Nameless gasped, "You're telling me you didn't do all this? You didn't create this new world to punish men? You... you..." Nameless choked. "You submitted to a man to have a share in all this?"

Yes.

Nameless slumped. "Then how are you supposed to help me?"

I did help you. I touched you, and gave you a little of my power. You can see the colors that breathe in each living thing. Your hands will bring a blessing to all you touch. And you will be able to hear the whisper of all living things, and speak in ways others will think are prophecy. You were meant to use that power against the Head. You would be my revenge.

"How long will I feel his hands on me?" Nameless shrieked. "How long will I feel him inside me?" Nameless could feel hysteria rising within her, and knew she could not keep it at bay much longer.

You think you are the only woman to suffer that way?

"Of course not. I suffer with many other sisters."

Then call me sister, too. It was the price I paid to be includ-

ed as one of the Six under the Head.

Nameless gasped as if she had been struck and fell over on her side. Her tears wetted the grainy sand which bit the side of her face. "You let... you let him..." She seemed to be speaking to herself. Eventually, she asked, "Why are you speaking to me at all?"

To tell you to care for the life inside you. He is important. And to ask for your help.

Nameless pushed herself into a sitting position again. "He? I am having a son?"

You have forced yourself not to think about it. But you know. You are Isis, soon to bear Horus.

"No."

You know it is true.

"You let someone rape you," she said. "You're not a real woman."

I will die unless you help me. I helped you.

Nameless pressed clenched fists into her eyes and said nothing.

Why do you think the ancient myths had so much violence? This is always the way of things.

"I don't believe you. It can't... it can't be like that."

I shared my power with you, but now I am dying. Touch me, as I touched you. It may help me.

The nameless girl pressed her palms into her eyes and screamed. "The power you got from him! From that man! And now it's in me? I've been raped twice!"

You will lose none of it in sharing.

The watery chaos started to churn more violently. A huge green face broke the surface of the water and long arms reached for the shore. The waves foamed around the goddess like hungry dogs. She drew her face close to Nameless.

171

Nameless saw the skin drooping from the goddess' face, the wild eyes, and the black water which didn't drip from her skin but wormed its way into it like maggots. "I guess you really are dying," Nameless said.

Help me.

"What the man did to me in that bookstore was awful. What you did was worse."

It is eating...

Nameless walked backwards up the shore. The goddess began to collapse into the foaming black water. She reached out a trembling hand and said, *You are Isis and Rachel and Eve. You are life.* Then she sank.

"No," Nameless whispered. "That is what you were meant to be. You're not worth believing in." *What I was meant to be* echoed from across the darkness, words toneless and dead compared to the warmth of her mother.

Nameless walked along the shore toward the line of the dead. They parted before she said anything.

*

She walked away from the shore toward the tunnel, but stopped when she saw the angry man walking toward her from the opposite direction. The cloud of red which always accompanied him fumed and billowed around him.

"I beat a suspect once," he said to her when he was near enough. "He was guilty but wouldn't talk. Three other cops had to pull me off of him." The swirling red crystallized around him into a thousand tiny flies which soon dissolved into a red mist. "I wish I could remember what that felt like."

Nameless looked at him.

"Where are you going?" Mason asked.

"To die."

The policeman nodded. "I never realized how being a cop made everything okay. Chase down the criminals, but even when I was home in the evenings, I knew who I was because of what I was going to be doing the next day. Never miss something 'till it's gone."

"Where are you going?"

"To get away from what I saw in there," he said, pointing to the void.

"What did you see?"

Mason's face blackened and he looked at the void. He stomped down toward the shore. A tall, dark figure rose from the abyss. In the fractured light its shoulders heaved, and black drops dripped off the dark circle of its face.

"Gentle, Mason, and tender," it said. Mason started to yell incoherently at it and splash water; the figure didn't react.

Eventually Mason walked away from the shore and his ghost sunk back into the void. His hands were fists; the red which swirled around him was almost a hurricane.

"Was that your voice?" Nameless asked.

"No!" he shouted. His body tensed as if he were about to throw a punch. When Nameless looked at him evenly, the policeman's shoulders slouched. "You going to go die?" he asked.

Nameless said nothing.

"Then let's go, sweetheart." He sounded as if he were chewing gravel.

They climbed together up into the light.

*

"You come to give yourselves to me," the Head boomed.

The nameless girl spoke as if hypnotized. "You said you would submerge us in the void."

The Head nodded.

As if manipulated by a puppeteer, Nameless slowly got to one knee, her neck straight and head up.

"Say I am your god. Worship me."

She remained with one knee on the forest floor and said nothing.

"Very well. I accept your worship," the Head rumbled. He turned toward Mason. The policeman didn't bow, but his straining, wide eyes seemed to smile feverishly at the Head.

"I accept your worship," the Head said.

"Is there... is there anything left to do?" Mason asked.

"My child, there is a whole world to build."

"Just gimme something to do," Mason said. The Head's aura gave Mason's grin a livid glow.

"What do you wish?" the Head asked, smiling.

"You've made everyone a criminal, so there's nothing left to chase down and lock up. But I still want something to punish."

"There are still pockets of survivors."

"I'll take 'em for you," Mason said. "All of them."

Slow lightning walked across the Head's aura like huge spiders and disappeared. "Very well. You shall be the keeper of the virus. You will be the new Resheph, god of plague."

The Head rose and turned to Oz, Masaaki, and Nameless. "Let us see what has become of the last two," he boomed. The Dead hissed in pleasure as his light played across their crater-like faces. His five servants followed.

*

When the Head had commanded his children to form prison walls around the seven survivors, Jack and Selene had been standing shoulder to shoulder. A line of Flowers, open faces livid and hissing, walked toward the twins. In the fading radiance of the Head's receding aura, Selene knew that the approaching dead would separate her from her brother. Expecting Jack to reach out for her or say something, she turned her back to him and walked away, giving the Dead ample room to walk between them. But when Jack said nothing, she turned back to him. In the growing darkness, Selene saw a dull, flat sheen on his eyes. He looked at her as if she were a beggar he would have walked past on the street. Then the line of Flowers blocked him from her sight. The darkness was relieved only by the occasional flashes of faint light which came from the waves of abyss.

She walked toward the edge of the shore and took the paperback copy of Dickinson from her back pocket. One by one she ripped out the pages and crumpled them, dropping them onto the lapping, licking waves. The pages burned away when they touched the water, as if dropped into a fire.

She lifted her eyes and saw a shape standing opposite her on the abyss. It was shrouded in darkness, but she could make out the sagging cheeks and bitter jaw of a woman who drove a rusting car home from an hourly wage job to a dirty trailer.

Selene laughed. "Are you what my own mother would have looked like, had she lived, or what I would have looked like if I'd lived?" But she shut her mouth quickly when *I am my mother when I get older* echoed across the churning dark.

"Does it matter which one?" the specter asked in a voice

hungry for another cigarette.

"Where does that echo come from?" Selene asked. *Where do I come from* sounded from the abyss.

"From inside you, sweetheart," her opposite said. "There wasn't nothin' here 'till you came."

"You're not me," Selene said. "You're not the kind of woman ever to even open a book." *I'm not a book you'll ever open.*

"Sweetheart," the apparition said, "the only reason it's talking to you is because you're here. It feeds off what's inside you."

Selene opened her mouth twice without being able to speak. Eventually she said, "Did I ever have a chance? Or was I always going to turn into the kind of woman my father would have married and then beaten? No matter how much I read?" *Did you ever have a chance to turn into a woman* sounded from the chaos. The smell of whiskey and the feel of week-long whiskers and ungentle hands and bruises was close to her.

The apparition tilted its head; Selene pictured it blowing smoke from a corner of its wrinkled mouth and giving her a tired look.

"What do you think?" it asked.

"So this is who I am." *This is who you are.*

Selene stood in the darkness for a long moment. She turned and walked to the line of Flowers that surrounded her. Only when she was close enough to touch them did the Dead closest to her seem to return from their reverie and focus on her.

"What can you see?" Selene asked. "What secrets do you know?"

The face of the Flower opposite collapsed and opened, its

starfish arms trembling in rigid lines. "It sees the nothing moving in everything," the thing hissed. "I see the void everywhere, and the motes of dust floating through it which are still alive."

"Let me talk to the Head," Selene said. The bitter old woman she had just spoken to laughed in the back of her mind. The line moved aside for her and she walked through, toward the tunnel.

She stopped walking when the gloom of the cavern started to brighten. The Head appeared at the mouth of the tunnel further up the shore. She squinted and held up a hand against the piercing brightness. When her eyes adjusted, she saw the glowing deity leading five human figures. Waves of Flowers followed them. A sixth figure was barreling toward the Head. Selene started running toward them, hoping she was not too late.

*

When she reached the Head, she saw the man who had been her brother standing before him, panting. The Head looked at him and thundered, "Well, worm?"

The same dull sheen covered Jack's haggard face as he locked eyes with the Head and said, "I've been weak my whole life." He looked at the Flowers behind the Head. "Now I'm the weakest of all. Zeke said I'd do all right if I kept going. He was wrong. I know that now. Make me strong and I'll serve you."

The Head stared at Jack intently from his single eye. A puff of mold escaped from his two dead eye sockets. "And if I asked you to show yourself strong against your sister?"

"I would do it."

"Why?"

"Because she's my biggest failure. I can't take care of her. So she has to change or die."

The Head boomed, "She refused my gift. She rebelled against me." He pointed to Selene. Without a word, Jack turned and walked toward his twin. Selene saw something in her brother's face she had never seen before. She held up her hands and backed away.

"Very well," the Head said. "You are my slave forever."

Jack stopped and turned back to the Head. "I am your slave forever," he said.

"And you, child?" the Head asked, moving closer to Selene. His upper lip curled in disgust. Selene felt an ancient fear mix with her new fear of her brother. Memories of shouting, broken dishes, bruises, drunken snoring washed over her.

"You are my Father," Selene said, her voice carrying clearly across the waves of dead. "More than you can know, you're him. I tried to read my way away from him, poetry and stories yielding secrets which would rescue me from his stupidity. But there's no more poetry left within your world." She shivered; she felt as if her soul was escaping with the words she spoke. "Now here you are, my Father, holding all the secrets. I want to know what you know."

The Head nodded. "Yes," he rumbled, and rose toward the roof of the cavern and floated past them over the void. When he reached it, the waves began dance beneath him in eagerness. He raised his hands. The open faces of the Flowers waved in something almost forming a pattern, like wind playing over grass. "My children," he boomed, "I intended that six from the old world should rule under me with bodies even more glorious than yours. But they were not strong enough for the privilege I gave them. They retreated into cowardice and betrayed me, and began to die themselves, as is only just. If they are not dead now, they soon will be. But I learned from one of them that there were six others who had a similar life waiting inside them. Now I have added to their number a seventh." He indicated Luke with a wave of his hand. "At first I thought a small failure had marred my triumph. Now I see the new world I have created bends itself to my wishes. We will baptize you and activate my seed inside you. Then I will begin my rule over my new creation through my mew filldren." The Head's single eye blinked. "My new children," he said.

Fourteen of the dead walked forward and took each of the survivors by the hand, leading them toward the abyss.

When the water was around their ankles, their guides started to stumble and bump into each other. Oz giggled. The Head's eye bulged and his fists shook; an angry roar came from his straining mouth.

"They can't see too good when they get close," Luke called to the Head.

"What? What?" the Head screeched.

"They can't see anything except the chaos you used to make them," Luke said in an urgent voice. "It's what they see with. But there's too much of it here and it's confusing them." He glanced behind him; as far as the god's aura shone, line upon line of Flowers stood, enthralled and somehow gazing at nothing at once. "That's why they're all mesmerized right now," Luke said.

"I don't care! Wet them in the fodder!" the Head shrieked.

With clumsy, drunken movements, the Flowers led their charges deeper into the lapping, black waves. At waist level, they stopped and dead hands leaned the seven survivors back into the water.

When the water closed over the faces of the seven survivors, they saw the image of human faces reflected in the dead faces of the Flowers holding them. Each of the seven humans knew, as one knows in a dream, that they were seeing the people these Flowers had once been.

The dead hands pulled away. The survivors began to sink.

The cold emptiness crept into their minds, and certain things became clear to them. The first was that there was no ground beneath them. The Dead were standing on nothing.

The second was the knowledge most of them had ignored: that they had been touched with preternatural new life by the Head's six rotting gods. As they sank, each felt that new life blossom inside and rise to meet the chaos entering them in an incestuous embrace.

The third was that the void was stirring, deep beneath them.

The chaos completed its hold on themand they sank beneath the feet of the Flowers. A rumbling sounded in the deep, like an earthquake gathering itself. The seven were sucked down into the crushing emptiness. A deafening roar erupted all around them. From a great distance, they saw the surface of the void explode and send the tiny figure of the Head spinning away. He shrieked as he fell into the void and was lost to their sight in a vast storm.

*

Down, ever further down until they could neither sink nor rise because they were beyond all direction. In the darkness, the faint outline of a globe became visible. Lines appeared on it. Perhaps they were the familiar outlines of the continents; perhaps they were the marks left by tentacles on the closed face of a Flower. The globe hung in the void, bereft of sunlight and stars, quiet and dead.

Light glimmered from somewhere. It grew stronger and shone on the globe, turning the memory of the Head's aura to a dirty yellow in the minds of the seven witnesses. The light caressed the surface of the globe like a great bird beating gentle wings, but the globe remained dark. It was as if an eternal dawn were trying to shine on a globe bent in on itself, forever brooding beneath the bright wings of morning. And whether it was anger breathing in each beat of the wings, or love, or both, none of the seven who had once been human could tell. But each could sense it would not wait much longer.

And inside each one of the seven survivors, something deeper than the void opened like a flower before the sun.

Sixteen

Twice Touched

Masaaki blinked and realized he was floating in something which felt like cold water. He tried to sit up. To his surprise, he rose slowly to his feet, as if underwater. He looked down: his feet stood on a river of jet black. Traces of silver and red and other colors he had never seen before flowed through the current.

Looking up, he saw the colors bend upward to either side of him. He realized he was at the bottom of a flowing valley. Above him, a dark expanse shimmered in occasional flashes of weak light.

He started. "Who's there?" he said, turning around and seeing only the slowly flowing black river. As he turned, the other presence stayed behind his head. He felt a frosty breath tickle the back of his neck.

He shouted, "Who are you? Would you kill me without showing yourself?" His voice reverberated across the plain.

You insist I show you honor when you have shown none? The voice was a raven's feather brushing against ice.

He turned again. "Why is it I cannot see you?"

Death is always unseen.

"You are Death?"

I was told I would be. He lied.

"Who?"

The fool you know as the Head.

His eyes grew wide. "You are one of the six board members."

Yes.

"Is it true you are dying?"

Yes. The cold itself seemed to be speaking.

"Why are you so angry?"

Because you gave yourself to him.

Masaaki felt the anger billowing behind him and fell to his knees and bowed his head. "End me." The hostility radiating behind him faded and a thin sigh breathed over the back of his neck. He shivered and waited, wondering when the blow would come.

Why do you yield to me? I betrayed the Head. Why am I not your enemy?

"I promised the man who killed the planet that I would help him only so I could understand it. I gave myself to a murderer and a tyrant. My death would be no great loss."

You gave yourself to the Head, but now you give yourself to me. Have you become nothing?

"No," Masaaki whispered, and sighed. "Yes. The void washed me. I remember my despair, but it is gone. I am empty. End me."

I am not going to kill you, Masaaki Shinogaido, because then I would have to kill myself.

His face crumpled. "You are not going to release me?"

You deserve death for trusting in the one you call the Head. But I did the same.

He stood. "The Head promised you immortality, but now you are dying," he said. The voice was silent, but he could feel sadness behind him. He said, "The Head thought our immersion would be brief, and we would soon begin our rule under him."

He told me the same.

"The Head did not intend to send me here."

He does not know it exists. You have been given another chance.

"One I do not deserve."

You have always sought to help others, and thus fulfill your duty. Even when you entered a foreign country, you sought to guide the people there. You thought the Head was holding every secret.

"Why are you repeating my useless history to me?"

Because it is not useless, nor is it past. Look up, Masaaki Shinogaido.

"I already have. It is the void through which we fell."

Look up.

Masaaki did. The endless gloom of the void faded, and he gasped at what he saw. At first he thought the long white arms were a huge starfish and he felt a pang of fear. But then he realized he was looking at the roots of a great white tree, thick toward their center and spindly and knotted as they radiated outward.

"What is this place?"

I do not know. I came here after my baptism, as you did.

"Why... why..."

What is it, Masaaki Shinogaido?

"I do not know how to say it."

Try.

"Why does it feel as if down is up? As if the center of gravity is above my head?"

Because it is. I am not sure, but I believe we are beneath the bottom of the void.

"Impossible."

Yes.

He looked up in silence for a moment. "That is no ordinary tree," he said.

Its roots reach into the abyss.

"Why could I not see it before?"

It takes time to see things here.

"What is it I am seeing in its branches?" His eyes watered as the images moved in and out of focus. "Is that... is that our camp?"

Yes.

"I am seeing the white tree in our camp? The corpse we burned?"

Yes.

"How... How could it grow so large?"

You all made camp over the Head's company. You did not know it, but you were drawn to the abyss which the Head had opened.

"How were we drawn?"

Because you were touched by the six board members. You had a little of the void within you.

"What about Luke?"

He only happened to live nearby.

"And this tree?"

The Head devised that his new creations would be able to grow back from any injury. But since you burned one of them, it was not able to regain its shape. It grew back as something like a tree instead. But it was close enough to the void that it was able to drink from the abyss. It has grown as large as the world.

"It did not look that way when I last walked past it."

You are not able to see all of it. Its roots grow deep, and are connected to other trees like it.

"My old house! How can I see it?"

You can see any part of the world by thinking of it.

"My house is smaller than I remember."

You are seeing it more truly than if you were standing in front of it. Now, look at your arms.

Masaaki did. His pale skin swirled with shifting patterns, like moth wings made of smoke.

I touched you in your world.

"The giant beetle that bit me in the forest."

It is the only form I can take in your world.

"That is why the Dead grow calm around me? Because I have been touched by Death?"

I can think of no other reason.

"Why did you do that?"

To try to atone for my mistake. To give someone something of the power given to me, that the evil of the Head might be undone, or at least contained. I spoke to the five other board members, and we each agreed to touch one survivor. Thus you and five others were led to that place nearest the abyss.

"And you have seen my life in the branches of the tree."

Only after you burned it and it began to grow.

"I have sorely disappointed you."

Yes. But much good may come of your betrayal.

"How?"

The chaos by which the Head transformed me and the other six is destroying us. Given enough time, the Head would have come undone as well.

"His speech became confused toward the end."

Given time, he would have died.

"But not the Flowers."

They are dead already. But it is different with you.

"What do you mean?"

How do you feel?

Masaaki breathed in the cold air. "At peace," he said.

As soon as I came here, I could feel the void eating away at me. But it reacted differently to you.

"Why?"

I do not know. Perhaps because you had the Head's disease in you already, and then I touched you.

"Why would that make a difference? Unless..."

The Head intended that I rule the Dead and watch over the void. I have passed this power on to you. You are in the deepest part of the void right now. Speak what you are thinking.

"Contact with the chaos unravels you. But if you already have a little of that chaos inside you, perhaps the opposite reaction occurs. Perhaps you grow."

Something flared behind Masaaki again. It was a moment before he realized it wasn't anger he felt behind him, but joy.

He let his hands fall to his side. The chill of the place had gripped him, but he didn't shiver. He took a deep breath. "It is very beautiful here."

Yes.

He said, "There was some kind of explosion as we were sinking. The Head was screaming."

Because of your immersion. There was a reaction the Head did not anticipate.

"Is the Head dead?"

He is inside the void. See for yourself.

He looked upward again among the branches until he saw a yellow shape in the watery gloom. Sometimes it was almost human in shape, sometimes a blob, sometimes a thing that looked like an octopus; but always its livid yellow eye stared.

187

"He is trapped within the void. How do I know that?"

This is your domain. You understand it better than anyone.

"Are we safe from him?"

As long as he lives, nothing will be safe. But you are safer than you were.

"Can he get out?"

I do not know. He is trying.

"I can touch different parts of the tree, can I not?"

You can travel anywhere these branches extend, which is very far indeed. But be warned that time will become fluid as you travel through the void. And you must not spend too much time in it—even you. The void is too powerful.

"You are implying I must leave," Masaaki sighed.

Yes. You must guide the other six... in death... The god's voice broke into a staccato chirping.

"Your end is near," he whispered.

Yes.

"One more thing. After I fell, I saw... it was either a Flower's head or our planet. Something that looked like a bird was brushing against it."

I do not know. You were lost to my sight during that time.

He stood, looking upward. The shifting images were coming closer to him. He couldn't tell whether he grew large or whether the sky above lowered itself, and didn't care. He brushed a hand across the shimmering underside of the void, and it rippled like water and then reformed its blurry window to the world above. His fingers tingled at the touch. His mind turned to his friends. In one part of the tree, he saw Luke, walking among white trees, bearded and haggard.

He came through before you.

He nodded, and then thought of Nameless, but saw only blurry images.

She has not yet resurfaced.

He nodded again. "She is carrying a pain too deep for words."

Would you carry it for her?

"Yes."

You may yet. And now you are thinking of the friend who hides his true name.

Masaaki nodded as he looked up at the tree. In a corner made by two crossing branches, swirling colors cleared to show a bald man inside a stone building at the top of a hill. The man was shouting at another human. A Flower was walking down the hill, face open. Instead of fear, something squeezed Masaaki's chest so that he could not breathe.

"A dead planet looking for a sun to orbit," he murmured. "Such a waste of life. It is so sad."

Like the nameless one, your friend is carrying a pain too great for words.

"Not Oz. The corpse walking away from them."

Are they sad, Masaaki Shinogaido?

He looked at the empty eye sockets. "Perhaps I am only seeing them smaller and more truly."

You cannot guide them. They are dead. They are the enemy.

"Perhaps."

There is no return to humanity for them.

"I wonder."

Another cold, thin sigh played over his skin. He turned so see a confusion of moth wing, pale skin, and folds of black robe. They fluttered and shifted, each trying to find its place.

I die, Masaaki Shinogaido.

"Thank you," he said to the thing opposite him. Amidst the waves of grief, he felt another pulse of joy from the dying

189

god. Then the shape dispersed into gray dots of ash.

He turned back to Oz and pushed his right hand into the watery image, then his shoulder, then his head. A great roar filled his waterlogged ears, and he knew he would forget his own name if he lingered in the emptiness. Thinking of Oz, he moved forward through the water. Soon he floated opposite the watery image of the hill. He walked through and felt the hot sun on his skin.

Standing opposite him, the professor was screaming.

SEVENTEEN

My Daughter is Dead

When Oz returned to himself, he heard a roaring wind. He opened his eyes to see nothing but the faint blue of the sky. He tried to roll over, but found he was suspended in the air. Whichever way he looked, he saw only the same sky-blue. Snatches of words sped past him: *gift... fool... trust... die.*

Oz tried to shout, but the sound was lost in the rushing air. He swung his fists. The effort made him start to spin in the wind tunnel. Far beneath him, white bordered by ocean-blue rotated into view and spun away and came back into view.

As he continued to struggle, the faint lines of a giant face appeared. Huge lips formed angry words which roared past him. He shouted back wordlessly. Behind the outline of the face, the earth rotated in and out of sight.

A huge sigh sounded and the wind died. He dropped like a stone.

*

When his consciousness returned, he was lying on spiky grass. He kept his eyes closed, knowing the Head was far away, and not wanting to see wherever he was now. Far off, like a star hidden in the daylight, pulsed the memory of the girl he had spoken to in the void.

He heard a rustling footstep near him and opened his eyes. A girl's face was staring into his.

"Who are you?" she asked.

"Where am I?"

"Near our shrine," she said. "Do you come from a different shrine?"

Oz sat up. A hill with short, spiky white grass was to his left. A collection of crumbling stones sat at the top. The grass didn't move in the slow, hot breeze.

"Is that the... the shrine?" he asked the girl. If she hadn't yet entered adolescence, she soon would.

"Of course," she said, her face blank. "Is your shrine different?"

"Is someone looking at us?" The face had disappeared behind a rock as soon as he saw it. He turned back to the girl, but she said nothing, her face cautious.

He stood and started to walk up the hill. The girl jogged at his heels, asking who he was, where he came from, was he an oracle, if they were near. He didn't look at her as he climbed.

He gained the top of the hill to find a dozen dirty, frightened faces staring at him from within the uneven circle of rock. There were a few broken pillars, and a floor of cracked stone worn smooth. One bald man with a black beard seemed the least frightened, so Oz said to him, "Where am I and where is the Head?"

The man with the black beard shot an accusing glance at

the girl standing behind Oz and said, "You are at the shrine of the Head, and I am his oracle. The Head is here, beneath us."

"Beneath us?" For the first time, Oz noticed the green weeds poking between the stones of the floor.

"Yes," the man said, and looked at one corner of the stone floor. Oz turned to see a small circle in the rock with black lapping water inside. He looked back at Black Beard and pointed to the water. "This?" he asked.

Black Beard said, "He appears to us there, and when I touch the water, I can hear his words."

"Large yellow body? Lightning and all that?"

Black Beard looked confused. "His eye looks at us from within the pool. The Head was about to begin ruling with his seven servants. Some of the stories say the servants became lost; some say his servants fled, frightened by his greatness. The Head moves within the channels of the new world he created, visiting his shrines and looking for his servants."

"Is that what the stories say?" The memory of the Head's scream sounded at the back of his mind.

"Yes," Black Beard said. The humans crouching around Oz showed fear and hope plainly on each face. "But once the Head finds his servants and reunites them under his rule, we will all worship him perfectly. In the meantime, he shares his life with us in his shrines. But now you have come, falling out of the sky. Surely the Head will return soon." The sun beat down on the rock; the surrounding white seemed radiant in its heat.

"Why haven't the Flowers overrun this place? How long have you been here?"

"One of my grandfathers helped to build this shrine."

Oz blinked. "What, during World War Two?"

"World War..." the man with the black beard murmured, his eyes wandering. "Are you talking about the old world our Head destroyed?"

"You don't remember the second World War?" Oz asked.

Black Beard looked at him blankly. "Was that part of the old world?"

His jaw dropped. He managed to ask, "How many years has it been since... since the dead came?"

"My grandfather was a boy when it happened," Black Beard said, and Oz fell into a sitting position. Black Beard continued, "Since my grandfather's time, we have waited for the Head. But here you are, falling from the sky and not hurt." Oz could hear the excitement in the man's voice.

"You should not trust the Head."

Black Beard blinked. "He shares his life with us. Come, I will show you." The oracle stood and motioned to a cluster of the seated men and women. They shuffled aside to reveal another larger hole in the stone. Despite himself, Oz walked over and saw a narrow descending staircase of rock. He followed Black Beard down into the darkness. A few dozen steps between narrow dirt walls brought them to the top of a huge cavern which extended down and away from Oz. Soft green folds of earth rolled like waves into a dim radiance. There were plots of gardens surrounded by vivid flowers on these hills. The air was misty and wet; tiny crystals of light flickered in the mist like fireflies. One curving wall of the cavern glistened as water continually dripped down its side. Oz pointed to it. "Is the pool at the top inside that wall? Where you say the Head appears?"

Black Beard nodded. "It is said that the Head scattered himself to find his servants, and as he did, he renewed parts of the earth. This is one of them. Someday he will reunite himself and make all the earth a paradise."

"Where does the light come from? It should be pitch black in here."

"I don't know. It's one of the Head's blessings."

Oz's eyes feasted on the green. He felt as if his ribs were opening, and something began to breathe which had slept for a long time. He almost resisted when Black Beard took him by the shoulder to climb back up. When they were above ground again, he had to squint as he stood on the stone.

Black Beard said, "The Head feeds us when we need to eat and gives us a safe place to sleep. We thank and worship him each time we do. He promises he will find a way to return to us and be our true father. He protects us from the children. In the meantime, we wait for the Head to return and reunite us." A hundred arguments rose within Oz, but they died as he looked at the humans sitting around Black Beard, frightened children waiting to be told what to do.

"How often do you eat?" he asked quietly.

"Perhaps once every other new moon. My grandfather said that in the old world, they slept and ate every day, but I don't see how that could be."

"How much do you know about what actually happened?"

"Not much," Black Beard sighed. "My grandfather would tell me stories of the old world. I couldn't make much sense out of them. It seemed like a hard place."

"Can I talk to him?"

"My grandfather went in search of the Head a long time ago."

"What do you mean?"

"He was old. One day he stopped breathing and his body grew cold. We laid him on the stone to keep him warm. He lay there, and after a while he sat up and walked away. He didn't seem to notice us. He was... different."

"Different in what way?" Oz asked.

A shadow passed over Black Beard's face. "He went to search for the Head," he said, without meeting Oz's eyes.

Oz sighed. "Why haven't the Dead overrun this place?"

"You mean the Children?"

"Yes."

"They don't seem to see it," Black Beard said. "Sometimes they wander here, and we hide in the cave. They have never gone down there. Are you one of the Head's servants? Why did you run from him? Can you bring him back?"

"Why would I want to bring him back?"

Black Beard blinked. "The Head said you would. The Head said you worshipped him."

"So why did I run? Your story doesn't make sense."

Black Beard shook his head. "But that is what the Head told us."

"What else has the Head told you?"

"Only to watch for his servants."

"And there are seven of them?"

Black Beard nodded. "His eye appears sometimes in the pool and he asks if we have seen them. You are one of them, aren't you?"

Oz looked at Black Beard for a moment. "When the Head returns, what will he do with the things you call the Children?"

Something in the atmosphere changed. The other members of the tribe eyed their oracle closely. He said, "I suppose he will destroy them."

"The Head told you as much?"

"No."

Oz opened and shut his mouth several times before saying, "You people are fools. The Head created the Children. If he ever comes back, you'll join them. Do not trust him." He looked around at the others as the hope in each face melted into confusion. He felt absurdly guilty, as if he'd just told a group of children that Santa Claus was a lie.

Black Beard walked past Oz to look at the tiny pool in the middle of the rock. The black water was boiling. Some of the tribe moved toward the staircase and started to hurry down, but stopped when Black Beard said, "There is no need to hide. This is one of the Head's fabled servants. He will save us."

Oz felt the eyes of the tribe heavy upon him. "Save you from what?"

"Whenever the water becomes rough, one of the Children is near," the oracle said. "It is said they were born in the water beneath the bottom of the ocean."

"That's truer than you know, but I can't save you from the Dead."

"Yes you can," the oracle said. "Let us wait and see."

They waited. The professor began to inch backwards. A smile formed within the oracle's black beard. "Mara," he said, "go see how close." The girl who had first met Oz stood and ran down the hill.

"What did you do that for?" Oz barked.

"We each have duties. She is quick. She should be safe."

"You would let a little girl go like that?" he shouted, and he was off and running down the hill. He didn't turn back when Black Beard shouted. A few steps and he was behind the girl.

A dozen paces away, the Flower walked toward them. The horizon of unending white fell away before the spiraling tentacles, the flicking, hissing tongues, the empty eye sockets, the gray, diseased feet, moving closer, closer.

*

Oz pulled the girl behind him. He felt the clear, cleansing coldness of the void as he stomped toward the Starfish and looked up. It stood two feet higher than Oz in its torn black robe; its curving starfish arms were the largest Oz had ever seen. A white swath of intermeshed, worm-like white tendons interrupted the dead flesh of one arm.

"Where is he?" Oz demanded. The question was a sword thrust into the cracked skin and empty eyes opposite him. The thing slowly turned to contemplate him. Something flared in its face.

"So hungry," it hissed.

"Where is the Head?" he asked again. A distant part of his mind was shouting at him to run. The rest of him was only cold.

The tentacles collapsed to form a parody of a human face. "You... you are back," it hissed. Then its tentacles whipped outward to full length. "You are different." Something flared in its face like a planet catching fire. "You are so beautiful."

It lunged, teeth snapping an inch from his face as he jerked back. One of its tongues fell to the grass and wriggled back toward its owner.

When Oz thought back on what happened next, he could remember only a jumble of images: he jumped, and the ground was far beneath him, and then his feet were standing on stone. Inside the circle of stone, the same set of frightened faces stared at him. Black Beard had a look of exultation on his face. Then a girl's scream from the bottom of the hill, another dizzying jump, a desperate pull to get her away from the thing wrapping its tentacles around her neck; another jump, and the same circle of frightened stares. The girl lay at his feet on the stone, gurgling and twitching.

Black Beard, gasped, "How did you do that?"

Oz blinked, his mouth open. No words came to him.

One of the women in the crowd said, "It's coming up the hill." Black Beard nodded to her, and they began to file down the narrow steps.

Oz turned to see black-green feet lifting and planting themselves in jerky motion as a livid black sun moved upward to shine atop the hill. "It will just follow you down," he said.

Black Beard shook his head as he waited for the rest of his tribe to file down the stairs. "The Head keeps us safe."

Beneath him, the girl groaned and arched her back. The ripped skin around the hole in her neck was waving as if heat were rising from the wound. Her skin was turning bruise-brown. One blind hand flailed and grasped Oz's. He stared at it, as if he wanted to pull away but couldn't. Her eyes locked with his without quite being able to focus. He stared at her with eyes that could focus on nothing else.

"I'm going to leave now," he said quietly. But his feet would not move away from her, nor his eyes from the dying girl's face as she shook and choked.

"You will be safer here until the Dead one passes by," the man with the black beard said.

"I have to leave..." Oz said. The shadow of the Flower's

head fell across the girl's face. He looked up. Its hissing face blocked the sun. Its gaze fell on them like the first beginnings of a fever. Clumsy, stumping footsteps shuffled on the uneven stone toward him.

Oz decided that he wanted to spend his last seconds of life looking at the fading traces of humanity in this girl. His eyes played over her nose and lips and forehead as pink faded into dull gray and green. Her hand began to tighten in his. He closed his eyes and hung his head and waited for the end.

And then he looked up. The Flower was shuffling past him and the thing which had once been a girl. He felt the fire radiating from it lessen. Its tentacles drooped. It seemed to be sleepwalking as it dragged heavy feet across the stone and down the other side of the hill. It didn't look back.

The hand in Oz's grew limp, and something ancient within him wept. A sigh escaped her. He glanced up as if he expected to see her spirit flying upward. He saw nothing and turned to Black Beard instead. He was sitting by the hole which led to the underground cavern.

"I'm going to leave now," Oz said. "I mean it." But it was the thing at his feet which moved, sitting up and pushing itself to its feet. It staggered in the same direction as the Flower. When its head was lost to view, he stifled a sob.

"Don't worry," the man with the black beard said. "They're blind in this place, and confused after they leave it. Usually they don't return."

"You don't care that your daughter just died and walked off?" His hands were fists.

"She is not..." the black beard said, and then shouted as the professor kicked him. He held his hands up, his nose trickling blood, a vivid red against the white horizon.

"You sent her out there?" Oz bellowed. "Among the

dead? Out of all these pathetic people, this pathetic tribe, you sent her?" He felt the strength go out of him. He collapsed into a sitting position on the stone opposite Black Beard. "Your own daughter," he said in a cracked voice. "That's how you treat her. Send her out among the dead. You're not a father. You're the opposite of a father. You knew something was wrong. You saw the signs, the listlessness, the lack of appetite, the pain deep in her eyes, but actually seeing what was wrong was too frightening, wasn't it? So you chalked it up to teenage moodiness, but you weren't surprised when you got the call from the police and they needed you to identify the body at the morgue and you went home and found the open bottle of sleeping pills in the bathroom. You sent her out among the dead! You!"

"That girl wasn't my daughter," Black Beard said, wiping his nose.

Oz stared for a second as it built inside him. Then he arched his back and howled. When his lungs had emptied themselves of their pain, he fell on his side, dizzy.

When Oz could focus his eyes again, he saw Black Beard's eyes grow wide. Oz pushed himself up and turned around. A billowing black cloud had appeared in the air above the slope of the hill. In the center, a confusion of moth wings fluttered around a human figure whose pale skin raced with patterns like smoke blown in the wind. He gasped and reached out a shaking hand.

"Finally," he moaned. "Finally, I will stop running. I am ready."

"Oz, it is I, Masaaki," the figure said. "We have much to discuss, and perhaps much to do." Oz's face blanched and he pulled his hand back as if it had been stung.

Black Beard scrambled to his feet and ran to the pool. Its

choppy waters danced with electricity and tiny waves spilled over the stone edge. "He comes!" Black Beard shouted. "The Head is coming!"

Not wanting to turn his back on the thing with Masaaki's face, Oz scrambled over to look into the pool, and almost lost his balance at the dizzying depth he saw in the water. A tiny spark of light was rising quickly. When it reached the top of the pool, it hung just beneath the surface and turned to show a yellow eye.

Black Beard touched the surface of the boiling pool with his fingers. Instantly, he froze and his eyes grew dim. His voice was half distant thunder, half quiet shriek: "You! Slave! Gather the others, and meet me in the forest. My other slave is there. There you will free me."

Oz looked back at Masaaki, who still floated within the billowing smoke. The living tattoos on his pale skin formed insect wings, Japanese characters, staring eyes. Oz looked back at the livid eye of the Head.

The professor looked into the distance and saw the thing which had just been a girl entering the crooked, white, leafless trees at the bottom of the hill.

He started to walk in her direction.

Black Beard pulled his hand out of the water with a grimace, as if it were glue. He shouted, "No! Wanderer, the Head needs you!" Oz didn't look back as he walked down the hill, nor when a cool whisper asked in his ear, "Why are you following her?"

Still walking, he said, "They speak what should never be spoken. They should just lie in their graves and let us grieve."

Masaaki said, "Every time you see one, you see your daughter."

A tear dripped from Oz's cheek, and he nodded; but he

didn't stop walking.

"She is dead, Oz. Stop trying to follow her."

"I can't. End me, or let me go."

Behind him, the former doctor said, "After the Head baptized me, I sank to a place beneath the void. It washed me. You were in the void as well, but not as deep as I. I will help you go deeper." A hand touched Oz's sweating back, and a cold seeped into his body which made the heat of the day feel like a fever. He gave a long sigh, and saw his breath plume in steam in the hot sunshine.

He stopped walking. The freshly dead girl walked out of sight among the bony trees. Oz breathed deep, relishing the cold. He turned and took a long moment to stare at the new being opposite him. "What is it that you see?" he asked Masaaki.

"I see you, Richard. I see your pain."

Oz gasped at the scenes appearing in Masaaki's aura. "You do, don't you?" He felt it rising in him again, and bent over as if he might vomit.

"You have lost much, Oz. Too much for words."

"Thank you. Thank you for... for knowing that."

The professor straightened up, but a third wave rose within him. He doubled over again, choking and moaning. When he could look Masaaki in the eye, tears streamed from his eyes. "My daughter is dead," he whispered. "Will the pain ever pass?"

"Not entirely. But it will not control you as it used to."

Oz nodded.

"Your daughter is dead, but you are not. When the Head immersed us, he awakened something in each of us. Let me find the others, and I will return for you." Oz gave him a stricken look and his eyes fell. "Why are you ashamed?"

Masaaki asked.

"The Head did not intend for us to be scattered, did he?"

"No."

"Am I turning into what the Head planned? A pet monster?"

Masaaki asked, "Do you still wish to serve him?"

"No."

"Then you are not what the Head intended." When Oz's eyes fell again, Masaaki said, "Still, you are ashamed."

He opened his mouth several times before he said, "If the others are alive, they won't want to see me. Or, they shouldn't."

"They are no less guilty than you. Are you not glad we have met?"

"More than I can say, Masaaki."

"Then let us all meet together."

The man who called himself Oz gave something close to a smile. "Very well." The billowing smoke folded over the apparition and Masaaki disappeared.

Oz turned to see Black Beard watching him at the top of the hill. He sighed again, hunched his shoulders, and put one foot in front of the other until he reached the top. Black Beard stared at him silently. Oz stood for a minute without returning the look. Then he said, "I have to find my friends. I want to see them again and I cannot wait. Do not trust the Head. That is the best help I can give you. I have to go. I'm sorry. I will come back and try to give you better help, if I can."

"If I do not trust the Head, who am I to trust? How will I lead my people? You must stay."

"Not me. But not the Head either. I'm sorry."

And then Oz was gone, a blue blur in the cloudless sky.

"The wind," Black Beard breathed. "He is the wind itself." He caught his breath as he saw three of the tall figures his father had called Walkers, but had never explained. One turned toward him and their eyes met. Then the three figures disappeared.

EIGHTEEN

Plague

Mason awoke and felt grimy sand beneath him. He scrambled to his feet and started to brush off the back of his arms and neck, but was suddenly dizzy and fell to one knee. Insects were buzzing between his ears.

Squinting, he saw painful sunlight and red sand in every direction. He looked around as long as he could before the burning brightness forced his eyes shut. He swallowed, a dry click in his throat.

When he opened his eyes again, he kept them on the red-stained sand. He must have a fever, that must be why he was hallucinating that he was in a desert. He was probably still back in that cave, being drowned so he could become the Head's watchdog. And that was why he felt a wonderful breath of cool air, why he saw a cloud of black smoke billowing around something with moth's wings. It asked him if he was hurt in a voice he couldn't quite place. The smoke surrounded him and something stronger than the earth pulled him down. He felt himself sinking beneath the earth and fought against it, swinging his arms and twisting his back. He felt the moth leave him as he lost consciousness.

When he came to, he was lying on the sand again, looking up at the night sky and shivering in the cold. Tiny raw stars pulsed in time to the pounding in his head. He got to his feet, swayed, and wrapped his shaking arms tight against his sides. In the distance, he saw a red body sitting against a rock, surrounded by piles of bony rags. A minute's stumbling brought him to it, and he saw that the piles of rags were Flowers, crumpled like they were asleep or dead. The rock was taller than his head, and the slumped body of the giant taller still. The body was deep red, eyeless, long dead but not decomposed, and covered with grains of sand which sparkled in the starlight. He closed his eyes, trying to think about where he was and what he was seeing, but his mind raced away from him.

One of the Flowers pulled itself up. Tentacles waving, it stood in front of him, a head shorter, blindly looking up at him. Another rose, and another. He was soon surrounded by short hissing bodies. As if on cue, they fell to one knee.

"You have returned," one of them hissed.

Their tentacles quickened, almost vibrating. The heat inside him seemed to radiate to them in slow waves. In his fever, Mason felt that the Flowers around him were hungry, and that they were somehow satisfying themselves without touching him. He felt his face: it hadn't blossomed like the Flowers, but the skin was sandpaper. He looked at his hand and saw the skin was red.

"Have I shrunk or have you grown?" he asked. His worshippers rose from their knees and stood before him, silent. As he looked down on the Flowers, it somehow seemed to him that they were the largest he had ever seen.

He closed his eyes and breathed. It was becoming easier to think, even though his fever was clouding his head. "I was going to bring the other humans to the Head," he said. "The survivors. Hunt them down like criminals."

"There is no need, Lord," one hissed. "They join us in death soon enough. Some tribes offer us sacrifice from their own members to please us. Or we catch them wandering." He couldn't tell which of the Flowers was speaking.

"I'll do it anyway."

"You must give more," the Flower said. "Many still live inside me, but it is never enough. I feed on them, but the void always hungers."

Mason's fever was not lessening, but he found himself paying less attention to it. "Where is the Head?" he asked.

"It does not know. So long, so long the Father has been gone."

"So what am I supposed to do?"

Each one hissed, and he felt their bottomless hunger.

"Who's that?" he asked, motioning to the red corpse.

"It is you," they said.

"The Head said I was the new god of plague," he said. The Flowers said nothing, their bodies rigid and attentive.

His hands were opening and closing, clenching into fists and flexing open. He made the fingers of one hand straight and drove them into the shoulder of the nearest Flower. Black mold exhaled from the wound before thin ropey feelers, white in the starlight, intertwined to cover the wound.

"You are displeased," the Flower he had wounded said.

"Can't punish something already dead."

He stood, hands at his side. His followers stood opposite him. The stars hung above them, silent.

*

Mason stood on legs which didn't tire as the night wore on. His fever sharpened and his thoughts cleared. He watched the world around him. In his mind, the ground and the sky became cheap stage scenery. The desert sand began to disappear beneath his feet until only a thin sprinkling of grains remained above the churning void, far beneath, the same void he had been baptized in. Dots of that chaos flew upward like thick spray from a waterfall, up into the desert, blotting out the stars, huddling on Mason's hands like insects.

"I can see the nothing moving through everything," a strange voice said. Mason looked around before realizing he had spoken. The Flowers standing nearby appeared only as outlines on which the chaos massed; but as he focused, the chaos grew transparent, and he saw their bodies as he used to. He let his eyes relax, and saw again the world transparent and stretched thin over the boiling void which streamed through everything.

The fever in his head was an unending thunder. He felt his own mind withering before it. The feet beneath him began to move.

"Where do you go, Lord?" the Flowers hissed.

"To find the Head," he heard the strange voice say, and somehow knew he spoke as well. He felt tiny within his own mind. "He lied to me. He's a criminal. I'm going to eat him."

The hissing behind him quickened, as if applauding.

*

So Plague journeyed across the desert. A growing train of Flowers followed him which inhaled the red mist coming off their leader. Plague didn't stop when the red sand changed to plains of white grass, each blade coated with ash or mildew. The white horizon was broken once by a hill topped with stone and green growth. Resheph could see the outline of humans hiding on top of it behind the stone, and the plague which lived in their bodies. He did not stop. The sun rose and set, rose and set. Twisted white trees began to appear. The fever hummed inside Resheph, burning its mind clean.

The trees thickened to a forest. Resheph walked into it, feeling the void pull him. White tree branches criss-crossed above his head, and a few trees much taller than these, standing like the bones of giants who had died as they walked. Memories of the man who had been Mason rippled across the surface of the mind of Plague. It did not stop walking.

Then Plague came to a gigantic tree. Its long knotted branches stretched across the faint blue sky as if to embrace it. Just beyond the tree, the ground fell away. Plague walked to the edge and stared down at what human eyes would have seen as churning mist. Plague could see past the mist to the chaos at the bottom of the world, spraying up into everything that is. It could also see the roots of the tree reaching down into the void. But it couldn't see any way down. Hundreds of Flowers waited behind their master for what was next.

Plague stiffened and looked to his right. "Come out," it shouted. Its voice was the grating of stones in a dark cavern.

A man crept out from behind a tree on all fours. He cast thin yellow light on the trees around him. The muscles in his long arms and legs bunched, as if he were ready to run.

The Flowers behind Plague hissed and staggered toward the man, teeth snapping; but a quick jump sent the man high into the branches of the great tree. Plague held up a single arm and the Flowers froze.

"Where is the Head?" Plague asked.

"Finally!" the man said. Short stalks of electricity raced up and down his arms, slowed, raced again. "What are you?" The man almost bounced in his excitement.

Plague stared at him. "The Head," it said. "Where?"

"Not even worth it. Not worth the trouble, and you don't want to go where he is." A southern drawl clung to the jittery words.

The red giant turned and started to walk away. The man blurted, "I can show you where I saw him last, if you'll tell me what you are and how you work. Part of him, anyway."

Plague turned to glare at the man trembling in the tree. The two stared at each other, and the man's face fell. "You're Mason. That's all you are."

"Mason is dead."

"I can still see him." His shoulders slumped.

Plague stared at the man. "You were the one called Luke."

"So?" the man asked.

"The Head said you were a genius. You were going to take the place of his scientists." The words were a slow avalanche.

The man held on to a branch with one hand and leaned so far over it looked as if he might fall. He shouted, "The Head had no idea what he was doing! When he dunked us in that stuff, it was about the stupidest thing he could'a done." The sparks playing across the man's body fell as he gesticulated and danced on the branches beneath him. "If I had had more time, I prolly could'a told him everything would blow up."

Plague looked down into the abyss.

"You can look down there all you want. You won't ever find anything worth looking at. I took what I could from the Head's old laboratory. Even found ways to power the equipment. Practically memorized everything on the computers. But it's like having a steam engine after a nuclear explosion. The Head changed everything. Everything."

Plague looked at the man. It noticed the scars on the man's wrists and the burns on his neck.

"How long have you been here?" Plague asked.

"I stopped counting years ago. Why?"

Plague said nothing.

The man who had been Luke said, "The abyss messes with everything. You can take a dip and come back a second later, or ten years, or before you went in."

"The Head. Where?"

Luke snorted. "Still a cop."

"Show me."

"Fine," the yellow man said. "But keep your leeches here. They're starving, and they'd love to get their hands on something like me."

Plague turned and glared at the Flower closest to him. It turned back to look up at Luke.

"So they're not comin'?" the man asked.

"Show me where the Head is."

Luke hesitated, then leapt far in the opposite direction, falling out of sight among the trees. Plague could see faint yellow light between the crisscrossing bones of branches. It followed the light and caught up with Luke a moment later. Luke was standing in front of a blur: dead white trees stood on either side of a no-space. Plague grimaced and forced its eyes to focus, and when it looked again, he saw a crude circle of stone. Weeds, flowers and green grass grew around it and poked through the cracks in the stones. The being which had been Mason stared, and saw, as if the rock and green growth were a thin film, a thick gray fountain spewing up from the hole in the center of the rock.

Luke was standing inside the circle of stone, looking into the pool. "He usually comes when I'm here. Some of the survivors built this place, but they ran when they saw me for the first time. Hey! You comin'?"

Plague stood outside the shrine.

"Mos' interestin' thing's happened this decade," Luke said to himself. He walked back toward Plague and peered at him. "You seen yourself?"

"The Head."

Luke shrugged and motioned to the shrine. "You wanna find him, most likely you'll see him in there."

"This is a perversion," Plague said. "This is not what chaos is meant to be. It's not meant to vomit more life that can reproduce and hurt itself. This forest is already perfect." It lifted one of the stones with its toe and made a sound of disgust at the weeds underneath.

The water in the pool started to boil. Luke said, "If you wanna see him, come now."

Plague grimaced and walked inside, stooping his head beneath the stone roof. It looked down into the pool. Something bright rose in the water in electric pulses and hung just beneath the surface. When the single livid eye turned to look at them, Plague reached a hand into the water to crush it. But as soon as its fingers touched, Plague froze, aware of the massive, incoherent body beneath, always in danger of dissolving and always recombining, and the long arm it had reached to one of the windows of its prison.

You! Tell that fool I made in my image that I can't speak to him unless he touches the water, and that he has to find a way to free me!

Plague wrenched his hand out of the pool, shuddering as the screechy voice echoed through his head. He grabbed Luke's shoulder. "You're in league with him, aren't you?"

Luke's long, dirty hair trembled as he shook his head. "He doesn't say nothin'. Just comes up and glares at me."

"He spoke in my mind when my hand touched the water."

A door closed behind Luke's eyes. "I never tried that."

"It never occurred to you to try that."

Luke said, "You sound more like the old Mason when you say things like that."

"How many times have you tried to kill yourself, Luke?"

Luke said nothing.

Mason's voice said, "You're a genius. The Head could see it in you. And you've been here for how many years, trying to keep boredom away, and it never occurred to you to touch the water? I think you'd rather die than talk with the Head again. But you can't even take your own life."

"You're the same as ever," Luke said in a tight voice. "Always seein' other people's faults and never your own. Do you know what you look like? The whole time in our old camp, all you talked about was how to kill the dead. You couldn't find a way, so you joined their leader. Then that didn't work out like you planned, so you try to kill their leader. You become what you hated. Why not aim that anger at yourself, Mason? It's gonna eat you eventually."

"Why is this place green?" Mason asked, his voice mixing with Plague's. "You must've thought about it."

Luke said nothing.

214

"Mason remembers that the Head screamed and disappeared in the explosion of water when he was baptized. But I felt him down there when I put my hand in the pool. I think he was scattered when the chaos touched him a second time. Have you found other places like this, Luke? Stone pools with green grass?"

"Yeah."

"I think the places the Head touches grow green because the Head is growing them. I don't think he wants to, but I think being touched by the chaos again changed him. And the Head touched you, and now you can't die. You've got a brilliant mind and more years to use it in than you can count, and what have you done? Lived like a caveman. You're still the white trash you always were."

Luke glared.

The red mist rolling off of Plague's body in a slow waterfall grew darker. It smoldered as he turned away and walked into the forest. Luke followed at a distance, watching trees burst into flame as Plague walked through them. At one point, Plague met one of the taller trees. It gave a high, thin scream as it erupted into flames and collapsed.

A minute's tramping brought them to the edge of the abyss. Plague's head hung as it looked down.

"Are you still lookin' for the Head?" Luke called. "Or you finally takin' my advice?"

Plague turned. Fire burned in its three eyes; the slit of its nose and its thin, flappy lips waved in the heat like gills on a shark. Then Plague fell backwards into the abyss.

*

From a distance, Luke watched the Flowers that had followed Plague. They stared into the void and hissed, waiting. He somehow sensed they were sad their provider had left, but none of them followed him. He slipped away and walked back to the shrine.

Inside, Luke kneeled and stared at the pool of water. He stayed there a moment, sighed, and pressed his hand into the cool liquid. He didn't hear his own sharply drawn breath as he felt the depth of the well, the miles of crisscrossing underwater tunnels rising from a measureless cavern, the faded outline of a huge body struggling to hold together. He felt that consciousness rising now, seeing him like a prisoner looking at a star. He kept his hand open so that the eye couldn't look at him.

The words sounded in his mind. *Finally, my son. Tell me how I can free myself and rule over my new creation.*

Luke thought, *You expect me to help you after what you've done?*

Anger raced up Luke's arm to explode in his head. Luke shouted, *Years I've been here with nothing while my mind eats itself!*

The Head thundered in his mind, *I was limited in my vision. I was meant to be even greater than I thought. My new body is evidence for it. Free me from this womb, my slave.*

Luke thought, *Come on out, then.*

He winced at the screech in his mind: *You think I haven't tried? The weight is crushing!*

I don't think you can survive up here. You've been in that stuff too long.

The Head said, *But think what wonders you will work with me when I am free.*

Of course, Master, Luke thought, and grabbed with his

hand, squeezing his fist as tightly as he could. But the eye dropped deeper out of his reach.

I can see your mind, slave, the Head screeched. *Freeing me will atone for this and your other sins. But do not test me or I will crush you.*

Luke stared at the pulsing yellow eye and thought, *I'll check your old lab again.*

Find a way, the Head thundered silently. The eye sank and the water quieted.

He walked out of the shrine, wiping his damp hand on his dirty pants. Dusk was falling. Luke walked through the white forest toward the edge of the abyss. When he reached the cliff edge, he followed the edge to his right, away from the great tree which had grown where they had made camp in a previous life. His faint aura became a lantern as darkness fell.

Eventually the trees began to thin and the ground dipped. The remains of a network of broken walls and staircases became visible in the deepening night. Luke wove his way downward to the long hangar he had visited as a human being decades ago. The roof had long since fallen in, and the hangar was only half its former size. Cutting across it was the same mist that bordered the forest. Half the rows of useless weapons and dead computers remained, covered in white mold, oblivious and silent next to the drop in the land and the swirling mist. He knew he only had to touch one of the computers to turn it on. He could still remember the systems and data he had studied time after time. He remembered the location of the weapons on the shelves, and the useless years he had spent learning to use them, only to run before dead bodies which always grew back.

He touched one of the laptops, closing his eyes. The tiny

stalks of lightning that played over his skin quickened. A tiny flame burst in the computer's side, growing quickly as it fed on the mold coating everything. Knowing it wasn't necessary, he started another fire a few desks down.

Soon it was a bonfire. He walked backwards up the stairs, staring at the flames. Eventually he sat on the top step and watched his world burn. Even when the heat became an oven, he sat. Then the flames started to drop and the fire died. Soon only the charred skeletons of desks and walls remained, lit faintly by glowing coals on the ground.

He sat, watching, as if he would never get up again.

A hiss sounded behind him. He jumped up and turned. He saw dark starfish-arms lit in faint, flickering orange from the remains of the fire below. He couldn't levitate like the Head, and there were no trees to jump to. He had tried to concentrate the energy in his body and electrocute the dead before, but it only slowed them for a moment.

As far as he could see in the darkness, waves of the Dead walked toward him.

"You have to obey the red thing," he shouted.

The hissing rose into a single word: *Hungry*.

His voice tight, he said, "You're hungry and you're tired of human flesh, but if you eat me, I can't bring the Head back. When I do, you can have your fill of him."

They stopped. "Our Father. He is alive?"

"I talked with him half an hour ago."

"We will worship him and be satisfied," they said, tongues licking, teeth clicking. "Then we will be satisfied with his slave."

Luke took a step toward them, but they didn't move: a wall of flaring tentacles and snapping teeth. "I can't conjure him up here. You gotta let me go back to the pool."

218

"The pool?"

"Those shrine things," Luke said. "With the rocks."

The hissing of the dead rose, but no words came.

"You can't see those things, can you?" Luke said to himself. "I seen you stumble around in 'em."

"Did you make this fire as an offering to summon the Head?" the hissing asked.

"Uh... yeah."

The Dead stood like angry statues, looking down on the burning world. "It will wait," the hissing said.

Behind him, one of the coals popped, and a charred wall fell over with a crack.

NINETEEN

The Sun God

As night wore on, Luke eventually sat on the steps and faced the burning embers of the Head's company as the Dead waited around him. Every time he wondered if he had done the right thing, the memory of the Head's screech washed over him like nausea. Memories of old faces and the vanished past played over his mind as he stared at the dying embers.

"Are any of you Bob?" he whispered, not daring to look at them. "Do any of you know him?"

A voice hissed, "It can remember the sack of flesh it used to be. None of us had that name."

"Do you talk together? Can you find him?"

"Why?" one of them hissed.

Luke's head sagged, and he moaned, "I did the best I could. The first shot took off most of his mouth. He couldn't talk, but his eyes were begging me. He just couldn't stand it anymore."

The Dead hissed behind him in the darkness.

"Can you find him? I want to tell him I'm sorry."

"Why?" they hissed.

Luke's mouth worked, and a tear slipped down his cheek.

When he could speak again, he said, "Must be nice to be you." He stood and turned back to the Dead. "I can't bring your Father back. He's stuck down there. I don't even think he can think clearly unless he comes up to the surface. And when he released the disease that made you, he changed how everything works. I can't figure anything out anymore."

The Dead stood, hissing, waving. "You cannot bring us the Father."

"No."

A tiny voice came from within the Flower nearest him. "Please, please, it is so cold, so gray, and only flesh is red and warm, but it is gone so soon. Please show us the Father, and that will be enough." The voice carried on its pleading, but the hissing around it rose. When it died down, the voice was gone.

"I can't bring you your Father," Luke shouted.

"You are like him," they said. The hunger in the words was a knife edge.

Luke took a step, and another, toward the nearest Flower. The cold starfish arm which stretched and wrapped itself around his neck quivered as if being electrocuted, but didn't let go. He didn't resist as the dead crater of a face loomed large above his own.

It stopped. In the darkness, he sensed its attention turn to something behind him. The tentacles loosened, and he fell to his knees, gasping.

When Luke could lift his head again, he saw how many hundreds of Flowers surrounded him, and also saw that their tentacles drooped and their heads hung forward, hypnotized. A dim radiance spread out over them, waving like the reflection of a pool. Still on his hands and knees, he turned to see what they looked at: a bright pale body, wreathed in smoke.

It turned its face and locked eyes with him.

He fell backwards against the legs of the Flower that had held him, and shouted in fear as Death floated closer. "Wake up!" he shouted, punching the thing's hard, cold leg. "Get me away from that! He's the real thing!"

Death reached a pale, cold hand and touched his shoulder. "Peace, Luke," it said, and Luke heard Masaaki's voice. He blinked in surprise and felt something untwist inside like a knot in a muscle loosening.

The Flowers nearest Luke were still stupefied at the sight of the dark being floating opposite them, but a hissing rose a dozen paces away. "No... no... he is ours."

Masaaki's face flared in alarm. He put both hands on Luke's shoulders. Curling smoke and moth-wing rushed toward Luke and enfolded him.

*

Water swirling in dark currents like a hurricane. Oceans and dry land and leprous vegetation, stretched above it as a thin film. A pulsing electricity beneath, a livid yellow eye, and long arms reaching toward them, and the cold grip tightening on his hand, dragging him up and throwing Luke onto the sand.

*

Luke pulled himself into a sitting position and sat on the beach, still as a statue. He looked out over the water. Eventually his chest rose and fell as he began to breathe again. He didn't brush the sand from his arms. His eyes remained on the endless ocean. He was cold, but he didn't shiver. The first glimmer of dawn appeared over the water.

"That was the void you were taking me through," he said, keeping his eyes on the water.

"Yes."

"The same void the Head pushed us into," Luke said.

"Yes."

"It's gotten bigger."

"Yes," Masaaki said. "Will you tell me why?" When Luke said nothing, Masaaki said, "Look at me."

"No, Bob."

"I am not him."

Luke turned his neck slowly. Masaaki's dark aura was becoming more visible as the sun rose, as if the rays of the dawn couldn't touch him. The shape of his face was close to the small Japanese man Luke had known before, except that his pale skin shone faintly against the velvet background of his aura. Heavy shadows played about his eyes and mouth as if a flickering candle were shining above his head.

"I thought you'd be so angry, Bob," Luke said in a wobbly voice. "I thought you'd kill me."

The first trace of irritation played over the demigod's face.

"I know you're not him," Luke whispered. "But you may as well be. Bob was the one that really mattered and he's dead. He was my brother. We couldn't'a been more different. But my old man didn't care who he slept with, and somehow he ended up with us two. I guess my mom didn't care about me, and neither did Bob's. My dad would'a killed us a long time ago, except he wanted other people around to torture when he drank."

"What do the Dead mean to you, Luke?"

223

"What?"

"Do you see your brother in them?"

Luke looked back out at the rising sun. "I tried to study 'em. Had a little book and took notes about 'em." He shook his head. "Useless."

"You feel you failed your brother."

"I did fail him." Luke stifled a sob. "Bob would steal science magazines and books from the library and tell me how I'd be famous one day and get us both out of there. I read all of 'em. Easy. Remembered everything without tryin'. My brother watchin' me the whole time and hopin'. He bet all his money on me, and I believed him. I really thought I was gonna be a famous scientist and take care of him 'n me. At least for a while. Then I started to realize how it wouldn't work. But I didn't say anything about that to Bob.

"Then one day my old man found the books, and... I really should'a taken Bob to a hospital. Bob just laid on his bed and whispered he was okay and coughed blood.

"After that, every chance I got, I started doing pushups. After a while I could do 'em from a handstand. I would go into the woods and punch trees until my knuckles were red. I guess the old man noticed, because he started pickin' on me more. I remember the first time I won. He had blood all over his face and he'd lost some teeth. I didn't have a scratch on me. He muttered something about going for a drive. He was too drunk to stand up straight, but I told him to go and not come back. Wasn't none surprised when we heard on the radio the next day about the driver who had crashed into the tree. They said they couldn't identify the body, but I knew who it was.

"The old man was finally gone, and Bob was all excited for my career to take off. Whenever I looked at him, he was grinning at me. We made a fire that night, and he was goin' on and on about how I was going to go places, and how he'd be with me the whole time. That part was true, at least. Eventually I couldn't listen to him and I told him I couldn't go to college 'cause I'd never been to high school. I couldn't even apply, because we didn't have an address. I can still remember the look on his face in the firelight. He'd gone all quiet." He didn't turn his eyes from the rising sun as a single tear slipped down his cheek. "Then he just carried on like I hadn't said anything. Weeks went by, and him carryin' on all the time about how great it would be. Then the Dead came, but not even that stopped him. The idiot still actually thought I was gonna make somethin' of myself." The different parts of Luke's face were grinding tectonic plates.

"I never made anything of myself, before the Dead came or after. One night in our camp, Bob finally couldn't lie to himself any more. Got real quiet. I could see the change in his face. I talked to him all night, tryin' to tell him how to be strong, that he had to be strong. Didn't work. I musta' dropped off, 'cause I woke up to a gunshot. My gun. He turned it on himself, but he couldn't even get that right. I had to help him even with that.

"The one person countin' on me, and I let him down. I made it worse for him, because I'd already faced down a monster, but he never had, and he was ashamed. I couldn't save him."

Luke hung his head. Masaaki put a luminous hand on his back and felt the tangled paths inside him which Luke's dazzling mind could never map.

Luke looked back at his guide. His face gathered itself a little as he said, "I've never told this to anyone. Why am I telling you?"

"The void unloosens us," the apparition said. "I experienced it myself."

"There was an old graveyard near my shack. We would hide there sometimes. I feel like I'm back there."

Masaaki said, "Confession is a kind of death. A truer death than what the Flowers give."

"They killed the world. There ain't nothing for me to do."

"That is why you promised to help the Head. You wanted to redeem yourself to your brother, even though he was dead."

Luke said nothing.

"And now you feel you are sealed in your failure forever. Sealed in your uselessness."

The misery in Luke's face was answer enough. He stood and walked toward the sea. When it covered his ankles, Masaaki called, "How do you know it will work?"

He turned. "The void unloosens everything. You said so."

"It will not be the end for you. The Head is still down there."

"Who knows? Maybe I'll end up like you if I go deep enough."

Masaaki's eyebrows furrowed. "Is that what you want?"

"You seem calm enough."

Death floated out over the tiny waves. "That is not your place, Luke. I am able to travel through the void because I was touched by the god who belonged there. Your place is here, in the sun. Your skin receives its light in a way mine cannot."

Luke walked further out. "Reckon I'll try anyway."

Masaaki followed him. "It is true there is a place beneath the void. It should not exist. The void itself is the opposite of

226

existence, so how can something exist even beneath that? But I was there. And I am at peace because I was."

"That don't help me none."

"After the Head immersed you in the void, your body changed," Masaaki said urgently. "Why?"

Luke continued walking without looking at Masaaki. "It don't matter," he mumbled. "I'm a freak. Always have been. Should'a never been this smart. You don't explain a freak."

"Why are you a freak, then?"

"The Head put his hands on the side of my head," Luke said. "It hurt, but something changed inside. Musta reacted funny with the stuff." His voice was flat. The water was at his waist.

"Why have the others changed as well?"

"The others?" Luke asked, stopping again and looking up at the spectre of Death, who floated above the water.

"Please come back to shore with me."

"Gimme a reason."

"The others from our camp. Each one of us was touched by one of the Head's chief servants. Now we are all different."

Luke blinked, and looked back at Masaaki. "I saw Mason," he said. "I didn't know about the others."

"This news does not make you glad?"

He shrugged. "There ain't nothin' for me to do. The Head reached down to the bottom of everything. Everything has been changed. Even if I had the same technology, I couldn't reproduce the results."

"There are new factors in play which the Head did not foresee."

"Name one that matters."

"The explosion. Do you know why the explosion

happened?"

"Only thing I can think is the void don't like itself. It was already inside us, then we got immersed again. It reacted."

"It is not much. But I want to gather the others. Will you join us?"

"I'm useless."

Death drew so close to Luke that their noses almost touched. Luke could feel the cold radiating from the other's skin. The shadows playing over the apparition's face seemed to accelerate as he said, "Stop thinking about yourself and your own failures. I do not care what you can or cannot do. I would be grieved if you did not join us. Come, and be useless with us."

The golden demigod turned and looked out at the ocean for a long moment. He turned and gave his guide a dark look. Then he waded back to shore. He stood, dripping from the waist of his ragged clothes and shivering.

"You are angry," Masaaki said.

Luke's face began to lose its coherence again. He opened his mouth, but couldn't speak.

"You are in pain, Luke. What I give is not much, and yet also it is a great deal." He floated forward and placed his hand on Luke's forehead. "Be at peace over your brother."

Luke closed his eyes and let out a long sigh, his breath appearing in the air as if it were freezing. When he opened his eyes again, they had lost their haggard look.

He looked out at the rising sun. His golden-yellow skin seemed to mirror its brilliance as he said, "You asked a good question there, Masaaki."

"You have a brilliant mind. Tell me what you think."

"The void should'a killed us. That's what it did to the six board members. Instead, the opposite happened to us."

"You think this significant?"

"I think when the Head immersed us, it was like the void was meeting itself. And it had the opposite effect. It made us more ourselves instead of undoin' us. It may be something. One of those new factors."

The ghostly figure nodded. "I think it would be wise to tell that to the others," he said.

"Where are they?"

"Two are near us even now," he said and pointed.

Luke looked down the shore. In the distance, a man and a woman walked toward them near the rolling waves of the beach. The man walked tall, long arms and wiry muscles unclothed despite the chill in the air. The scabbard of a long, curved sword was strapped around his side. His sister walked in cautious contrast to the man's long stride. Luke felt something flutter inside as he watched her approach and remembered Selene's ivory skin, her raven hair, her softly burning eyes.

Luke tensed. "You think those two are gonna' be as calm as you about meeting me?"

"They are no less guilty than you. Or I."

The two soon stood in front of them. When Jack reached out his hand, Luke couldn't meet his eyes. But he reached out his own hand and met Jack's. He almost cried out at the strength of the former bank teller's grip, but forced himself not to. When Jack finally let go, Luke risked a glance at Selene, but saw no hatred in her eyes.

Standing on the shore of the ocean at the end of the world, they stood in the cold blowing wind and the crashing waves and faced each other.

TWENTY

The Moon Goddess

After she was immersed by the Head, Selene sank in darkness. Like the others, she saw the great wings of light beating against the starfish head. She was a dust mote before the titanic energy reaching out toward the dead world, and knew she was not safe, and didn't care. She could make out six other tiny figures turned toward the light, and wondered if they felt the same joy beating against her ribcage like fluttering wings.

The vision dimmed; Selene's joy mellowed but did not fade. After a no-time of minutes or hours, she saw something luminous and wavy high above, but couldn't tell whether it was a woman's face or the full moon. Not wondering why she didn't need to breathe, she swam upward. When her head broke the surface of the water, she saw the moon just above her, larger than she had ever seen it, almost close enough to touch. Whispering light fell on the choppy waters.

She sputtered and coughed, and when she looked again, she saw a woman floating over the waves toward her from within the circle of the moon. The whiteness of her skin was the luminosity of the moon, the curve of the moon's craters were the lines of her eyes and lips. She took Selene's hand and lifted her so that they both floated over the waves.

Daughter, the woman said. *We meet again.*

"You. I did not dream it? That night, that wondrous night, after the dead had come, when I followed Jack to the ocean, and he saw the snake, and I saw you?"

You know you did not dream.

"You said nothing, but I knew that I was different after meeting you."

I did not have much time. The Head would have been attracted to my presence if I had stayed.

"I knew I was supposed to do... something. But I ignored it. It was just too much. But, oh Mother..." Selene gave the goddess an agonized look.

There is much sadness and much joy in you. Tell me everything that is in your heart.

"I failed you, Mother. I pledged myself unto the Head." She shuddered. "It was like marrying a boyfriend who had beaten me. But still I'm almost glad, I mean, I am glad, because unless the Head had put us in the water, I never would have seen the... I don't know what it was. A bird or a flower or sun. It was... it was even more beautiful than you, Mother. Don't you know the thing I saw?"

I have never seen it.

"Oh, Mother, who am I and who are you? I tried to keep reading after the Dead came, but I failed. The words just weren't the same. I talked to myself when the Head kept me by the void. I talked to the tired woman I might have become, the kind of woman my father married and abused."

You are not trapped inside that woman.

A tear slipped down Selene's cheek. "Thank you. Thank you, Mother. But down there, in the pit, it frightened me so much I gave up and joined the Head. I'd have done anything to avoid becoming her. But the Head doesn't understand the new world much more than anyone else. And now I've seen something so beautiful, I'm ruined forever. Everything else will forever be plain in comparison. And still I feel your touch. Who am I? And who are you?"

I am a traitor, daughter. I was part of his company, and I was hungry for the same things the Head wanted. But the drug the Head gave us changed us in ways he could not anticipate. I am not the woman I was. Besides, you cannot see the things I have seen and remain the same.

"What did the Head intend for you to do?"

I do not really know, and I do not think the Head knew. He prattled on about ruling the night, and it is true that I can see everything which happens by night. But I can do nothing but watch. Watch how the Dead ate the living. Her words carried an ocean of sadness.

"You mean the best I can do is watch what happens?"

You are different from the woman I touched on that beach, daughter. You turned to books after the Dead came, did you not?

"I always read a lot, but even more so when they came."

The moon goddess gave her a long look. Selene felt naked beneath her gaze. The goddess said, *You used reading as a way to escape your father, daughter. You were trying to avoid your pain and master it. But as you say, the words are dead. Now you will read hearts. You will discern the dark places of truth where others stumble, and guide them where they cannot go alone. The night is now your domain.*

"I don't understand."

You will. The moonlight sighed, and Selene felt the ancient, dusty rock that the moon was. *I sense your brother is near. You must comfort him. I do not know if you can change what the Head has done. But now I can finally rest. Let us go to your brother.*

They floated over the shifting waves, hand in hand, saying nothing. The faint outline of the shore in the darkness came far too soon for Selene. She stepped onto the cold, rocky sand, and turned back to her mother to speak again. But when she turned, she saw only the moon. She stood, looking for a long time at the fading traces of the woman's face, until she saw only a rocky skull in the sky. She stared at it for a long time, holding on to the feel of the mother she'd never had like someone trying to keep a sputtering fire alight. When she was sure the memory would not be totally lost to her, she turned and looked up and down the beach. The sand dunes lit up wherever she looked. Eventually she saw a man with a thin beard and ragged clothes sitting with his head down. A group of broken buildings stood behind him. She walked toward the man, and as she did, she saw a tall, ghostly figure standing behind Jack, looking down on him. Selene opened her mouth to speak, but as soon as she did, the figure looked at her and stepped back into the nighttime darkness. Her brother looked up with wide, tired eyes. He said nothing, caught within the searchlight of her gentle radiance.

"Jack," she said.

The man blinked, as if remembering something. Without standing, he shifted in the sand to bow on one knee. He placed his sword on the sand in front of her. "Lady," he said, "I do not know how you know my name, but I pledge to fight for you always, if I might have your blessing."

"What, have you become a knight?"

"Yes," he said, his head still bowed.

"And now you magically can save me from the dead.

You."

"Not by magic. By training."

"A traitor is inside you. Your training cannot hide him."

Even with his head bowed, Selene could see her brother's face tighten. "The light of the moon shines in your face," he said. "You see everything. I did betray my... someone who depended on me. But my very soul has been hardened by years of training, and it will never happen again."

"If your betrayal means nothing now, then why does it still haunt you?"

His head sank, and he bit his lip. "The world was evil before the change, Lady, and now it is even worse because of the Dead, and because of me. But if everyone unworthy gave up, all hope would be lost." He looked up, and the grief in his eyes pierced Selene. "And even though I don't deserve it, I would be glad for your blessing, whatever you are."

Something broke inside her, and she sat down next to Jack and put her arm around him and smiled at him.

Jack stared for a moment before recognition flooded his face. "Selene! I thought you were dead! And it was my fault!"

"Yes," she said. "I did die. So did you. And that was my fault. But here we are, and I am so glad to see you again." Jack blinked and shook his head. When he met her eyes again, the fatigue was still in his face, but the grief was gone.

*

"What happened to you, Jack? Where have you been? What has happened?"

"What happened to you? You're practically glowing. How can you look so excited and serious at the same time?"

"I spoke with my mother again."

Jack shook his head. "We never knew her."

"Something happened before we came to Oz's camp that I should have told you about. That night you swam in the ocean? And saw the huge snake, like you told the group? I followed you and sat on the sand, far behind you. And I saw something too. The moon came and spoke with me. I know how silly..."

"It doesn't. You were calmer and wiser after that night. And whenever the moon was full, you could practically narrate someone's soul back to them. And now look at you."

She smiled. "My true mother, Jack. She came to me."

"You mean one of the old gods. The Head's pantheon."

She nodded and wiped a tear from her cheek.

Jack said, "And then you lost her. You finally met her, and then she dies. I'm sorry. Really sorry." He held her hand, and they were quiet for a moment in the deep dark, lit by tiny stars. The wind played over their skin with cold fingers.

Eventually he said, "So where have you been living and what have you been doing?"

"I just got here. We were back in that cave getting baptized minutes ago."

His jaw dropped. "How..."

"That's the sort of thing Luke or Oz would understand. I suppose we all came through at different times. What I really want to know is how you changed. When you looked at me in the cave... it was like you were a statue. Did you see your god again? The snake? Was that it?"

The muscles in his arms bunched unconsciously, and something passed over his face like a storm at sea. His sister touched his hand.

Taking a deep breath, he began to speak.

235

Twenty-One

Jack's Ordeal

"When the Head baptized us, I went under that water, but I kept sinking. There was some kind of explosion, and the Head was shrieking as he fell into the void. Eventually I saw that horrible light flowing around the giant corpse's head."

"It wasn't horrible!" Selene gasped. "It was too beautiful for words!"

He paused. "I was still angry and frightened when I saw it. But that's how I remember it."

"Do you know what it was?" Her eyes were wide and hungry.

"I always thought we were seeing the virus the Head had released into the atmosphere."

"I think it was the opposite of that."

"I'd trust your guess more than mine. Anyway, I floated away from it and after a while I realized the water had become sort of green. There was something moving in it. It was huge, Selene. Even its eye was bigger than me, staring at me as it circled me in the water. I could almost feel the strength rippling off of it. Then it started to squeeze me. Everything went dark, and I thought I was going to die. But it sort of unraveled. It wasn't there any more, just giant chunks of its body and disintegrating snake skin. I started floating upward, and pretty soon waves were shoving me up onto the shore. Two brothers helped me to my feet."

"Brothers?"

"Two other students. I'll get to that soon. They were helping me walk along the shore to a stone building while I puked seawater. I turned and saw a giant eye break the surface. It seemed like it was staring right into me. I still have dreams about that sometimes. I think it was trying to kill me, but it died just in time. It just came undone. Then it was staring at me with its last wisp of life and saying, I see you and I know the coward you are. But then the eye capsized in a giant bubble of water and floated out to sea.

"I guess I blacked out, because the next thing I remember is lying on one of our thatch mattresses and hearing the shouts from..." His voice cracked.

Selene sensed that his words were stopping, and gave him a tender smile.

The words started again in bumpy hiccups. "It's all gone. This place is all wrecked. You can't see them now, but there are ruins further up the shore. I left and when I got back... This! Broken buildings and dried blood."

She looked full upon her brother until he turned back to her. His face relaxed a little and he said, "I'm not answering your question. This was a place for people to train, as best they could, to fight the dead and stay alive. You can't kill them, but there are ways to use their strength against them. We would train every day, wrestling and with swords. Then we'd eat a little in the evenings and tell stories."

"Why are you looking at me that way?"

"I think some of them might have been about you. They were about the moon, anyway. I'll tell you later. They made me do work—clean things and stuff like that—but nobody ever talked to me about training until the Master pointed me out to everyone. One group was doing handstand pushups and the other was doing wrist locks." He smiled. "You should have seen it. One brother would grab the other's wrist or shoulder, or just reach for him, the way the Dead do. The other brother would grab it and twist, hardly any movement at all, and the first one would just go flying into the mattresses they laid out on the stone courtyard. Within two years, most of us would be strong enough to throw one of the Dead reaching for you.

"Anyway, our Sensei stopped everyone and pointed to me. 'You see that outsider? He wants to train with us, but he's too frightened.' I was carrying two buckets of water and froze. Everyone stared at me, but no one laughed."

"That was a cruel thing to say," Selene said.

"That's the way he was. I knew he loved me, but nobody's ever been harder on me. I thought he was trying to egg me on at first, but as I just looked at him sitting at the head of the courtyard, I wasn't so sure. I think that's how I remember him best. Him sitting with his stick across his knees in front of his potbelly, his handlebar mustache grinning at me. There was a lot of laughter in that grin, but something wolfish about it too.

"Anyway, I put the buckets down and walked toward the wall where the weapons hung. 'OK,' I said. 'I'll train.' I picked up one of the staffs, about my height. Sensei was still giving me his grin as he nodded to one of the brothers, who turned toward me. I threw him another staff, and he started to twirl it back and forth the way he had been taught. I swung my staff and my brother was lying on the ground holding his arm at a funny angle and clenching a scream between his teeth. The staff the brother had been holding was broken in half. I stared at Sensei and squeezed my fist, and my own staff splintered in my hand. Then I did a goofy kung fu pose and a little yell.

"Sensei was across the courtyard in maybe three paces. I dodged two swings from his cane before the third snapped the side of my head. Everything went blurry and I collapsed onto the ground.

"Holding my head, I gasped, 'See why I don't want to train?'"

"'You want me to agree with your self-pity?' he growled. He was fat and old, but I'd never seen anyone move like him.

"I shouted, 'I'm a freak!'

"He knelt in front of me and stared into my face. 'You think that means you're excused? You think the Dead will leave you alone? You think they'll leave the ones you love alone?'

"I got to my feet and faced him. 'I don't have anyone left," I said. "It'd be a relief if they ate me. You want to beat me, go ahead. I deserve a lot worse.'" I remember being distantly surprised at how cold my voice was.

"Sensei stared at me like a wolf about to bite. Then he told two brothers to take care of the student whose arm I'd broken. He walked toward the big wooden doors at the far end of the courtyard. I realized I'd never seen those doors open. Everyone was staring at me as Sensei gave one of them a push. It swung slowly, groaning, like it would crush whatever stood in its way.

"Sensei turned and looked at me. The serpent's eyeball flashed across my mind.

"I swallowed and looked at my feet and put one step in front of another. When I was outside the doorway, I looked back at the courtyard, our sleeping quarters, and the crashing sea beyond. Most of the brothers had smiles on their faces, as if something good was going to happen. Sensei told me to shut the door. I had to lean against it with both arms and strain for a while before I got it moving. When it was finally closed, I felt totally alone.

"'How did you open that so easily?' I asked Sensei, panting from the effort. I could feel a bump rising on my head where his cane had landed.

"'That is one of the things I hope to teach you,' he said. 'You are already stronger than me, but you do not know how to use it.' He turned to pick his way among the jagged rocks that made up the beginnings of the mountain above us."

Selene looked at her brother with unhurried curiosity, as if she could see the scenes as she heard them.

"I feel like this night is going to last forever," he said.

"It will give us the time we need. But dawn is coming soon. Tell your tale."

Jack did.

*

We climbed all day. Sensei had to wait for me to catch up a lot. If the biting wind bothered him, he never let it show. We met three of the dead, climbing at an angle to catch us. Sensei didn't even put down his cane; a few twists of his wrist, and they were bouncing down into the mist below.

The sun was setting in bloody orange when we reached the cave at the top. I lay on the stone floor and gasped while Sensei gathered a few sticks and put them in a dip in the rock floor. There was a pile of books inside and a long sword leaning against it.

"How did anyone drag books up here?" I asked when I had breath.

Sensei's wrinkled face was lit by a small fire in the middle of the cave. "My father and his men took them up here. He thought it was the safest place for the relics from the old world."

I staggered to my feet and looked down. It was getting dark, but the outlines of the sharp rocks were still visible.

I asked, "What's to stop me from..."

"Nothing. But I doubt it would kill you. You've been touched by Ouroboros, the serpent who encircles the world."

"How did you know?" I asked.

"How did I know about the serpent, or that you had been touched? Because I've seen the serpent before, and because parts of it were floating out to sea when you washed up on shore, and because of your impossible strength. You know there's a rumor going around that you killed it? Why are you laughing?"

"If you really saw it, you'd know how huge it was. Even touching it was something I'll never forget."

"So the rumor is not true, then?" Sensei asked.

"You can drag me up here for who knows what reason, but don't make fun of me."

Sensei's face was rock. "I would never do that, Jack. I'm one of the few who knows the whole story. My grandfather worked at Horus Industries. He knew what they planned, and found a way to keep himself and his family alive when they released the serum that raised the dead. He told my father, and my father told me. But I'm beginning to think you know even less of it than I do, even though you have lived it."

I still stood at the edge. Sensei looked at me with the leaping flames reflected in his eyes. "I see the weakness in you, Jack," he whispered. His voice was as gentle as I had ever heard it. "Look at me."

"I am."

"No," he said. "Stop looking at me as an opponent. Stop looking at me in relation to your own fears. I'm weak too. I'm a traitor. I was a child, maybe nine or ten, when the dead took my father, and I ran."

"That's not treachery. You were just a kid."

"And you'll say the fact my father was yelling at me to run is another strike in my favor. It is treachery. If those who love you need you, you fight. You do not consider the odds against you. If you run, you are a traitor." Then Sensei sighed, and his face softened. "Every one of those students down there has the same story of failure. That's why they're here, to grow strong. But you will remain stunted until you look your failure in the face and admit you can never repay the debt you owe to the people you failed."

"I already told you I deserved death."

"You said that because you wanted me to seal you in your self-pity. Look at me. I see you, and I don't hate you, and none of the brothers do. Or jump, and be alone with yourself forever."

I looked away from Sensei and down the mountain again, to the darkness waiting for me at the bottom.

Sensei said, "At a certain point in their training, I take every student here. There is a pool at the back of this cave. Each student looks into the pool and takes one sip of its water—no more than that, or strange things can happen. I doubt you, who have been immersed in the void beneath the earth, will need to drink anything. But come and look all the same. I warn you that it will be a far harsher ordeal than anything you might suffer in my school. And more difficult than running away by throwing yourself off the mountain."

I stared at Sensei for a moment. If he had not warned me, I'm not sure what I would have done. But when he said that, something twisted inside me. I left the darkness far beneath the mountain and walked past him. The light from the small fire wasn't strong, and with my back to it, I was soon staring into darkness. It felt good.

"I can't see where I'm going," I said.

"Even at full noon," Sensei said, "that part of the cave is dark. Press on."

I took a few more steps and felt water splashing over my feet. In the rippling water, a glowing image appeared.

*

Jack shut his mouth and hung his head. It hurt Selene to see the look on her brother's face. She knew he couldn't say what had happened next. She took his hand, guessing what it was he saw, and knowing she could not utter it for him.

Jack looked at her and whispered, "I saw a lot of things I don't want to talk about, but I will say this: I saw Father standing over a crying boy. Except, the boy's face was Father's, and my face was on the man." The first orange streaks of dawn showed the tears on his cheeks.

Selene gave her brother a luminous smile, knowing her grace would fade when the sun rose. "You saw truly," she said, "but your seeing it prevented it from ever coming true."

Jack shuddered, and the flow of words began again.

*

I walked backwards away from the pool and turned around. Sensei was still sitting at the fire. Not looking at me. Looking like he could sit there forever and be content.

I got the sword from next to the bookshelf, went to Sensei, and got on my knees in front of him. Pressing my forehead into the cold floor, I held the sword out to him.

"I will not do it."

"I'm a monster," I said. My tears dripping into little pools on the stone floor. "I killed my sister, and it's just as well she got away from me. I'm worse than the Dead. They just caught a disease and changed. I... I'm my father."

"And your father was an evil man, I see. And thus we see your choice. You can become a brute like your father. Or you can accept my invitation, and become truly strong."

(Jack paused, his face as radiant as it had been horrified just a moment before. "Sometimes it feels like I'm still there, my knees stinging on the floor, the earth spinning beneath me," he said to his sister.

"In a sense, you are," Selene said.

"You can see everything I'm telling you, can't you?"

"The moon is above us," Selene said. "I can see what it means to you.")

Still on my knees, I craned my neck up at Sensei. I couldn't speak.

"You wish to be a great warrior," he said.

"I am a coward."

"Yes. But you could have thrown yourself off this cliff. Why didn't you?"

The world seemed to hold its breath as his question echoed through me. "I want to see the darkness for what it is.

The terrible secret at the heart of the world. And you said I couldn't find it at the bottom of the mountain. You said I could find it right here."

"Did you?"

"I think so. Kind of."

"Are you sorry you looked in that pool?"

"No. I would do it again."

"Then," Sensei said, "you are a great warrior."

"I am a great warrior." Only after I said it did I realize it was true.

"You have never told this to anyone."

"No."

"It is a secret you carry deep within you, too precious to share," Sensei said. "And no matter how many times you leave it behind, it never leaves you."

"Yes. I wish to be a noble and valorous warrior." It somehow seemed appropriate to stay on my knees.

"Do you understand, brother, that our way lies in death?"

"I thought our way lay in escaping death. For ourselves and others."

"Yes. But to do that, you must face death and feel its cold breath on you every day. And you must accept that everyone loses in the end. Death will come for you soon enough. You cannot fight unless you remember that."

"Then there's no point fighting," Jack said. "I may as well stay a coward."

Sensei looked at me sharply. "Is that what you want?"

"No."

"But you cannot give yourself a reason to keep fighting?"

I nodded.

Sensei sighed. "Are your knees hurting yet?"

"I can't feel them."

"Then sit up."

I sat opposite him by the fire, holding the sword in my lap. He stared at the fire for a while. It felt like the world had given up holding its breath and had just stopped breathing.

"Do you know how I started this custom of bringing students up here and having them look in the pool? It was an accident. I came up here years ago by myself. I was going to leave and I didn't want to be followed. So I thought I would wait here for a while and let my students search for me. After a while, they'd give up and I'd be on my way."

"You were going to leave? Why?"

"For a while I told myself rebuilding the world was possible. That's what we were fighting for. Even if we couldn't reconquer the world, we could carve out a place for families to live safely. But it wasn't long before I knew it for a lie. The more babies born, the more we are adding to the ranks of the dead. We will never outnumber them, ever. Eventually all human life will stop. As a result, it does not matter if we are courageous now. Whether we fight or not, we lose in the end. And yet, like you, I did not want to stop fighting. I could not. But I had no reason to give myself, and so my desire felt absurd. I turned the matter over and over in my mind while I waited in this cave and became more certain of my decision. But after a few days, one of my older students climbed up here, looking for me. My father had carried these books up here with his friends, to store relics from the old world. That student had known about it. We fought and I threw him to the back of the cave. He stayed back there, in the darkness, quiet, where I couldn't see him. I waited for him, thinking it was a trick; but after a long time, he walked past me without even looking at me and started climbing down. I never saw him again." Sensei's face clouded. "Another whose blood is on my hands. I didn't know what he had been doing, so I walked back there. And I saw something in the pool."

"What? What did you see?"

"I saw death. I thought I had faced the inevitability of the Dead swallowing everything. But I saw it as I never had before. And I saw you, Jack, right in the middle of it."

I gaped. Nothing he could have said would have surprised me more.

"Why do you think people see visions when they look in that water?" Sensei asked. "The pool must be deep. Very deep, reaching past the bottom of the world, past the order of time and space. I suspect there are other pools like it, after what the Head has done. Every time I go back, I see the same thing. I never remember everything. But I remember death swallowing all. And I see you, surrounded, fighting, fighting death and fighting in death. And I saw..."

"You saw me die?" I asked. "That's what you saw?"

"I do not need a vision to know we both will die. And I did not see it in any case. But..."

"But, but Sensei, if I'm going to die and join the Dead, just like you, how can I do anything now that matters?"

"I do not know. As I was trying to say, no matter how many times I look, I cannot quite remember what I see. One sees beyond all time and space in that pool, so one's mind cannot organize what one sees. But I know you are different, Jack. All of your brothers fight and die. For all of us, these two are very close. For you, they may be even closer. That is all the guidance I can give you. Will you walk this path?"

"Sensei," I whispered, "it is too much."

"Yes. But do you wish to see that darkness at the heart of the world?"

"More than ever."

"Then I have little else I can teach you. Now stand up."

I did, and Sensei embraced me, and said gruffly, "Thank you. Because of you, I did not give in to cowardice and run. Because of you, I have a reason to fight."

I was glad he was hugging me then so he would not see the shame on my face, that someone like him would say something like that to me.

He let me go and looked at the sword on the ground. "I give every student who survives their ordeal a gift," he said. "Surely this sword is to be yours."

I took the long handle in both hands and flicked it around like a stick. One half of the blade flowed with cloudy blue, another with milky white.

"My father brought that sword up here with his books," Sensei said. "He said it had been touched by a god." When I gave him a questioning look, he said, "He looked in the pool in the back of the cave often." He laughed quietly. "He said one could see far in it because it reached so deep, like a man at the bottom of a well seeing stars clearly which are invisible to others."

We talked into the night, and I began to see more the man he was, not the pillar of strength I had known before. As the conversation drifted toward sleep, he said the only thing I've ever heard that never made sense to me. He told me that even if I had thrown myself over the edge, he wouldn't have loved me any less.

We slept on the hard cave floor that night. Or, after he started snoring, I crept to the mouth of the cave and looked over the darkened world and the cold stars above, and wondered where my darkness lay, and what fighting it might mean. I started training the next day.

Jack stopped talking and his eyes fell. The brightening dawn glowed orange on his face.

Selene said, "Something grieves you." She drew in her breath sharply. "Your community was destroyed, wasn't it? Otherwise you'd be there now." She turned to the buildings behind them further up the shore. "It was right here, wasn't it? This was your home."

He sighed. "It's a long story. Sensei would send us out, once we had finished training. You may not like this next part."

"I doubt it can be worse than the things I've seen over the last few weeks."

"He never forced any of us. But he did tell us that if we left by any other way, we'd be weaker for it, and he was right. There was a pit beneath our building with tunnels. All of them eventually opened miles away from our compound."

"And the dead were down there, weren't they?"

The look he gave her was answer enough.

"That's cruel," Selene said. "But it was necessary, wasn't it?"

"It's crueler to send us out only to succumb later. After that, facing one of the dead out in the open was never as frightening. If one of us made it out, they'd come back and wave to everyone else, waiting along the wall, and we'd all cheer."

He paused, and she saw, in the fading light of the moon, the long, dark corridors he had crept through, flinching whenever he heard hissing, turning and twisting whenever he felt the grip of dead fingers on his arms to pin the dead thing to the ground and run. She saw the part of her twin that had

249

begged him to go back and plead with his brothers to let him up through the trap door, and saw as well the part of him that would have rather joined the dead than give in.

After a moment, she asked, "You said you were sent out?"

"There are different wells where things still grow. Everything is white now. The Head really did kill the world. But there are little oases where plants can grow. Sometimes pockets of humans live there and keep gardens and dig places underground to sleep and hide from the dead. We were sent to find these places, protect and help them any way we could, and tell them about the Head and what he did."

"Why..."

"Why would they need to be told? I don't know exactly how long I was in the void, but most of the humans still alive were born after the disaster. Hardly any of them know what really happened."

"Why did you come back?"

"The first oasis I came to, they tried to kill me when I wouldn't join their group. They were keeping slaves and trying to worship the Flowers. The next group I found was similar, except I realized that they hated the groups next to them as much as they were hated by them. I didn't know what else to do, so I went back to tell Sensei what was happening and ask his advice." He shook his head. "I haven't really told you what it was like to be with my brothers. The evenings were the best. We'd tell stories. Some were serious, but some were so funny my sides would hurt as I laughed. And do you know that when I got back, I heard the brother whose arm I had broken wanted to talk to me? I got ready to be contrite and apologetic. But when he saw me, his arm still in a sling, he just smiled and shook my hand and said he wanted to train with me as soon as he was better. That's the kind of place it was."

Selene gave him a smile. "So you came back to find the only real home you'd ever had in ruins," she said, turning to see the rubble of buildings behind them. "And your father and brothers dead." His face hardened, and she looked long on the cold, dark currents, deep beneath the surface of his face. "Is that why you pledged yourself to protect me when you saw me? Something new to fight for?"

He nodded. "I still will." His face was a storm at midnight.

"Jack," she said, "we've all changed. All of us were touched, and being in the void activated whatever was put into us. I'm something of a guide."

"Your face shines in the moonlight."

"Yes. I can see in dark places. I know this sounds silly, but I can sort of see the world now. Like the image of the moon in the daytime sky, I can see the miles and miles of the Flowers. But Jack, I don't know how to guide you. What can I say that your master hasn't already? And how are you supposed to fight the Flowers? Or the Head? They're both stronger than you."

His hands flexed. He said, "Yes."

"Then what can I say to help?"

They sat in the rising sunlight and said nothing for a long time.

Eventually she looked down the long line of the shore. Two figures stood near the crashing waves. The long blonde hair of the one caught the sunlight in fiery curls. The other stood in what looked like a rippling black coat. She stood and walked toward them, knowing her brother would follow.

*

Jack and Selene stood before Masaaki and Luke in silence. Luke looked back and forth between the twins with tenderness in his eyes, as if he wanted to speak but was too shy. He shifted from foot to foot but didn't look away. Their Japanese friend was calm as ever, standing within curling black smoke as Japanese characters and images of humans and the dead played over his white skin. Jack reached out and shook Luke's hand; Luke seemed to relax a little.

Masaaki said, "I have found the others. I will bring us together."

"Is there anything we can do?" Selene asked.

"I do not know," Masaaki said. The darkness folded over him and he disappeared.

Luke's eyes were flitting back and forth between Selene's face and her feet. She smiled at him and waited for him to speak. When he did, the words were almost lost in the noise of the waves: "It's good to see you again, Selene. Is it..."

"Is it good for me to see you?" She looked paler and smaller than ever in the morning light, compared to the fiery athlete who stood opposite her. "Yes, Luke. I am glad to see you."

TWENTY-TWO

The Healer

In the dark cavern, Nameless let herself be led toward the infinite abyss by dead hands. Her skin crawled at their touch, but she didn't pull away. The glowing man above her was ranting about his power and the new world he had made, the new world they would soon join him in ruling. The fool thought she was going to serve him, but Nameless knew she would soon be gone. Nothing could survive the void, not even the being she had thought of as her mother. Everything came from the void, and everything returned. She was going home. It was the way of all living things.

She stepped into the cold lapping waves. Soon the water was at her waist. She closed her eyes as they leaned her back and the water closed over her head. She began to sink. A muffled boom sounded above the water, and a scream that sounded like the Head's voice. Nameless didn't open her eyes. Perhaps his time had come as well.

She sank deeper, waiting for oblivion. She wondered if it would happen all at once, or if she would feel her consciousness unravel in slow tendrils in the water. The pain of her violation, a pain which followed her every day, grew large within her and burst like a firework into glowing embers.

She felt those still-burning embers sink deep within her and was glad she would not have to carry her pain much longer.

She sank. She waited.

Some time later, she realized she was still waiting. She felt her eyelids open, but the unbroken darkness was the same. She wasn't cold. If she was still sinking, she couldn't feel it. She felt a jab of fear. In the old world, where her name had been Cindy, she had seen a TV show where government agents had blindfolded a prisoner and made him listen to random sounds. After ten minutes, they took off the head-phones. The prisoner was weeping and had thought it had been an hour.

How long had she been down here? Minutes? Years?

She started to struggle. She felt her arms and legs moving, but there was no water for her to push against. And even if she could have moved, where would she go? To the world above, ruled by men?

Faint light fluttered beneath her. It looked small at first, so that she felt like a bloated giant above it; but then she realized it was huge, and only looked small because of her distance from it. She moved toward it, a comet pulled to a star.

She saw wings of light enfolding a dark planet. The globe opened like one of the Flowers and hissed without noise, as if to consume the light embracing it, but the great light only continued its great gentle strokes. Her arms and legs stiffened in terror as she realized how wrong she had been, how coldly and narrowly she had imagined the Mother-Love which hovered over the face of the deep. How she had dishonored the Mother-Spirit! Nameless felt the dogma she had nursed against the world of men slip away from her like a ragged doll she had treasured as a child.

One of the waves of light moved toward Nameless. Fear choked her. But instead of a blow, the wave flowed through her in peace, pure peace.

*

If she had floated as a speck in front of the light for years, it still would not have been long enough; but eventually her slow orbit took her down and away from the great wings of light. Something in her wanted to try to stay, but she sensed it would have been ungrateful to struggle. She drifted, content.

The water began to lighten. Far above, she saw a wavy circle of pale light. She realized it was the sun and wondered if it would ever look the same after the light she had seen. Beneath her, a stain of bloody red spread slowly outward. She felt anger radiating from it and thought of Mason. She remembered the contempt she had held for the man, but felt none of it.

As she floated, she saw something beneath the blur of red: a yellow cloud which crackled lightning. And in the center, a single, pulsing eye.

A wave moved inside Nameless, and the sweetness of the great Mother-Spirit breathed in her. Not knowing how she moved so swiftly through the water, she dropped until she could grab the mass of moving red. Her hand sunk into it like hot tar. It burned her skin, but she didn't let go. She pulled Mason up toward the surface.

She looked back once and saw the cloud of lightning rising behind her.

*

Her head broke the surface of the water. She grabbed the circle of stone around her and pulled herself out of the well and collapsed to the stone floor, coughing water from her lungs. When she finally sat up, she saw that the red thing had pulled itself out as well. It sat on the other side of the well, water streaming from its spongy sides.

She was surrounded by muscular women dressed in rags. One of the women, old and bent, pointed a long, wrinkled claw toward her. The woman's other hand gripped a long staff. The trinkets hanging from her neck tinkled.

The ground beneath Nameless trembled.

"Bring them," the old woman hissed. Nameless could not tell whether it was fear or joy in her voice, and didn't have time to wonder, for rough hands were pulling her to her feet and away from the well and across white grass which crumbled beneath her steps like ash. When she stumbled at another tremor, her guards squeezed her arms and dragged her.

A loud crack sounded. She turned and saw four more women dragging a gooey red mass, wincing as if it burned their hands. Behind them, a split appeared in the earth, moving from the well and across the white field toward a sparkling lake. The split widened and a long golden arm reached out of the crack, its flesh sagging. The huge dome of a head appeared with a single vivid eye in its forehead.

The women pulling Nameless began to run. A trap door in the ground opened for them and they tumbled down a flight of stairs. Rough hands threw her in the corner of a dark, dirty room.

A series of narrow slits had been dug in the underground

chamber. The women (and a few men) crowded around to look, but the windows were high enough for Nameless to look through them. She saw great yellow limbs drag the sagging torso of the giant past their hiding spot. Electricity crackled up and down its body. Then it was lost to their sight.

*

Nameless and the red thing were herded further into the bowels of the underground shelter and thrown into a small room. A sheet metal door closed the only entrance. She heard urgent female voices whispering just outside and knew the prison was guarded. She moved to sit against the far wall of her prison, exhausted.

The red thing glowed in the darkness next to her. Sitting against the wall, she saw the human form within the melting blubber. Its long mouth opened in wordless moan. Then it moaned again, a single, long word: "Ha-ate."

"You're Mason, aren't you?"

A look of purest misery passed over the thing's three eyes, its long mouth, the long slit of a nose. "Sti-ill Mason," it warbled.

She crawled to the red thing and sat opposite it. "I saw something when I was in the void," she said. "I saw what I had always believed in, and saw how badly I had believed in it. It touched me, and I felt how loved I was, even though I was hurt, and trying to hide it by being strong."

An echo of that light washed over her, and she placed her palms on the thing's face.

*

Remember, she told herself, remember what you saw, as she felt the void churning inside Mason, remember the spiraling petals of light, as the chaos rose from within Mason and stung her hands, remember, remember how it loved the dead world, remember through her hands kissing the hatred inside Mason.

*

She pulled her hands away and crossed her arms and squeezed her hands under her armpits. When the burning lessened a little, she looked at the red giant. His third eye had receded into his skull so that only a bump remained. His mouth and nose, though still long, were no longer flat slits. He was still two or three sizes bigger than the man she had known, but his skin glowed red only faintly.

Mason took deep, slow breaths, as if recovering from a run. When he spoke, the metallic, grating tone in his voice had faded enough for Nameless to hear his old voice. "Who are you?"

"I'm the girl from your camp. The one who lost her name."

"The angry one? The one who... who had been hurt?"

She winced, glad Mason couldn't see her. "Yes," she said.

More panting in the darkness. Then: "You were glowing. Glowing white. What did you do to me?"

"I tried to help you."

"Why? You hate me."

She gave him a smile which few men see and none deserve. "Because of the Mother-Spirit who let me see her and who touched me," she said. "And because of the story you told when that tribe locked us up. About the girl you were trying to save when her father shot her in front of you. I don't think you heard it, but I heard your sadness as you spoke. And because... because if people got treated the way they deserve, we'd all be dead pretty quick."

"I wanted to die. I talked to Luke, and I went back to the void to die, to see the Head and die with him. It was working. I was coming undone. You pulled me up, didn't you? How did you know it was me down there? I didn't even know myself."

"I've been different ever since I was touched by the earth goddess. The one the Head made. I could tell it was you."

"The fever is gone," Mason said. "I can still feel it, back there, but I can think. You're amazing. Thank you."

The red-haired girl smiled again. Without thinking, she reached a hand to touch her belly. When the red god's quick eyes saw it, she dropped it to her side and looked away.

There was a scraping sound as the sheet metal door was moved aside. The bent figure of the old woman stepped into their prison, the trinkets on her neck clinking. Nameless thought again of the Mother-Spirit embracing her dead world, and wondered what the long, hard years of survival might have done to these women, and what they might do to her.

Twenty-Three

The Matriarchy

Nameless blinked in the dim light as she looked up at their captors. The old woman leaned on her staff and seemed about to speak, but stopped when she saw Mason. A motion of her head brought a candle from one of the women behind her. She snapped her fingers on the wick and it caught light. The woman stared at the giant in the flickering light. Her skull was visible under her papery skin. She blew the candle out and handed it back to the woman.

"What do you to have to offer me and my tribe?" she asked in the darkness. Her voice was the wind whistling over white bones.

From the midst of his steady breathing, Mason shifted his massive frame and chuckled. "What makes you think we got something to offer you?"

"I summoned you," the old woman said. "I was leading our tribe in the ritual of the seventh day. My knowledge of the deep summoned you." When he chuckled again, the witch thumped her staff against the dirt floor. "Don't trifle with me!"

He lumbered to his feet and stepped toward the old woman. Red light glistened over his thick arms like sweat.

260

Stooping within the dark prison, his glow deepened. "Gimme a reason not to," he murmured.

The witch nodded again. One of the guards stepped forward with a long knife in her hand. Although the fear in her face was plain, she walked toward Mason, raised the knife, and brought it down on his wide chest. The metal bent and melted onto the floor in bubbling ribbons. The woman dropped the handle and stepped back, eyes wide.

Her face covered in darkness, the witch said, "I am the leader of this tribe. I know the secrets of the deep. I know who the dead are, and what they mean. I know of the Head, and of the Six she appointed to rule. I know of their rebellion against her. And I know that one day she will return to rule again. That is why we honor her as Seventh and offer a sacrifice on every seventh day in her well."

"Uh, it's a he," Mason said. "The Head."

The witch laughed. "So all men think."

The red-haired girl couldn't help herself. "What sacrifice?"

"Many years ago, our mothers found one of the dead pinned beneath a rock in a cave. They built their home around this prize. Its fingers grab and its mouth still bites, but every seventh day, the smallest piece of its flesh is cut from it and dropped into the void with our prayers. The wise among us, of whom I am chief, are allowed to go and sit with it and learn wisdom. And when one of us has proved herself worthy through a lifetime of service to the tribe, she eats of the smallest portion from it, and leaves the cave to join the dead who live in the light of the new world. It is said that our body will not be consumed entirely before our Head returns."

"So did you know that was him, crawling past us, all giant-like?" Mason asked.

The witch was silent and perfectly still for a moment. The women behind her shifted. The witch thumped her staff again and hissed, "Silence!" even though none of them had spoken.

Mason turned to Nameless. "You're comin' with me," he said.

Nameless took a deep breath as she got to her feet and stood behind him. To the witch, he growled, "Take it from me: don't listen to the Head or anything the corpse tells you. I've seen the Head. I even said I'd serve him. He's crazy and he don't care about you."

He looked at the women standing behind the shaman. "Who are you gonna believe, me or her? You can kill her, but you can't kill me." It occurred to Nameless that he was doing to this tribe what he had done many times before in police stations: turning suspects against one another.

"I'm leavin' now," said Mason, "and if anyone takes a stab at me or my friend here, I'll kill 'em."

The women at the door of their prison parted, and Mason and Nameless walked through the doorway to see a dirty chamber with longer tunnels extending in different directions. Other women stood, and a few men huddled and stared as they walked past.

He retraced their steps to the wooden doorway outside. He reached to open it, but Nameless said, "No, Mason. You'll burn it and leave them open to the Flowers." She walked in front of him and pushed it open and walked out into the wind and blinding sunlight.

They walked, but Nameless soon looked back at the faces huddled in the still-open tunnel. Mason asked her what was wrong.

"We've upset the order of their tribe."

"Worshipping the dead ain't no order."

"I know," she said, still looking at the cave they had left. "But after what you did, I'm not sure that old woman will be safe. And even if she is, that's no life for them, even in this world."

She walked back to the trapdoor and called, "Let my sister the witch, who knows the mysteries of the deep, come out and talk with me." She waited a few breaths before the old woman poked her head out of the trapdoor and limped toward them. One hand squeezed a long wound on her arm. Blood trickled through her fingers.

Nameless spoke loudly enough for those inside the cave to hear. "You know about the Head and how this new world was created. You have kept your tribe safe, in a sense. Your people will probably be worse off without you. But would it mean anything to you if I told you you should not pray to the Head? He cannot hear you, and his help will only hurt you."

The witch looked at the ground.

Nameless looked back to the opening of the cave. "You," she called. "Brother, with the scar. Come to me." A single face among many crammed in the doorway cringed in fear, but the man walked out of his cave, crouching low and dragging one hand on the ground so he could sprinkle white dust on his bald head as he approached.

"We do not allow our men to go above ground," the witch said softly. "It is too dangerous."

Nameless was about to tell her to shut up, but the words died in her mouth as she realized she was risking the lives of them both: if any of the dead came along, she would not be able to protect the man who was bowing before her or the witch who was jealous of her.

Her red curls moving in the gentle breeze, she told the man to stand. He did, but would not meet her eyes. Her fingers traced the scar which started on the man's temple and ended below his jaw. In a flash, she saw the knife descending toward her own face, and the rage of the wife who held it. The pain of the cut and the long years of the man's shame washed over her. She felt as well how much more frightened this man was of the goddess who had commanded him to come out into this strange new place than he was of his wife.

Nameless pulled back, and the man fell backwards into a sitting position. His scar was gone. She picked up a withered piece of vegetation. When she handed it to the man, it was a flower in full bloom, vivid against the endless white. The man contemplated it with wide, glassy eyes.

Eventually the witch made a noise and moved her head, and the man blinked, got to his feet, and walked back to the cave. The other men and women watched him with unhidden wonder, parting for him as he descended.

Nameless turned back to the witch. She had her head down. Nameless walked close to her and whispered, "I know what it's like to taste power and not really understand it. The Head is no god. I've seen Mother-Spirit that gives life to everything. If you knew how much she loved even you... Treat your people better. Especially your men. You may see her eventually if you do." She thought of the hatred she used to have for men, and what she had seen. She whispered, "And you may see her anyway." The witch gave her a sharp look.

Nameless turned and walked away. Mason walked beside her.

They hadn't taken many steps when they heard a shout

behind them. She turned and saw the women of the tribe streaming out of the doorway. Some had surrounded the witch and were striking her; the witch cried out again as she fell to the ground and threw her arms around her head. More women were running toward Nameless.

Nameless heard Mason grunt. She said, "Don't hurt them."

The women surrounded her. The red giant was left outside the circle; none of the women looked at him or even seemed to be aware of him. "Come, goddess," one of them said. "Rule us."

"You have your witch," she said. She heard the old woman cry again and tried to look past the women to where the witch was, but couldn't see her.

"You will rule us," another said. The circle started to walk, herding her back to their cave.

"Don't hurt her!" she said.

None of the women replied, but Mason growled, "I ain't leaving her."

She looked back at him. "My friend comes with me!" she shouted. The women in the circle looked at each other as they walked. No one said anything, but the circle opened. Mason moved to walk beside Nameless.

As they herded her through the door, she looked back to see the witch, bloodied and crawling on the ground toward them. She groaned and reached out with a shaky arm. Behind her, a tall figure stood. Nameless gasped and felt her heart flutter inside her chest. Then the door to the compound was shut.

The green-eyed goddess looked at the captors surrounding her wildly. "Did you see her? The other one? Who was she?"

One of the women said, "We see them from time to time. The Walkers. No one has ever spoken to them. But now we have you."

Nameless said, "Your leader. We have to help her. She'll die out there."

"You are worthy. She is not."

She crossed her arms. "Not if you treat people like this."

The women surrounding them became very still. The cave suddenly felt cold and dark. Without a word between them, the women circled the pair again and walked them back to the room they had been imprisoned in.

When they reached the door, Mason growled, "I ain't goin' back in there."

Nameless whispered in a rush, "Mason, I'm asking you not to hurt them."

He gave her a long look and walked inside. She followed.

After the door locked, a voice said, "Think about the wisdom you have to share with us. Think about how you can lead us in worship. Think about how the giant might be a good sacrifice for us. Tell the guards outside your door when you are ready." Footsteps walked away.

In the dull glow of Mason's heat, they looked at each other.

"I can bust us outta here no problem," he said. "But you won't let me, will you? So what do you want to do?"

"I don't want to stay here. They're asking me to lead them, but they already know what they want. But if we try to leave, either they'll get hurt or we will." She dropped her head into her hands. "The old world was bad, but this is worse. Women get a chance to rule, and this is what we come up with."

They sat.

Mason rumbled, "Even if we could get out, what would we do? You can at least heal people, but what can I do? Burn stuff?"

"Healing people won't matter much when they just die anyway." She stiffened. "Who's there?"

The darkness seemed to concentrate itself in the corner of their cell. A thin, pale ghost appeared within it. "My friends," it said. "I finally found you. The void is dense here."

"Masaaki!" Nameless gasped.

"Mason," Masaaki said, "you are better. I am glad. The others are assembling on the shore of an ocean thousands of miles from here. Let me bring you there."

"How are you going to do that?" Nameless asked.

"I have been given control of the void. We will cross the distance easily."

The burning demigod stood. Nameless got to her feet and started to scratch on the dirt wall of their prison.

"Do we even know if they can read?" Mason asked.

Nameless said, "No," without turning around. When she was finished, she turned toward Masaaki. "Is this... will this be frightening? Going back to the void?"

"I am not sure. I am at home there. And I will be with you."

The darkness surrounding Masaaki enfolded them.

*

The flame-haired goddess sank, feeling that Mason and Masaaki were still near. The world faded into a shimmering mirage, as if it were a window, and the tears of the Mother

Spirit were running down it. Nameless saw plain and mountain and forest and sea, and the dead wandering everywhere, and the humans who tried to hide and always failed in time. She saw the great white tree near their camp, and how deep its roots ran, and how many other trees were like it. A wild hope flared in her, and she looked for the light of the Mother Spirit; but she saw only the void, around and beneath them, storming and trying to become an agony. She looked away from it, and saw, in the middle of the world, an ugly tower of wood and steel, with Flowers swarming over it like ants. Then Masaaki was pulling her up and she was sitting on cold sand.

TWENTY-FOUR

I'm Sorry

Billowing black smoke appeared and pulled back to reveal a young woman with glowing green eyes and red hair, a smoldering red giant, and a moth in human form. Some distance away, a woman with pale skin and jet black hair was walking toward them, waving. Behind her, a bald man, a muscular man with golden-tinged skin, and a man carrying a sword ran toward them. They stood on the endless shore of the crashing ocean. None of them smiled. The wind blew over the sand dunes.

Mason stared at the people he had shared a camp with in another life. The skin on Luke's muscular arms and legs was golden like his hair. Tiny stalks of electricity walked up and down his arms. For the first time, Mason saw no shiftiness in his face. Selene's pale face seemed almost to hang above her body; Mason blinked when he realized he had been staring at her too long. Jack stood with bare chest to the biting wind; Mason knew that if he were to rush Jack, Jack would spring out of the way easily. Oz sat on the beach with legs crossed, a perfect statue.

"Friends," Masaaki said, "what is wrong?"

"Six days you have been gone," said Selene.

"We didn't know if you were comin' back," said Luke.

The spectre dropped to his knees. "My friends, I am sorry. I will no longer travel through the void unless I must. I remember now what Ezekiel said..."

"There's somethin' else," Luke said.

"What is it?" Mason asked.

He motioned with his hand. They followed.

There was a pit in the sand which had been dug about three feet deep, and something inside. Sand had crusted onto the side of its head. The white feelers coming out of its neck had been tied in a knot, as had the feelers coming out of the stumps where most of its tentacles had been. Only two tentacles remained. They waved weakly, occasionally touching the sand to rock the head back and forth.

Jack said, "It dragged itself here soon after you left." He seemed to be trying not to vomit.

"All seven," the thing rasped. "So lovely, so lovely. You glow within the gray."

Nameless stammered, "What does..."

"It came to make us an offer," Oz said.

"Why would they decapitate one of their own?" Masaaki asked.

"Won't say," Luke said. "My guess is if they sent a whole one, it wouldn't be able to help tryin' to eat us."

"So hungry," the head hissed. Three black tongues flicked in the sand. "So empty. It is going to summon our Head from his home. You will help. Then we will worship."

"Is it talking about itself?" Oz asked.

Luke said, "They say 'it' when they're talkin' about themselves, or all of 'em."

"You will help," the head said. "You will come to the center. You will join it, all of it there. Then it will summon our

Father from below, and it will worship him. So hungry."

"Your Head is gone," Luke said. "Good as dead. He ain't never comin' back."

"Dead?" the blind thing hissed.

"Uh..." Nameless said. "Can we talk where that thing can't hear us?" She glanced at Mason, but his dark eyes were fixed on the thing in the pit.

"Dead?" the thing on the sand asked again.

"What part of dead don't you understand?" Luke asked.

"I am death," it said. "If the Head is dead, where is he?"

No one had anything to say to that.

"We should have gotten rid of this thing a long time ago," Oz whispered to Luke.

"I will carry this thing to the ocean," Masaaki said. "It will sink to the void and may dissolve there."

"Come, come to the center. Join it. It will worship the Head, and you will be worshipped too."

Masaaki stepped forward, but Mason whispered, "Wait." He walked forward. Water ran down his scaly red cheeks and hissed when it hit the sand. He knelt in front of the pit.

"Who were you before you died?" he whispered. The thing's tongues flicked out of its mouth like snakes being crushed; it rocked back and forth on its two tiny arms in excitement.

"She was in love," it hissed. "She would marry in a month. So in love. The whole world sang for her." The thing paused, then said in a slightly different but still reptilian voice, "So sad, so sad I was. All I had was money. All I ate. Now I am eaten." Then: "Mommy? Are you there? Why doesn't it hurt?"

"Are you in pain?"

"None of us are alive. There is no pain."

The giant turned to Masaaki. His face was a volcano about to erupt. Masaaki floated forward, picked the mutilated thing up in his white hands, and moved toward the waves. Mason watched Death move toward the ocean, his shoulders shaking as he wept silently. Nameless went and stood beside him, putting her hand on his shoulder. A hissing sounded when her skin touched his, but if it hurt her, she didn't show it. Selene saw her brother's eyes grow wide as he watched. Jack glanced at his sister and forced his face into a mask.

*

Masaaki floated back toward them. He said, "My friends, I did not see the Head in the void. And now I remember I did not see him there when I brought Mason and the Nameless one back to us."

"You can see to the bottom?" Luke asked.

"And past it. It is my domain."

"There's something deeper than the void?"

"Yes. But where is the Head?"

Nameless' vivid green eyes were wide as she murmured, "It's my fault." She suddenly looked very small compared to her friends, who waited quietly for her to speak. Eventually she said, "I'm so sorry for how I treated you in the camp. I'm sorry I gave up and let the Head drown me. I thought it would kill me and I'd be free of him."

"Each one of us is sorry," Selene said, looking around. "None is free of guilt. But we're still here. And we're glad that you are here."

Nameless took a deep breath and said, "My name is Rachel. That's not the name my parents gave me. But the old earth goddess, the slave of the Head who touched me, said I was Eve and Isis and Rachel. And that's what I should be called. I can make things grow. And I'm..." Her eyes fell and her hand went to her belly.

Selene gasped. "You're pregnant?"

She nodded.

"Who you bin sleepin' with?" Luke asked. Rachel shook her head.

"From the... from your attack?" Selene asked. Her voice was gentleness itself.

No tears came from her eyes, but the lines of her lovely face were etched in pain. "And I love him. My baby son, inside me. I can feel him. I am a mother." Cold, salty air from the sea brushed her red hair as she spoke, as if the gray clouds were ready to weep.

Oz said, "I know how improbable it is, but there may be a hospital still standing which may have..."

She gave a heartbreaking smile. "Life, Oz," she said.

"We need to get you vitamins," Selene said in a rush. "Somewhere we can find..."

"Sister," Rachel said, "I can feel him inside me. When I touch dead plants, they turn green. When I touched Mason, he returned to himself. It's the power the old goddess gave me. I know my son is healthy. I can still see the colors, but I can see now that they're blurry, like the Mother Spirit is weeping over how the Head violated her children. I know that Mother-Love wants to bring life out of this. So that's what I want, too." She paused, and said, "When I was being raped, I tried to beat the man at his own game. This way is better."

They sat for a while as the waves crashed on the beach

and the cold wind played over their skin. Oz sniffed and turned away as tears streamed down his face. "I'm sorry," he said, his back turned and shoulders shuddering. "My daughter took her own life in my previous existence, and it was my fault. Mostly. Masaaki talked with me about it, and something inside me opened up and I can't shut it."

"We are your friends," Selene said. "You honor us."

He turned back to the group. Selene gasped when she saw his face; but then the pain passed, like a summer shower blowing itself out. "You are my friends, too," he said. "And Rachel, you are a brave and noble woman." Rachel favored him with a deep smile. "Now, what did you say about Mason?"

The red man growled, "After I stabbed you all in the back and told the Head I'd be his right hand man, I sank into that stinking watery stuff like we all did. When I came to, I was in a desert. I wandered for a while and found the corpse of the board member I was replacing." He paused, and his huge, ruby head fell. "I thought the Head had won. All I wanted was something to punish. I thought it'd be satisfying. It wasn't.

"Eventually I found Luke, and he told me the Head was down there, in the void. So I fell in. To kill him or join him or both, I dunno. Then Nameless here... I mean Rachel, she dragged me up. I was mostly blubber after being in the void so long, but Rachel touched my face, and..." His voice grew soft. "I know I still look like a monster, but at least I can think straight."

"So how does the Head fit into this?" Luke asked.

"After the Head put me in the void," Rachel said, "I saw Mason floating down there. Beneath him was a mess of arms and a huge yellow eye. I grabbed Mason and pulled. We came up through a well, and the Head followed us. The earth split, and the Head dragged himself out."

"How come he didn't come out sooner?" Mason asked.

"He can't think down there," Luke said. "That's what he told me, anyhow. He mustah been followin' Mason."

The group stared at Luke.

"Hey, I ain't in cahoots with that psycho," he said. "Him comin' back is worse than the dead wanderin' everywhere. You know he's gonna try to make us his slaves again."

"Maybe not," Mason said. "He's gigantic now. I think he can barely survive up here. I got a glimpse of his face. I dunno how coherent he'll be."

"Maybe he's coming back to himself," Luke said. "Maybe he'll be stronger than ever. Maybe he's organizing the Flowers, and they're all comin' for us right now."

"The Head is not doing that, but..." Oz said. He seemed about to speak again, but closed his mouth. When he saw everyone looking at him, he said, "The Dead have surrounded this whole beach. They've been standing there since their little messenger came. They haven't moved." Mason opened his mouth to say something, but Oz waved a hand. "How do I know? I can move faster than any of you. And I can be silent when I wish. The Dead have the beach surrounded. I don't believe they are offering us a choice."

Jack asked, "What did their messenger mean, go with them? How are they going to summon the Head?"

Luke said, "I'm pretty sure that when they say 'worship' they mean eat. Otherwise, I have no idea."

"We can't possibly accompany them," Oz said.

"Why not?" Luke asked. "I ain't disagreein' with you. Jus' trying to think it through."

"It'll end in death. With them, it always does."

"We may not need to eat any time soon," Luke said, "but Zeke never said we could live forever. And we can't drink the seawater."

Silence. The wind blew. The waves whispered of decay and loss as they broke and washed away, broke and washed away.

Mason turned and looked at the horizon of the sea. "I've got some things I want to say." His words were loose boulders. "But first I wanna ask... are you really a genius, Luke? Really?"

The eyes of the golden statue narrowed and the electricity which constantly played over his arms quickened. Masaaki put a hand on his shoulder and said, "He is, Mason. But remember Luke has had to hide his whole life. Tell us what you wish to say."

The giant's raspy voice cracked as he spoke. "How come you guys didn't turn me out when I showed up? And how come none of you are scared of me?"

Something lightened in the atmosphere. Oz, his hairless face cracking in a smile, asked, "Why didn't you turn us out, Mason? Why are you with us? Is it only that you have nowhere else to go?"

Mason blinked. "Nope. I mean, I'm useless. I got this big ugly body as a reminder of what I did, and it can do things no human can. But what do I do with it?"

"Kinda true for all of us, isn't it?" Luke said, and looked around. "Check me out. What am I supposed to do with these?" He held up his crackling arms.

Still smiling, Oz said to Mason, "Answer my question."

Mason shrugged and held up his hands. "Okay. You win. I'm glad to see each one of you. Really glad." He looked out at the ocean again. When he looked back at his friends, a deep distance had entered his face. "Thank you for not turnin' me away."

Jack said, "The message. What do we do?"

"Do we really have any options?" the red man said. "I mean, we got a dead world that don't mean nothin' any more. There's probably the ruins of Chicago and New York and L.A. still around, but the places are gone. We got leeches crawling all over the place so hungry they'll eat anything. We got pockets of survivors who are mostly miserable and ignorant—if they ain't actually worshiping the dead, that is. We got a psycho who caused it all, who's back and maybe stronger than ever." He gave a hollow laugh. "The leeches don't seem to know that yet. But they'll learn. And even if they don't want our help bringing back the Head, they ain't gonna leave us alone. So what can we do?"

"There's more," Rachel said. "I saw... I guess it was a person, but it was tall, and..."

"The Walkers," Jack interrupted. "I've never seen any, but two of my brothers have. They look like humans, but you talk with them, and you know they're not. That's why I didn't recognize you at first, Selene. I thought you were one of them."

"And the Great Mother Spirit," Rachel said. Oz frowned, and Luke shook his head.

"Are you talking about that big butterfly thing?" Mason asked. "You saw that too?"

Jack asked, "Why do you call it Mother?"

Rachel shook her head. "I just..."

"I don't know if it was really feminine," Selene said, "but it's good you bring it up."

"If it was real," Luke said.

"Real?" Rachel said. "Of course it's real. It's how I healed

Mason. It has to be real. It just is."

"Even if it's real," Jack said, "how does it change our decision right now?"

Luke took a deep breath. "Let's think this through. We don' have to go with the Dead. Masaaki here can take us through the void."

Masaaki said, "We should not count on that. It is dangerous. We may not resurface for years, and we do not know how it might change us. It changed Mason, after all."

"Okay, but this is a dangerous situation. May not have a choice. Jus' thinkin' out loud here. We can get off by ourselves. World's a big place, and without long distance communication it's a lot bigger. There are those wells. The dead can't see 'em. Anybody want to try?"

Rachel was shaking her head; her red hair bounced. "Mother Love was embracing the whole world, even though it was dead."

Luke said, "Okay. Anyone wanna disagree?"

Nobody spoke until Masaaki asked, "Do you wish to, Luke?"

"Not unless everyone else wants to."

"And what is your reason?" The apparition's aura was curling around him in sinuous black fingers.

"I spent years alone. I came through sooner than any of you." He shuddered and his eyes fell to the sand. "Hiding ain't no way to live. Living for yourself ain't living." The decades echoed in his wide, haggard eyes. Masaaki smiled.

Oz asked, "Is it somehow possible to turn everything back? Neutralize the chemical that's in the air?"

"I don' think so," Luke said. "The lab the Head used is destroyed, and even if it wasn't, the Head changed how things worked. If we were still livin' under the same scientific laws, it might be possible. But we ain't. You'd need to write a whole new code for the universe."

"Good," Selene said. "I know how horrible that sounds. But am I sorry that my former life is dead? No. I don't want to go back. Ever." Several of the others nodded.

"Okay then," Luke said. "Are we sure we don't have a way to destroy the Dead? I can't think of nothin'. But anybody have any ideas?"

Oz said, "What about the void? It undoes everything. Can we lure them in?"

"My friends," Masaaki said, "I am sorry to say this, but the dead who have wandered into the ocean are still there. I have seen them. They float. Some find their way out. I think the void is too much like them to damage them. However, the one we burned at our camp became a tree. If we can lure them into a fire..."

"That don't kill them," Luke said. "I spent a lotta time in the forest our old camp was in. There are a lot of those tree things there, and they're still alive. The branches reach for you and there's these slits in 'em that I wouldn't stick my hand in. Tongues in there, too. I saw one twistin' once like it was trying to walk. It couldn't, but it might someday."

"They just keep finding a way to come back," Jack said. Luke nodded.

Oz gave the group a tentative look. "There is one option we haven't yet considered. We could try to offer terms to the Head. I'm not hopeful, but perhaps a truce could be reached."

"He wouldn't listen," Mason grated.

"We've got more cards to play this time round. We're not human."

Jack said, "Say we offer terms and the Head rejects them,

which he will. Hiding is not an option. We've got one choice left." His words seemed to hang in the air.

"I kill the Head," he said. He turned and walked up the beach.

TWENTY-FIVE

Hopeless

The wind whipped through Jack's hair as he walked. He wondered when he would see the lines of hissing faces on the dunes. Behind him, a silvery voice called, "What do you mean, 'I'?"

He stopped and turned around. "You can't go with me."

"And why is that?" Selene asked.

"Too dangerous. Especially for you. What are you smiling at?"

The red god spoke, his voice a gentle rumble and his black eyes trained upon his friend. "Kid, if you just go to war, what'll keep you from bein' any different from the Head? The Flowers want something to worship. Even if you can kill that thing, how do you know they won't put you in the Head's place?"

"He who fights monsters," Oz murmured.

Jack noticed the look Rachel was giving him. His palms felt sweaty. He said, "Sorry, Masaaki, what did you say?"

"You are most brave, Jack. But it is foolish to go alone."

Jack felt something shift among his friends as they turned back to their conference. He walked back to the group, wondering why he didn't feel embarrassed.

Luke said, "The Head was confused in the void and couldn't get out. Is there a way to get him back in?"

The giant said, "You're sayin' we go along with what the Dead want. Maybe find some way to trick the Head."

"And then, assumin' we're not dead already, which is more likely, we find ourselves the biggest well we can and get as many of the survivors together. It won't be much of a life, but it will be somethin'." The ocean breeze was tugging at his shaggy hair.

"But the virus is still present in the atmosphere," Oz said. "When we die, we will join the Dead."

"Maybe not all of us," Luke said, giving Rachel a significant look. She looked back, uncomprehending.

Oz's eyes widened. "The seed of a goddess..." He had to raise his voice to be heard over the whipping wind.

"You think her child will be different?" Mason asked.

Luke shrugged. "Maybe. And if the child can grow up and have kids, then... What's the deal with this wind?" He was practically shouting.

Rachel stood and ran further up the beach, disappearing behind a sand dune. The rest followed her, Jack carrying his sword. They found her standing in front of a small whirlwind. The sand blowing in the wind stung their faces.

"Quick," Rachel shouted. "An offering. Do we have anything for an offering? Food? Stop blinking at me and find something!"

Selene shook her head. "Nothing!"

Rachel turned to Jack. "Your sword, warrior." With a sweep of his arm, Jack unsheathed it and held it out to her. Rachel pulled her palm across it, pushed her fist inside the tiny whirlwind, and squeezed. Drops of green blood streaked like rain across a windshield. The whirlwind became a green cloud. Within it, the lines of a face appeared.

Oz's face flared, as if someone were pinching a nerve. His mouth opened as the lips inside the sandstorm moved. *Hopeless*, a long, low voice said from Oz's mouth. *Go with them.* The face disappeared and the whirlwind quieted. Rachel's blood dotted the sand. Grass sprouted from the dots, but white spots quickly appeared on each blade and they withered.

Oz trembled and fell to his knees. His eyes rolled back into his head. Rachel went to him and touched his shoulders; blood dribbled down one arm of his dirty shirt. For a second, the others could see pale blue flaring around him; then he leaned over and gasped, blinking rapidly. Rachel let go, and the blue swirling around Oz disappeared.

Jack tore a strip of cloth from the bottom of one pant leg, went to Rachel, and tied it around her hand. His eyes stayed fixed on her hand as he tied.

"Can heal others, but not myself," Rachel murmured. "Thank you, warrior."

"Don't thank me yet," Jack said, motioning with his head across the dunes.

A figure rose and fell as it made its way over the dunes. Only a green-black head was visible at first, but soon they could see the lines where tentacles had closed over its face like stitches.

"Friends," Jack said, his eyes on the Flower, "what do we do?"

"What was that?" Mason asked.

"Someone else claimed it was hopeless," Oz said. He snapped his fingers. "Ezekiel."

"It was Ezekiel," Rachel said. "I could tell."

"What do we do?" Jack hissed.

The Flower stopped a dozen paces from them. Sand crusted the dead skin of its feet. It stood taller than any of them except Mason.

"You come," it hissed. The syllables slid across the dying wind. "It sent a messenger, as you would have." It took a step closer.

Selene moaned, "I don't want to go with that thing!"

Jack took a step toward it, his sword high.

"It has... accommodated," the Flower said. Another step. "You brought the Head up. Now bring him to us." Another step. "It must worship." Two more steps. Its face flared open. Their new world walked toward them, arms outstretched.

Jack stepped forward to meet it. Twice, a third time his sword flashed. He turned to his friends. "It will stand again soon," he said. "What do we do?" He shook his sword free of the gray fluid snaking its way up the blade toward his hand.

"I think we have to go with them," Rachel said quietly.

Mason was the first to walk forward. Something passed in the air between him and Rachel as he looked at her. He walked past, away from the ocean. Selene put a trembling hand in Rachel's and the two of them followed. Luke looked at Oz.

The former professor shrugged. "If we are to die, let us at least do it together."

They followed. Masaaki floated behind. Jack sheathed his sword and followed his friends. After a dozen paces, he looked back and saw an arm, a head, and a torso crawling toward each other.

A dozen more paces up the sand dunes and the waves of unnumbered dead were visible in the distance, stretched as far as the horizon, and the path the Dead had made for them to walk through their midst.

*

A few minutes' walking and the sand ended in a flat plain. White stalks of grass extended in a broad highway in front of them. On either side, an endless flowing mass of green-gray-black. The Dead stood silent and still and endless, alert and blind.

They walked.

*

At one point, when their road turned, they walked closer to the line of dead. Faces flared in the front row of corpses and they walked toward the travelers. The sword cleared its scabbard in a quiet hiss, but the red giant walked toward them, palms up.

"Go back," he said.

Something which was not recognition passed over what had once been their faces, and the corpses moved back.

The survivors walked on.

*

Eventually night came and the path in front of them grew dark. They sat. Soon the darkness covered even the dead. There was no sound. Faint light shone from the dull red of the giant and from the electricity moving up and down the blonde man's muscular arms.

"I feel so alone," one of the women whispered. "I know they're all out there, but it feels like we're alone. Almost like we're floating in mid-air." Her twin put his hand on hers.

A bald head nodded. "Like the darkness before creation. Was that truly Ezekiel earlier? Speaking through my mouth?"

"I felt him."

The bald man asked, "How did you know to cut yourself?"

"To help him come through."

"But how did you know to do that?"

"I... I..."

"You've always understood this new world better than any of us," the man with the sword said. The red-haired woman stared at him.

"Regardless, please don't do that again."

"You don' like being controlled, do you?"

The bald man's voice trembled. "After my daughter killed herself, I was being controlled. I became someone else with my wife. No, I don't like it." He hung his head. "I think that's why I survived when everything changed. It didn't feel terribly different from my former life. But I don't want to be someone else again." Tears dripped from his cheeks. "And yet, I cannot help but wonder: what further transformations might await us? What else will we leave behind, and not care?"

No one spoke until the man with the sword said, "You can run, Oz. You move too quickly to be seen. And you don't stay on the ground, do you? You could just leave. I don't think anyone here would blame you."

The bald man sat as still as a stone. The red light from the giant played over his face like orange flames. Eventually he said, "Running away won't stop me from changing. Nothing can stop it."

"That's the thing that frightens you the most, isn't it?"

"Yes, Selene, that is what frightens me most. Now, can

someone explain to me how Ezekiel might still be alive? Or if not exactly alive, at least existing in some form?"

"When you touch the void, it undoes you. Makes you less. 'Cept, that's not it. It brings out the nothin' you already were. Most of our bodies are empty space anyway. But... touchin' it again, like we did... it was like the void saw itself in us, and the opposite happened. We become even more of what we was."

"And you are suggesting that's what happened to Ezekiel? That his second baptism preserved him?"

In the darkness, the golden man nodded.

"Then what about the Flowers Masaaki saw floating in the void? Their second contact hadn't changed them."

"They're already dead. You can't get more deader."

"Does this mean the Head will be stronger, as we are? He was in the void once before."

"My guess is he was down there too long."

The man with the sword said, "None of this is the real question. Was Ezekiel right? Is it hopeless? Can we lure the Head into the void? Can we find a place safe from the Flowers? Will Rachel's son be different enough to make any difference?"

How long they sat, each waiting for another to speak, none of them could tell.

Eventually the pale woman said, "I wish the moon were out."

"I remember how you guided us when we were locked up. That was wonderful."

"Sis, I'm sorry this is hurting you, but if I'm going to die, I want to know what I'm dying for. Or if there's anything left worth dying for."

"There is another option. Bushi Jack possesses a sword."

No one spoke.

The pale Japanese man said, "He is an honorable warrior. If we let him go last, he would dispatch himself."

"What..."

"You can't mean..."

"Jack wouldn't let us do that," the pale woman said; but her brother's face was a mask.

"We'd just get up and join the dead."

"Perhaps not. Jack is skillful enough. When it first happened, I saw bodies too damaged to walk and feed."

The small Japanese man spoke. "Well, friends? If we are going to proceed, let us be sure it is what we wish to do. Oz?"

"I can't answer Jack's questions. I don't know if it will do any good whatsoever. But I will not run again. Ever." The Japanese man nodded.

"I can't pay Bob back," the golden man said. "But I ain't gonna give up and join him, either."

"I don't know if you really mean it," the red giant said, "but you're asking me to become as pathetic as those things. No."

The swordsman asked, "What about you, Masaaki?"

The pale Japanese man said, "I am so close to death I doubt your sword would be effective. But if the rest chose so, I would leave and not return. And you, Jack?"

The swordsman looked at the sword in his lap. "During my training, we would sit and talk in the evenings. We didn't have wood for a fire, so we'd look up at the stars. It was good, being there. I knew what I had done to Selene was bad, but that they had all acted badly too. They were accepted like me. And the longer I stayed, the angrier I got. I thought about the children who had screamed as their parents ate them. Or the parents who screamed. And the better it was inside, the more I wanted to get out. But I can't just go slicing up the dead. What does that do? And if I were to kill the Head, what would that mean? He was a fool. Had no idea what he was doing. He isn't equal to the disaster he's created. But something is. There's some secret. I want to find it and cut it in half and see what's inside." The warrior looked at them all. "Not if all of you were dead, not if all of my bones were broken, not if the dead were inches from me. Not if it turns out there is nothing worth fighting for. Not even then would I give up."

The bald man sighed. "How could we do it? Humanity has brutalized itself before, but this? Who can take the measure of it?" He shook his head. "May I ask something else? Something which may discourage?"

No one spoke, but they leaned in closer to listen.

"Let us say our fondest hopes come true, and the Head is trapped and we find a safe place to raise Rachel's child. Will even that make a difference? Luke said the Head rewrote the code of the universe. How do we know we won't simply reproduce the code? Will we ever be anything else to the Dead but objects of worship? Things they hunger for?"

"The Mother Spirit," the woman with red hair said.

"You really believe in that, don't you?"

"She doesn't depend on my belief."

"I know I saw something," the bald man said. "But you must confess it is passing strange."

"As weird as the Dead walking again?"

The bald man smiled. "Well said. If this evil can be true, why not that great good?"

The red-haired woman's eyes flared open and she pointed wordlessly. They turned back to see a human face just outside of their circle, stepping back into the shadows. The giant stood, his body glowing bright red; but the man was gone.

"A walker," the swordsman said. "A walker has come to us." Hope pulsed in his voice.

TWENTY-SIX

The Tower

Three more days they walked under a dead sun, breathing the hollow air.

None of the Dead moved.

They didn't speak at night. They lay on their backs and looked at the stars, pinpricks in a velvet fabric pulled over the dead world, hiding some unimaginable light.

The tower was visible in the dim distance of the flat plain on the fourth day. By the fifth, they stood before it, a stumpy, vast circle. Except for a few areas of wood and stone, it was mostly covered with white scabs. Endless rows of Flowers circled it. Faces opened and closed in an unguessable code. Huge fires burned at different spots near the tower. In jerky rhythm, corpses walked into them, screamed and ran, pulling themselves up the tower with melting hands as their bodies liquefied into white plaster. Some hardened with their faces facing outward and continued to wave feeble white feelers and flick thin white tongues.

In the distance, storm clouds gathered above an unearthly yellow glow.

As the seven drew near and stood before the tower, each of the thousands of faces turned toward them. A hissing rose from the endless waves like a swarm of insects. *The Head dwelt below, so it built this opening so our Head could return. But he is not below. He wanders above. He does not see us his children. You must summon him to us.*

"Why do you want him?" Jack called.

He made us for himself. We must worship and be satisfied.

Masaaki floated toward the tower and placed a hand on one of the few remaining spots of wood and concrete. His head fell. In a still, clear voice, he called, "How did you bring the void to the surface?" His voice was as close to anger as it ever came.

It breaks through wherever it can. It hungers for life.

"Just as you do."

Always it hungers, bottomless, endless. You are no different.

Masaaki was floating back to his friends as Mason called, "How are we supposed to summon him?"

You all have his power within you. You are his chosen servants. Summon, or it will worship you.

"The Flowers are getting closer to us," Selene hissed.

Jack said in a tight voice, "I can't fight all of them, but if Mason and Luke help, we might be able to get away."

"You know there's too many of them," Selene said. Jack opened his mouth to argue, but his shoulders fell.

Summon him.

Oz asked, "Masaaki, can you take us through the void again?"

"I can move through it, but it would be difficult for me to take all of you. And the Dead would find us again eventually."

Mason rumbled, "At least Oz can get away. No sense in him dying with us."

Oz shook his head. "I will not leave you to commit suicide. Don't ask me to do that."

Summon. The waves of Dead started to walk toward them. The seven backed toward each other as the first wave drew closer, closer.

"What do we do?" Jack asked. Luke saw the same question on every face.

"All right," Luke said. He closed his eyes and rose from the ground above their heads. The lightning on his skin began to accelerate; soon Luke's body was only a dark outline inside a storm of electricity. His six friends had to shield their eyes, but not before seeing a giant bolt burst upward toward the sky with a crack of thunder. A great crack of lightning from the storm on the horizon sounded in response.

He dropped to the ground, reeled, and collapsed. He was grimacing and shaking. His friends surrounded him.

"What did you do?" Mason asked.

"I sent him a signal. He was near anyway. We're connected. Never told you."

"We can't give in to them," Jack said.

"You hurt your forehead," Selene said.

Luke shook his head, and Selene gasped when the skin on the bump on Luke's forehead pulled back to reveal a vivid yellow eye.

The hissing rose around them: *You have brought him. He comes.*

Rachel put a hand on Luke's head, wincing as the electricity played over her hand. She gave an urgent look to her friends.

"Can you heal him?" Selene asked.

Selene shook her head. "It's too deep for me."

"What now?" Jack asked.

Luke groaned, "Need to know if the Head's coherent. Might be able to get 'im back into the void."

"I will see," Oz said, and was gone in a blur of blue which rushed above their heads toward the storm.

In the distance, the storm clouds drew closer. The yellow glow beneath it was streaked with lightning.

*

Watching him go, Rachel put a hand to her belly. She felt a calloused hand touch her arm, and looked to see Jack standing next to her. His face was a shy question.

"Say the word," Jack said, "and I'll leave you alone. Forever." Smiling at him, Rachel took his hand and squeezed.

Breathless, Jack whispered, "For you, I would..."

"I know," Selene whispered, and brushed her lips against his rough cheek, and felt him shiver. She turned to the sad giant staring at her from the infinite distance of a few feet away. "I know you as well, Mason," she said, releasing Jack's hand. "You have my love, and my blessing."

The red giant's head fell. "More than I deserve," he whispered.

Masaaki asked Rachel, "Do you still believe that what you call the Mother Spirit will come for you?"

She felt her belly again and said nothing.

"I hope you are right," Masaaki said. A faint blue shape was rushing toward them in the air.

"Why?" asked Luke.

"I do not think there is any other help for us."

Suddenly Oz was standing before them, inhumanly still.

"Well?" Mason asked.

"I don't think we'll have to worry about the Head much longer. He's incoherent. The void ruined him."

"Then how are we going to trap him back in the void?" Jack asked. "We can't force him in."

But no one was listening: they were all looking at the waves of the Dead, which had turned away from them and toward the approaching storm. Soon a gaunt yellow giant was visible in the distance, crawling toward them on his hands and knees. The dead moved to make a path for him toward the tower. The sound of Jack's sword clearing its scabbard was lost in the rising hiss of the Flowers as they welcomed their Sun.

The Head crawled toward the tower and lay before it, panting. Even on his hands and knees, he was taller than the tower the Dead had made. The seven had to crane their necks upward to look at him. The Head's eye was wild and staring. His flesh sagged and rippled as electricity sparked and danced from it. A stream of words came from his mouth, as if the Head didn't know he was speaking: "Worship, worship, I will be worshipped, the seven will serve me, everything I created will serve me in death, in life, in death, I will be whole, somehow whole, never enough, but I will be whole, I will eat them if I have to, eat my seven and my dead, eat death..."

The words droned on as the Head grasped the sides of the well and lowered his face into it. When he pulled it out, some of the wildness had left his face. His eye focused on the seven.

"You," he said. A huge yellow hand reached toward them. Jack's sword flashed and lightning crackled from Luke's body; a finger larger than any of them fell to the ground. Wriggling white feelers grew out of the finger and started to drag it back toward the Head. When the seven looked up at the Head, the emptiness in his face had returned. He dropped his head into the well as if it was too heavy to hold up.

The words floated around them: *This is not our Head. This is nothing.* A pause; the faces of the dead seemed to open and close in quickening circles as whatever passed for thought moved among them. Their hissing sharpened to a knife edge: *It will worship and be satisfied. First the Head, and then you.*

"Luke," Selene whispered. "What have you done?"

Still wincing, Luke sat up and opened his other two eyes. They were blank gray. "No choice," he huffed. "But get ready. When they say worship, they..."

The Head bellowed and jerked his head from the well. Giant drops of water flew from his face, hissing as they landed on the white ground. The Head looked back at his ankle, lying a quarter of a mile away. A tiny figure with waving tentacles was pressing its face into the Head's skin. Another, closer to the well, broke ranks and ran to one of the Head's hands. It unhinged its jaws wide and sunk its jagged teeth into the Head's flesh.

The Head shouted again, a hoarse, muffled sound, as if coming from underwater. He tried to pull his hand away, but it seemed too heavy for him. He looked back at his leg. It was covered by swarming Flowers up to the knee.

"Help," the Head said to the seven. "I cannot die. I must be whole. I must be worshipped."

"You are," Mason said. His friends stared at him when they heard the pity in his voice.

The dead began to swarm over the Head like ants, crawling over each other to move higher up his body. Their

296

tentacles trembled as they feasted. The Head looked back at the seven, and something shifted in his face. "Let my children worship me, then. I will live in them, my body." He lay his head against the side of the well. Soon Flowers were crawling over his entire body like ants.

The massive shape on which the dead feasted began to sink. Flowers began to run past the seven to the diminishing feast.

"Are they ignoring us?" Oz whispered.

Jack, eyes wide, said nothing as he turned and took a few steps into the waves of dead moving past them. They didn't turn toward him. He turned back and motioned to his friends.

Mason knelt and pulled one of Luke's arms over his own shoulders and helped him stand. The red giant's skin began to char black as the electricity crackling on Luke's skin bit into his. They moved through the lines of running flowers which still stretched for miles to the horizon.

"Do you think we might make it?" Selene asked Jack.

He turned to answer, but said nothing as his mouth dropped open. He pointed behind. They turned and saw something black and bright flying in the sky from the well toward them. It descended to a few inches above the ground a dozen paces in front of them. The Flowers who had been walking toward the well stopped and circled it.

The thing in front of them was a Flower with its face closed. Its empty eye sockets stared at them for a moment. The diseased, green-bruise color of its skin had changed to charred black. Its tunic had been burned away. Electricity sparked and danced on its dead flesh. Then its face flared open, and above its two eye sockets, a third eye of vivid yellow opened and stared at them.

"This, this, is what I was meant to be," it said. "I have eaten, and I am finally full, and still I hunger." Electricity ran up and down its body as it levitated. It opened its arms and looked up at the sun.

A crash sounded in the distance from the well. They looked and saw that the Head's body was almost entirely consumed. The side of the well on which the Head had leaned had collapsed inward. Dark water was spilling through the hole in the wall over the plain, making a shallow lake in which the Dead splashed as they moved.

"Are they... are they eating each other?" Mason asked.

No one answered, but even from a distance they could see those still feasting on the Head beginning to bite each other and not let go. Chains of Flowers connected at the mouth began to form. Soon long, thick tentacles radiated outward from the ruins of the well, half submerged in the water of the void which continued to seep outward.

"Come to me," the Flower said. The seven turned back to see the new Flower, still floating above the ground, holding its arms out and its palms to the sky. The surrounding Flowers were taking bite after bite from the new Flower. After each bite, its flesh quickly grew back in white which charred black when electricity touched it. As each eater walked away, electricity burned their bodies black, a third eye opened, and they rose from the earth to float in the air.

"Worship me," the Flower said to the seven. "Your own pain will be healed, and your own void satisfied. We will rule together. We will be our own Head, in living death." Its black tongues flicked. The surrounding Flowers floated around their new leader, their eye fixed on him.

None of the seven moved.

The Flower fixed its eye on Rachel. "You have something

beautiful inside you." It floated toward her.

Jack leapt forward with his sword, but it was too late: the Flower touched a single blackened finger to Rachel's womb. Electricity swept over Rachel and she collapsed.

Jack shouted and decapitated the Flower with a single sweep of his sword. Before the corpse's head touched the ground, white feelers were already drawing it back toward its body, which hung unmoving in the air. As the head was pulled back to the neck, it said, "And now more beautiful still."

When it was whole again, it held its arms out toward them. "You will worship me."

Selene turned and grabbed her brother's hand. "Jack!" she cried. "It's hopeless! Hopeless!" Jack would not look at her.

Masaaki rose and spread his arms over his friends. Darkness covered them.

Twenty-Seven

The End

Selene opened her eyes. She was lying on the ground. Ghostly white tree branches crisscrossed above her; a few fragile stars shone in the night sky. An echo of what she saw in the void sounded within her, the sharp scream of an angry woman, her father's giant shouting face, and her brother's.

She sat up. A dozen paces away, a muscular golden body lay trembling on the ground. Masaaki sat next to him, scratching in the dust with a twig. The pulsing, crackling light from Luke's body shone on the former doctor's furrowed face. Masaaki ignored Selene when she called his name, continuing to scratch in the dirt. Just beyond Luke and Masaaki, the trees ended in a long trail of mist which extended as far as Selene could see.

In the still night air, a tree branch stroked her shoulder. She jumped and brushed it away, shuddering.

"They are alive," Masaaki said. Japanese characters appeared on his white arms and blurred into nothing. "If the fire is intense, the Flower is not able to recombine. But it does not die. If these trees could move and eat, they would. They never stop. Ever."

Luke opened his two eyes. The bump on his forehead

300

remained closed. He stared up into the night sky. "Masaaki? You still there?"

"There is nowhere else to go."

"Is Selene awake?"

"Yes."

"Has she seen me?"

"I'm here, Luke," Selene said. Luke put both of his hands over his forehead and closed his eyes.

Selene looked up at the thumbnail curve of the moon. Thin as it was, she felt it shining on her, and understood. "You don't need to feel ashamed," she said; and though she usually sensed the effects of her words on others when the moon was high, she felt nothing then. She said to Masaaki, "I recognize this forest."

"Yes. We are back at our camp."

"How..."

"I did not know what else to do, so I tried to take us through the void, but I was not able to hold on to everyone, or control where we landed."

"You saved our lives, then," Selene said.

"So we can lose them now."

"Why won't you look at me, Masaaki?"

He stopped scratching in the dirt. His eyes met hers, and Selene shivered. "I cannot understand this world," he said. "I can only guide those in it. But it seems we have come to the end of our path." He turned back to his scratching. "Too soon, too soon. There was supposed to be more. More I wished to see."

Selene looked at the moon again, sighed, and got to her feet and walked toward them. Her foot struck a root and she had to catch herself to keep from falling. A hissing rose from the ground, and a few sparks like fireflies.

Masaaki said, "You were not awake during the day, so you have not seen it. But..." Selene started to walk to her right, but Masaaki said, "I would not advise that."

"Why not?"

"You are cut off from us."

"What?"

"Long black roots with many mouths reach through the forest. And eyes. Yellow eyes look at us."

"From the trees?"

"No," Luke moaned, his forehead still covered. "The Flowers ate the Head, and became like him. And the void got mixed in. Everything got mixed together." He shuddered again, as if he was cold.

Selene looked down to see a yellow eye open a few feet to her left. It stared at her, and she could feel its hunger like a wave of heat. "I don't understand and I want to come over there," she whispered.

"They are eating the world," Masaaki said. "I saw it when we were travelling in the void. Many still crawl on its surface, but many more have joined themselves into one large Flower. It is eating its way through rock and soil."

"Tell me where the root ends so I can come to you."

"By day, I could see no end," Masaaki said.

"Then I'll jump," she said, backing up.

He shook his head. "It is higher than you think. The tongues from the mouths are long. And..."

Luke twisted on the ground and groaned. Eyes still closed, he reached a trembling hand toward Selene. The light from his aura shone toward her, and she gasped: the root in front of her rose a foot off of the ground. In the flashlight glow of Luke's light, a dozen tongues rose from it and trembled as high as her waist. More yellow eyes opened and stared at Luke; tiny stalks of lightning began to appear on the root's twisted surface.

Luke let his trembling hand fall, and the root fell into darkness.

"It is larger than it was by day," Masaaki said. "It is growing."

"Growing everywhere," Selene said. "Everywhere." She stood in the darkness and watched as Masaaki scratched in the dirt and Luke shuddered sparks of light.

*

Luke sat up. Lightning still played over his body, but his trembling had stopped. His third eye opened, and a loud voice came from his mouth; but before Selene could distinguish any words, he clapped his hands over his mouth. His eye bulged and pulsed as if trying to signal in Morse code what his mouth could not say. Eventually the shouting stopped and the eye closed and he fell over again, shaking.

He moaned, "Move me toward the root."

"Why?" asked Masaaki, as if he were not paying attention.

"Don't want to become him. The Head."

"I will push you into the abyss."

"No, that won't stop it. Better join 'em before I turn into something worse."

Selene said, "Luke, no."

He opened his two gray, blind eyes and stared in Selene's direction. "Nothin' I don't deserve. I summoned the Head. Sent him a signal. Because of me, the Flowers changed again. Got even worse. My fault. Would'a been better for all uh you if I had jus' died."

"Luke..." she said, and gasped, "Masaaki, what are you doing?" Tears blurred the sight of the Japanese man dragging Luke by the armpits, grimacing as lightning shocked him.

Masaaki stopped. "It is what he wished," he said. "I have no other guidance."

Still prone, Luke's mouth shouted: "Get your hands off me! Don't you bring..." The rest was muffled as Luke clamped his hands on his mouth.

Selene's mouth dropped, her tears forgotten. "That's the Head's voice," she said.

Masaaki nodded. "I do not believe we have a choice," he said.

"But he will turn into one of... *them*," she wailed.

"And perhaps an even more terrible Flower than any of the rest. But would you have Luke turn into a new Head? Would you condemn him to that? At least, when he joins the Dead, he will not care anymore."

She hung her head.

"It does not greatly matter. These roots will soon grow until they cover everything. And each one has many mouths."

She turned heavy eyes toward Masaaki again. The strange voice in Luke began to shout, but Luke didn't seem to have the strength to stifle the words of domination and hate.

"I don't want to watch Luke die," she said. "I'll go first." She stepped toward the root. It hissed beneath her. She heard, but could not see, teeth clicking.

*

When she thought about it later (as she did many times after she died) it seemed to Selene that the being who spoke next had been there all along, and that Selene had known this, but had not been able to pay attention to it. It was as if someone had been watching her sleep and decided to speak inside her dreams. When the voice spoke, Selene felt that she woke, and dreamed deeper still.

"Do not step any closer," a voice said behind her, and she stopped without thinking and turned.

A human figure stood some paces away, two heads taller than her, with broad lips and wide forehead. Two more stood beside... Selene could not decide whether to say "him" or "her." The first was dressed in a long robe of pale fiery white; the second, black, and the third, gold. The three didn't glow so much as appear to be untouched by the inky dark.

"Please, ma'am," she asked, "can you help my friend?"

"He is dying," the speaker said. "You must understand that."

"Then you cannot help?"

"I did not say that."

No one spoke. Selene sensed a hint of impatience from the two behind the speaker, but also that they were more interested in what she had to say. Feeling like a child too young to say anything but the truth, she said, "Your voice reminds me of something."

"Of what does it remind you?"

"Of the voices I heard within the void. The cave in which the Head imprisoned us. Except not ugly."

"Walkers," a shrill voice said behind Selene. She turned (thinking only when she turned away from them how beautiful they were, so beautiful she should have been frightened) to see Luke floating above the ground. His yellow eye glared.

"You're what the slave Jack called Walkers. What do you want?" Masaaki stood behind him. Selene couldn't tell if it was fear or wonder that transfixed his face.

The three stared at Luke.

"You won't get it!" the voice from Luke shrieked. "You'll never have me!"

Selene turned back. "Please, ma'am, why is he speaking that way?"

"You love him."

Selene said nothing.

"Your love for him is a precious thing, Selene. We cherish it with you. He is talking that way because, when Luke summoned the Head, he used what the Head had put into him; but as he did, the seed grew into a plant."

"Luke would never act like the Head," Selene said.

"The serum the Head used to transform himself was mostly taken from the void. The void corresponds to everything inside you, even your intention and will, whether it is self-sacrificing, or self-worshipping, as the Head's were. The Head transferred this to Luke with his touch. But it would not have taken root if it had not found receptive soil inside him." The speaker paused, and then said, as if it were difficult, "The same would have happened to all of you eventually. The seed inside you would have blossomed, and you would have turned into different versions of the Head's original servants, as corrupt as they."

The one in the black robe said, "But it is sacrifice of which we must speak."

"Do you hate the Dead?" the third asked. Selene blinked and said nothing. She felt she was having a conversation with the moon, the sun, and the night.

"Luke has the least time," the golden one said.

The three moved past Selene. She realized once they stood opposite Luke that she didn't see how they made it past the root which separated her from Luke; but she forgot her question as she stared at them again.

"Luke," said the one in the golden robe. Luke's yellow eye bulged, and he roared at them.

"You must help him a little," the one in the black robe said. The one in the golden robe seemed to hesitate, and then touched Luke's two gray eyes. The yellow eye drooped as if drugged and he sank back to the ground. Selene saw a little of the light blue come back into his other eyes.

"Do you hate the Dead?"

Luke looked too confused to do anything but say exactly what he was thinking. "No," he mumbled. "My brother's one of 'em. Hate the Head. Hate myself. Don' hate 'em."

The black robe said, "You said earlier you wished you were dead, Luke. But which death? If you turned into another Head, that would be a kind of death, but not one you wish for. Joining the Dead would be a deeper death. If you joined them, you would not forget your mistakes, but they would mean nothing to you. Nothing would mean anything to you. A void would open within you, and you would be forever hungry and empty. If you were still alive, it would drive you insane. But as one of the Dead, you would not truly feel the void within. Is that the death you long for, Luke?"

"No," Luke mumbled. "Not enough."

None of the three showed any reaction to this, but Selene sensed something change in the air between them.

"There is another kind of death. You know that the Dead have started to join together, and to join themselves to the earth. Soon there will be no difference between them and the

307

earth. Already a great mouth is forming below us in the void."

Luke blinked. "They'll eat everything?"

"The entire planet will become a Flower."

"Don't make sense," Luke muttered.

"No. But this is death you are facing, Luke. Your intelligence is already far beyond that of your friends. It could be a hundred times greater, and still you would not understand death. Will you surrender yourself instead? Without despair, or any hatred of what is consuming you?"

"I'll jus' turn into one of 'em."

The atmosphere among the three speakers tightened. The one in the golden robe said, "No, Luke. You will not return as one of them. You will truly die. Is that what you wish?"

"Yes," he said; and Selene hung her head as a tear slipped down her cheek.

"You will die in agony, Luke. You will experience what the Flowers are more than they ever do, because you will still be alive. You will taste the wrongness of what they are."

"An' leave everyone else here. Jus' leave 'em."

"We will give your friends the same choice."

"No, I mean the Dead. The things that used to be people."

None of the Walkers spoke, but the tension between them sharpened.

Luke started to shake his head. "Tell me what I don' know. Tell me how I can fix things..."

"Death would contaminate all your calculations. You would only make the world worse. It must die, and so must you."

"I'll really die? I won't join 'em?"

"Yes. Do you believe us, Luke?"

"I don' deserve it. They're worse now, and it's my fault."

"Nevertheless. Will you truly die, Luke?"

"Yes," he said, and smiled.

The one in the golden robe said, "We will push you into the void, and you will taste true death. You will drink its bitter agony."

Luke's yellow eye started to blink.

"Remember, as you sink, that there is no other way. And remember your brother."

The three guided him so that he stood with his back to the void. They placed their hands on Luke's head for a silent moment. Then they removed their hands and he fell backwards. Selene saw the old blue of his eyes for an instant before the mist covered him. Seconds later, light flashed from deep within the mist, showing the outline of a dark circle with long arms. A thunderous howl rose from below, as if the entire world were screaming in its hunger.

*

As Luke fell, he saw a hillbilly drinking himself to death in a lonely hut in the sticky Georgia heat; a man with shaggy blonde hair staring into the face of a Flower; the same man forcing himself not to weep as they dragged his brother's body away to bury it; and a terrible golden figure, crackling with electricity, floating above the worshipping Dead: each one a hell of his own making. As he slowly dropped into the massive, gaping mouth in the void, he felt glad none of them was alive, and that he was finally over.

*

"And you, Masaaki."

The shepherd of the Dead knelt and pressed his forehead into the dirt. A stream of Japanese syllables came from his mouth.

The one in the black robe said, "Please rise, honored Shinogaido Masaaki."

Masaaki replied, "It is not fitting that one should stand in the presence of *kamigami.*"

"Then we should not stand in your presence, Shinogaido Masaaki."

He stood, but kept his eyes low. "There is so much I do not understand. And much you understand which you will not say."

"Always you have sought to guide others, Shinogaido Masaaki. But you know that every path ends in death. You have both feared and desired this ending. Will you accept guidance from us, and fall into the void, and truly die? Or do you choose the lesser death of joining the Dead, or remaining as you are?"

"My soul is not one within me." Something broke in Masaaki's face, and tears began to drip from his pale cheeks to the ground. "May I ask one question?"

"Very well."

"Is it really so simple? Submit to the Dead without malice, and you do not join them? If so, why didn't more of those bitten stay dead?"

"You seven are different, Shinogaido Masaaki," the Walker in the black robe said. "The constitution of your bodies has been changed by the Head's minions who touched you." The Walker paused. "You have come to love those you guided, Masaaki. You would have sacrificed yourself for them."

"Yes. But..."

"Speak, Shinogaido Masaaki."

"I am grieved I did not see more of my friends' stories. I would have liked to see them."

"You see beauty in them where they saw none. But the end of each of their stories would have been corruption."

"It is better this way."

"Yes," the Walker said.

Masaaki gave a shuddering sigh. "I have sought to guide my friends. But now I feel I cannot walk this path."

"Would you wander alone in the few weeks left to the world while your friends took their final journey?"

"No. No, I would not."

"Then let your love for your friends be your guide to true death."

Masaaki closed his eyes, gave a shuddering sigh, and nodded.

The three turned to Selene. A coldness gripped her in a way she had never felt in the presence of the Flowers.

"I know," she said, as tears streamed down her cheeks. "The same choice falls to me. I do not wish to join the Dead, and I don't hate the Flowers. They're a horror, but they make me sad. But please, sir, what did that Flower mean when he said that we were no different from them?"

"Like them, you have a void within you. All of you do. Like them, you consume things in order to fill it. The Dead call this worship, and they speak truly."

"Is reading poetry really that bad?"

"No. You used it to save yourself from becoming the kind of woman your mother was. But the void remains within you still, and if you had borne a daughter, she would have turned to something else to keep from becoming you."

Selene wrung her hands. "Am I really that useless? Does it always end badly, no matter what I choose?"

"You are not useless. You can see in the dark where others cannot, and help them."

"But I haven't at all!"

"You surely have," the Walker said. "Your brother will remember your final words. He trusts you."

"You mean when I said it was hopeless?"

"You spoke the truth."

"That's all?" Her face twisted as her tears continued. "That's the best I can say?"

"It is the best anyone can say about the world you have created. Do you wish to stay here for however long it lasts? Or will you let the void swallow you, and thus escape? It will be no less terrible for you than Luke or Masaaki."

"Please, sir, who are you?"

"We have no names, for we do not yet know who we are."

The one in the pale white robe placed her hand on Selene's forehead. Selene felt the moon above her, and knew what she was going to do.

The Walker said, "May your peace remain, even as you die." She pulled her robe around Selene and walked with her to the edge of the mist. Selene was too frightened to wonder how she was able to walk through the root that had separated her from Masaaki and Luke, but she felt something cold which passed through her leg. She looked for a moment at Masaaki's face, ivory and chiseled in the faint light. Then the two of them turned so that their backs were to the void. The Walker in the pale white robe touched her forehead again and she fell backwards. The mist closed over her and she sank swiftly through the cold water. Her last thought was not of the books she had given so many hours to, nor of her brother, and how she admired him and wanted to protect him. She did not even think of Luke, or wonder, as she often had, what kind of man he might become if she was with him. It was her father she thought of as she sank. She realized how lonely he had been, how sad and pathetic. Her mind filled with an image of a man who would never let her embrace him, no matter how much she wanted to. She was glad she would not feel that pain much longer.

A massive complication of arms, blacker than the surrounding gloom and somehow greater than the void it filled, opened to receive her. She sank and didn't struggle, and entered the yawning void, and pain, and death.

*

Jack stood on the plain, saw the newly transformed Dead moving toward them, and felt despair grip him. Then the ground was suddenly far above him, and he knew Masaaki was pulling him through the void. He sensed rather than saw that Masaaki was pulling the rest of his friends as well, and that the demigod wouldn't be able to hold onto them much longer. A giant face opened in the murk beneath Jack, and he saw the face of his father following them from below. Tentacles peeled off of his father's face and reached for him. Gripping Rachel's hand tight in his, he swung his sword until his arm felt like lead; but always new tentacles reached for him.

After an endless no-time, he felt Masaaki let go. He swam upward. His head broke the surface of the water and he felt a wave of sadness as Masaaki rushed away. He whipped his head back and forth to clear the water from his eyes and saw Rachel floating nearby.

By the time he had pulled her to shore, she was coughing water. They staggered up the beach and sat next to each other, shivering, too tired to wonder about the long black arms that reached through the sand into the ocean like giant cables, too tired to move to the ruined stone buildings further up the beach to their right.

As the sun set, he saw a red figure slowly treading water toward them. The water boiled and hissed in his wake. He was too tired to worry about how Rachel might try to comfort him. He only thought of the baking warmth which Mason would bring.

*

The three huddled together that night, the warmth from the giant their last comfort. They tried not to notice the winking yellow eyes which stared at them in the darkness.

Jack put his arm around Rachel and said, "Try to sleep."

He felt Rachel shrug her shoulders and lean into him even more. "You know there's no point," she said.

The sun rose and shone its light over the beach. He saw Mason's smoldering eyes moving back and forth between himself and Rachel. The giant stood and walked away from them, further down the beach.

Jack felt Rachel stiffen beside him, and saw the look in her face. Something broke inside him and he called, "Mason, come back." The giant stopped and turned, and Jack saw the resolution in his face. But the giant's expression broke in surprise. He pointed wordlessly.

Behind him, a voice said, "Jack."

"Yes," he said.

"Stand."

They stood and turned. Three figures stood opposite them. Jack took Rachel's hand in his own and tightened his grip on his sword in the other. He felt warmth as Mason moved to stand behind him, but Jack didn't turn away from the three standing opposite.

"You once said you wanted to find the secret of the world and cut it in half. But you have seen the secret of your world in each one of the faces of the Dead. If you cut it open, it will only form itself again, and you will learn nothing."

Jack's face tightened. "So there is no secret."

"I did not say that. But you will not find it in this world. Do you wish to make that journey?"

His stomach tightened, but before he could say anything, Rachel asked, "Sir, will my son be safe?"

The second of the three, dressed in a robe of deep green, stepped forward. "You would have had a healthy baby boy, Rachel. And he would have been different, as you hoped. But the Flower who touched your belly has claimed him for the Dead. If your son had been born, he would have become an even more terrible member of their race, so terrible you would lose your mind if you saw him."

Although Rachel didn't move, Jack suddenly felt she was far away. "If?" she asked.

"None of you will live long. There is not much time left in the world."

"What..." Jack asked, but Rachel interrupted, "How do you know? How do you know that? How do you know my baby has turned?" He pulled his arm away from her and stared at her when he heard her voice. Rachel didn't seem to notice.

"We have seen it."

"And you expect me to believe that?" she snapped.

"You do believe me."

The color drained from her face. "Are our friends at least safe?"

"No," the one in the red robe said. "Luke and Selene and Masaaki are together, but soon they..." All three suddenly lifted their heads, as if they heard a sound too high for the human ear. A light flashed from within the ocean, huge and distant. "Yes," said the one in the robe of deep blue. "All three have just died."

Jack's jaw dropped. "Are you happy about that?"

"No. They go to agony."

"And Oz?" Rachel asked.

"He has not yet come through the void."

Mason rumbled, "But it's only a matter of time." He turned and walked down the beach, a setting sun in the darkness.

The one in the robe of red said, "You can never make this right, Mason."

Mason stopped but didn't turn around. "Ain't there any release?" he rasped.

The one in the red robe stepped toward him. "All your life you have carried the wrongness of the world inside you. You felt it even before that girl you were trying to save died in your arms. You have arrested it and imprisoned it, but always it remains. Then the Dead came, and it only grew worse. You will never make it right."

Mason's head sank. "I know."

"Do you know what these arms are, which reach through the ground, Mason?"

"Does it matter?"

"Perhaps. You remember what happened as the Dead consumed their Head?"

"They kinda became like him. They got even worse. I didn't think that was possible, but they did."

"And they began to latch on to each other, and to the earth. The void was spilling over them."

The giant's red eyes widened.

"Soon there will be no earth left for you to stand on," the Walker said.

"The whole world becomes like them," Mason growled. "It becomes a Flower."

Rachel gasped. "Our vision," she whispered.

Mason didn't seem to hear her. He said, "So I die and become what I hate."

"And be denied even the release of pain and remorse," his Walker said, "for you will care for nothing as one of the Dead." An indescribable look passed over Mason's face, and the Walker said, "There is a way out. Will you give up and let the void consume you? Will you surrender to the wrongness you hate?"

"And that will get me out of here?"

"You will truly die. You will not join the dead."

"And my friends?"

"They must make their own choice. Either way, they will die soon as well."

"And if I say yes?"

"You will fall into the abyss and it will consume you. You will feel the wrongness of the world, and your place in it, and how all your attempts to make things right made it worse. You will feel it more keenly than you ever have."

"My own personal hell."

The Walker nodded. "Will you surrender to it without hating it?"

"What does that matter?"

"The void reacts to everything inside you. If it touches hatred inside you, it will produce something hateful, and you will not be delivered from its grip."

Mason hung his head. Molten heat radiated from him in waves.

"Think of the girl," the Walker said. "She is among the dead now. Is she worthy of your hatred?"

"No."

"Are not all the Dead like her? Are none of them worthy of pity?"

He kept his head down and said nothing.

They turned toward Rachel. She took a step behind Jack, her eyes wild. "Stay away from me," she said distinctly.

The Walker in the green robe stepped toward her. Rachel backed away and shrieked, "Don't you touch me! You'll never have my son!"

The one in the green robe turned to the two other walkers. They both shook their heads, but the green one said, "I do not think there is any other way." The green one moved toward Rachel and caught her hand. As Rachel screamed, a light shone, and disappeared just as quickly. Jack blinked, feeling something within him stretch out after the light he just had seen, trying to remember it even as it slipped from him.

*

For Rachel, there was no forgetting. It was not so much that the Walkers grew bright as much as the surrounding world dimmed for a heartbeat. If she could have caught her breath, she would have gasped at the beauty she saw.

A beauty which smiled at her.

*

"You," she said. "You are what I have wanted, all along. You are what woman was meant to be. And more."

"I am a reflection," Rachel's Walker said.

"A reflection! What are you reflecting?"

"Something which has not yet come to be."

"Tell me!" Her face was twisted in her longing.

"If I say more, it may never come to be. Do you trust me?"

"You are so strange, but I feel like I know you," she said.

The Walker's eyes grew wide for an instant before her face became impassive. "Do you trust me?" the Walker asked again.

She said nothing.

"Would it help if I told you I cared for your son as much as another could, and would not lead him to ultimate harm?"

"Yes," she said, her voice trembling. "I trust you with my son."

Jack swung his fist toward the Walker who had been speaking with Rachel, but the Walker in the robe of deep blue stepped forward and caught his wrist. The Walker spun him around and twisted his arm behind his back.

"You would keep the woman under your protection for

yourself? And destroy her?" the Walker asked. His voice was a calm thunderbolt.

Pain twisting his face, Jack shouted, "You want her to surrender to defeat?"

"It is the only way," the blue Walker said, and released him. He stumbled backwards, caught his balance, and dropped his sword. He rushed at the Walker as Rachel screamed for him to stop. Jack raised his right fist in a long right hook, letting it fall at the last instant as his left hand shot toward the Walker's undefended face. Without blinking, the Walker ignored Jack's feint, caught his left wrist, and gave a small twist. Jack was suddenly on the ground, the Walker standing above him and twisting his wrist at an angle that made Rachel worry it would break.

"What would victory look like in this new strange world?" the Walker said. "What would it take to defeat them and really live?"

Grimacing, Jack growled, "I don't know!"

"Neither do I," the Walker said, and released him. He stood and made two feints before the Walker grabbed another wrist and threw him again.

"You have the strength of the sea within you," the Walker said.

Jack stood. "You have the same in you."

"Am I anything like the Dead, Jack? Do I move like them?"

"No. You are the opposite of the Dead."

"Tell me what your Sensei said on your first day of training."

Still grimacing, he said, "He took me to the shore of the ocean and told me to walk in." He paused and his body relaxed a little as he spoke. "The waves were huge and the sea was pulling at my legs like snakes. Sensei was standing on the shore. He called to me, 'You must flow with the waves. Stand, and do not resist.' I knew he wanted me to go deeper. The sea was so rough, but I waded in. I realized I didn't care if I drowned."

The Walker said, "Your training involved facing your weakness and your potential to be a monster. But you have not yet finished your training. If you turn away from us, you will live a little longer, and grow stronger. What the Head's servant put in you will grow until it overwhelms you. You will change into something which would horrify you if you could see it."

Jack wobbled as if he had been struck. He gave the Walker an agonized look.

"What does fighting mean to you, Jack?"

"Purging evil."

"What evil?"

"Mine."

"Yes. But everyone loses eventually. Will you lose, and still fight, and be purged? Will you complete your training?"

He looked down the beach. "We're near the ruins of my old school, aren't we?"

"Yes. It was a good place for you to be, but it has served its purpose. It is dead now."

Mason rumbled, "I'm ready." Jack and Selene turned to look at him. "I can't make anything right. But I don't want to join it. I'll do what you say."

The Walker in the red robe took him by the hand and led him into the ocean. His Walker had him turn around and then touched him on his shoulder, as if in farewell. Mason fell backwards into the water. For a long time, they saw him sink in a red cloud, growing ever more faint until it merged with the gloom.

After a minute, the image of giant tentacles flashed deep in the ocean.

*

"Where did they go?" Rachel breathed.

"There is a steep drop just a little ways out."

"That's where you're taking us?" The two remaining Walkers said nothing.

"What about the vision we saw? What about the Mother Spirit?"

"Was it a mother, Rachel? A mother only?"

"No," she said in a soft voice. "Not only a mother, although it was that. When will it come?"

"How do you know it is not already here?"

Her eyebrows furrowed. "Because if it were, the world would be so much more beautiful."

"Do you trust us, Rachel?"

"You're not going to give me an answer. Yes, I trust you."

She looked out on the ocean for a long time and then turned toward Jack. He embraced her, and she trembled against him for a moment. She lifted her head and pressed her lips against his. In the sweet friction of their kiss, he felt Rachel's longing and regret. He held her tighter.

She pulled away. When he could open his eyes again, the flowers which had sprouted in the ground around him were already withering. Rachel was wading into the ocean, accompanied by her Walker. She didn't look back, and he understood why, and didn't have the heart to call to her.

But then she whirled and called, "Help me, Jack! I can't!"

he rushed into the surf, embraced her again, and then walked with her deeper, struggling to stand in the strong undertow. When the water was near their chins, they saw it: a deep black, like an oil spill, far beneath the wine-dark waves.

"Remember your vision," the green Walker said.

"It's true? What I saw will happen?"

Rachel gave Jack one last look before turning round. The green Walker touched her forehead and she fell backwards. The waters covered her head. She dropped.

Jack looked around. The Walker in the green robe was gone.

"You have one more question to ask," the Walker who had fought with him asked.

"My Sensei. In the cave. If I threw myself down and tried to kill myself, he said he would have loved me no less."

"If you do not know what that means, I cannot explain it to you in a way you would understand. But it is true whether you understand or not."

"What does it matter, if he's dead?"

"You are still loved, Jack. Even if you were a coward, which you are clearly not, you would still be loved. By your master, and by me."

"My sword, back on the beach. You can have it."

"I need it no more than you. It has served its purpose."

He saluted his Walker in the way he had been taught, which only members of his tribe were allowed to do. Then he ducked his head under the water and swam away. The current caught him and he sank into the darkness. He sensed a massive hunger beneath him. He felt the hard years of training rise unbidden within him and coalesce. He finally understood what all his training had been for, and understood that he had been waiting for this moment all his life.

*

It was Oz who surfaced from the void last, and who had the most difficulty finding a place on land.

His head broke the surface of the water. He treaded water for a moment, looking at the land far away. He flew upward, a pale blue blur high in the wind. From that height, he saw the Dead who still floated above the surface of the earth. He saw their skin charred black by the electricity dancing over their bodies. He saw the intelligence in their single yellow eye which pulsed above their two vacant eye sockets. He saw the crisscrossing patterns as other Flowers fastened to each other, and others latched onto the earth, and ate. He saw how the Flowers were becoming the only earth there was. He saw the pattern of spiraling tentacles which the Dead formed, and the center to which they pointed in the sea.

Eventually he saw a hill of white in the surrounding black and landed. He turned and stared at the sea of black around him, glistening and oily under the pale blue sky, peppered with blinking yellow eyes. The wind blew sharp, but he wasn't cold. He heard a rustling and looked at his feet. The black roots seemed to be closer to his feet than when he had landed. He walked further up the hill, then turned outward to look at the only thing there was to see.

Further up the hill, there stood a tall figure in a robe of pale blue.

"I can help you find what you want, Ozymandis."

"That is not my real name."

"It is not the name you were given at birth. But it is your

true name."

A look of sadness passed over Oz's face. "You can help me find what I want?"

The Walker looked at him.

"And what is it that I want?" Oz asked.

"When the Dead first came, you ran from them to flee the death of your daughter. But whenever you looked at one of the Dead, you looked for some sign of what your daughter had become. Always you have sought resolution for your daughter's death, now fleeing it, now staring at it. But you have not found it. Will you come with me?"

Oz looked at the roots creeping up the hill. "Where?" he asked.

"Follow." Then the Walker was gone, a blur in the air which no human eye could have traced.

Oz followed.

*

When Oz alighted, he was on a small outcrop near the top of a jagged peak. The wandering sun shone on the miles of black earth like a pale stranger. The restless sea whispered in the distance. A few ragged clouds hung on the horizon.

The Walker said, "Come inside." He followed the Walker into a dark cave. A small pit in the middle held the cold remains of a fire. A pile of books and scrolls stood against one of the walls. The Walker picked up a scroll and handed it to him.

Oz unrolled it and read, "It was a week ago when it happened. Exactly a week when I heard the stomping on the front porch. I remember it sounded like someone was drunk." His mouth soured, and his eyes ran down the paper. "Or perhaps without any home to come back to, all one can do is run. But if so, why is there no comfort in the thought?" He tossed the scroll into the cold fire pit.

"You are displeased with what you wrote? Your journals were copied out carefully. If humanity had survived longer, they would have become sacred."

"The scribbling of a coward who was glad to have a reason to keep running? Nothing sacred there."

"So you are no longer the man who wrote those things."

He collapsed into a sitting position against the wall of the cave. "No, I am not. Where are my friends?"

The impassive face of the Walker didn't change, but Oz sensed a flicker of warmth in his features. "They are all dead, Oz. Truly dead."

"What do you mean?"

"Your friends have not returned as Flowers. They are gone, and you can join them. There can be a resolution to your pain. You will be freed from your old life."

Oz's eyes flared. "The Head made the same promise to me."

"A promise he could not keep. But perhaps he spoke better than he knew."

"Isn't there anything to be done for the other survivors?" His voice cracked and his face twisted in pain.

"Why?"

"Anyone who would take what I wrote as sacred needs help. Anyone who would trust the coward I used to be is barely better than the Dead."

The Walker said, "You are a coward no longer." It was a simple assertion.

"Is there anything at all that can be done?"

"It will not bring her back."

"I know that. You think I don't know that? I know that."

"There is almost no one left to help. The few survivors who live now will soon be swallowed."

Oz's head fell. "It is the end of all things, then."

"Not yet. Reality exists on many different levels, physical and otherwise."

"I'm not sure I want to hear this."

"And yet you must. As things stand now, the entire globe will become a Flower, but it will hunger still. The disease which makes the Dead what they are will ride on the waves of particles which pass through this planet to other worlds and infect them. Soon those planets will become giant Flowers, like ours. Every atom will be infected. Eventually the universe will eat itself, and hunger still."

A brutal roar sounded from outside. Oz stood and went to the mouth of the cave and looked at the ocean. A giant black mouth had broken the surface, surrounded by tentacles miles thick which reached past the horizon.

"What have we done?" Oz asked. "What great evil have we awoken?"

"If you surrender to the Dead, without malice toward them, and let them consume you, you will truly die, and not become one of them. There will be an end to your pain. It will be agony to reach it, but you will be released. Do you hate the Dead?"

"No. But how is it possible I can escape the Dead?"

"You and your friends are different from everyone else. You were touched by one of the pantheon of the Head, and then immersed in the void."

Oz's eyes narrowed. "Is there nothing left to do but escape? Is there *nothing* that can be changed?"

"Everything you tried has failed."

"We tried, at least. We knew it was probably hopeless, even though none of us could say it. But we tried."

The Walker gave the faintest of smiles, as if the sun were about to come out from behind the clouds. "It could not happen otherwise: you are dealing with Death."

"So there is no hope, then." He glanced sideways to see how the Walker would react. The Walker stood, beautiful, statuesque, impassive.

"What is it?" the Walker asked without looking at him.

"I met a man once who told me it was hopeless, but he said it was good news. He's gone now. But I don't think he's dead."

Something imperceptible played over the Walker's features. It hung between the two like a secret neither could name.

"I have seen you before," Oz said. "You're not going to tell me anything more, are you?"

"If I do, it may not come to be. But I will tell you that human eyes are normally not able to see us. However, when we concentrate on you, we become visible to you. That is why you have seen us from time to time."

"You've been watching us?"

"Your stories are precious to us. Even in their failure."

Oz turned back to the sea and the black behemoth which was slowly dragging itself toward the shore. "This is cheating, you know. You're a *deus ex machina*."

"I am no god."

"No?"

"I am a reflection."

"A reflection of what?"

The Walker paused. As if speaking unwillingly, he said,

"You once said a walking corpse was like death reaching backwards through time. I am the same, and yet opposite."

Oz shrugged. "I know you won't explain that to me. But this still sounds like the god from the machine."

"Perhaps. But a great many rules have been broken in this story. May not another be broken in your favor?"

"So if I let myself be eaten, I'll really die?"

"If you go without malice or envy of the dead, yes."

"And... I will stop hurting?"

"Yes."

"I'm not a hero," Oz said. "I'm a coward."

"A true coward would never admit it."

"Did my daughter ever come back?"

"Even if we could find her, you could not bring her with you to true death. But there is a depth of care for her and for you which you cannot imagine."

"I don't even know what that means. But I don't want to run anymore. I don't want to abandon anyone."

"There is nothing you can do. Nothing, except increase the ugliness by joining it."

Oz hung his head. "You sense what I'm feeling, don't you?"

"Yes."

He kept his head down, knowing that at least the Walker shared his grief. After a moment, he asked, "Why don't you feel like a stranger to me?"

"Do you trust me?"

"I have no reason to."

"Do you trust me?"

The Walker's face peeled back in waving starfish-arms. Although the face still held the unearthly hints of colors for which Oz had no name, he saw the same cavernous face of a

Flower. Then the Walker's face re-formed, without any scars.

Oz gasped, "How..."

"I hold death within me, yet am not overcome," the Walker said. "Do you trust me?"

He stared into the face of the Walker and the lively solemnity, the joyful gravity he saw there. Unable to speak, he nodded.

"Then let that serve for an answer."

"What kind of strange new world is this?" Oz whispered.

"A strange one indeed. So strange that the world can die, and hope not die with it. I give you mystery after mystery. I am sorry. It must be this way. But remember, if you had not joined the Head and been baptized, you would have joined the Dead long ago. Now, our time has grown very short. You must get as close to that mouth as you can." The Walker pointed to the thing in the ocean.

Oz looked to see the ugliness below wriggling onto the beach. He saw many other smaller mouths opening to consume the sand and drink the sea water. "How could we do it?" he asked. "How could we eat death that way? How could we stare at the sun until we went blind?"

"A stronger light creates a darker shadow."

"What?"

"It is a very great evil," the Walker said.

"I'm glad," he said, staring at the monster beneath him. "I'm glad for every minute I had, every minute of pain and loss and life." And then he was gone, a faint blue blur which sped across the sky and dropped onto the giant Flower. He stood near the mouth, smaller than an ant next to its gaping maw. Tentacles wrapped around his legs and pulled him in. He disappeared.

*

The Walker who had spoken to Oz stood on the high mountain, sensing Oz's fear and agony as he sank. After a time, the black tentacles creeping up the mountain gained the place where he stood. The Walker lifted from the ground and watched still.

A trace of color appeared in the ocean.

Without turning, he sensed another and said, "You came to watch."

"How could I not?" the second Walker asked. "It is the beginning of what I prophesied to you when I was alive."

The two rose into the sky. More colors appeared in the void: green, red, blue, white, and others which did not yet have names. When the colors brushed against the gigantic Flower, half on the ground and half in the ocean, it shuddered and shrank away from them.

TWENTY-EIGHT

The Initiation of Zerah

The priest found Anah working in the garden with three other women. She was on her hands and knees, pulling weeds from the rows of tomatoes and carrots and squash. The overhanging trees shaded the garden, and the wind whispered its way through the green branches, but sweat still dripped from Anah's nose into the moist soil. The priest stood on the edge of the garden and waited for her to stop working, but she only pulled the weeds more quickly.

The priest said, "Anah." She stopped pulling and turned toward his feet, but didn't look at his face.

The priest said, "Tonight, then," and walked away. When he glanced back, he saw one of the other women making the sign against evil to his back.

*

At dusk, the priest went to the border of his tribe's land and looked out at the unbroken white desert. The priest glanced back at the short stake he had driven into the ground the day he had been ordained. The stake marked the boundary between green and white. It was now almost completely hidden in the undergrowth of long grass and weeds. Through the crisscrossing branches, the priest saw the light from the fire which his tribe lit every night. He could hear the singing coming from the campfire.

The sun set. The priest watched the desert. Flickering yellow lights appeared on the horizon.

A faint *click* of a stone being thrown against the well sounded. The priest could hear the mumbled prayer which always accompanied the casting of the stone. He stood and walked back toward his stone hut. Anah stood next to the well, waiting with her left hand pressed against her forehead in a fist. The priest waited, wondering what she would do when he didn't come out of his hut as she expected. She only stood, hand to forehead, trembling in the darkness.

The priest walked to Anah and touched her on the shoulder. She flinched and turned to him. "This way," he said, and walked back to the edge of the desert. The priest sat and stared at the shining dots on the dark horizon. After a while, he heard Anah's footsteps behind him.

"Are they getting closer?" she whispered. The priest turned and saw her standing among the trees.

"You are not in danger," the priest said. "They will not come within our borders. Please sit with me." He turned back to the desert. She stayed under the cover of the trees.

A minute later and the sparkling yellow dots were a stone's throw from the green garden. They floated above the parched white, each with a vivid yellow eye, seemingly disembodied as their black bodies melted with the night. Then they moved on. When they were out of sight, Anah moaned.

The priest said, "They always come more often when

someone is about to be taken." He turned and looked at Anah. Her eyes fell to the ground, as they always did. "I think your son Zerah might be next," he said.

She slumped to the ground and pressed her forehead into the soft grass. She stretched her hands toward the priest. "Please," she moaned. "Spare my son."

The priest turned so his back was to the desert. He said, "It is not my choice. And Anah, you need not fear me." She looked up from the ground, a look of surprise on her face.

"You guard our border," she said, "and send those who have been chosen to the Dead."

The priest sighed as she pressed her forehead into the ground and began to weep. He stood and went to sit next to her.

"Sit up, woman. Dry your eyes." She did, but seemed not to listen when he said, "I mean you no harm, nor your son."

"You walk through the desert and send our sons and daughters to the Dead. And your skin. Some say..."

The priest clenched his fists. "I know what they say."

"That you are one of the Dead yourself," she finished, looking him full in the eye.

The priest turned away. "Your son is angry."

Her voice shaking, she said, "About his father. He cuts himself."

The priest nodded. "And fights."

They sat for a silent moment beneath the dark night sky.

"If I ask," the priest said, "will you send him to me?"

"No."

"I have seen the like of him before. I suppose I was not so different when I was young. His anger may grow into murder if it is left alone."

"What is that?"

"He may hurt the body of one of our tribe so that they join the Dead."

With a shuddering sigh, Anah nodded. She stood and walked back to the fire without waiting to be dismissed.

*

The priest sat on the edge of the green. More of the Dead appeared in the distance and moved in strange patterns which reminded the priest of things he had not yet seen. When the sun rose, he walked back to the well. He sat and waited.

The priest heard footsteps behind him and knew Zerah had come, but the priest said nothing. Knowing the boy had stared at them many times already, the priest let Zerah look once more at the symbols which flowed like smoke over his skin. Then the priest asked, "Do you know how my skin came to have these moving shapes, Zerah?"

Behind him, the boy said nothing.

The priest asked, "Will you walk through the desert with me?"

"That's forbidden," the boy said, and took a step closer to the priest.

"And with good reason. The Dead rule that place. But you have walked there already, as far as you dared. Will you walk farther with me, out of sight of your home?"

Zerah said nothing. The priest turned and saw the hunger in the boy's eyes.

The priest stood and walked through the shrubs and trees toward the tribe's border. He could hear Zerah walking behind him, crunching and rustling the leaves and sticks which covered the short paths through the tribe's land.

The priest stood for a moment at the border, waiting. "Where..." Zerah asked, but the priest held up a single finger. The lines and figures which formed and re-formed on the priest's skin coalesced into straight lines, and the priest walked out of the green and into the hot white desert. He turned.

"I can feel which path we must take, but not for long," the priest said. With a grimace of determination, Zerah put one bare foot on the hot white ash, then another. The priest smiled.

When they had walked for almost an hour, the priest said, "Your feet sting. They are not used to this."

"How much farther?"

The priest glanced at the boy's pale, sweaty face and chapped lips. "Not much. There will be a pool where you can drink." He stopped, listened, and veered off to the left. Zerah trudged after him.

A few minutes later, the ground dipped into a small green valley. The priest walked to the tiny spring in the middle and motioned for Zerah to drink. The boy did, loudly slurping the water for a minute or more. When he was done, the priest had him sit in the one place where there was shade, under a tall shrub.

"You are not sweating," the boy gasped.

"I do not feel the sun."

"Why not?"

"I will explain, if I can. But there are other things I need to explain first. You know the Dead are coming to our borders more often."

"Are we safe here?"

"As safe as we are around the well. The Dead can enter

our place, but they hate it. It used to make them blind, but it does so no longer." The priest felt a wave of sadness, swallowed, and said, "It is time to initiate you into the mystery of our tribe."

The priest began to speak, and continued all through the afternoon and long into the cold night. The exhaustion in the boy's face changed first to fear and then to wonder, and the priest's heart grew ever heavier.

*

"You know the border of our home, Zerah, for you have walked it many times."

"You can walk it a hundred times before the day is half done," the boy said.

"You have walked outside our borders as well." The boy's jaw tightened. "I did the same, when I was young," the priest said. "But never so far that I lost sight of my home. Do you know what you would find if you did walk far?"

"The desert. Then the ocean."

"And beneath us?"

"The void. Mother says the ocean and the void are the same, but that does not make sense."

"That is another matter. Did you know that there are other settlements like ours? Other wells, where green grows, and the unborn live?"

Zerah's face hardened and he said nothing.

The priest asked, "Why are you angry?"

"Another thing Mother lied to me about."

"She probably does not know herself. She does not know where your father is, either. But I do, and I would like to tell you." The boy's face softened, and the priest continued: "Even if she does know, she may not have told you because these oases are so far apart that we would never reach them if we tried. We would die in the desert, or meet the Dead."

"Mother says the Dead are the true rulers of the world."

"She is right," the priest said. "What else does she say?"

"That we are their unborn children."

The priest nodded, and asked, "Has she told you that it was not always so?"

Zerah shook his head.

The priest said, "The world used to be a net of roads and cities and buildings..."

"What are roads and... the other things you said?"

"A road is a path the ancients used to travel between cities. Cities were their homes, where many thousands of the Dead would settle together. Buildings were tall huts, very tall, made of wood and stone."

"They settled together? What were they doing?"

"They were trying to conquer the world and re-make it in their image. Many things were different, then. The Dead could not fly, and they had two eyes, like us, not one. I was told by the priest before me that they dug pits for themselves for when they fell asleep and called them graves, and had many other strange customs I do not understand. But whatever the ancients did, they did it to shape a world as an image of themselves, so that they might worship themselves. Then one of their kind found a way for the Dead to achieve in one moment what they all desired. He released a substance into the air, so fine it could not be seen or felt.

"Have you seen, Zerah, how the seed of a plant will grow another of its kind? And do you know how adding compost, made of refuse and dung, makes the thing grown from the

338

seed stronger? So it was with the ancients. One of the Dead found a way to release a mixture made from the void into the air, and the true seed of the Dead was revealed. The Dead grew into stronger versions of themselves.

"The one who did this gave himself a new body and named himself the Head. He appointed six to rule under him, each with bodies different from the newly born Dead and different from himself. They made themselves different from the Dead so they could rule over them, but they soon began to die themselves. The Head had released death into the world, and could not escape it. The six appointed to rule grew angry with their Maker for this, for they were starving for power. They appointed six from the unborn, people like us, to overcome the Head. They shared their power with these new six and made them like themselves, giving them powers even I cannot understand. But when the Head confronted them, the new six cowered before the Head and promised to serve him. This pleased the Head, and so he added a seventh to their number in his own image. Because their new powers had not yet fully taken effect, the Head immersed these new seven in the void again. And then... Do you know what the void is, Zerah?"

"It... it's the void."

"That was not the best way to ask that question, for the void is not anything. How is a shadow made?"

"You hold your hand up when the sun is high and it makes a shadow."

"Light is blocked. Exactly. Dung is the refuse which is made when someone eats something nourishing. There cannot be a corpse unless something was first alive. That is all the void is. It is the refuse and shadow and corpse of everything that is alive. Many of the ancients thought that the void was first, and was that out of which all else arose. But that is like saying a corpse gives birth to a human being, or a shadow creates light. The void could not exist without a much greater life above it."

"What happened to the new seven when they were immersed?" the boy asked.

"They sank beneath time and space, and saw both from the outside. They saw the very worst that might come to be, and the best. They saw that great Life from which all life is derived, and they saw the Dead consuming everything, until all that remained was Death."

"Then what happened?"

"They rose from the void and resolved to kill the Head. But before they could, the Dead, who hunger always, turned on the Head and ate him. Because they did, they became like him, more cruel and more intelligent. In their hunger, the Dead also began to consume the earth and sky. If you traveled far enough, Zerah, you would see the soil give way to the intertwined bodies of the Dead."

"Are they still eating everything?"

"No, they are not; or at least, they are eating only slowly. This is the mystery of our tribe, which I guard. The new seven saw that the Head had already been killed, and that they could do nothing against the Dead, and that they would soon join the Dead. In despair, they threw themselves into the void. But they did not know that their despair would lead to so much good. The new seven were now strange creatures. They had breathed in the substance which the Head had let into the air, had been touched by the old seven, and had sunk within the void once already. They carried the void within themselves. And when they, who carried the void within themselves, sank into it again, something strange beyond reckoning happened." The priest looked up at the newly twinkling stars.

"What happened?" the boy asked.

"I hope you will see for yourself soon. It will help you. What happened was the void itself changed. I do not entirely understand it myself, but that is what I was told. It is still the shadow of the world, but it is no longer the hungry, frightening thing it was. It is more like a womb now. When others sink into it, they can rise with new bodies as Walkers. The change in the void also kept the Dead from eating everything so quickly. And it created in those seven a new nature, people who held death within themselves, but were more alive than you or I ever could be. We call these new ones Walkers. Have you ever seen one, Zerah?"

"I don't think so."

"If you had, you would know. The Walkers can move through the void at will, and so can move through time and space. It harms them not at all. And when they rose from the void, they realized how fortunate their submission to the Head and their final despair had been. But they were also troubled. Because they could sink beneath the world, they could move through all possible times. Time is not a straight line, but a river, which can wander in different currents and eddies. The Walkers moved through these eddies, and watched their past histories. But they moved through other currents where their past selves took a different path. Sometimes they saw themselves not going into the void a second time, but joining the ranks of the Dead and becoming terrible new gods to them."

"I don't understand. They saw something that never happened?"

"They saw a possibility, which may have happened in another stream of time. And it troubled them."

"Why?"

"They feared that other stream might break through into ours. The people of the old world learned that matter and time are not so different from each other. If the Dead ate all matter, they worried Death might eat away the very fabric of time itself, and bleed into all times. So the Walkers decided to resurface in their own past, and guide their own selves to that true defeat which would be their greatest happiness. But they feared to speak too much to the past."

"Why would they be afraid when they were so powerful?"

"They feared that if they said too much to their past selves, they might corrupt the sacrifice which their past selves were required to make, and the void would reject it. I do not understand that, but that is what I was told."

"What does this have to do with my father?"

"Your father is dead, Zerah."

"My mother told me he was taken."

"It is the same thing. We... I understand you are angry. I understand what it is like to have it burn and burn within you. You may not believe that, but I do. You can let your anger eat you. Or you can ride your anger to the secret heart of the world. Look." He pointed outward. The Dead were circling the edge of the valley, floating in midair, crackling faintly in the twilight and hissing. Their starfish arms unfurled slowly. "They are hungry for you, Zerah. You can join them. Or you can become a Walker yourself."

"How?" The boy's eyes were wide in the darkness.

"When someone is ready, the Walkers come and lead him through death and into a life like theirs."

"How do they do that?"

"They lead them into the void and into death. Eventually, they rise from the void, transformed."

Zerah asked, "Why does it have to happen that way?"

"The void touches each one of us. It is within each of us. We all return to it eventually. The only way to be free is to sink within it past its bottom."

"Is that what happened to my father?"

"No. He was taken in a raid by the Dead. They loathe the green of our home, but they are so driven with hunger that sometimes they overcome their loathing and take some of us to eat. I am told it never satisfies them. But that is what happened."

"Will my father become a Walker?"

"It is possible." The priest's voice was soft. "There are two ways it happens. If you lived out your life in our tribe, you would come to love it. It is a better life than many of the ancients had. And when you died, you would stand up and leave your home and join the Dead. This is what happens to many. But sometimes the void calls for one of the unborn early. I do not know why this happens, but I have seen it.

"But hope is not lost for those who have joined the Dead, for sometimes something sparks inside one of the Dead. They have the void within them. But the void was changed by the sacrifice of the Seven, and sometimes it calls to one of its children to return to it and be changed. Then the Walkers lead it through the void, holding it by the hand, and it joins their ranks as one of them. There is no telling when or how one of the Dead goes to the Walkers, for the void is random. But it happens."

"How do you know the Walkers want me?"

"I was touched by a Walker and given a gift. That is how I gained the priesthood." The priest sighed, looked up at the ancient stars and the Dead surrounding the valley. "Will you join the Walkers, Zerah?" The priest forced his voice to be steady.

"My father is not a Walker."

"He may be. He may have felt the void calling to him."

"You do not know that."

"No, I do not."

Zerah stood and moved off to another part of the valley. In the darkness, the priest could not see him.

*

When the son rose the next morning, Zerah stood and walked toward the priest. The boy's eyes were haggard. He looked at the priest and asked, "You didn't sleep?"

"Even since I became a priest, I have been too close to death for sleep."

"Doesn't it hurt?"

"No. Are you jealous?"

He glared at the priest and then walked up the slope of the valley and stood on the edge of the desert. The Dead swarmed close to him, crackling and alert in the dawn light on the boundary between green and white. "Rule with us," they hissed. "We feel no pain or loss. You need not trust a priest. You can trust yourself."

The priest shouted to the boy, but he did not turn away from the Dead. The priest ran and stood behind Zerah.

"Do you know my father?" the boy asked in a tiny voice.

In a rushed whisper, the priest said, "You cannot find your father this way. You would never recognize the body he once was, and even if you did, you would not care about him or even remember why you wanted to see him."

"My father," the boy said, his back to the priest.

"You do not need him," the floating Dead hissed. "You can be a father to yourself."

Zerah turned to the priest. The priest's heart sank when he saw the look on the boy's face.

"I'm going with them," Zerah said. The priest opened his mouth to plead, but Zerah turned and stepped onto the burning ash of the desert.

The Dead reached for him, arms out, mouths open, eyes wide, tongues flicking.

And then stopped, frozen in midair.

The Dead rotated slowly. A man was walking toward them across the desert. The Dead's constant hissing fell into silence. Their eyes flicked back and forth as they looked at the man, as if they could not focus on him.

The Walker's face was the wind on a bright summer day, free and wild and clear. There was a brilliant darkness which played about his face, bright shadows caused by a light the priest could not see. The man walked through the Dead and stood opposite Zerah. The boy craned his neck back to look full on his face.

"You have lost one of your family," the Walker said.

Zerah said nothing, but his face cracked in pain.

"I have as well," the man said. Something passed over the man's face, and Zerah gasped as if he had been struck; and the priest knew that the Walker had shared something with Zerah without words, as their kind are able to do. A tear slipped down the priest's face as he wondered what he had missed.

The Walker took Zerah by the hand and began to lead him through the stationary Dead, into the desert and away from the priest. The Dead followed in train, silent for once and somehow not frightening. The priest shouted and ran to fall at the Walker's feet. He felt the scaly hands of the dead on his back, and felt them pull away at a single word from the Walker. The priest craned his neck upwards to see the Walker regarding him.

"Why don't the Dead eat you?" the priest gasped.

"Because I am dead like them," the Walker said, and turned away.

"Please," the priest said. "It's bad enough when I do the ceremony for one of us who has died and is about to get up and join the Dead. It's worse when I lead someone still alive to the edge of the mystery and cannot join them. How much longer? When will you come for me?"

"A brother of mine initiated you into many mysteries," the Walker said. "But he did not tell you everything. Have you seen the long shadows cast by the morning sun? My kind and I are those shadows, cast by the sun which will rise on the last morning of the world. That great Life will some-day rise, and even now it is casting its rays backwards through time. They shine on you, faint but true. And you are guiding others to that light."

The priest got up from his hands and knees and held open his hands in a gesture of helplessness. "Lord, I do not understand."

"I will show you, then, so that it will be easier for you to wait." He took the priest by the hand.

The priest tried to squint but could not: a brilliant light from the Walker's face forced his eyes open. The world around him dimmed. The priest saw the same light shining on Zerah's face, and saw the Dead as he always had, but realized for the first time the rotting corruption which they really were.

The priest saw his tribal home, across the desert in the distance, as clearly as if he were standing in front of it; but the green of the grass and bushes was faded and frosted with ash, the trees were withered and decrepit. The ground was dry and cracked and ancient, heavy with time. Black roots burrowed through the ground, through the green of his home, eating. The trees and bushes disappeared. There was only level black ground, yellow eyes which stared at nothing, and waving tentacles.

The priest looked further and saw a great tree, its roots reaching to the void and its branches enfolding the world.

The priest saw the void, the cold depth of it, and saw as well a flickering radiance at the bottom of it, a bright shadow which hummed.

The priest saw the giant Flower lying in the ocean, and saw its tentacles reaching through the entire world, eating and eating until there was no difference between the two. The globe opened like the face of a Flower and gave a shuddering groan. Giant tentacles waved and scattered red particles into space.

And the priest saw shimmering waves of light surround the dead planet. The Flower opened its mouth and the bird descended inside it. The Flower shuddered and began to grow bright, so bright the priest could not bear it. The priest held up a hand to shield his eyes, and screamed in pain when the light shone through his hand. He felt the Walker squeeze his other hand, and the priest fell on to the hot ash of the desert. He blinked, looked around, and saw the world as he knew it, and Zerah staring at him, and the Dead.

The Walker said, "I have shown you the world's last day. You have seen the final victory of death. We changed the void with our sacrifice, but that slowed Death only a little.

Eventually Death will conquer the entire planet and every other world. But it must be so."

"What was the... the..."

"You saw, as best it can be seen, that uncreated Life which gives life to all else."

"It fell... it sank..."

"Yes. It will fall into the void and let itself be eaten. Thus it destroys Death. How do you think I am able to stand here now? Only because of what will happen on that last day. I am an echo of a song which has not yet begun."

"What good is it if I am long dead when these miracles happen?"

"You will not be. I have shown you only what you will someday see for yourself. I could never have taken you there otherwise. So wait in patience, and guide those unborn."

"Lord, how can all this be?"

"I do not have any answer to that. But know that as the light shines on us from outside time, it created a deeper shadow and spawned the Dead. But the shadow will pass."

The Walker turned to Zerah. "It is time for your baptism and death. Will you come?" The boy nodded.

The Walker turned to the Dead. "You hunger for something to worship, and always you are frustrated. Does the void call any of you? Are any of you ready to lay aside your living death for true death, and true life?"

One of the Dead hissed, "You were what I always wished to be. I will follow." It sank to the ground and bowed its forehead to the ground. Two others followed suit.

The Walker touched the three of them on the shoulder. They stood, and walked with the Walker and Zerah into the desert. When they had walked some distance, the priest saw seven other shimmering figures, both strange and familiar, as all the Walkers were. One was dressed in a black robe with strange characters moving over his skin. The priest recognized him as the Walker who had ordained him. He raised his hand in salute, and the Walker raised his own. Another Walker had a mane of golden hair and a yellow beard, standing taller than the rest, a king among equals. One stood dressed in a robe of deepest sea-blue, and another stood close to him in a robe which shimmered calmly like the full moon. One stood in bright red, one in verdant green, and another behind the green one, with features so similar they looked like mother and son. The faces of each shone with that light the priest had seen in his vision, and he thought he understood what the Walker meant when he said they were a reflection.

And then they were gone. The priest knew the Walkers had taken Zerah and the three Dead to the void, but he still looked for them, feeling that the trees behind him and even the dead ground beneath looked as well, as if their presence had turned the landscape into a sanctuary. Even the Dead looked to where the Walkers had been, faces open and tentacles waving, as if waiting for that sun which would someday rise.

THE FAT CHEF

Raoul, fat Head Chef of Le Metro, the top hotel of Paris, hardly notices the Nazi invaders occupying the city – until they threaten his beloved demi-sous chef Natalie.

From acclaimed author Fredrik Nath, *The Fat Chef* is a wartime tale of unrequited love, heroism, and a rather suspect Béchamel sauce.

www.fingerpress.co.uk/the-fat-chef

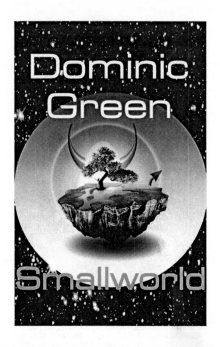

SMALLWORLD

A captivating novel from
Hugo-nominated author Dominic Green

Mount Ararat, a world the size of an asteroid yet with
Earth-standard gravity, plays host to an eccentric farming
community protected by the Devil, a mechanical killing
machine, from such passers-by as Mr von Trapp (an escapee
from a penal colony), the Made (manufactured humans
being hunted by the State), and the super-rich clients of a
gravitational health spa established at Mount Ararat's South
Pole.

www.fingerpress.co.uk/smallworld

CPSIA information can be obtained at www.ICGtesting.com
Printed in the USA
LVOW080518100413

328188LV00003B/50/P